Outstanding Praise for Kristina McMorris's
Letters from Home

"This sweeping debut novel is ambitious and compelling . . . will appeal to historical fiction fans hungry for a romance of the 'Greatest Generation.' "
—*Publishers Weekly*

"*Letters from Home* is an absorbing debut, combining the emotional power of *The Notebook* with the stirring history and drama of *Saving Private Ryan*. An evocative and compelling storyteller, Kristina McMorris gives us a novel to savor and remember."
—Ben Sherwood, *New York Times* best-selling author of
The Death and Life of Charlie St. Cloud

"McMorris gives readers a poignant and resonant 'Greatest Generation' story of love and loss during wartime."
—*Booklist*

"*Letters from Home* is a heart-grabbing story of love and war in the era of big bands and among friends keen on small deceptions. Full of period detail and characters you root for, Kristina McMorris offers up a stellar debut novel readers will cherish."
—Pamela Morsi, *USA Today* best-selling author of
Last Dance at Jitterbug Lounge

"A beautifully told story. The characters are well developed and the motivations for their actions and misunderstandings are clearly shown. The tale is emotionally moving and the end is heartwarming. This is a tough book to put down!"
—*RT Book Reviews*

"A great read. From beginning to end, Kristina McMorris spins a compelling tale of chemistry, love, deception, and the labyrinth of emotions that leads to the human heart."
—James Michael Pratt, *New York Times* best-selling author of
The Last Valentine

"This poignant novel digs deep into the emotional and physical effects of war and is well written and well researched. . . . The heart-tugging scenes interspersed throughout *Letters from Home* serve to highlight the harsh realities of both war and human nature."
—*New York Journal of Books*

"This is a debut novel for McMorris, who writes of the people and the period with a great deal of insight and compassion. Through the three heroines she captures a cross section of the myriad experiences and coping mechanisms of the women left behind with their hopes and dreams and fears."
—*Historical Novel Reviews*

BRIDGE OF
SCARLET LEAVES

Books by Kristina McMorris

Letters from Home

Bridge of Scarlet Leaves

Published by Kensington Publishing Corp.

BRIDGE OF SCARLET LEAVES

KRISTINA McMORRIS

KENSINGTON BOOKS
www.kensingtonbooks.com

KENSINGTON BOOKS are published by

Kensington Publishing Corp.
119 West 40th Street
New York, NY 10018

All Kensington titles, imprints, and distributed lines are available at special quantity discounts for bulk purchases for sales promotion, premiums, fund-raising, educational, or institutional use.

Special book excerpts or customized printings can also be created to fit specific needs. For details, write or phone the office of the Kensington Special Sales Manager: Attn. Special Sales Department. Kensington Publishing Corp., 119 West 40th Street, New York, NY 10018. Phone: 1-800-221-2647.

Kensington and the K logo Reg. U.S. Pat. & TM Off.

ISBN-13: 978-0-7582-4685-1
ISBN-10: 0-7582-4685-4

First Kensington Trade Paperback Printing: March 2012
10 9 8 7 6 5 4 3 2 1

Printed in the United States of America

*For those whose voices stayed silent
so that one day others could sing*

ACKNOWLEDGMENTS

As the daughter of a Caucasian American mother and Japanese immigrant father, I fell in love with the idea of creating a story set during the Second World War that combined the unique perspectives with which I was raised. The more research I did, however, the more responsibility I felt to accurately depict the experiences of those who survived this tumultuous era. If I achieved anything close, it is from the help and patience of a great many people.

First and foremost, my gratitude goes out to the following Japanese American WWII veterans for so generously sharing their time and, most of all, their memories: Military Intelligence Service members Ken Akune, Don Oka, George Fujimori, James Murata, Ralph Kaneshiro, Frank Masuoka, the late Dick Kishiue, and 442nd Regimental Combat Team member Tets Asato. Your collective courage is surpassed solely by your inspiring humility.

I extend my appreciation to former relocation camp evacuee Sets Tomita and Park Ranger Richard Potashin of the Manzanar National Historic Site, both of whom endured an endless peppering of questions. The only person who quite possibly answered more is my research buddy and friend Wes Burritt.

For providing me with a crash course on historical baseball, I thank 1940s USC ballplayers and WWII veterans Al Spaeter and Hank Workman, as well as Scott Taylor, Jim Klee, and Pat Egan. And for aiding me in tackling the portrayal of legendary coach Justin "Sam" Barry, I am grateful to his godson and namesake, Justin Dedeaux, and USC Sports Information Director Tim Tessalone.

My Army Air Corps scenes would have struggled for liftoff without the help of fellow historical author Sarah Sundin and WWII airmen Robert Gilbert and Kenneth Tucker. All three of you are my heroes in various ways.

I am eternally indebted to others who guided me with their diverse areas of expertise, among them: concert violinist Emily Day-Shumway, the late Allied-POW historian Roger Mansell, vintage car enthusiast Neil Handy, Louisiana native Connie Cox, National Railroad Museum curator Daniel Liedtke, Japanese American National Museum docent James Tanaka, archivists at The Juilliard School and Stanford University, the Multnomah County Library Research Department (my new phone-a-friends), and Tomoko Hirata, who kindly reviewed my Japanese phrases with care, no doubt preventing inadvertent obscenities.

For the privilege of borrowing her poem, which so poignantly captured the essence of my story, I thank the very talented Deanna Nikaido.

As ever, I am grateful to my fabulous readers Julia Whitby, Darcy Burke, and Elisabeth Naughton (who ensures there is actually "love" in my love stories); to Whitney Otto, Tatiana Hulser, and Graceann Macleod for their valuable enthusiasm and input; to my unyielding group of cheerleaders for accompanying me every step on this often-bumpy yet never-dull road: Michelle Guthrie, Sunny Klever, Tracy Callan, Stephanie Stricklen, Lynne House, Jennifer Sidis, Sally Ramirez, Delilah Marvelle, and my mother, Linda. And, of course, to my grammar gurus Sue McMorris and Kathy Huston, whose generous spirits and contagious zeal should be packaged and sold in a heated auction.

Once again, I offer my immense appreciation to my editor, John Scognamiglio, and my beloved literary agent, Jennifer Schober, both of whose support and faith made this experience not only possible, but utterly fulfilling. To the entire Kensington team: Thank you for rolling out the red carpet on this unforgettable journey. And to my film-rights agent Jon Cassir at CAA for stretching that red carpet ever closer to a childhood dream.

Lastly, above all, my heart goes out to my husband, Daniel, and our sons, Tristan Kiyoshi and Kiernan Takeshi, for serving as my constant reminders of true success; for understanding that a B-17 ride far outweighed any other possible Mother's Day gift; and for continuing to be the unwavering bridge upholding my life. I love you more than words.

PART ONE

Every leaf while on its tree sways in unison;
bears the same light and shadow,
is sustained by the same sap that will release it in blazing color.

It is that moment before falling we all live for,
to see ourselves for the first time,
to hear our name being called from the inside.

—Deanna Nikaido,
daughter of a Japanese American "evacuee"

✤ 1 ✤

November 1941
Los Angeles, California

At the sound of her brother's voice, flutters of joy turned to panic in Maddie Kern. "Cripes," she whispered, perched on her vanity seat. "What's he doing home?"

Jo Allister, her closest girlfriend and trusted lookout, cracked open the bedroom door. She peeked into the hall as TJ hollered again from downstairs.

"Maddie! You here?"

It was six o'clock on a Friday. He should have been at his campus job all night. If he knew who was about to pick her up for a date . . .

She didn't want to imagine what he would do.

Maddie scanned the room, seeking a solution amidst her tidy collection of belongings—framed family photos on the bureau, her posters of the New York Symphony, of Verdi's *Aida* at the Philharmonic. But even her violin case, which she'd defended from years of dings and scratches, seemed to shake its head from the corner and say, *Six months of sneaking around and you're surprised this would happen?*

Jo closed the door without a click and pressed her back against the knob. "Want me to keep him out?" Her pale lips angled with mischief. Despite the full look of her figure, thanks to her baggy hardware store uniform, she was no match for TJ's strength. Only his stubbornness.

"My brother seeing *me* isn't the problem," Maddie reminded her. She glanced at the clock on her nightstand, and found cause for remaining calm. "Lane shouldn't be here for another twelve minutes. If I can just—"

The faint sound of an engine drove through the thought and parked on her words. Had he shown up early? She raced to the window, where she swatted away her childhood drapes. She threw the pane upward and craned her neck. Around the abandoned remains of her father's Ford, she made out a wedge of the street. No sign of Lane's car. She still had time.

"Hey, Rapunzel," Jo said. "You haven't turned batty enough to scale walls for a fella, have you?"

Maddie shushed her, interrupted by creaks of footfalls on the staircase. "*You* have to do it," she decided.

"Do what?"

Warn Lane, Maddie was about to say, but realized she needed to talk to him herself, in order to set plans to meet later that night. Come tomorrow, he'd be on a train back to Stanford.

She amended her reply. "You've got to distract TJ for me."

Jo let out a sharp laugh. Pushing out her chest, she tossed back stragglers from her ash-brown ponytail. "What, with all my stylish locks and hefty bosom?" Then she muttered, "Although, based on his past girlfriends, I suppose that's all it would take."

"No, I mean—you both love baseball. Chat about that."

Jo raised a brow at her.

"Please," Maddie begged. "You came by to help me get ready, didn't you? So, *help* me."

"Why not just tell him and get it over with?"

"Because you know how he feels about my dating." *A distraction from her future,* he called it. The same theory he applied to his own career.

"Maddie. This isn't just about any guy."

"I know, I know, and I'll come clean. But not yet."

A knuckle-rap sounded on her door. "You in there?"

She sang out, "Hold on a minute," and met Jo's eyes. "*Please.*"

Jo hesitated before releasing a sigh that said Maddie would owe her one. A big one.

"I'll come right back," Maddie promised, "once I head Lane off down the block."

After a grumble, Jo pasted on a smile, wide enough for a dentist's exam, and flung open the door. "TJ," she exclaimed, "how 'bout that streak of DiMaggio's, huh?"

Behind his umber bangs, his forehead creased in puzzlement. "Uh, yeah. That was . . . somethin'." His hand hung from a loop of his cuffed jeans. Nearly four years of wash and wear had frayed the patch on his *USC Baseball* sweatshirt. Its vibrancy had long ago faded, just like TJ's.

Diverting from Jo's unsubtle approach, Maddie asked him, "Didn't you have to work tonight?"

"I was supposed to, but Jimmy needed to switch shifts this weekend." His cobalt gaze suddenly narrowed and gripped hers. "You going somewhere special?"

"What?" She softly cleared her throat before thinking to glance down at her flared navy dress, her matching strappy heels. She recalled the pin curls in her auburn, shoulder-length do. The ensemble didn't spell out a casual trip to a picture show.

Jo swiftly interjected, "There's a new hot jazz band playing at the Dunbar. They say Duke Ellington and Billie Holiday might even be there. I'm dragging Maddie along. A keen study in music. You know, for her big audition."

"I thought you were practicing tonight," he said to Maddie.

"I am—I will. After we get back."

"You two going alone?"

"We'll be fine." As everything would be, if he'd let up long enough.

"All right," he said, rubbing the back of his neck. "I'll just grab a bite in the kitchen then come along."

Maddie stifled a gasp. "No, really. You don't have to."

"At the Dunbar? Oh yeah I do."

Criminy. Was he going to hold her hand as they crossed the street to reach the bus stop too?

"TJ, this is ridiculous. I'm nineteen years old. Dad used to let us go out all the—"

He lashed back with a fistful of words. "Well, Dad's gone, and I'm not him. You don't like the deal, you can stay home."

Stunned, Maddie stared at him. He'd spoken the word *gone* as though their father had died along with their mother.

Jo waved her hands, shooing away the tension. "So it's settled. We'll all go together." Maddie widened her eyes as Jo continued, "And hey, while he's eating, you'll have time to drop off your neighbor's letter. The one the postman delivered by accident."

The letter . . . ?

Confusion quickly gave way to disappointment. Maddie now had an excuse to sneak out, but only to cancel rather than delay her date with Lane. She hated the prospect of missing one of his rare visits from school.

On the upside, in two weeks he would be back for winter break, offering more opportunities for quality time together.

"Fine, then," she snipped at her brother. "Come if you want."

What other choice did she have?

While Jo bombarded TJ with questions about the World Series, Maddie strode down the hall. Her urge to sprint mounted as she recalled the time. She made it as far as the bottom step when the doorbell rang.

Oh, God.

"I'll get it!" She rushed to the entry. Hoping to prevent the disaster from worsening, she opened the door only halfway. Yet at the greeting of Lane's perfect white smile, all her worries evaporated like mist. The warm glow of the portico light caressed his short black hair and olive skin. Shadows swooped softly from his high cheekbones. His almond-shaped eyes, inherited from his Japanese ancestors, shone with the same deep brown that had reached out and captured her heart the first time he'd held her last spring, an innocent embrace that had spiraled into more.

"Hi, Maddie," he said, and handed her a bouquet of lavender lilies. Their aroma was divine, nearly hypnotic, just like his voice.

But then footsteps on the stairs behind her sobered her senses.

"You have to go," was all she got out before TJ called to him.

"Tomo!" It was the nickname he'd given Lane Moritomo when they were kids. "You didn't tell me you were coming home."

The startle in Lane's eyes deftly vanished as his best friend approached.

Maddie edged herself aside. Her heart thudded in the drum of her chest as she watched Lane greet him with a swift hug. A genuine grin lit TJ's face, a rare glimpse of the brother she missed.

"I'm only in till tomorrow," Lane told him. "Then it's straight back for classes." Though several inches shorter than TJ, he emitted a power in his presence, highlighted by his tailored black suit.

"Term's almost over," TJ remarked. "What brought you back?"

"There was a funeral this afternoon. Had to go with my family."

Surprisingly, TJ's expression didn't tense at the grim topic. Then again, Lane always did have the ability—even after the accident—to settle him when no one else could. "Anyone I know?"

"No, no. Just the old geezer who ran the bank before my dad. Came away with some nice flowers at least." Lane gestured to the lilies Maddie had forgotten were in her grip. "Priest said they didn't have space for them all."

TJ brushed over the gift with a mere glance. "I was gonna take the girls to some jazz joint. Any chance you wanna come?"

"Sure. I'd love to," he said, not catching the objection in Maddie's face.

Her gaze darted to the top of the staircase, seeking help. There, she found Jo leaning against the rail with a look that said, *Ah, well, things could be worse.*

And she was right. Before the night was over, things could get much, much worse.

2

Cigarette smoke at the Dunbar swirled, adding to the fog of Lane's thoughts. Since arriving, he had been struggling to keep his focus on the Negroes playing riffs onstage. Now, with TJ off fetching drinks, he could finally allow his eyes to settle on the profile of Maddie, seated across from him. Her jasmine perfume, while subtle, somehow transcended the wafts of beer and sweat in the teeming club.

From above the bar, blue lights danced over the crowd united in music and laughter—racially integrated, as the entire world would be when Lane was done with it—and rippled shadows across Maddie's face. The narrow slope of her nose led to full lips, moist with a red sheen. Her hazel eyes studied the musicians with such intensity that he chose to merely watch her.

Amazing that he'd known her for more than half his life, yet only months ago had he truly begun to see her. The ache to touch her swelled, along with a desire to make up for lost time. He reached over and brushed the back of her creamy hand resting on their cocktail table.

She jolted, her trance broken. "Sorry," she said, and returned his smile.

"Pretty good, isn't he?" Lane indicated the saxophonist. The long, haunting notes of "Summertime" made the guy's talent obvious even to Lane.

"Yeah, I suppose."

"You don't think so?"

"No, I do. It's just—the structure's so loose, with all those slurs, and the downbeat going in and out. Plus, the key changes are too quick to feel grounded. And during the chorus, his timing keeps—" She broke off, her nose crinkling in embarrassment. "Gosh, listen to me. I sound like a royal snob, don't I?"

"Not at all."

She exaggerated a squint. "Liar."

They both laughed. In truth, he could listen to her talk forever. "God, I've missed you," he said to her.

"I've missed you too." The sincerity in her voice was so deep, he could lose himself in that sound for days. But a moment later, she glanced around as if abruptly aware of the surrounding spectators, and her glimmering eyes dulled, turned solid as her defenses. She slid her hand away, sending a pang down his side.

He told himself not to read into it, that her aversion to a public show of affection wasn't a matter of race. She was simply fearful of jeopardizing her relationship with her brother. Understandable, after all she had been through.

"So," she said. "Where did Jo go?"

"To the ladies' room."

"Oh."

Awkwardness stretched between them as the song came to a close. They joined in with a round of applause. When the next ballad began, it occurred to him that a slow dance would be their only chance for a private, uninterrupted talk. His only chance to hold her tonight. He gestured to the dance floor. "Shall we?"

"I . . . don't think we should."

"Maddie, your brother won't get any ideas just because—"

A booming voice cut him off. "Evenin', sweet cakes." The guy sidled up to the table near Maddie, a familiar look to him. Beer sloshed in his mug, only two fingers gripping the handle. He had the sway of someone who'd already downed a few. "Fancy seeing you here."

Maddie shifted in her seat, her look of unease growing. "Hi, Paul."

Now Lane remembered him. Paul Lamont. The guy was a baseball teammate of TJ's, ever since their high school years, subjecting Lane to occasional encounters as a result. Even back then, the towhead had carried a torch for Maddie subtle as a raging bonfire.

"What do you say?" Paul licked his bottom lip and leaned on the table toward her. "Wanna cut a rug?"

"No thanks."

"C'mon, doll. You don't wanna hurt my feelings, do ya?"

Lane couldn't hold back. "I think the lady's answered."

Paul snapped his gaze toward the challenge. He started to reply when recognition caught. "Well, lookee here. Lane Moratoro." Beer dove from his mug, splashed on Lane's dress shoes.

"It's Moritomo." Lane strove to be civil, despite being certain the error was purposeful.

"Oh, that's right. Mo-ree-to-mo." Then Paul yelled, "Hey, McGhee!"

A guy standing nearby twisted around. His fitted orange shirt and broad nose enhanced his lumberjack's build. "Yeah, what?"

"Got another rich Oriental here who wants to rule our country. Thinks he's gonna be the first Jap governor of—no, wait." Paul turned to Lane. "It's a *senator*, right?"

Lane clenched his hands under the table. "Something like that." Out of the corner of his eye, he glimpsed Maddie shaking her head in a stiff, just-ignore-him motion.

Paul's lips curled into a wry grin. "Well, in that case, maybe you can help a local citizen out." He put an unwelcome hand on Lane's shoulder. "See, my pop's been truck farming for twenty-some years, working his fingers to the bone. But wouldn't you know it? Jap farmers round here just keep undercutting his damn prices. So I was thinkin', when you're elected senator you could do something about that." His mouth went taut. "Or would your *real* loyalty be with those dirty slant eyes?"

Lane shot to his feet, tipping his chair onto the floor. He took a step forward, but a grasp pulled at his forearm.

"Lane." It was Maddie at his side. "Let it go." The lumberjack squared his shoulders as she implored, "Honey, forget him. He's not worth it."

At that, Paul's glance ricocheted between her and Lane. He scoffed in disbelief. "Don't tell me you two are . . ."

Lane knew he should deny it for Maddie's sake, yet the words failed to form. Again, her touch slipped away, leaving the skin under his sleeve vacantly cold.

Paul snorted a laugh, thick with disgust. "Well, Christ Almighty. Who'd a thought."

Lane's nails bit into his palms. He felt his upper back muscles gather, cinching toward the cords of his neck.

"We got a problem here?" TJ arrived at the scene and put down their drinks.

"Everything's great," Maddie announced. "Isn't it, fellas."

Jitterbug notes failed to cushion their silence.

"Paul?" TJ said.

Paul nodded tightly and replied, "Just fine, Kern. I'm surprised, is all. Figured you'd be more selective about who made moves on your little sister."

TJ's face turned to stone. "What are you sayin'?"

Once more, a denial refused to budge from Lane's throat.

"What, you didn't know either?" Paul said, but TJ didn't respond. With a glint of amusement, Paul shook his head, right as Jo returned to their table. "Goes to prove my point," he went on. "Every one of them filthy yellow Japs is a double-crosser, no matter how well you think you—"

His conclusion never reached the air. A blow from TJ's fist stuffed it back into the bastard's mouth. Paul's beer mug dropped to the floor, arcing a spray across strangers' legs. Shrieks outpoured in layers.

A wall of orange moved closer; McGhee the lumberjack wanted in on the action. Lane lurched forward to intervene. Diplomacy deferred, he shoved the guy with an adrenaline charge that should have at least rocked the guy backward, but McGhee was a mountain. Solid, unmovable. A mountain with a punch like Joe Louis. His hit launched a searing explosion into Lane's eye socket.

The room spun, a carousel ride at double speed. Through his

good eye, Lane spied the ground. He was hunched over but still standing. He raised his head an inch and glimpsed TJ taking an uppercut to the jaw. TJ came right back with a series of pummels to Paul's gut.

Lane strained to function in the dizzy haze, to slow the ride. He noted McGhee's legs planted beside him. The thug motioned for Lane to rise for a second round. Before going back in, though, Lane was bringing support. His fingers closed on the legs of a wooden chair. He swung upward, knocking McGhee over a table and into a stocky colored man, who then grabbed him by the orange collar.

"Cops!" someone hollered.

And the music stopped.

"Let's scram, Tomo!" In an instant, TJ was towing him by the elbow. They threaded through the chaos with Maddie and Jo on their heels. They didn't stop until reaching an empty alley several blocks away.

Lane bent over, hands on his thighs, to catch his breath. The echo of his pulse pounded in his ears, throbbed his swelling eye. Still, through it all he heard laughter. TJ's laughter. That carefree sound had been as much a part of Lane's childhood as Japanese Saturday school, or strawberry malts at Tilly's Diner.

Maddie rolled her eyes with a glower. "Well, I'm glad *someone* thinks that was funny."

"See, I was right." Jo nudged her arm. "Told you that joint was jumpin'."

"Yeah," she said, "it was jumpin' all right. Too bad we almost jumped straight into a jail cell." When TJ's laughter grew, Maddie's smile won out. She hit her brother lightly on the chest. "You're off your nut."

Lane grinned. "And this is new news?"

Jo peeked out around the brick wall. Water drizzled from a drain spout. "Coast is clear," she reported.

The ragged foursome treaded toward the bus stop. On the way, Lane turned to TJ and quietly offered his thanks—for what he did, for defending him.

"Eh," TJ said, "what're friends for." He used a sleeve to wipe the trickle of blood from his lip, then slung an arm over Lane's shoulder. "Besides, I can't think of the last time I had that much fun."

The vision of TJ hammering out his aggressions on Paul came back in a flash of images. "I'm just glad I'm not your enemy," Lane said with a smile—one that faded the moment he recalled what had initially provoked the fight.

3

It was on nights like this that Maddie missed her most, when her love life seemed a jumble of knots only a mother could untangle. More than that, her mom's advice would have fostered hopes of a happily ever after.

The woman had been nothing if not a romantic.

She'd adored roses and rainstorms and candlelight, in that order. She had declared chocolate an essential food for the heart, and poetry as replenishment for the soul. She'd kept every courtship note from her husband—who she'd sworn was more handsome than Clark Gable—and had no qualms about using her finest serving ware for non-holiday dinners. Life, she would say, was too short not to use the good china. As though she had known how short hers would be.

Maddie tugged her bathrobe over her cotton nightgown. Unfortunately, no amount of warmth would relax the wringing in her chest. Always this was the cost of remembering her mother. The one remedy Maddie could count on was music.

She placed the violin case on her bed. Unlatching the lid, she freed her instrument from its red velvet–lined den. The smooth wood of the violin, of the bow, felt cool and wonderful in her hands. Like a crisp spring morning. Like air.

An audience of classical composers—black-and-white, wallet-sized portraits—sat poised in the lid's interior. Mozart, Mendelssohn, Bach, and Tchaikovsky peered with critical eyes. *Do our works justice, Miss Kern, or give us due cause to roll over in our graves.*

She rosined and tuned in systematic preparation. Then she positioned herself properly before the music stand. Bach's Partita No. 3 in E major. The sheets were aligned and ready. She knew them by heart but took no chances. She placed the chin rest at her jaw, inhaling the fragrance of the polished woodwork. A shiver of anticipation traveled through her.

Eyes intent on the prelude, she raised her bow over the bridge. Her internal metronome ticked two full measures of allegro tempo. Only then did she launch the horsehairs into action. Notes pervaded the room, precise and sharp. Her fingertips rippled toward the scroll and down again, like a wave fighting its own current. The strings vibrated beneath her skin, the bow skipped under her control. And with each passing phrase, each conquered slur, the twisting on her heart loosened, the memories faded away.

By the time she reached the final note, the calculated stanzas had brought order back to her life. She held her pose in silence, waiting reluctantly for the world to reenter her consciousness.

"Maddie?"

Startled back, she turned toward the doorway.

"Just wanted to say good night." Her brother held what appeared to be ice cubes bound by a dishcloth on his right knuckles. His scuffle with Paul suddenly seemed days rather than hours ago. "Got a game tomorrow morning. Then I'm taking Jimmy's shift," he reminded her.

"Are you sure you can do all that, with your hand?"

He glanced down. "Ah, it's nothin'," he said, lowering the injury to his side.

TJ's hand could be broken into a thousand pieces—as could his heart—and he'd never admit it.

"That sounded good, by the way," he said. "The song you were playing."

She offered a smile. "Thanks."

"You using it for the audition?"

"I might. If I make it past the required pieces."

"Well, don't sweat it. I know you're gonna get in next time." In contrast to this past year, he meant, when she had blown the audition at I.M.A.

Under the Juilliard School of Music, the Institute of Musical Art had been established in New York to rival the best of European conservatories. Maddie's entrance into the program was a goal her dad had instilled in her since her ninth birthday. He'd gifted her with a used violin, marking the first time he had ever expressed grand hopes for *her* future, versus her brother's.

"You know, I was thinking. . . ." Maddie fidgeted with the end of her bow. "When I visit Dad this week, you should come along."

TJ's eyes darkened. "I got a lot of stuff to do."

"But, we could go any day you'd like."

"I don't think so."

"TJ," she said wearily. "He's been there a year and you haven't gone once. You can't avoid him forever."

"*Wanna bet?*" Resentment toughened his voice, a cast shielding a wound—that wound being grief, Maddie was certain. She had yet to see him shed a tear over their mother's death, and those feelings had to have pooled somewhere.

After a long moment brimming with the unspoken, his expression softened. She told herself to hug him, a sign she understood. Yet the lie of that prevented her from moving. Their father, after all, had never even been charged. How many years would TJ continue to blame him?

TJ studied his ice bag and murmured, "I'm just not ready, okay?"

Maddie knew better than to push him, mule-headed as he could be. Besides, she couldn't discount his admission, which held promise, if thin. And truth, the core of his existence.

"Fair enough." She tried to smile, but the contrast of her ongoing deception soured her lips.

Lane.

Her steady.

It had been Maddie's idea to keep their courtship a secret, at least until the relationship developed. With TJ's temperament heightening along with his protectiveness of her, why get him hot and bothered for no reason? His friendship with Lane aside, society's resistance to mixed couples wouldn't have helped her case.

Tonight, though, from her brother's old smile to his old laugh, his defending Lane with gusto, she saw an opening for his approval. She needed to act before the opportunity closed.

"Well, good night," TJ said, and angled away.

"Wait."

He looked at her.

The words gathered in her throat, but none of them suitable for a brother. She didn't dare describe how a mere glance from Lane could make her feel more glamorous than a starlet. How his touch to her lower spine, while guiding her through a doorway, would cause a tingle beyond description.

"What is it?" TJ pressed.

Time to be square with him. She clutched her bow and hoped for the best. "The thing that Paul said," she began, "about me and Lane . . . together . . ."

He shook his head. "Ah, don't worry."

"Yeah, but—"

"Maddie, it's fine."

Stop interrupting, she wanted to yell. She had to get this out, to explain how one date had simply led to another. "TJ, I need to tell you—"

"I already know."

Her heart snagged on a beat. She reviewed his declaration, striving to hide her astonishment. "You do?"

His mouth stretched into a wide grin. The sight opened pores of relief on her neck before she could question how he'd found out.

Of course . . . Lane must have told him. In which case, how long had her brother gone without saying so? All these months spent fretting for nothing. She couldn't decide which of them she wanted to smack, or embrace, more.

"Seriously," TJ mused, "the two of you dating? That's the stupidest thing I ever heard." He bit off a laugh, and Maddie froze. "Lane's part of our family—the only family we've got left. Even if he ever did get a wild hair to ask you out, he'd come to me first. He's not the kind to go behind a pal's back. Paul was just drunk, and he was egging for a fight. Don't let anything he said get to you, all right?"

The implication struck hard, shattering Maddie's confession. "Right," she breathed.

"Listen, I'd better hit the sack. Sleep well."

"You too," she said with a nod. Though with her uncertainties and emotions gearing up to battle, she expected anything but a restful sleep.

4

"Shhh." With a finger to his lips, Lane reminded his sister to keep as quiet as a ninja. Her analogy, not his. Emma gave him a conspiratorial smile. In her blouse and pleated skirt, black bob framing her round face, she stood next to him behind his bedroom door. Their secret quest lent a twinkle to her chocolate, Betty Boop eyes.

He donned his sunglasses, a necessary measure. Not as protection from the cloudy morning light, but to prevent a scolding should they fail to sneak past their mother. Although he felt rather proud of his inaugural fistfight, the bruises encircling his puffy left eye would hardly earn parental praise. At least Maddie wouldn't see him like this. His train would depart hours before she'd be off work.

Lane pushed aside his suitcase that barricaded the door. His clothes were packed, ready to nab once he and Emma returned, en route to the station. One cautious step at a time they crept down the hallway. The polished wood floor felt slick beneath his socks. Navigating a corner, hindered by his shaded view, he bumped something on the narrow table against the wall. Their mother's vase. The painted showpiece teetered. Its ghostly sparrow clung to a withered branch as Lane reached out, but Emma, lower to the ground, made the save.

He sighed and mouthed, *Thank you.*

Emma beamed.

They continued down the stairs. A Japanese folk song crackled on the gramophone in the formal room. The female singer warbled solemnly about cherry blossoms in spring and a longing to return to Osaka, the city of her birth.

It was no coincidence the tune was a favorite of Lane's mother.

From the closet in the *genkan,* their immaculate foyer, he retrieved his trench coat with minimal sound. His sister did the same with her rose-hued jacket. Their house smelled of broiled fish and bean-curd soup. The maid was preparing breakfast. Guilt eased into Lane over her wasted efforts, yet only a touch; he always did prefer pancakes and scrambled eggs.

He pulled out a brief note explaining their excursion, set it on the cabinet stocked with slippers for guests. Then he threw on his wingtips and handed Emma her saddle shoes. As she leaned over to put them on, coins rained from her pocket. This time she reached out too late. Pennies clattered on the slate floor.

"Get them later," Lane urged in an undertone, and grabbed the door handle.

"Doko ikun?"

Lane bristled at his mother's inquiry. "I'm . . . taking Emma to Santa Monica, to the Pleasure Pier. Remember, I mentioned it yesterday?" He risked a glance in his mother's direction to avert suspicion. Even in her casual plum housedress, Kumiko Moritomo was the epitome of elegance. Like an actress from a kabuki theatre, never was she seen without powder and lipstick applied, her ebony hair flawlessly coiffed. A small mole dotted her lower left cheek, as dainty as her frame, underscoring the disparity of her chiseled expressions.

"Asagohan tabenasai," she said to Emma.

"But, *Okāsan . . ."* The eight-year-old whined in earnest, an understandable reaction. What child would want to waste time eating breakfast? Cotton candy and carousel rides were at stake.

Their mother didn't bother with a verbal admonishment. Her

steely glare was enough to send the girl cowering to the kitchen. "*Ohashi o chanto tsukainasai,*" their mother called out, Emma's daily reminder to use her chopsticks properly. Crossing the utensils, though it more easily picked up food, symbolized some nonsense involving death. One of many bad omens to avoid on the woman's tedious list of superstitions.

She shifted to Lane and jerked her chin toward the formal room. "We have an issue to discuss," she said in her native tongue. Despite having immigrated to America with her husband more than two decades ago, she spoke to them only in Japanese, which Lane now honored in return. The show of obedience might help at least delay a stock lecture.

"Why don't we talk when Emma and I get back? Before the train. I did promise to take her this morning."

"We will speak *now*." She turned to fetch her husband from the den. Negotiating wasn't an option.

Why couldn't she have had a Mahjong game scheduled? Or her flower-arranging class? Either activity, required by her societal ranking, might have prevented whatever was to come.

Lane shucked off his shoes. In the formal room, he dropped into a wingback chair. The surrounding décor emanated a starkness that carried a chill. Decorative katana swords and encased figurines created a museum display of a heritage to which he felt little connection.

He bounced his heel on the ornate rug, checked his watch. Perhaps if he could guess the impending topic, he could speed things along. The laughing fit he and his sister had barely managed to contain at yesterday's funeral seemed the most likely possibility, given that the high hats of Little Tokyo had been in attendance.

But really, who could blame them?

Pretending to grieve for their father's predecessor, the widely despised manager of Sumitomo Bank, would have been hard enough without the suffocating incense and silly Buddhist rites. The frilly green dress their mother had forced Emma to wear—complete with an onslaught of matching gloves and bows—befit a Japanese Shirley Temple. The sole element lacking absurdity had been the priest's droning chant. Surely the audience would have fallen asleep if not for the blinding altar of golden statues. Another prime lesson from the ancestors: gaudiness to celebrate humility.

He scoffed at the notion, just as his father entered. Although Nobu was several years short of fifty, more salt than pepper topped his lean form. His Kyoto dialect reflected the gentleness of his eyes. He wore his usual *haori,* a twenty-year-old kimono jacket, simple and humble, the same as him.

"Good morning," he said in Japanese.

Lane proceeded in his parents' language. "Good morning, Father." A slight bow sent his sunglasses down the irksomely low bridge of his nose. He nudged them upward to conceal his wound.

In the corner, his mother tended to the gramophone. Her song had ended, giving way to a loop of static. As she stored the record, his father settled on the couch across from Lane and absently rubbed dried glue off his thumb. Assembling his latest model airplane had tinted his fingernails red and blue.

Lane was tempted to kick-start the discussion, an acquired habit from his collegiate council position, but refrained. His family didn't operate as a democracy.

Finally, his mother moved to the couch and claimed her space. She folded her hands on her lap. Prim. Poised. A usual gap divided the couple, as if flanking an invisible guest.

"Your father would like to speak to you," she prompted, a verbal tap of the gavel.

"Mmm," his father agreed. He folded his arms and let out a deep exhale that stirred Lane's curiosity. "It is the matchmaker in Japan. He has been working very hard for you, searching for a well-suited prospect."

Shit, Lane thought, *not this again.*

He didn't realize the words had slipped out of his mouth until his father narrowed his eyes. "Takeshi!" It was Lane's birth name, spoken with more surprise than anger.

Right away, Lane regretted not mirroring the respect his father had always shown him. "I apologize. I didn't mean to say that." *Only to think it.*

His mother tsked. "You are in your father's house, not a dorm at your American university. If this is how you—" She stopped short. "Remove your glasses when we are addressing you."

For a moment, Lane had forgotten he was wearing them, and, more important, why. His mother's gaze bore through the lenses. Bracing himself, he unmasked his suddenly not-so-prideful mark, and his parents gasped in unison.

"What is this?" His father leaned toward him.

"It's nothing. Really. It looks worse than it is."

"Nothing?" his mother said, incredulous, but his father continued on with concern.

"What happened? Were you robbed?"

"No, no," Lane assured him. "I was just at a club last night, when a brawl broke out." Not the most tactful opening. Better to expound with highlights considered heroic in their culture; violence as a means of unconditional loyalty was, after all, a samurai staple. "Some chump I went to Roosevelt High with was there. He was being disrespectful, not only toward me but against all Japanese. So"—better to keep things anonymous—"a buddy of mine came to my defense. And when I tried to hold the bigger guy back—"

"Enough," his father said. His eyes exhibited such disappointment, the remainder of the story stalled on Lane's tongue. "I did not raise you to be a lowly street fighter. You have been afforded a better upbringing than that."

Lane's mother turned to her husband. Shards of ice filled her voice. "Did I not warn you? He is twenty-one years old, and because of you, he remains a child. All the idealistic views you have put into his head, to speak up when it suits him. As always, the nail that sticks out gets hammered down." To punctuate the ancient adage, she flicked her hand to the side. The gesture effectively illustrated the quiet criticism she sent the man in every look, every day. An unyielding punishment, it seemed, for trading the dreams she'd once held for his. But his dreams were also for his children. Lane had always known this without being told.

Japan was a tiny island, crammed with farmers and fishermen and conformists, all bowing blindly to an emperor roosted on an outdated throne. Here, possibilities floated like confetti. Los Angeles was the city of angels, the heart of Hollywood, where imagination bloomed and promise hung from palm trees. Hope streamed in the sunlight.

America was their home, and Lane's need to defend that fact took over.

"There's nothing wrong with wanting to make a difference in this country. My country. *Emma's* country." His delivery was gruffer than intended, but he wouldn't say "sorry" this time. His sister, if no one else, deserved a safe place to plant the seeds of dreams and watch them grow.

Lane's father straightened. He rested his hands firmly on his spread knees in a contemplative, Buddha-like pose. Outside of his job, his greatest displays of strength were reserved for these kinds of moments. Moderating. Keeping the ground beneath their family level.

"Your mother is right," he said evenly, and continued before Lane could argue. "You are a man now. You must settle down. Carrying another's needs on your shoulders will focus you on your future." In banking, he meant. A baby rattle made of an abacus had established the reference since Lane's birth. "Therefore," he added, "we are pleased the matchmaker has found you a suitable bride, and he will make the necessary arrangements."

Bride.

Arrangements.

The sentence replayed in Lane's mind, pulling him back to the original subject.

"She comes from noble lineage," his father explained. "The matchmaker has ruled out all the usual imperfections—tuberculosis, barrenness, and such. Her family's financial troubles make your pairing a sensible one. Her younger sister has found a match as well, so you must marry first. The family will sail over from Tokyo in time for the new year."

"Hopefully," his mother muttered, "our son will look presentable by then."

Lane scarcely registered the gouge. His mind was too consumed with the timetable his father had laid out. The rush of it all, the solidity. "But—what about school? I still have a whole semester left."

"She will live with us after the wedding," his father said with a small nod to his wife, as if crediting the source of the solution. "Once you graduate, you may make other plans if you wish."

Lane's thoughts moved in a rapid tumble, blending into a mass of confusion. From that blur emerged a simple voice of reason. *Tell them the truth. Confess, as you've wanted to all along.*

Before he could reconsider, he tossed out his protest. "I can't. I'm in love with somebody else."

Tension of a new level swept through the room, conquering every inch of space. No one moved. No one spoke.

Lane wondered if anyone was breathing.

"You've met her before," he said, easing them in. "She grew up here, in Boyle Heights. She's a talented violinist. And she's charming and beautiful, responsible . . ."

"Her name?" Lane's mother spoke through lips that barely moved.

"Maddie."

"Maddie," she repeated as if judging the name by its taste, expecting a release of bitterness. The women had crossed paths on only a few occasions, during which his mother sustained disinterest. "I do not know of this girl. Who is her family?"

First names meant little in their community; at least a third of the "Nisei," those born in America to Japanese immigrants, were called George or Mary. All significance lay in the surname, an indication of nobility, of lineage. Of race.

"If you mean Maddie's last name," Lane hazarded to admit, "it's Kern."

His mother blanched. The lines spanning his father's brow deepened.

"She's TJ's sister," Lane added, hoping their fondness of his friend would somehow permit a bending of their rules. Yet their scowls made clear there was no exception.

"You have made fools of us," she hissed.

"Why? Because she's not Japanese?"

There was no reply. Which said everything.

"Father, you're the one who's so proud of your kids being American. That's half the reason you came to this country. So why should it matter where Maddie's parents are from?"

Lane's mother patted her chest, grumbling under her breath, until her husband raised his hand, stilling her. His rigid words hovered above the quiet. "The final decision has been made."

A humorless laugh shot from Lane's throat. "A decision I haven't been a part of." He rose to his feet. "Shouldn't I have a say in my own future?"

"This is not about you alone," his father said, meeting his stance. "This is about the honor you bring to your family."

"What if I say no? What if I want to make my own choices?"

When his father hesitated, his mother supplied the answer from her seat. "Then you will disgrace this family. And you will *not* be welcome in this home. Ever."

Lane felt the stab of her tenacity, a knife between the ribs. He stared at his father in a desperate plea for support. Surely the man wouldn't be willing to disown his only son. Emotions aside, a male to carry on the name and bloodline was a fundamental basic.

"*Okāsan.*" Emma entered from the kitchen. "I finished my breakfast. Can Lane and I go to the Pier now? Can we, can we?" Not receiving a response, Emma resorted to the parent whose soft spot for her was a reliable constant. "Papa," she begged, "*onegai.*"

Lane held his father's gaze for an eternal moment. Every second sent a mixture of frustration and sorrow through his veins. He felt his limbs sag with each devastating pulse.

At the point of futility, Lane replaced his sunglasses. He would never look at his father the same. "Get your shoes on, Em," he told her. "We're leaving."

5

The song had died. TJ scuffed his spikes on the mound, wishing for the life of him he could remember the tune. For all those high school shutouts and championships, an internal humming had carried him through. Its reliable rhythm had added a zip to any pitch from his hand.

Now, score tied at the bottom of the seventh inning, all he could hear was wind through the trees at Griffith Park and cheering from an adjacent winter-league ball game. Morning clouds soaked up any other sound.

The USC catcher flashed the sign. A curveball. TJ's old bread-and-butter.

A senior from St. Mary's continued at the plate. He was a lanky walk-on TJ used to cream with fractional effort. Even sophomore year, just weeks after the holiday that had sledgehammered TJ's life, the guy couldn't compete. But that was before. Before TJ's world had turned silent and grim.

The hitter waggled his bat, waiting. Two balls, one strike, bases loaded with two out.

TJ tucked the ball into his glove. Worse than his sore jaw, a bone-deep ache throbbed from his knuckles. What the hell had he been thinking last night, throwing a right instead of a jab? Thankfully, Paul Lamont hadn't shown today, banged up as he must have been. It wouldn't have taken a genius to put two and two together, and the last thing TJ needed was the coach to think he'd become a hotheaded scrapper.

Blinking against the dusty breeze, TJ lowered his chin. He reared back with knee raised, adjusted the seams, and let the ball fly with a snap of the wrist. It broke low and away. A decent bend—just outside the strike zone.

"Ball!" the umpire declared.

Damn it.

TJ spat at the ground. He caught the return throw and tugged at the bill of his cap, blew out a breath. Gotta clear the melon. Start fresh without the clutter or a pitch didn't have a rookie's chance in hell. He loosened his neck, shook the stiffness from his hand. Strove to look calm.

The St. Mary's batter smiled. He crowded the plate, his confidence growing.

But confidence could be a tricky thing. It lasted only if the person either had forgotten or didn't realize what they stood to lose.

TJ wished he had the leeway to send a reminder. Nothing like a knockdown pitch to wipe a smirk off a slugger's face.

Just then, the catcher tilted his head and shifted his eyes toward the third-base foul line. It was a warning, understood in a game of silent signals. TJ glimpsed a figure he recognized in his periphery. Bill Essick was approaching their dugout. The Yankees' scout, a periodic spectator of Saturday league games, had once been a follower of TJ's career.

Time to turn up the heat.

The catcher appeared to understand. He pointed one finger down, a fastball high and inside.

TJ rose to his full height and grasped the ball in his glove. He paused, ears straining. Where was the song? *Where was it?*

In a pinch, he closed his eyes and forced himself to picture his father's face. On cue, anger boiled toward an eruption. Memories of the accident poured in a heated stream. The panic of tearing through the hospital halls, the police officer and his endless questions. The stench of the morgue, the lifting of the sheet.

He unshuttered his view and hurled the ball in a torrent—*smack* into the glove.

"Steee-riiike!"

Wiping his mind, TJ struggled to reduce his emotions to a simmer. He scuffed the mound again, hard.

Coach Barry nodded beside the dugout. A look of approval from the man, a praised coach of three sports for the Trojans, never lost its impact. He continued to be the major reason, in fact, that TJ attended University of Southern Cal.

But right now, Essick's opinion was all that mattered.

TJ rolled his shoulder muscles for the impromptu review. He could feel the scout's gaze on him. Just one more. All he needed was one more to smoke by the batter, one more to wrap up the inning. If he kept it up, he might even close out the game, from start to finish like the old days. Wouldn't that be swell.

The hitter set his stance. He gave home plate a little more space.

Catcher signed another fastball. It was a cocky choice though relatively safe, given the solid zip on the last pitch and drag on the swing.

Problem was, safe choices never led to greatness. Legends were made of risk takers armed with the skills destined for success. A display like that could be just the thing to regain Essick's interest, to see a winning thoroughbred in a stable of foals.

TJ grabbed hold of that risk, that sample of greatness, and shook off the catcher. "Come on," he murmured, "something to dazzle 'em."

The catcher complied: slider.

Now we're talkin', TJ thought. With a 3–2 count, the hitter wouldn't be expecting a pitch that chanced ending up out of the zone. And when done right, a slider gave the illusion of a fastball, up until it fell off a table the last several feet.

TJ readied for the windup. But just as he was about to close his eyes and dip once more into his cage of fury, a question snuck up on him: What if his rage soon tired of being locked up? He could feel its power increasing each time he let it loose to breathe and stretch. Brought out too often and that rage might end up refusing to go back in.

He squashed the thought and threw the ball with all the strength he could muster. Down the pipe it went. The seams spiraled away—a wall of wind seemed to slow every rotation—and laid tracks that led directly to the bat. *Crack.* The white pill soared overhead while the runners rounded the bases. Every footfall was a stomp to TJ's gut. Only for the mile-length arms of the left fielder did the ball not reach the ground.

The inning was over. TJ had pushed the batter to a full count and gotten the out, but once more he alone hadn't closed the deal. When it came to risks, the thinnest of lines separated a legend and a fool.

Quiet applause broke out while the USC players jogged toward the dugout. Following them in, TJ dared to seek Essick's reaction—not a total disaster; they were still tied, after all.

But the guy had already left.

⚜ 6 ⚜

Apprehension reverberated through Maddie's body, a concerto plucking away the minutes. Inadvertently sticking her callused finger with another straight pin served as a reminder to concentrate on the job at hand. At least until Beatrice, the manager, arrived after a doctor's checkup. Then Maddie would be free to leave her father's tailor shop early, in order to present Lane with her decision.

She scooted her knees another few inches on the scarred wooden floor, dark as the paneled walls, and tacked up more hemline of the jacket. Emerald silk enwrapped Mrs. Duchovny's robust form. A regular customer since Maddie's childhood, the woman had spent her youth as an opera singer. Her endless chatter in the full-length mirror evidenced her sustainable lung capacity. Even more amazing, she gesticulated as quickly as her lips moved, taking only tiny breaks to fluff her pecan-brown curls. None of this made marking her garments an easy task.

"Of course, you know more than anyone," she was saying, "I have enough holiday suits to clothe all of Boyle Heights. But with Donnie coming home on leave, I just wanted something special to wear for Christmas dinner. Especially after missing him over Thanksgiving. We only have three weeks to go, which doesn't give

Bob much time. He's trying to surprise our Donnie with an entire wall of custom-made bookshelves in his room. That boy could read two books a day if he wanted. Did I ever tell you that?"

Maddie glanced up at the unexpected pause. "I think you've mentioned it." She pretended Mrs. Duchovny hadn't already reported the same news about her Navy son a thousand times. Often Maddie wondered about the true reason the woman had insisted on becoming her benefactress for Juilliard. A charitable act of kindness? Or an investment in a potential bride for her son?

Mrs. Duchovny prattled on, continuing to drop matchmaking hints, until Maddie announced, "All finished." Then Maddie snatched two stray pins from the floor and pressed them into the cushion bound to her wrist. She rose, wiping a dust mark from her apron.

"Madeline, dear." Mrs. Duchovny faced her, suddenly serious. The corners of her eyes crinkled behind her thick glasses. "Are you feeling all right?"

And there it was. The dreaded question Maddie had heard more times than she cared to count.

"Yes, I'm fine. Thank you." She forced a smile, feeling anything but fine, as always seemed the case when delivering the phrase. Fortunately, frequency of use had worn the roughness off the lie, turning it smooth as sea glass.

"Are you *sure* about that?" said Mrs. Duchovny, resonant with disbelief. Before Maddie could repeat herself, the woman cracked a wide grin and displayed her right arm. "Because I think you've forgotten a little something, dear."

The other sleeve. Maddie had only tacked the left. "Good grief, I'm so sorry." She resumed her tucking and pinning as Mrs. Duchovny chuckled.

"I'm actually relieved. For a minute, I was worried one arm had grown longer than the other."

Maddie's lips curved into a full smile. Soon, though, she recalled her meeting with Lane. Today. At the Pier. And her anxiousness rose like the tide.

Oh, how she wanted to get the conversation over with.

She had planned to inscribe her thoughts in a letter, but just as she'd flipped over the *OPEN* sign this morning, Lane had phoned. He'd said he was headed to Santa Monica with his sister, and that he and Maddie needed to talk before he left town.

It's about us, he'd replied ominously when she asked if everything was all right. There had been a heaviness in his voice throughout the call, yet it was the word *us* that had landed with a thud, a trunk too burdensome to carry.

Clearly, he too had been pondering the impracticality of it all: A couple weeks for winter break and he would be back at Stanford; by summer's end, she could be off to New York for who knew how long. There would be no harm done should they simply put their relationship on hold, revert to friendship for now. If they were meant to be, destiny would reunite them.

The bell above the entry jarred Maddie back to the room. Beatrice Lovell entered—at last!—hugging a sack from the corner diner. It took two shoves for her to fully close the door. The sticking latch was among the list of repairs the seamstress had been chipping away at since becoming the shop's overseer.

Maddie hastened a review of Mrs. Duchovny's sleeve lengths. Satisfied, she secured the second one with more pins.

"Lord 'a' mercy," Bea exclaimed with her residual Louisianan accent. "I thought I'd left hurricane weather behind me." She set the paper bag on the counter. Outside the windows, red ribbons flapped on storefront wreaths. Passing pedestrians looked to the pavement, hats held to their heads in a tug-o-war with nature.

Mrs. Duchovny clucked in response. "I tell you, this wretched wind is a lady's enemy," she said while Maddie eased her out of the jacket, guiding her around the exposed metal points. "You should have seen the scattering of clothes that ended up in my backyard this morning off my neighbor's line. Good thing Daisy sews her name into her undergarments, because I wasn't about to go door-to-door in search of their owner."

As Maddie hung up the coat, Bea dabbed two fingers on the tip of her tongue and tamed the silvery strands that had escaped her signature bun. Her pursed mouth created a coral embellishment on the wrinkled fabric of her skin. "Brought us back an early lunch," she told Maddie, and unloaded two wax paper–wrapped sandwiches.

Maddie opened her mouth to explain that she had a last-minute . . . well, errand to run. But Mrs. Duchovny interjected, "Ooh, I almost forgot. Donnie's favorite dress shirt is missing a button." From a shopping bag near the sewing machines she produced a white, long-sleeve garb pin-striped in blue. "I was hoping you might have one to match."

"I'd be right surprised if we don't." Bea turned to Maddie. "Sugar, would you mind peeking in the back?"

Maddie strained to preserve her waning patience. How could she deny her patron a measly button?

"Not at all." She accepted the shirt and hurried toward the storage room. Mothballs and memories scented the air, luring her inside, in every sense. It was here, between the racks of now dusty linens, that she and TJ used to hide, still as mice, awaiting a familiar waft. The fragrance of rose petals and baby powder. Their mother's perfume. A sign she'd returned from shopping at the market.

The giggling youngsters would huddle together as two sets of hands swooped in for the capture. And with their small bodies cradled in their parents' arms, a sound would flow through the air, lovelier than any sonata could ever be. For try as she might, Maddie had yet to hear a melody more glorious than their family's laughter. A four-part harmony never to be heard again.

Enough.

She wadded the thought, tossed it over her shoulder. There were plenty more where that came from, and the clock wasn't slowing. Lane, with a train to catch, would only be at the Pier another hour.

Refocusing, she scoured an old Easter basket filled with abandoned buttons, found a decent match, and headed down the hall. She was rounding the corner when she caught the women in hushed voices.

"Goodness me," Mrs. Duchovny lamented, "I forgot how terrible the holidays must be for them."

"Aw, now. You shouldn't feel bad, for having discussed your family gatherin'."

"I suppose. Just such a shame, the poor girl."

There was no doubt whom they'd been talking about. The same family everyone was always talking about. After two years of rampant whispers, Maddie should have been used to this.

Bea popped her head up with an awkward abruptness. "Any luck, sugar?"

Maddie swallowed around the pride, the voiceless scream, lodged in her throat. "I found a button that'll work."

"Splendid," Mrs. Duchovny gushed, her cheeks gone pink. With arms appearing weighted by guilt—or pity—she reached out for the items.

"No." Maddie stepped back, her reply a bit sharp. She held the shirt to her middle and softened the moment with a smile. "That is, I'd be happy to do it for you. No charge." She would have offered normally anyhow, yet it was her sudden inability to unclench her hands that left her without choice.

Mrs. Duchovny conceded, followed by a rare moment of quiet. "I'd best be getting home. Bob will be sending out a search party soon." She shrugged into her fur-collared overcoat and covered her locks with a brimmed hat.

"We'll call y'all when everything's ready," Bea said, and ushered her to the exit while they exchanged good-byes. A burst of air charged through before the door closed, rocking Maddie onto her heels. And not for the first time, she was surprised to discover she was still standing.

7

"Kern!" Coach Barry's voice shot over the departing spectators at Griffith Park. "Need a word with you, son."

TJ fought a scowl as he zipped up his sports bag. Since being pulled for the last two innings, he'd been counting down the minutes to leave. Their closing pitcher had held on for a 7–5 victory, but TJ wasn't in the mood to celebrate.

He slung his bag over his left shoulder and hid his purpling bruises by dangling his right hand behind him. Thankfully, only a muted yellow tinted his cheek.

Coach Barry strolled toward the outfield, a signal for TJ to join him. A private talk. Not a good thing, considering TJ's mediocre showing today. The solid, dark Irishman carried a thoughtful look, hands in the pockets of his baseball jacket. A taunting wind blew past them. It flapped a lock of the man's slicked hair, receding from the effects of close-call games and concern for his players.

As they passed the pitcher's mound, TJ mined his brain for arguments to defend himself. He wasn't about to surrender all hope of regaining his slot in the starting rotation for USC's upcoming season. When his game had gone to hell last year, a compassionate demotion landed him in the bullpen. Now he wanted out. He was a prisoner who knew what it was like on the other side of the fence, and could feel his cell closing in on him. Telling the coach about a new pitch he was honing might aid his cause. A "slurve," they called it. The slider-curve combo could break wide enough to raise some brows.

He was about to volunteer as much when Coach Barry asked, "So how's your father been?"

Your father.

Swell. Was there anything TJ wanted to talk about less?

"The same," he answered. Which meant mute in a convalescent home, nearly too depressed to function.

Coach Barry nodded pensively. "I'm sorry to hear that."

TJ squeezed the strap on his bag. Redirecting, he said, "My sister, Maddie, though—she's doing great. Her violin teacher says she's a shoo-in for Juilliard this year, if her audition goes well. Just gotta keep her on track till then."

"That's good, that's good." Coach Barry smiled. "I'm sure you've done a fine job looking out for her."

TJ shrugged, despite feeling as though caring for Maddie was the one thing he was still doing right.

"What about you, son? How you doing these days?"

"I'm gettin' by." The reply was so reflexive, he didn't consider the bleakness of the phrase until it was too late to reel the words back in. "'Course, if you're talking about baseball, I can assure you, my pitches are coming back more and more every day. You just wait and see. By spring practice—"

Coach Barry held up his hand, bringing them to a stop. "Look," he sighed. "I'm gonna cut to the chase. Your professor, Dr. Nelson, paid a visit to my office last week. It's about your grades."

The path of the conversation, in an instant, became clear. A detour TJ resented. He didn't need their sympathy, or to be ganged up on. That woman had no business stirring up trouble on the field.

"It was a couple lousy tests," he burst out. "I've told her that. Got plenty of time to make it up."

"And the rest of your classes?" The challenge indicated Coach

Barry was well informed of the situation. That his former-ace pitcher was barely skimming by, tiptoeing on the fence of a scholarship lost.

TJ clenched his jaw. He wrestled down his anger, to prevent it from seizing control.

Coach Barry rested a hand on TJ's shoulder, causing a slight flinch. "I know you've been through a lot, son. But you've got less than a year left, and I, for one, don't want to see you throw it all away. Now, if you need a tutor, you just say so. Or if you need more time for studying, we can certainly see about cutting back your delivery hours. . . ."

Less time dedicated to his on-campus job was a nice thought, particularly on days of lugging cadavers from Norwalk State Hospital for the Science Department. Yet a nice thought was all it was. Besides school expenses, TJ needed all the dough he could get for house bills and Maddie's lessons and everything else in the goddamned world that chomped its way through a pocketbook.

"I'll be fine, Coach," he broke in. He repeated himself, taking care to stress his gratitude. "Really, I'll be fine." If it hadn't been for the guy's encouragement, TJ would have dropped out of college long before now.

Coach Barry rubbed the cleft in his chin before he heaved a resigning breath. "All right, then. You know where to find me."

TJ obliged with a nod. He remained on the faded lines of the diamond as his coach walked away and disappeared from sight. At that moment, in the wide vacancy of the ball field, TJ suddenly realized why he had always been a pitcher.

Because alone on the mound, he depended only on himself.

8

Maddie stood on the Pier, searching, searching. Though unbuttoned, her long russet coat hoarded heat from her anxious rush across town. A current of strangers split around her like a river evading a rock. An ordinary rock, medium in size, nearly invisible. And Maddie preferred it that way. Only when channeling another's composition through her bow did she now find comfort in the spotlight.

Scanning faces, she hunted for Lane's distinct features, his sister's pint-sized frame. Outside the Hippodrome was where he had asked Maddie to meet them. But they weren't there, and she didn't have the luxury of time to wait patiently. It was a quarter after noon. She had but fifteen minutes to spare. He couldn't have left early; she'd told him she would be here as soon as she could. She needed to find him, before he left, before his train.

Before she lost her nerve.

"Lane, where are you?" At the very moment she whispered the words, she spotted the back of his familiar form blinking between passersby. His golden skin peeked out between his short black hair and the collar of his coat.

She prepared herself while striding over the wooden planks to reach him. "I'm so glad you're still here," she said, touching his arm. He turned toward her, revealing the face of a man with sharp Italian features. Mustard stained his large lips.

"Pardon me," Maddie said. "I thought you were somebody else." Then she streamed into the mass, head down. Blending.

The smell of onions from a hot-dog stand caused her stomach to growl. In her haste, she'd left the lunch Bea had insisted she take for the bus ride over. Macaroni salad and a baked-bean sandwich. Maddie had grown to love both as a child, long before she could comprehend which meals were served solely to survive the shop's less-profitable months.

But she couldn't think about any of that now. She had ten minutes to find—

"Maddie . . ."

She focused on the vague call of her name, filtering out the crowd's chatter. Notes of "In the Mood," from the band on a nearby stage, took greater effort to block; music dominated her hearing above all else.

"Maddie!" At last, the soprano voice guided her to Emma's china-doll face. The girl was scurrying toward her with a smile that made perfect little balls of her rosy cheeks. Maddie used to secretly babysit her when Lane was in high school. Naturally, he had preferred outings with TJ over watching his pesky little sister. He'd been adamant about paying by the hour, though Maddie would have done it for free. And one look at the youngster reminded her why.

"Hiya, pretty girl."

Emma leapt into her outstretched arms. Adoration seemed to flow from the child's every pore. It filled Maddie's heart so quickly she had to giggle to prevent her eyes from tearing up.

As their arms released, she noted a substance on Emma's hands. "Ooh, you're sticky. Let me guess, cotton candy?"

"*And* a caramel apple," Emma boasted. Then her smile dropped. "Don't tell my mom, okay?"

"My lips are sealed." An easy promise to make. Running into the woman, unreadable in her stoicism, had always occurred by mere chance, and Maddie's talk with Lane would do anything but change that. "Say, Emma, where's your brother?"

Emma twisted to her side and pointed. There was Lane, weaving around a family ordering ice-cream cones. He wore a trench coat and sunglasses. A bright red balloon floated on a string clutched in his hand. When Maddie caught his attention, he flashed a smile, the breathtaking one that seemed crafted just for her. She felt a warm glow rise within her.

"I was getting worried," he said, once they were close.

"Sorry it took so long. We had customers, so I couldn't leave until Bea showed up."

Emma tugged her brother's sleeve, looking troubled. "I thought you were gonna get yellow?"

Lane glanced at the inflatable swaying overhead, as though he'd forgotten it was there. He squatted to her level. "Turns out they were out, kiddo. But since Sarah Mae's favorite color is red, I was hoping this would do."

Emma contemplated that, and nodded. "Good idea. Sarah Mae loves balloons."

Maddie smiled at the reference to the girl's doll, equally ragged and beloved, while Lane tied the string around his sister's wrist.

"*Onīsan,* can we go down to the sand?" Emma asked him. "I didn't get to collect shells yet."

The Japanese term for "brother" was one of the few things Maddie understood about Lane's foreign culture.

He checked his watch. "I guess we can. We only have a few minutes, though, so don't go far. And don't wade too deep into the water."

"Okay, okay."

"You promise?" he pressed.

Emma sighed, her pinkie drawing an *x* over her chest. "Cross my heart," she said, and rolled her eyes, not in rebellious defiance, but in a gentle manner. As if at the age of eight, she could already see his barriers for what they were. An expression of caring. It wasn't so different, Maddie supposed, from the strict guidelines TJ had instilled after assuming their father's role.

Except that she herself wasn't eight.

Side by side, Lane and Maddie walked toward the beach. Strangers with rolled-up pants and buckets and shovels speckled the sandy canvas. A choir of seagulls cawed as they circled yachts in the harbor, muting the hollers of a teenage boy chasing a scampering black puppy. The dog was yipping toward a pair of brilliant kites dancing in the air. With attentive eyes, Lane watched his sister sprinting like the pup, bobbing beneath her flag of a red balloon.

The picture of him as a father hit Maddie with a swell of emotion she swiftly shoved into a box, stored away for the future.

"How's your eye?" she asked.

He shrugged, half a smile on his lips. "It's still there."

"Could I see?" Noting his reluctance, she added, "I'm sure it's not as bad as you think."

Slowly, he reached for the glasses and slid them free. In the swollen bruising she discovered an irony of beauty she didn't expect. He'd always projected such certainty in her uncertain world that strangely she found the sight comforting, proof of his vulnerable side. A symbol of commonality she could actually touch.

"Does it hurt?" Her fingertips brushed his skin before she could remind herself to keep her distance.

"It'll heal."

She nodded and withdrew her hand. Her gaze shifted to the distant figure of Emma, whose raised arms couldn't reach her fleeing balloon. Already twenty feet up, it zigzagged a path toward the ceiling of clouds, away from the chaos, the worries of life. Maddie had the sudden desire to be tethered to its string.

"I don't have much time," he said. "But we need to talk. . . . It's about us."

That phrase again.

He gestured to a thick, weather-beaten log. "Why don't we sit down?"

She didn't reply, simply led them to perch on the bumpy seat. Waves before them lapped the sand, weakening the shore layer by layer. She clasped her hands on her skirted lap. So close to Lane now, she could almost taste the fragrance of his skin. It smelled of citrus and cinnamon and leaves. At the Pico Drive-in, where they'd spent numerous dates necking through double features, Maddie would inhale that lovely mixture. Afterward, she'd sleep in the cardigan she had worn, to savor his scent until it faded.

Would their memories together just as surely disappear?

She banished the thought. She needed to concentrate, to review the practical reasons to loosen their ties. Their usual outings, for one: hidden from crowds, cloaked in darkness. Lookout points and desolate parks. Only on occasion would they venture to the openness of a bowling alley or skating rink, requiring them to refrain from acts of affection.

Just like now.

Lane hooked his glasses in the V of his royal-blue sweater. He stared straight ahead as he continued. "Last spring, you told me you thought it was best if we didn't tell anyone about our dating, and I went along with it. I lied when I said I agreed." He wet his lips, took a breath. "But the truth is, you were right. It was better that we didn't say anything. My family wouldn't have understood, what with our . . . differences. God knows, they wouldn't have taken us seriously. They might have even thought I went steady with you to make a point."

Their racial diversity had, before now, seemed an off-limit topic. An issue to deny through tiptoeing and silence. But more striking than this new candidness was his usage of the past tense. *Went steady with you. Wouldn't have taken us seriously.*

He wasn't asking for her opinion. To him, the relationship was already over.

"I'm tired of sneaking around," he said. "I don't want to lie anymore. I don't want *you* to lie anymore. Especially to TJ. He's more than a friend, he's like a brother to me."

She couldn't argue. None of this had been fair, to any of them.

"Maddie . . ." Lane's mouth opened slightly and held. He seemed to be awaiting the arrival of a rehearsed conclusion, a finale to their courtship. He angled toward her with a graveness that wrenched her heart. "There's something you don't know. Something I should've told you before, but I wasn't sure how."

Maddie blinked. What was he talking about? What had he been keeping from her?

"It's my parents," he said. "They've arranged a marriage for me."

The word *marriage* entered her ears with a calmness that, in seconds, gained the piercing shock of a siren. "To whom?" she found herself asking.

He scrunched his forehead, a revelation playing over his face. "I'm not sure, actually. The *baishakunin*—the matchmaker—found her in Japan. Tokyo, I think they said. Anyway, her family is supposed to be a good fit."

"I . . . didn't realize . . . they still did that." The response was ridiculous, trite. Yet the blow was too great to formulate anything better.

"The custom is crazy, I know. But as their oldest son, their only son, it's my responsibility to do what's best for the family." Annoyance projected in the timbre of his voice. He shook his head. "It's no more than a business negotiation. Same as my parents were. And they want to bring her over right away."

A scrapbook materialized in Maddie's mind: a portrait of Lane in a tuxedo, beside him a wife as exotic as her wedding garb; their children waving to the procession of a Chinese New Year parade; a snapshot of the family at Sunday supper, a foursome with identical almond eyes.

"All of this," he said finally, "is why I needed to see you." He laid his hand on hers, a sympathetic gesture. "I've given it a lot of thought, and there's only one thing that makes sense for us."

The breeze blew a lock of her hair that caught in her eyelashes, a shield to hide her welling tears. She lowered her lids and waited for the words: *to break up.* She'd been foolish, so foolish to believe she could walk away unscathed.

"Maddie," she heard him say. "Will you marry me?"

Once the question fully soaked in, her eyes shot open.

"What?"

He smiled. "Marry me."

She couldn't answer. Her thoughts were a jumble of fragments. An orchestra of musicians, each playing a different piece.

Lane brushed the strands from her face and tucked them behind her ear. He tipped his chin down, peering into her eyes. "The only way they'll ever accept us is to not give them an option. Maddie, I love you. I want to see you every morning when I wake up, and fall asleep every night next to you. I want us to raise a family and spend our whole lives together. And if you feel the same"—he tenderly tightened his grasp on her hand—"then marry me."

Logic. She grappled for any shred of logic. "We can't though. It's—not even legal here." A fact she'd known yet never liked to dwell upon.

"Just the wedding isn't. The marriage would be perfectly valid. A college friend of mine is from Seattle. He says interracial couples get married there every day."

"Seattle?"

"That's right," he said. Then his smile faded into something tentative. "But sweetheart . . . we have to do it next weekend."

Next weekend? *Next weekend?*

The very idea was rash, and insane. She tried to protest, yet her sentence amounted to a whisper. "That's so soon."

"There's no other choice. They plan to bring the girl's family here before New Year's. I don't want to hurt other people, just because we've waited too long." He caressed her cheek. "I know we're meant to be together. Since the first time I kissed you, I've known it with everything in me."

The warmth of his fingers on her face revived the memory of that day. He'd been there when she came home from visiting her father, another one-sided exchange. Lane had been in town for the weekend, relaxing on their couch while TJ finished up at the ball field. She'd walked in to find a fresh envelope from the Juilliard School of Music. Even though she'd predicted their decision—a surety after her poor audition—reading the actual form rejection had struck her with a reality that ripped through the seams of her soul. The reality of lost dreams, a lost life she had taken for granted.

Until then, she had been proud of how dignified she'd been about it all. The perfect portrayal of strength in the face of disaster. But with the weight of that letter in her hands, dignity became too much to carry. When her strength buckled, Lane was the person who'd caught her. She literally cried on his shoulder, soaked his shirt with pent-up grief. He held her close and safe, stroked her hair. And once their lips joined, more than passion flowed through her; it was the peace of finding someone whose heart felt tailor-made to match hers alone.

Now, with Lane's hand on her cheek, her skin melting into his palm, she felt the same overwhelming emotion. The family she'd been raised in was gone, but she and Lane could start a family of their own. The kind she'd always dreamed of. Together, they could be happy.

"Yes," she answered.

"Yes?" A request for clarity.

"Yes." She smiled. "I'll marry you."

Recognition settled in his eyes and a grin across his face. He jumped to his feet and drew her up into his arms. Their hearts were pumping at the same rapid pace. "Oh, Maddie, I love you so much," he said against her temple.

"I love you too," she whispered. She had conveyed the sentiment plenty of times, on notes she'd snuck into his pockets, or in letters she'd mailed to Stanford. Yet only now did she become aware of how much she meant the words.

He leaned back and gazed at her, his eyes glinting with joy. Then he placed his curled fingers under her chin to bring her in for a kiss. Their mouths were a few inches apart when a voice cracked through the moment.

"*Onīsan,*" Emma yelled. "I found one!"

In an instant, they stood a respectable distance apart, though Maddie couldn't say who had created the gap. How could she have forgotten where they were? That Emma, too, could have been watching?

"Look!" The girl ran toward them, holding up something round and white. "It's a whole sand dollar. And it's not broken or chipped or anything. It's a sign of good luck, right?"

Lane gave Maddie a brief glance and grinned again. "Definitely."

"Did you know there's five doves inside?" Emma asked Maddie. "And the North Star is in the middle, and an Easter lily's around it?"

Unable to speak, Maddie nodded.

"Wow." Emma studied the shell. "I can't wait to show Papa. He's gonna love it. Can we go home and show him? Can we?"

Lane looked at his watch, then sighed. "I guess we'd better go. My train . . ."

"Of course," Maddie said, regaining her voice.

He turned to his sister. "Hey, Em. Race you to the snack stand?" He didn't have to ask twice. She automatically assumed a runner's starting pose. "Ready?" he called out. "Set . . . go!"

Unlike Emma, Lane didn't dash away. He stepped back toward Maddie and, picking up from where he left off, he leaned in and placed his lips on hers. Although she closed her eyes, she saw a vision of strangers walking past, pointing, whispering their disapproval. And when the kiss ended, she couldn't help feeling relieved.

"See you next Saturday?" he asked.

She prodded herself to nod.

"You promise?"

"Cross my heart," she said lightly, pushing out a smile.

He touched her check once more, then jogged off to catch up to his sister. After the two faded into the crowd, Maddie lowered herself onto the log. A chill from the wind prickled her neck. She crossed her arms and stared out into the endless ocean that stretched straight up into the clouds.

Remembering Emma's balloon, she panned the sky for what had become a tiny red dot. When it vanished from sight, she wondered how much pressure she, too, could take before bursting into nothing.

9

"Got any idea what you're lookin' for?"

TJ turned from the hardware store's shelves to find his sister's friend Jo. Her tone made clear she doubted he could find the right part on his own. Just the kind of conversation he needed after the lecture from his coach.

"I got it handled." He swung his attention back to the bins of gaskets, the same ones he'd been staring at for the past five minutes. The smells of kerosene and turpentine were making him lightheaded, compounding his frustration.

"Problem with the sink?"

He edged out a nod.

"Kitchen or bathroom?"

"Kitchen," he muttered, picking up a random gasket to study the thing. He was hoping she'd take her cue to move on to another customer roving her family's store.

But she didn't. She continued to watch him, hands in the pockets of her gray work uniform. Her lips bowed in amusement. "You know, I could save you a whole lotta time if you let me help."

Was there a skywriter over his head today announcing he needed charity?

He snapped his eyes to hers. "I said I got it."

Pink spread over her cheeks, a look of surprise, then aggravation. "Suit yourself." She pivoted sharply on the heel of her loafer. By the time she exited the aisle, TJ saw himself for the jerk he'd been.

"Shit." He flung the gasket into the bin. Abandoning his sports bag on the cement floor, he trudged after her, ready to smooth the waters with the *I'm-just-tired-and-have-a-lot-on-my-mind* spiel. Sure it was only half the story, but no one needed to hear more. He rounded the corner and bumped a display of paint cans. The pyramid held its ground. Jo's loose ponytail in his sights, he trailed toward the cashier's table in front. He was about to call Jo's name when a voice from the side stopped him cold.

"TJ," was all she needed to say and he knew it was Cindy Newman.

The harsh fluorescent lights did nothing to take away from her stunning face, her knockout figure. The girl was known to pass as Veronica Lake any day of the week, and today was no exception. Her golden hair draped long and styled, her sundress snug around the curves. Her full lips shimmered in the same red that had tainted his shirt collars more than once.

"Hi, Cindy."

She smiled broadly. "How have you been?"

"Doin' all right. You?"

"Terrific, thanks." The difference between their answers was that hers sounded genuine. "So," she said after a pause, "who won?"

It took him a moment to follow the question. He'd forgotten he was wearing his baseball uniform and jacket. He wished he could as easily forget about the game. "We did."

"That's grand. You were pitching?"

"Yeah." He left it at that.

"Then I'm not surprised." She offered another smile, though this one wasn't solid enough to block the awkwardness rising between them. She fidgeted with her purse handle and glanced down and away. It was the same look she'd given at the end of their last date, a look that said she didn't expect to hear from him again. No question, she had put in effort. She'd tried to talk to him, to kiss him until he would open up. But his wall of fury had sealed her out.

He realized now, more than a year later, that he'd never explained that to Cindy. Never told her it was nothing she'd done.

A grizzled man in overalls wandered past with a shovel, the cash register rang out a sale, and TJ decided another place would be more appropriate for this conversation. "You know, maybe, sometime," he said, "if you're not busy—"

Jo's brother Wes was marching in TJ's direction. The oldest of the five Allister boys, he'd been a quiet but popular linebacker. Latest word had it he was on a winning streak of boxing matches around the city. A guy you didn't want to piss off by insulting his sister.

TJ was about to speak up but didn't make it that far. Wes took the first shot—by scooping Cindy up by her waist. "There you are," he said, and nuzzled her neck, inducing a giggle.

"Were you worried I'd gotten lost?" she teased.

Wes gazed at her with pure adoration, oblivious to any others' existence. "I'm all finished here with inventory. How about a movie at the Palace?"

She groaned. "Is there any picture we *haven't* seen this month?"

He held her close and whispered in her ear, prompting more giggles, her face to blush. TJ did his best to pry away his focus. He felt intrusive, irritated, regretful. And yeah, jealous. Not of being with Cindy necessarily. Just of any guy who could truly be that happy.

The couple headed for the door. As her boyfriend held it open for her, Cindy angled back. An afterthought. "It was good seeing you, TJ. You take care."

He nodded, staring after her. She'd moved on, as she should have. She was better off with someone who had his head on straight.

"Anything I can help you with, sonny?" From behind the counter, old man Allister regarded him over the rims of his bifocals.

Jo touched the man's shoulder. "It's all right, Gramps. He's not one who takes kindly to help." After flicking TJ a cool look, she pushed through the swinging half-doors of the storage room. It was then that TJ recalled why he'd trailed her through the store. Yet the urge to follow her was gone.

❧ 10 ❧

L ane wasn't aware his mind had been wandering until something hit him in the forehead. He jolted back in his cushioned leather chair. A wad of notebook paper had landed on his leg. He could guess the culprit before looking up.

"At least we know he's alive." Dewey Owens smirked at the other two guys in their study group before turning to Lane. "I was getting worried that punch had bruised more than your eye."

Lane pitched the crumpled ball right back. But with Dewey's eagle eyes, a match to his beak-like nose, he ducked in plenty of time.

"Have to be faster than that!"

A student in the corner of the common room sent a curt, "Shhh," to which Dewey retorted, "Relax, bookworm. Finals ain't till next week." No doubt, he'd thrown out the grammatical error just to grate on the stuffy kid's nerves; Dewey had been born to a wealthy L.A. family, same as Lane. Both saddled with the tedium of properness.

"So where were we?" Lane flipped forward in his economics book. Envisioning his rendezvous with Maddie wasn't going to speed up the week. "Did we already cover the graph on page one-o-one?"

Dewey reclined with feet on the coffee table and addressed the classmate beside him. "Gotta love my roommate. Almost four years now, he's been pretending to cram just for my sake. Bastard aces his classes without even trying."

"That's not true," Lane said.

"Oh?"

"I try. A little."

Dewey laughed. "Imagine what you could do if you were actually interested in your major."

Lane had imagined it all too often, and to no point. Political Science wasn't an option according to his family's conditional funding. In contrast, Dewey's Economics degree—using numbers merely to support the conceptual and theoretical—would serve as a small rebellion against his father, the owner of an accounting firm.

"Lane Moritomo in here?" some guy called out.

"Yeah, that's me!"

"Girl's on the phone for you."

Fighting a grin, Lane set aside his book. He had been hoping all afternoon that Maddie would ring him back once her brother left the house. "That's gotta be my sister," he told his study pals.

"Pass along my thanks," Dewey said, "for making those paper birds." The origami cranes were what he meant, folded by Emma's tiny hands to bring them luck on their exams.

"Sure thing." It drove Lane crazy not being straight with his roommate.

Soon that would change.

At the phone in the hall, Lane brought the handset to his ear. A pair of athletes in Cardinal sweatshirts strolled into the dorm. For privacy, he spoke just above a whisper. "Maddie?"

"Am I speaking with Lane Moritomo?" It was indeed a woman, but he didn't recognize the voice.

"Uh, yes. This is Lane."

"Mr. Moritomo, this is Congressman Egan's office."

"Yes?" he said again, thrown off guard.

"Sir, I'm phoning to inform you that you've been chosen for an internship."

Her sentence lit a fuse. It traveled through him, gaining potency and speed, until he exploded with excitement. "I can't believe it! My God—I mean, my gosh." A small circle of students glanced over. Lane cranked his volume down. "I . . . don't know what to say."

"How about, you accept the offer?" A smile broke through her businesslike tone.

"Of course. I definitely accept."

"Congressman Egan will be delighted to hear that. Your enthusiasm and fresh ideas made quite an impression." Lane strove to listen, despite his yearning to scream while sprinting through every corner of the Quad, around Lake Lagunita and back. "You'll receive more details by post, but feel free to contact us with any concerns. Otherwise, we look forward to seeing you in June."

"Details. In June." Thoughts tumbling, he barely remembered to add, "Thank you, ma'am. For letting me know."

"My pleasure."

The line went dead, but Lane was afraid to release the handset, as though the phone were his sole link to the internship.

Among all the politicians in the region, Egan most closely shared his visions of equality and civil rights, community outreach. Of immigration and landowning laws needing to be reformed. Ongoing peace talks between Japan and the U.S. were dandy, but why stop there? Increasing American commerce in the East would benefit everyone.

To each of Lane's points, the congressman had listened, and concurred. Egan maintained that the government existed to serve the public, not the other way around. He was a doer, not a talker. And somehow, Lane's foot had managed to wedge into that esteemed man's door.

Granted, it was only an internship and the pay wouldn't be much, but it was a stepping-stone toward a brighter future. A future he couldn't wait to share with Maddie.

Maddie. She was the first person he wanted to tell.

The operator connected the call. He started tapping his thumb on the phone after the first ring. By the fourth, it felt like forty.

"Kern's Tailoring."

He was so thankful Maddie had answered he plunged straight in. "The internship. At the congressman's office. Sweetheart, I got it. I got it!"

"Wow, that's wonderful," she said. "I'm so proud of you."

"I thought I had a good shot, after the interview, but . . . there were so many applicants—" He heard Maddie talking to someone, her voice muffled from covering the mouthpiece. "Maddie?" He waited. "Honey?"

"Sorry, I'm here. And I do want to hear more, but there's a whole wedding party being fitted."

He squelched a budding of disappointment. "No problem."

"I'm happy for you, though. Truly I am."

"It's fine, I understand," he assured her, then remembered the upcoming weekend. "Besides, I can tell you more in person, when we meet on Saturday."

"Oh, right. Saturday," she agreed. But there was a catch in her voice that tugged like a hook in his chest. He was about to investigate the cause when the reason became clear.

Egan's office was in California; Juilliard was in New York.

"Don't worry about this affecting your schooling, okay? We'll figure it out, no matter what."

Muffled again, she spoke to a customer, then, "Sorry, Lane, I have to run. Talk to you soon."

"Okay then, take care. I—" *Click.* "Love you."

The hallway went eerily quiet.

By the time he hung up the phone, he chose to brush away his senseless worries. There was too much to celebrate. The internship of his dreams, a key to his future, had been dropped into his hands. Maybe there was magic in those lucky cranes after all.

He sped to the commons and shared the news with Dewey, who demanded they toast at Danny Mac's Pub to commemorate the triumph.

Later, once the elation and beer began to wear off, they crashed in a happy stupor on their beds. And that's how Lane remained until late that night, when he awoke from a nightmare, sweat beading his face. The scene imprinted in his mind left him unable to sleep: At Seattle's Union Station, he stood on a platform, awaiting his future bride—who never showed.

Dreariness hung in the air, rivaling the pungency of medications and disinfectant. The odors, however, didn't bother Maddie. With each visit to the convalescent home, her nose had grown more tolerant of the strange, sterile surroundings, as had the rest of her senses. The sight of elderly residents struggling to feed themselves over-boiled food, or getting agitated at relatives they no longer recognized, had gradually lost its impact. Even glimpsing shriveled bodies holed up in their beds, disguised chariots headed for the afterlife, caused Maddie only occasional pause.

She pondered this while rosining her bow, preparing for her performance. As she stood alone in her father's assigned room, it dawned on her how accustomed she had become to the bland, beige walls and scuffed tiled floors, the clusters of wheelchairs and muted floral paintings. A sadness rose within her.

He wasn't supposed to be here this long.

The doctor had recommended a change in scenery to help cure his depression, some place free from the memories of his wife. Beatrice Lovell had been quick to highlight the amenities of the rest home owned by her husband, as if selling a vacation house on the Malibu shore. Of course, more than the vastly discounted rate communicated her unspoken favor. Given that Maddie and her brother had both been in school, and lacked any close relatives, Bea had secured the care their father needed. Perhaps even rescued him from an asylum.

What else did authorities do with people whose grief stripped their desire to function?

"Mr. Kern, look who's here," a nurse encouraged. She guided him into the room in a slow shuffle.

"Hi, Daddy." Maddie dredged up a smile, held it as his glassy blue eyes panned past her face. The routine persisted in delivering a sting.

Before the window, the nurse eased him into a chair. He angled his face toward the glass pane. "Your daughter's going to play for you today. Won't that be nice?"

Holiday garland swagged above him. The fading afternoon light bent around his slumped shoulders. For an instant, time reversed. It was early Christmas morning. He wore his bathrobe over his pin-striped pajamas, his brown hair disheveled. Bags lined his eyes not from aging sorrow, but from a late night of assembling Maddie's new dollhouse, or TJ's bicycle for the paper route. Maddie could still see her dad settling on the davenport, winking at his wife as she handed him a cup of strong black coffee. Nutmeg and pine fragranced a day that should have lasted forever.

"If you need anything, I'll be at the desk," the nurse said to Maddie, doling out a smile. The pity in the woman's eyes lingered in the small, stark room even after her departure.

Maddie shook off the condolence and retrieved the violin from her case. She methodically tuned the strings. Photographed composers stared from the lid, always in judgment.

Today, theirs wasn't the approval she sought.

She took her position before the music sheets. Each lay in sequence side by side on her father's bed. Height-wise, the pages weren't ideally located, but she knew the composition forward and backward. The wrinkled papers, strewn with penciled finger markings, merely served as a security blanket.

"I've been working on a Paganini caprice for you. His ninth, one of your favorites."

He didn't respond, not so much as a blink.

She reminded herself that the title alone would carry little impact.

As she nestled the violin between her chin and collarbone, she played the opening in her mind. There was no room for error. The perfection in her phrases, her aptness of intonation, would wake him from his solitary slumber. Lured out of his cave and back into their world, he would raise his eyes and see her again.

She lifted the bow, ticking away two-four time in her head. Her shoulder ached from relentless practices. Scales and arpeggios and fingered octaves had provided escape from gnawing doubts over her looming nuptials.

If only life could be as well ordered as music.

Maddie closed her eyes, paced her breathing, and sent the bow into motion. The beginning measures passed with the airiness of a folk dance in a gilded palace, where women with powdered unsmiling faces and tall white wigs tiptoed around their buckle-shoed partners. Soon, the imitative notes of a flute alternated with dominant horn-like chords, and after a brief rest, the strength of the strings pushed through an aggressive middle section. Maddie's fingers leapt up and down the fingerboard. The bound horsehairs hastened through ricochets and over trills. Any ending seemed miles away until a soft high-B floated on melodic wings. Only then did the prim courtiers return. They lent their limelight to a ruler's abrupt pronouncement, before trading bows and gentle curtsies. When the final note drifted away, Maddie opened her eyes.

Her father's seated form appeared in blurred lines. As they solidified, her anxiety climbed the hill molded of hope and dread. Her technicality had been pristine, a rendering her instructor would deem "admirably spotless."

But had she chosen the right piece? The right composer?

Violin held snug to her chest, she watched and waited for the answers. In the silence, her father inched his face toward hers. A trembling of anticipation spread through her. Their gazes were about to connect when an unexpected sound robbed her focus. At the door a matronly nurse stood behind a woman in a wheelchair, pit-patting their applause.

Maddie jerked back to her father—whose attention had returned to the window. His expression remained as dispassionate as those of the composers in her case. Once again she stood before him, alone and unseen. She'd become the beige walls, the tiled floor. An insignificant fixture he passed in the hall.

She sank down onto the bottom corner of his bed. Instrument resting beside her, she leaned toward him. "Daddy, it's me . . . Maddie. I know you can hear me."

At least she hoped so. Even more today than usual.

Suddenly she recalled her impromptu audience. She glanced at the empty doorway before continuing. "Since my visit last week, some things have happened. You see, the thing is that Lane—the Lane you've known for years—well, he proposed to me. In a couple days, we're supposed to get married."

For a second, she envisioned her father shooting to his feet, outraged she had accepted without his consent, a sure sign he'd heard her.

He didn't react.

"I love Lane, I honestly do. It's just happening so fast. We've only been dating since the spring, and he's been away half the time at school. Then there's Juilliard, and now he's got a job offer in California . . . I'm not sure of anything anymore. And even if I were, how can I do any of this without you?" She went to touch his hand, but reconsidered. Grasping fingers that made no effort in return would crumble the strength she'd rebuilt, day after day, note by note.

Maddie tightened her grip on her violin, growing more insistent. "You're supposed to walk me down the aisle. You're supposed to tell me what a good choice I've made, and that we're going to live happily ever after." The impossibility of it all brought tears to her eyes. "Please, Daddy," she urged in a whisper, "talk to me."

He continued to stare out the glass. He didn't utter a sound.

Her answer, however, came regardless. From a cavern of truths, it echoed from deep inside. All she had to do was listen.

12

Hunched over the kitchen table, TJ attacked the page with a vengeance. He scrubbed at his lead markings with a pencil eraser, but the layered numbers still peeked through. Five layers to be exact. That's how many times he'd been stumped by the blasted stats equation.

Such a waste. Waste of an evening, wasted effort. Baseball had already taught him all the math he ever wanted to use. Measurements from the mound to every point of the plate, the trajectory of hits, angles of pitches, addition of runs, the subtraction of players.

He'd chosen Business as his major. It seemed the least specific option. In actuality, a degree was never part of the plan. His vision of the future had been nothing but stripes. Not of the flag, a symbol of patriotic roles meant for guys like Lane. No, his own allegiance lay with the good ol' Yankees, with those dapper stripes, their top-notch talent. And TJ's name could have been—should have been—added to their roster long before now.

Freshman year, only one teammate besides himself had been recruited on scholarship. The second baseman, a fellow All City player, signed last year with the Red Sox. Yet here was TJ, still stuck in Boyle Heights, trying to rid his life of another mistake that couldn't be wiped clean.

Although that didn't keep him from trying.

Rubber shavings scattered as he wore down the eraser at an angle. When the nub snapped off, the pencil's top skidded across the paper. The metal rim tore a rut through the single problem he'd actually gotten right.

He chucked the pencil across the room. Growling, he crumpled the page. "Stupid, useless piece of—" He reared back to pitch the wad, but a discovery halted him.

Company.

At the entry of the kitchen, Jo Allister leaned against the door-jamb. Her oversized peacoat hung open around her overalls. "Don't let me interrupt," she said. A baseball cap shaded her face, though not her bemusement.

"Don't you ever knock?"

Her mood instantly clouded. "I'm looking for Maddie. If that's acceptable to you."

This made for the second time this week he'd misdirected a vent on his sister's friend. He surrendered the balled paper onto the table, tried his best for a nicer tone. "She's not here."

Jo upturned her palm as if to say, *You wanna elaborate?*

"She . . . went to see our dad." Based on periodic reports from the nurses, any visits were pointless. Maddie just hadn't accepted that yet. "Afraid I don't know when she'll be back."

"Fine. Then tell her I swung by." With a scathing smile, Jo added, "I'd stay and wait, but you might take up throwing knives next."

Once again, he watched her ponytail shake with fuming steps away from him. She certainly had a knack for jumping straight into his line of fire.

"Hold on," he called out weakly. Her shoulder flinched, indicating she'd heard him, but she didn't stop.

He marched after her. "It wasn't you, okay?"

Ignoring him, she opened the front door. He caught hold of her sleeve.

"Jo, please."

She didn't face him, but her feet held.

"I just got a lot on my plate, with baseball and finals and . . . everything."

Gradually she wheeled around. Her bronze eyes gave him a once-over. "That supposed to be an apology?"

TJ found himself without a response. He had lost the skill of presenting a proper sorry. It was tangled up in the net of regrets that a million apologies couldn't change.

"You're welcome to stay"—he gestured behind him—"if you wanna wait for Maddie." Padding the peace offering, he told her, "No knife throwing, I swear."

A reluctant smile lifted a corner of her mouth. She glanced past him and into the house, considering. "I dunno."

Man, was she going to make him crawl over hot coals for her forgiveness?

"Looks like we've both been cooped up too much," she said. "Come on." She waved a hand to usher him down the steps.

He had to admit, it was a nice night. From the smells of leaves burning and cookies baking next door, he sensed his stress dissolving, making her offer tempting. Still, he felt the tug of obligation, recalled the equations that weren't going to solve themselves.

"Stop your fretting," Jo said. "Your books aren't gonna run off. Or your pencil—wherever it landed."

He gave in to a smile. "All right, all right. Let me grab a jacket."

TJ glued his gaze to the asphalt to avoid the lineup of houses they passed. It wasn't the string of gingerbread cutouts that made him want to scream, but the normalcy.

Middle class to upper class, nearly every ethnicity peppered the neighborhood—Russians, Mexicans, Jews, you name it. The families' after-supper scenes, however, varied little. Fathers smoked their pipes, slippered feet crossed at the ankles, reading newspapers or books, or playing chess with a son eager to turn the tide. Mothers in aprons tended to children all bundled in nightclothes; they double-checked homework or darned socks beside the radio; they nodded to the beat of a youngster plunking away at a piano. Some even had the gall to hang Christmas decorations—December had scarcely arrived!

TJ was so intent on blocking out these lousy Norman Rockwell sketches, he didn't give any thought to destination until Jo spoke up.

"This is it." She jerked her thumb toward the sandlot.

"This is what?"

She rolled her eyes, making him wish he'd just played along. "You know, TJ, you're about as good at apologizing as you are at listenin'." She continued into the ballpark, collecting rocks from the lumpy dirt.

TJ slogged behind. By the light of the moon, he took inventory of the place he hadn't visited in at least a decade. The park was even more run-down than he remembered, and smaller. A lot smaller. When the new ball field had opened several blocks away, complete with kelly-green grass and shiny cages and splinter-less benches, kids had immediately shunned the old hangout. It was a toy they'd outgrown and dumped in a dusty attic.

Only now did TJ detect a sadness etched like wrinkles in the sandlot's shadows.

"Right over there." Jo pointed out a set of sagging bleachers. "That's where I carved my initials, front row on the left. My own VIP seat. Every weekend Pop and I would come here and watch my brothers play. I tell ya, we missed a heap of Sunday Masses, but never a Saturday game." She jiggled the rocks in her hand as if seasoned at throwing dice. Even TJ would think twice before going up against her in back-alley craps. "One day the coach got so tired of me nagging about wanting to hit, he put me in. Thought it would shut me up."

"Well, obviously *that* didn't work."

Without warning, she flung a pebble that TJ barely dodged.

"And that, buster, was with my left arm."

TJ shook his head. A quiet laugh shot from his mouth as he dared to follow her.

On the sorry excuse of a mound, level as the Sierra Madres, Jo planted her loafer-clad feet. A pitcher's stance. She transferred the rocks, save for one, into her coat pocket. With her right hand, she drew back and slung the stone at her target, the lid of a soup can dangling from the batter's cage. *Plunk.* The tin rattled against the warped and rusted fence.

Not bad. For a girl.

"So, how'd you make out?" he asked. "Up at bat?"

"Walked," she said with disdain. "A beanball to the leg." She flipped her cap backward with a sharp tug and set her shoulders. Sent out another nugget. *Plunk.* "My brother Otis was pitching. Told his buddies he wanted to teach me a lesson, which was baloney. He was terrified of his little sister scoring a home run off him." She wound up and threw at the lid again, as hard as her expression. Another bull's-eye. Three for three. Without daylight.

TJ tried to look unimpressed. "How long ago all this happen?"

"I dunno. Eight, maybe nine years back."

A smirk stretched his lips. "And . . . you're still holding a grudge?"

She pondered this briefly, rubbing a fourth stone with her thumb. "Irish blood," she concluded. "Forgiving wasn't exactly passed down by our ancestors."

TJ, too, had a dash of Irish mixed into his hodgepodge of European descent. Perhaps this explained his shallow well of forgiveness. He dreaded to think what other traits he'd inherited from his father.

Averting the thought, he focused on the road that had delivered them there. "I gotta get back."

"No," Jo said.

He turned to her. "No?"

"Not till I show you why I brought you here." She tossed her rock aside and sat on the mound. Then she slapped the dirt beside her twice, peering at him expectantly.

He scrunched his face. "Um, yeah. As nice as it would be to hang out and tell ghost stories, I do need to get some studying done." His future at the university sadly depended on it.

"Two minutes and we'll go."

"Jo, I really need—"

"Would you stop your moanin' and take a load off?"

Clearly arguing would get him nowhere. And he couldn't very

well leave a girl, no matter how self-reliant, alone at night in a deserted park. Safety aside, it was just plain rude.

"All right," he muttered, "but make it quick." He took a seat on the packed slope.

"That wasn't so hard now, was it? Now, lie back."

"What?"

She groaned at him. "Just do it."

Concerned by her intentions, he didn't move. The two of them had never really hit it off, but if any other girl had invited him to cozy up like this, he'd know where it was leading.

"Don't flatter yourself," she spat as if reading his thoughts. Then she lay back, head on her hands, convincing him to recline.

The coolness of the ground soaked through his clothing, sparking a shudder. "Now what?"

"Relax." She took a leisurely breath. "And look up."

He cushioned his neck with his fist and dragged his gaze toward the sky. The lens of his vision adjusted, intensifying the spray of white specks. Clear as salt crystals on an endless black table. Were the stars tonight brighter than usual? Or had it simply been that long since he'd paid notice?

Within seconds, everything else faded away. He was suspended in space, floating among those specks like he'd dreamed of as a kid. He was an adventurer visiting other galaxies, a fearless explorer. There were no responsibilities anchoring him in place. And for the first time since he could remember, TJ felt free.

"This is what I wanted to show you." Jo's voice, like gravity, yanked him back to earth. Again, he lay in the old ballpark. "My pop," she went on, "he knew everything about the stars. Was a big hobby for him. He's the one who taught me about constellations making up pictures and whatnot."

"Yeah?" TJ said. "Like what?"

She gave him a skeptical side-glance. Seeming satisfied by his sincerity, she raised her arm and pointed. "You see those three running up and down in a row?" She waited for him to respond.

"I see 'em."

"Well, they're the belt hanging on Orion, the hunter. And next to it, right there, are three more dots that make the line of his sword." She picked up speed while motioning from one area to the next. "Above him is Taurus, that's the bull he's fighting, and on the left are his guard dogs. The lower one is Canis Major, and the star at the top of it is Sirius. That's the brightest star in the night sky. Believe it or not, it's almost twice as bright as the next brightest star. . . ." Not until she trailed off and cut to his gaze did he realize he was staring at her. "Swell." She looked away. "Now you think I'm a nut job."

"Actually, I was thinking . . ." He was thinking that he'd never noticed what a pretty face she had. Had a naturalness about her. She wasn't one for wearing makeup, and he sort of liked that—though he wasn't about to say it. "I was wondering how you remember so much about all of them. The constellations, I mean."

"Oh. Well. I don't remember them *all*. Those are just some of my favorites."

"What's so special about them? Compared to the others?"

She lifted a shoulder, signs of embarrassment having fallen away. "I like that they have a whole story. Plus, you can see them from anywhere in the world. It's kinda nice, don't you think? Some stranger in a faraway country's gotta be looking at those very shapes right now."

Jo turned back to the sky, and after a beat, she quietly added, "Mostly, though, I guess they remind me of my dad. I like to think of him as Sirius, the brightest one. Way up there, watching over me and my brothers."

Normally TJ would bolt from a moment like this, averse to poking and prodding, yet he felt compelled to hear more. "What exactly happened to your parents?"

"Depends. Which version you lookin' for?"

He understood the dry response. The local rumor mill had churned out plenty of whoppers about his own family, so he didn't give much credence to anything he'd heard about Jo's. When she and her brothers moved into town, to live with their granddad, stories had spread like wildfire. Some claimed her mother ran off with another guy, supposedly a traveling missionary from Canada; others said friendly fire took out her father during the Great War. TJ could have asked Maddie for the real dope, after the girls met in junior high, but he hadn't considered it any of his business.

Probably still wasn't.

He decided to nix his question, but then Jo up and answered.

"Plain truth is, my ma died while giving birth to my brother Sidney. I was only two, so I don't remember much about her, outside her photo. As for Pop . . . on the dock where he was working, some wire on a crane broke loose. A load of metal pipes dropped. Folks said he pushed another fella outta the way and that's why he bought it. Wanna know the screwy thing? It wasn't even his shift. He was filling in for another guy who'd come down with the flu." A sad smile crossed her lips. But then she heaved a sigh, and the moisture coating her eyes seemed to evaporate at will. "Just goes to show you. Of the things we're able to control, death sure ain't one of them."

"Pffft, right." The remark slipped out.

Jo angled her face toward his. She hesitated before asking, "You wanna talk about it? About your parents?" The glow of the moon highlighted a softness in her features. She looked at him with such profound understanding that he genuinely felt the relief of someone sharing his burden.

The cost of the moment, however, was remembering.

Suddenly that horrific night, usually flashing in pieces, stacked like a solid wall of bricks. He closed his eyes and the emergency room flew up around him. His father lay in a hospital bed, forehead and shoulder bandaged, gauze spotted with blood. Bourbon oozing from his pores.

Once he's conscious, we'll need him for questioning, the policeman said. There was an accusation in his voice. When TJ's mind stopped spinning, he found himself in the passenger seat of the officer's car. Rain hammered the roof as they drove through the streets, shrouded in darkness. With every passing headlight, he saw his father's sedan winding down the canyon road, colliding with the oncoming truck. He imagined the spontaneous sculpture of bloodied bodies and twisted metal, saw the New Year's Eve party the couple had left only minutes before the accident.

Cars honked in ignorant celebration as TJ mounted the steps to the morgue. Round and round "Auld Lang Syne" played in his head as the coroner pulled back the sheet—*Should old acquaintance be forgot*—and TJ nodded once in confirmation. If not for her gray pallor, the absence of breath, his mother could have been sleeping. A doctor arrived to identify the other driver, a widower lacking a family member to do the honors. *We'll drink a cup of kindness yet . . .* TJ drifted out the doors. He thought of Maddie, and the task of telling her the news when she returned full of laughter and tales from her group holiday concert in San Francisco.

It had been at that moment, outside the morgue with drizzle burning cold down his face, that TJ swore two things: He would protect his sister at all costs; and he would never, for anything in the world, forgive his father for what he did.

"Maybe it would help," Jo said, "if you talked about it." The tender encouragement opened TJ's eyes. "I know it helped me an awful lot when I finally did that with Gramps."

A sense of comfort washed over TJ, and he couldn't deny wanting to purge the memories. But how could he put those images into words? And how could Jo truly relate? Her dad was a hero; his own, a murderer. Sure, an inconclusive investigation had prevented any charges—whether it was the truck driver or his father who'd crossed the median, whether booze or the slick road was to blame.

Yet to TJ, the key evidence lay in his father's reclusion and, more than that, his inability to look his children in the eye.

Jo kept watching, in wait of an answer.

"Another time," he said, almost believing it himself.

She twisted her lips and nodded thoughtfully.

Rising to his feet, he extended a hand to help her up. She dusted off the back of her overalls, her peacoat. "Home?" she asked.

"Home," he replied, the word sounding distant and hollow.

❧ 13 ❧

The morning crept by, chained at the ankles. Lane stole another glimpse at his watch. *Don't worry,* he told himself. *She'll be here. She'll be here.*

For three nights in a row, the same scenario had plagued his dreams. Clear as the aqua sky now overhead—unique weather for a Seattle winter, according to passersby—he had visualized himself in this very spot. On a platform at Union Station, waiting futilely for his fiancée's arrival.

To quell his concerns, he had contemplated phoning her again from his dorm. Yet calling without warning meant the possibility of reaching TJ or Beatrice and raising unwanted suspicions. Thankfully the charade would soon be over. At last he could tell her brother the truth—presuming cold feet hadn't kept Maddie from boarding her train.

Although Lane tried to dismiss it, he'd sensed her uncertainty, both at the beach and on the phone. And how could he blame her? A sudden rush to the altar should rightly cause reservations. He just hoped her love for him would be powerful enough to conquer any doubts.

Excited murmurs swirled. A train appeared in the distance,

chuffing on tracks that led toward Lane. An eternity bloomed, then wilted, before the dusty locomotive chugged to a standstill. A cloud of steam shot out like an exhale of relief, of which he felt none.

He bounced his heel on the weather-stained concrete, hands fidgeting in his trench coat pockets. Minutes later, passengers poured from the coaches. Men in suits and fedoras, ladies in coats and brimmed hats. Lane's gaze sifted through the commotion. Families and friends reunited. Children squealed, set free to release their bundled energy. At a faraway glance, he mistook a lady for Maddie, clarified when the stranger angled in his direction. He rose up on the balls of his feet for a better view. But still no sign of her.

Lane confirmed with the conductor that this was the overnighter from Los Angeles—both good and poor news. Could she have missed her train, taken another?

The likelihood of the more obvious taking hold, dread rushed through him. Somehow only with Maddie at his side did defying his parents make sense. Fighting the muzzle that would bind his future to a stranger would require, while hopefully only temporary, a break from his family. Without a strong incentive, rebellion would be hard to justify. Even to himself.

Once more, Lane reviewed the train cars. The crowd was thinning, hope growing sparse. What was he to do now?

He started toward the station's Great Hall, needing to regroup, to process, until a sight ensnared him.

Maddie . . .

In a burgundy suit jacket and skirt, she lugged a suitcase down the steps of the lead coach. Sunlight added radiance to her creamy skin, her swaying auburn hair. She spotted Lane and sent an enthusiastic wave.

Grinning, he hastened to meet her. He picked her up and held her close, savoring the fragrance of her jasmine perfume. It flowed like her music into his heart. That's where he'd stored every note she had played at her last performance. Her movements had been so entrancing; if not for Jo nudging him to applaud, he'd have forgotten that TJ, or anyone else in the audience, was there.

"Gosh, I'm so sorry you had to wait." She spoke with a lingering panic as he set her down. "I almost missed my connection, so I didn't have time to check my baggage. Which was fine, until the darn latch caught on a seat while I was carrying it off and my clothes scattered all over the aisle. People offered to help, but I just couldn't accept. My undergarments and nightdress were in there and . . ." She put a gloved hand to her face. "Good grief, I'm rambling, aren't I?"

He rubbed her blushing cheek with his thumb and shook his head. "You're perfect."

When she smiled, he drew her in for a kiss. Her lips tasted of mint, their texture like Japanese silk. But even more wondrous, he sensed a new comfort in her display of affection. From the discovery came an instant desire to sweep her off to their hotel. It was an urge he would have followed if not for the importance of one other stop.

He pulled his head back and Maddie slowly opened her eyes. "So, Miss Kern," he said as though suggesting an afternoon stroll, "how would you feel about tying the knot today?"

A knock announced the message: It was time.

"I'll be right out," Maddie called to the closed door. She finished smoothing her hair in the tall oval mirror and straightened her suit jacket. Dust motes danced like fireflies in the spill of light through the window. A four-poster bed, two Victorian chairs, and a square table with a bowl of peppermint candies filled the makeshift dressing room, leaving little space for her nerves to jump and jitter.

Another rap sounded on the door.

What was the hurry? There weren't any other couples when they arrived here, a minister's residence on the outskirts of the city. A few more minutes to prepare for this momentous step seemed reasonable enough.

On the other hand, eliminating time to dwell would be wise. Little good would come of imagining the very different wedding she had pictured as a child, with the smashing gown and mile-long veil, the church pews teeming with friends. And most of all, her mother's sweet fussing, her father's arm to guide her.

"May I?" Lane asked, poking his head in.

"Of course."

Inside, he shut the door with his heel. Approaching her, he paused and tilted his head in concern. "Is something wrong?"

Pondering her parents must have left clues in her expression—signs Lane could mistake for second thoughts on marriage. "I just thought it was bad luck," she said quickly, "seeing each other before the wedding."

"I didn't think you believed in old wives' tales."

"Better to play it safe, don't you think?" In truth, she didn't want to taint their day with mentions of past sorrows. "Honey, you need to go. The ceremony will be starting."

"Without us?" His eyes gleamed. "Now, pick a hand."

Until then, she hadn't noticed he held his arms behind his back. "What is it?"

"Pick a hand," he repeated.

Neither of his bent elbows gave a hint. "I don't know. This one." She tapped his right shoulder. He flashed an empty palm.

"Now which one?"

"Lane," she grumbled.

He laughed softly before presenting her the gift. A bundle of peach roses, each bud a flourish of perfection. White ribbons bound the thorn-less stems.

"Can't be a bride without a bouquet," he told her.

She barely deciphered his words. The flowers in her hand, their reminiscent color and scent, pinned her focus. "These roses," she breathed, "they were . . ."

"Your mom's favorite," he finished when her voice faltered.

She nodded, amazed he had logged away such a detail.

"And let me tell you"—he smiled—"they weren't the easiest things to find in Seattle in December." Growing more serious, he moved her hair off her collar. His fingers brushed past the side of her neck. "But I thought you might want something of your mother with you today."

The bittersweet sentiment tightened Maddie's throat, just as he added, "I've got one more thing for you."

What could possibly top what he had given her?

To her surprise, he went to the door and signaled to someone in the next room. The recorded notes of a solo violin entered the air with a slight crackle. Bach's Chaconne. It was the final movement of his Second Partita, by far among his grandest works. Which was why Maddie's father used to listen to it on their phonograph so often. Somehow the piece had slipped through her repertoire.

She felt moisture gather in her eyes, unaware a tear had fallen until Lane returned to her and wiped it away. "Thank you," she said, unable to verbalize the scale of what the presents meant to her. She leaned in for a kiss, but he gently put a finger to her lips.

"Not yet," he whispered.

Maddie beamed in agreement, remembering the impending ceremony. Then a revelation struck. "Oh, no."

"What's wrong?"

"I didn't give *you* anything."

"Yeah, you did," he replied, confusing her. "You said yes."

Such power lay in a single syllable. *Yes.* Scarcely a word, a reverse gasp really, it was an answer capable of forever altering the landscape of a person's life. And yet, to Lane's proposal of marriage, she would say it a hundred times over.

"I'll be in the other room," he said. "Come out whenever you're ready."

Once he'd left, she brought the bouquet to her nose. At the old fragrance of home, she recalled a memory of Lane and her family. A slow month at her dad's shop had elevated nerves while they awaited a scholarship offer for TJ. A rise in the cost of Maddie's lessons clearly hadn't helped. Seated at supper, each Kern drifted so far into thought, no one realized Lane had built a tower of biscuits twelve layers high. Maddie was the first to notice his attempt to crack the tension. He gave her a knowing wink, a secret traded between them. By the time her family caught on and all broke into smiles, something small but deep in her had changed. In a single look, she'd finally seen Lane as more than her brother's friend.

She held on to that moment now, a scene of the two of them surrounded by her family's joy. It wasn't hard to do, thanks to the gifts Lane had given—her mother's favorite scent, her father's beloved notes. She drank them in as she opened the door and headed for the aisle.

In what appeared to be a dining room, lacking a table to hinder the cozy space, she walked in time to the Chaconne; its harmonic middle section resembled a church-like hymn. A stained-glass cross glowed red, blue, and gold in the window. The watercolor of light projected a kaleidoscope over her open-toed heels, guiding her to Lane. Beside him, the Methodist minister waited, wrinkled as the leather Bible in his hand. The man's wife looked on in delight from the corner, where she supervised the Victrola.

Bach continued to roll out the carpet of chords. Once Maddie turned to face Lane, the music miraculously faded from her mind, as did everything in the room but him. Lost in his eyes, she listened as he vowed to love, honor, and cherish her. In kind, she devoted herself through good times and bad, through sickness and health, till death would they part. She embraced him as their lips met, sealing her heart and name: Mrs. Madeline Louise Moritomo.

The day unfolded with more enchantment than Maddie had imagined possible.

Never one to break a promise, Lane had handled every detail from the marriage license to the rings, gold bands perfect in their simplicity. She wasn't a fan of jewelry that would impede her playing, and he'd understood this without being told. He understood everything about her.

For their first night as newlyweds, Lane had reserved a hotel room downtown. The accommodations were going to be nice, he'd said. Nice. His tone was one Bea would use to describe a Mint Julep or Mrs. Duchovny's son. Perhaps a little girl's party dress with bells sewn into the petticoat. *Nice* didn't come close to describing their gilded suite.

If not for Lane carrying Maddie over the threshold, she might have fainted in the marble entry. *Splat.* There went the bride.

What a story that would have made for the bellboy behind them balancing their luggage. As Lane directed the placement of their belongings, Maddie explored the lavish furnishings. Copper-hued satin draped from the ceiling in a waterfall of luxury over an enormous bed. Claw-footed chairs flanked an oversized window. At the center of the framed view, a burnished sun slid behind a train station. The building had inarguably been modeled after the Campanile di San Marco. In high school, she had studied the famed bell tower of Italy. The redbrick structure boasted an arched belfry, a pyramidal spire, and a cube displaying images of lions and the female symbol of Venice, La Giustizia. *Justice.*

Somehow, a time machine had zapped Maddie into the drawing room of Giovanni Gabrieli. No wonder the Venetian composer had contributed such significant works to the High Renaissance. With a view like this, motets and madrigals must have flowed like water from his quill.

"What do you think?" Lane's arms looped her waist from behind. "Not a shabby way to kick off a marriage, huh?"

Rooted back in reality, she noticed the bellboy was gone. She and Lane were alone. In a room where all barriers would soon be removed, her nervousness strummed.

"It's marvelous here," she said, gently breaking away. She retreated to the curtains, projecting a fascination with the embossed ivy and fleur-de-lis pattern. "Are you sure we shouldn't go someplace else, though? This must be costing a fortune."

"Well," he drew out. "It does help that I secretly rob banks for a living. Including my father's."

She kept her eyes on the fabric and felt him getting closer. "Really, Lane, I didn't expect all this extravagance."

Right behind her again, he stroked the back of her hair. Each strand tingled as he offered a level explanation. "When I was in high school, my father put some funds in the bank for me, a nice start for after college. Of course, you and I will have to find a modest home at first. But that'll change, once my internship turns into more. Or I'll find an even better opportunity near Juilliard."

It suddenly hit her that she hadn't considered any details past their nuptials—where or how they would live, before and after his graduation. Everything had happened with the force and urgency of a tornado. Besides thoughts of her father, the sole concern crouching in the back of her consciousness had been her brother.

As far as TJ knew, she was traveling with Jo to visit the Allisters' cousins in Sacramento for the weekend. To cover her bases, she'd told Jo she would be away for a performance. This time, more than any other, she'd despised fibbing. She just couldn't jeopardize complicating her decision with others' opinions. Better to ease them into the news once all was solidified.

Lane turned her around with care. "All of that," he said, "we can talk about later. This is our wedding night, and I don't want you to worry about anything." He pressed her hand to his chest. "Just know, I'm going to take care of you, Maddie. So long as we're together, the rest will work out."

The assertion cradled her, as solid and real as the throbbing of his heart. With every beat, the trust he had nurtured expanded, pressing down her defenses.

She linked her hands behind his neck and brought him to her. Lane trailed kisses across her cheek, into the curve of her neck. A soft moan escaped her. No longer would they hide in the darkness of a drive-in, shadowed by worries of who might see. From the freedom they'd been granted—in the eyes of God and the law— she yearned to be closer than ever before.

Sensibility, nonetheless, reminded her to do this right. She forced herself to pull away from the magnetism of his hold. "I'd better freshen up," she rasped.

He paused before yielding a nod, his breathing heavy.

Regaining her composure, she slipped into the bathroom fit for a palace. Steam crawled up the mirrors as water filled the porcelain tub. She unboxed a bar of honey-milk soap and, when the bath was ready, twisted off the faucets. In the vaporous space dripping with gold and marble, she removed her clothes, then remembered. She'd left her nightgown in her suitcase.

Drat.

A problem, yes, but easily remedied. She threw on a plush hotel robe from the door hook. To fetch her garment, she would sprint both to and from her luggage. That was the plan, anyhow, until she stepped into the room, its fabric-lined walls aglow with candles on the nightstand.

"Thirsty?" Lane's voice came gently from the side, inches from her ear. The smell of champagne sweetened his breath. Candlelight flickered over his bare chest and down the muscles of his stomach. At the sight of his pajama pants, relief battled disappointment, her curiosity swelling.

She ignored the flute of champagne in his hand and ran her fingers along the contours of his shoulders. For years, while he and TJ played basketball at the park, she had witnessed a younger, leaner version of this very chest, these same arms. She'd pumped away on the swings, on a pendulum in her own universe. That girl had no inkling that one day the touch of his skin would ignite passion that stole her breath.

Lane set aside his glass and led her to the bed. When he lowered her onto the cream comforter, billowy with down, she closed her eyes. His fingers traced the collar of her robe and edged the fabric away from her body. Her breasts prickled from a tepid draft of air. Her mind grew dizzy approaching the act she knew little about, outside scandalous passages from a book Jo once swiped from beneath an older brother's mattress.

"My nightdress," Maddie murmured, recalling her mission.

Sensing his movements had stopped, she lifted her lids and discovered him gazing at her, his head propped on an elbow. A tender smile crinkled the skin bordering his eyes. "I don't think you'll need it," he said. "But if you're saying you want to slow down . . ."

The compassion in his voice soothed her unease, drawing her into another dimension like she'd thought only music could. She rose up and placed her mouth on his. Their bodies soon discovered a natural rhythm, and all reservations fell into an abyss. For it was here, safe in the heat of his arms, Maddie came to believe anything was possible. The rest of the world be damned.

Like their night of lovemaking, waking up next to Maddie—his *wife*—surpassed any expectation. Lane never wanted to leave the surreal bubble encasing them. Only from the incessant grumbling of his stomach did he agree to her suggestion that they venture out for a meal. It was, after all, almost noon.

With her arm hooked snugly around his, they emerged from the hotel. Once a block down, he pointed to a restaurant across the street. "That's the one."

"Let me guess," she said. "It's the fanciest diner in town."

"Nope. Just the closest. I'm starving."

She laughed. "Oh, and whose fault is that?"

He whispered in her ear, "I'm happy to take the blame. Last night was worth it."

"*And* this morning," she reminded him.

Her growing brazenness made him want to flip around and head straight back to their hotel room.

They'd make it a quick meal.

Inside the diner, the aroma of bacon caused his stomach to complain yet again. He led her to an empty booth by the window. The seats were easy to nab with so many customers clustered around a radio on the counter. Too late in the year to be listening to the play-by-play of a Rainiers game. The announcer must have been relating the latest of FDR's policies. When else would a crackling transistor warrant this much attention?

Usually, Lane would join in, craving every word from the President's mouth. But not today. "I'm ready to order when you are."

"Hold your horses," she said, grabbing a menu from behind the napkin dispenser. "Let me see what they have at least."

"Better make it snappy, 'cause my belly isn't about to wait."

"Jeez. What happened to chivalry? You *are* my husband now, aren't you?"

"Hey, I swore to love and cherish. Never said anything about putting you before hunger."

Mouth agape, she batted at his forearm, and they broke into laughter. When they settled into smiles, he clasped her fingers. She stared at their interwoven hands.

"Why do we have to go back to California?" she sighed. "Why can't we just stay here?"

Lane mulled over the idea. It wasn't impossible. He had plenty in savings to afford a couple more nights of heaven. "Who says we can't?"

"Yeah, sure."

"I don't have exams till Friday. And you said there's nothing you have to rush home for."

She studied him. "You're serious."

"What's stopping us?"

"Well . . . I told TJ I'd be back tomorrow. . . ."

"So, you'll send him a telegram and let him know you're staying a few more days."

She hesitated, taking the suggestion in. "I guess I could. But—I didn't pack many clothes."

He leaned forward and answered in a hushed tone. "Mark my words. I'll make sure you don't need any of them."

Her eyes widened, looking embarrassed. Then a giggle won out.

"Well, what do you say, Mrs. Moritomo?" His finger rested on her wedding band. "Want to treat this like a real honeymoon?"

She bit her lip, her cheeks still blushing. At last she nodded in earnest.

"Good." He grinned. "Now, let's eat, so we can hurry back to the room." He twisted around to find a waitress and muttered, "Isn't anyone working here?"

Through the dozen or so people gathered across the room, Lane spied flashes of pastel-blue diner dresses behind the counter. He waved his hand to no avail. The gals were too far away for a polite holler. Rising, he groaned before his gut could beat him to it.

"I'll go get someone," he told Maddie. As he moved closer to the group, mumbles gained clarity.

"Dear God."

"How many were there?"

"What does this mean?"

He sidled up to a bearded stranger in back of the bunch. A faded denim shirt labeled the man approachable. "What's going on?" Lane asked.

The guy answered without turning. "We been bombed," he said in a daze of disbelief. "They've finally gone and done it."

"Bombed? What are you talking about? Where?"

"Hawaii. They blasted our Navy clear outta the water." The man shook his head. "We're going to war, all right. No way around it."

"But who?" Lane demanded. "Who did it?"

The guy angled toward Lane, mouth opening to reply, but he suddenly stopped. His eyes sharpened with anger that seemed to restore his awareness. "You oughta know," he seethed. "Your people are the ones who attacked."

* * *

The train's whistle stretched out in the tone of an accusation. Once the locomotive had cleared the claustrophobia of Seattle's looming buildings, Maddie forced her gaze up. *The Saturday Evening Post* lay limply on her lap. She'd absorbed nothing of the articles. Their print, like the universe, had blurred into smears of confusion.

She scanned the coach without moving her head. Her neck had become an over-tightened bow. Her wide-brimmed, tan-colored hat served as an accessory of concealment. Suspicious glares, however, targeted the suited man beside her: Lane, who hadn't spoken a word since leaving the hotel. Lane, who could always be counted on for a smile. A guy who could conjure solutions like Aces from a magician's sleeve.

Lane, her *husband.* The word hadn't yet anchored in Maddie's mind, and already dreams for their marriage were being stripped away.

In the window seat, he swayed with the rattling train car. A dull glaze coated his eyes as he stared through the pane. She yearned to console him, to tell him he wasn't to blame. The Japanese pilots who'd decimated Pearl Harbor, a place she had heard of only that morning, had nothing to do with him.

You're an American, she wanted to say, *as American as I am, and we'll get through this together.*

But the sentence wound like a ball of wire in her throat, tense as the air around them. Any utterance would carry the projection of a scream in the muted coach. Helpless for an alternative, she inched her hand over to reunite with his. She made a conscious effort to evade scrutinizers' eyes. Closure around Lane's fingers jarred him from his reverie and he turned to face her. A warm half-smile rewarded her gesture. Then he glanced up as though recalling their audience, and the corners of his mouth fell. He squeezed her palm once, a message in the release, before leaning away.

For the rest of the trip, this was how they remained. Divided by a wall they'd had no say in constructing. Through the night hours, she heard him toss and turn on the berth beneath her; through the daylight hours, his gaze latched onto the mountains and valleys hurtling past.

Upon their debarking in Los Angeles, the contrast between Friday and Monday struck her like a slap. It seemed mere moments ago when she had stood on this platform, the same suitcase at her feet. Yet everything had since changed.

"Extra, extra!" the paperboy in the station hollered. "U.S. going to war! Read all about it!" His pitch carried easily over the graveness of the crowd. In small huddles, customers followed his order with newspapers propped in their hands. Headlines blared in thick black letters.

"Do you want me to come home with you?" Maddie asked Lane as they exited the station. The rustiness of her voice underscored the length of their silence.

"Nah, you'd best get home."

"Are you sure?"

"Your brother's got to be worried about you. It's better if I check on my family alone."

Of course. Nobody back here knew about their secret excursion. Now was hardly the time to announce their blissful news.

Lane added, "I'll have a cab drop you on the way to my house, all right?"

She agreed, relieved they'd be together a little longer before facing the unknown.

A peaceful sunset glowed orange and pink as they approached the taxi stop. Lane swung open the back door of a Checker cab, inviting Maddie to slide in. He ducked in after her to take his seat.

"Whoa there, buddy!" the driver called out. "Uh-uh, no way. I ain't driving no Jap."

Lane became a statue, one leg in, one out.

"You heard me, pal!" The cabbie white-knuckled his steering wheel. Bystanders paused to observe the scene, pointing, not bothering to whisper.

"It's okay," Maddie assured the driver, "we're getting out." She scooted back toward Lane, who blocked her from rising.

"No," he told her. "You go ahead."

"But, Lane . . ."

"I'll take the next one."

"Well—what if they won't—"

"Then I'll ride the bus."

The driver's steely look bounced off the rearview mirror. "You goin' or not, lady? Make up your mind."

Lane tenderly touched her chin. "Honey, don't worry. I'll swing by as soon as I can." The surety in his tone caused her to relent. She made room for him to place her suitcase beside her. He had barely closed the door when the cabbie screeched away with the speed and power of fear.

Maddie strained to keep Lane in her view until the taxi veered around a corner. Grip on her luggage, she sat back in her seat.

Seven days, she told herself as they rumbled down streets that now felt foreign. In seven days God had created the Earth. In a single day mankind had turned it upside down.

~~14~~

Free hand curled into a fist, TJ waited for the call to connect. Any more pacing and his shoes would leave a permanent groove in the floor. His ear felt feverish against the metal receiver. Behind him in the living room, a floor model radio delivered seeds of hysteria. The quiet of dusk amplified the man's reports: mandated blackouts, potential sub sightings, a climbing toll of Navy casualties, a list of precautions to keep families safe.

At last came a buzzing on the line. Years lingered between each ring.

"Answer it," TJ snapped.

Another ring . . . and another . . .

"Allisters." It was one of Jo's brothers, didn't matter which. They all sounded alike.

"It's TJ Kern. I was wondering—"

"*Who?*" The question competed with chaotic conversations in the background.

"TJ," he repeated louder.

"You callin' about the meeting?"

"Meeting?" TJ said, thrown off.

"The block meeting." The guy sounded annoyed. "For standing

guard at the beaches. We're figuring out shifts. You wanna come, we'll pick you up on the way."

Jesus. Were enemies invading the coast? TJ had never even held a rifle before. Apparently it was time he learned.

"Uh, yeah. Okay."

"Fine. See ya soon."

Then TJ recalled his greater concern. "Wait, don't hang up."

A mumbled response trickled through, indiscernible amid the noise.

"I was looking for Maddie. I know she and Jo were supposed to be up north, visiting—"

"Hang on." He yelled in a muffle, "Shut your traps, will ya?" The volume lowered half a notch. "Now, what're you sayin'?"

TJ rubbed his thumb over the knuckle of his fist, bridling his own annoyance. "I was asking about Jo."

"Hey, Jo! Phone's for you!" TJ winced from the guy hollering into the mouthpiece. A rustling and a clunk followed.

As TJ waited, relief swept over him. Jo was back in town. That meant Maddie must have stopped over at the Allisters' on the way home.

"Hello?"

"Jo. Thank God. Is Maddie still there?"

"TJ, is that you? Here, let me go in the other room." More sounds of rustling with the handset and cord, then the chatter dimmed. "I swear, I can't hear myself think in this place."

No wonder she retreated to the ballpark to find some peace.

"I was just trying to find Maddie," he said, "since I hadn't heard from her yet."

"Oh. I don't know. She didn't tell me what time she'd be home from her trip."

"I—don't understand. Didn't you two travel together?"

"Together? No. Why's that?"

He wasn't in the mood for razzing, if that's what this was. "To visit your cousins. In Sacramento." The lengthy pause reinstated his panic. "Jo, where the hell's my sister?"

He heard her exhale, at a loss. "I don't know, TJ. . . . I don't know."

"I repeat," the broadcaster declared, *"we are in a state of emergency. Authorities recommend that everyone stay inside and tune in for further details."*

A state of emergency. The death count rising.

In a combustive flash, he saw his father on the hospital bed. His mother lay lifeless on a silver table so shiny he could make out his own reflection. The memory of rain pelted his eardrums, interrupted by the screech of brakes.

But that screech was real. A fresh sound. He turned to the window.

"TJ? You there?" Jo said.

Maddie was stepping out of a taxi in a coat and hat, yet relief had no chance of regaining its footing. "She's here," he said, and slammed the handset onto the cradle. The bell inside pinged.

TJ faced the door with arms crossed. Air labored through his nose. He was a bull preparing to charge.

She didn't see him until she'd closed the door behind her and set down her case. Her demeanor shrank beneath his gaze.

"Where the *hell* have you been? And don't you dare lie to me again."

Flushing, she fumbled for a reply.

"There's a goddamned war going on out there. You understand that? Got any idea what that means?"

She straightened, lifting her chin in feeble defiance. "As a matter of fact, I do."

"Yeah? Then why don't you prove it by telling me where you've *really* been." He pressed her with a hard stare.

"I . . . think we should discuss this later. When you've had a chance to calm down."

The challenge to his temper only inflamed it more. "Well, that ain't gonna happen for a while. So why don't you start explaining yourself."

She locked on his eyes and replied firmly. "You're not my father, TJ."

"You're right. But maybe I shoulda been. I guarantee, then, you wouldn't be traipsing all over the place with God-knows-who, doing—" An impossible sight cut through his words. A gold band gleamed from Maddie's finger. Her wedding finger.

She wouldn't . . . couldn't have. Yet the evidence was smack in front of him.

"You got married?" he breathed.

Her gaze fell to the ring. The answer was clear. What he didn't understand was why. Why'd she run off and elope? Why'd she keep it from him? His mind seized the most obvious reason, and the air in his lungs turned to lead.

"Maddie, are you pregnant?"

Her forehead bunched. "Oh, God, no." She gave an insistent shake of her head. "No, it's nothing like that." She reached for his arm, but he moved backward.

TJ wanted to feel grateful, but all he could think about was which asshole was responsible. Which one would trade a girl's innocence for lustful kicks. Why else would a guy have persuaded her to sneak around? Anyone with good intentions would have been up-front, not treated her like a dirty secret. Like a mistress. Like a whore.

He muscled down the thoughts. Left to roam free they just might unlock the cage inside, setting loose the constant rage that prowled back and forth behind the bars.

A succession of honks summoned his face toward the window. The silhouette of a pickup appeared, its headlights off.

"Come on, Kern! Let's move it!" Jo's brothers, plus a few other neighbors, crammed the truck from cab to bed. The fading sunset outlined their rifles pointed straight at heaven.

TJ grabbed his jacket from the coat tree. With any luck, he could take his fury out on an enemy bomber orphaned from its flock.

"Where are you going?" Maddie asked as he headed for the door. "TJ . . . ," she pleaded.

In need of escape, he simply walked out.

~~15~~

From the far corner of the lawn, Lane stared at the crime scene, his senses gone numb. No lights shone through the windows. By government order, darkness draped the city.

Men in black trench coats, black hats, even blacker eyes, swam in and out through the front door. They carried boxes off the small porch and down the driveway, loaded them into two old Packards with rear suicide doors.

FBI agents.

He recognized their type from the picture shows. That's what this had to be—a movie set. It wasn't real. At any moment, the word *Cut!* would boom from a director's horn and Cecil B. DeMille would leap from the trimmed hedges.

"Sir, you're gonna have to clear out." The man approached him on the grass. His features were like Gary Cooper's, but spread over an elongated face.

When Lane didn't respond, the guy sighed, took another tack. "I can see you're concerned about the family. But right now, they're part of an investigation. So I gotta ask you to move on till we're done. I know you people like your privacy, and I'm sure the Moritomos are no different."

The mention of his surname—Moritomo, how did the fellow know that?—tore Lane from the surreal dimension of his hopes. There would be no intermission between reels, no velvet curtains or salted popcorn. Dramas crafted for the silver screen were morphing into the reality of his life.

"Listen, pal." The agent planted a fist on his hip. "I've asked you nicely, but if you're not gonna abide—"

"They're mine." Lane's reply emerged with so little power he barely heard it himself. "The family in there is mine."

The man studied him and licked his bottom lip. He nodded toward the house. "Well, then you'd better go in. Agent Walsh will have some questions for you."

Lane scarcely registered the path he traveled that led him into the foyer. He was a driver after a weary day who had blinked and discovered he'd already reached his destination.

"*Onīsan!*" Emma came running. She latched onto his waist. Her little body trembled.

He set down his suitcase to rub the crown of her head. "What's going on, Em? Where's Papa?"

She peeked over her shoulder and pointed toward the kitchen. Her manner indicated that the monster trapped in her closet had found a way out. Lane knelt on the slate and clasped his sister's hands. It dawned on him how rapidly she had grown. He once could cover her entire fist with his palm. "You go to your room while I figure out what's happening, okay?"

"But those men, they keep going in there."

"Your bedroom?"

She nodded with a frown. "They're looking through all my stuff. They took Papa's work books, and his radio, and his camera. Some of my Japanese tests too—even though I don't care about that." Then, cupping her mouth, she whispered, "I hid Sarah Mae so they couldn't find her."

He was about to assure her that the doll he'd given her two Christmases ago wouldn't be in jeopardy. But who knew what they were looking for, or what other absurd belongings they would confiscate.

"Good thinking," he told her. "Now, you just sit on the stairs here. Everything's going to be all right."

Reluctantly, she stepped back and sat on the middle step. She gripped the bars of the banister and watched him through a gap.

Lane paused while passing the parlor. Cushions of their empire couch had been slashed. Its stuffing poured out like foam. Scraps of papers dappled the rug. His father's prized katana swords had been pillaged from the wall.

A man's husky voice, presumably Agent Walsh's, led Lane into the kitchen. An oil lamp on the table soaked the room in yellow.

"You're not lying to me, are you, folks?" The guy, thick with a double chin and a round belly obscuring his belt, loomed over Lane's parents, who sat stiff and humble in their chairs. He held up a small laughing Buddha statue. "'Cause I don't want to wonder what else you might be hiding from me."

"We telling the truth," Lane's father insisted politely, taking obvious care to pronounce his words. "We Christians. Not Buddhists. Christians. This only Hotei-*san.*"

"This is what?" Walsh said.

"Hotei," Lane replied, turning them. "It's a lucky charm. My mother brought it from Japan when they first moved here."

"Uh-huh. And who might you be?"

"I'm their son."

"Is that right," Walsh said slowly, and glanced at Lane's father. "I was told you were away at a university. How 'bout that, now?"

Lane fought to control his tone. If his dad possessed any trait, it was integrity. "My train just got in. With a war starting, I thought I should be with my family."

"Sure, sure. I understand," the agent said, as though not accusing. He returned to Lane's mother in a gentle appeal. "Got a family of my own. Nice, pretty wife, two kids. Boy and girl, just like yours. So I know how it is, wanting to do everything I can to protect them. Which is the reason we need to ask all these questions." He put the decoration on the coffee table and motioned at Lane. "Have a seat. Make yourself comfortable." The arrogance of his invitation, implying a staked claim on the house, bristled the tiny hairs on Lane's neck.

Due to alien land laws, and Asian immigrants being barred from citizenship, his father could only lease the place. Although it was common practice, Lane hadn't felt right about purchasing it in his own name to bypass the rules. He preferred to change the system and guide society's evolution.

That system, however, was turning out more flawed than Lane thought—starting with Agent Walsh, who eyed him, waiting for compliance.

"I'm fine standing," Lane bit out.

"Uh-huh. Well, I'm telling you to take a seat."

"And I said I'm fine."

Their invisible push and pull raised the temperature of the room.

"Takeshi, *suwarinasai.*" His father intervened, a stern command to sit.

Lane's gaze shot to his mother. The woman would never stand for such humiliation. After all, they had nothing to hide. But she remained rigid, her eyes fixed on the agent's dress shoes, another insult to their home. That's when Lane remembered he, too, hadn't taken his off.

"Boss," a voice called out. The Gary Cooper agent entered the kitchen. "I think we got something here."

Walsh accepted a stack of large creased pages. Flickers from the lamp concealed the content from Lane's view. The man flipped through them and drew out a whistle. "So you like airplanes, do you, Mr. Moritomo?"

"Yes, yes." Lane's father perked with a touch of enthusiasm.

"American bombers . . . fighter planes . . . all kinds, looks like."

"Yes, yes. I paint for, *ee* . . ." He searched for the word, found it. "Hobby. Is hobby."

"Any chance you've been sharing some of these drawings with, oh I don't know, friends back in Japan?"

Blueprints. That's what they'd found. Blueprints for his model aircrafts. The same ones any kid could buy for a few nickels at Woolworth's.

"This is ridiculous," Lane blurted. "Are you trying to say my father's a spy?"

Walsh crinkled the paper edges in his hands. "Better watch that tone, son."

"I'm not your son. And my father's not a criminal." This wasn't how America worked. Justice, democracy, liberty—these were the country's foundational blocks that creeps like this kicked aside like pebbles.

Lane's father stood up and yelled, "Takeshi! *Damarinasai.*"

"No," Lane said, "I won't be quiet. They can't come in here and do this. We haven't done anything. We're *not* the enemy." Holding his gaze, he implored his father to fight for the very ideals with which Lane had been raised. Yet the man said nothing. His Japanese roots had taken over, dictating his feudal servitude.

"Eh, Boss, we're all set." A third guy appeared. The brim of his fedora shaded his features from nostrils up. "Boss?"

Walsh relaxed his glower. "Yeah?"

"All the major contraband's packed up."

"Right." He jerked his layered chin in Lane's direction. "Then, let's take him in." The two other agents crossed the room, the faceless one pulling out a pair of handcuffs.

Lane's stomach twisted. "What is this? You're gonna arrest me?"

"Got a reason we shouldn't?" Walsh said.

Gary Cooper raised a calming hand at his supervisor. "Al, you're tired. You need some food, some sleep. Go on home and rest up. We got this."

Walsh exhaled, rubbed his eyes. Eventually, he mumbled his concession and handed off the blueprints. He had just left the kitchen when Lane heard two metallic ripples. The third agent had handcuffed his father, explaining it as a formality.

"*Nani ga atta no?*" Lane's mother demanded, now on her feet.

"We just need your husband for some more questioning," the agent said. "He'll be back by morning."

"*Shinpai suruna,*" her husband assured her weakly as the men began escorting him out. "*Shikata ga nai.*"

Lane despised the old adage. *It can't be helped.* No culture needed to be so damn passive.

"You can't do this!" Lane marched behind them. "Where are you taking him?"

"The Justice Department will be in touch," one of them answered, right as Emma charged down the stairs, begging him to stay.

"Papa, *ikanaide*." She shook his bound arms. "Papa, Papa! *Ittara dame!*"

He offered her phrases of comfort that did little good. Then he turned to Lane and in Japanese stated in an even tone, "From now on, you are responsible for the family."

These were his final words before being ushered into the backseat of the agents' car, the last instructions before Emma chased them two full blocks. She wailed out useless pleas as her mother retreated into the dishevelment of their house. Neighbors peeked from windows.

Yet for Lane, none of this—not the groundless arrest, not his sister's cries nor their mother's isolation—caused the physical blow that came from the look in his father's eyes. A look of utter shame.

⤜16⤛

She couldn't stand the wait anymore.

Maddie threw her coat back on, not bothering to fasten the buttons. She had tried phoning Lane, to confirm he'd made it home. Then to warn him not to come over. But the calls wouldn't go through. The only person she'd reached was Jo, who had more questions than Maddie felt up for. A third attempt to ring Lane's house had failed. The chaos of the switchboard was likely the problem, the operator had said. Told her to try again after a spell.

Maddie, though, didn't have time to spare. TJ could return at any minute—having gone to a meeting, Jo claimed. Right or wrong, TJ needed a chance to cool off before connecting her wedding band to Lane. And that's precisely what would happen if the three of them shared an exchange. After the intimacy of her wedding night, how could she possibly hide her feelings in Lane's presence?

In the morning, once TJ's shock had settled, she could explain everything. Rarely did she deviate from tracks laid in reason. He knew this. He knew *her*.

At least the brother she used to know did.

Headed for Lane's, she hurried from the house and down the front stairs. The tip of her shoe caught on the splintery bottom step, sending her tumbling. Exhaustion from the day wilted her body. No chance to rest. She heaved herself up and brushed off her gritty palms. A hole tore through her silk stockings, among the few she owned. Yet the misfortune had become a meaningless hiccup in the grand scheme.

She continued toward the street with a hindered stride. At this pace, the walk would stretch to a good twenty minutes, widening the opportunity for the guys to cross paths.

Should she go or stay? Which option would be worth the risk?

Frustrated by her own indecision, she wagered her hopes on a car approaching from the end of the long suburban street. The vehicle rumbled in and out of moonlight slanting between houses. Its chrome grille had the opened fish-mouth shape of a Buick's.

"Lane, please be you." She focused on the windshield, breath held.

"Are you all right, dearie?" a woman called. It was her elderly neighbor, leaning out from behind her screen door. "I was just watering my pansies in the window when I saw you take a fall."

"Oh, yes, I'll be fine." Maddie flung the reply behind her.

"I have some peroxide if you scraped yourself up. You remember what I told you about my nephew's ankle, after he didn't care for it properly. Ended up almost dying in the hospital."

No matter how dire the situation, Maddie knew better than to entrap herself in the house of a person who took pride in enumerating worst-case scenarios.

"I appreciate the offer. But I'll be okay." Maddie stretched her neck toward the street.

"What are you doing out here, exactly? If you pardon my asking."

"Just waiting for . . . a friend," she said, at last determining that Lane—thank goodness—was the driver behind the wheel.

"Well," the woman replied, "if you change your mind."

A creak indicated the screen door had shut, but Maddie could sense the peering of curious eyes.

Thoughts roaming in a fog, Lane pulled over slowly to the curb. He didn't notice Maddie waiting outside until she bolted around the hood to reach him. As he stepped out of the car, she spoke in a quiet rush.

"TJ's on a rampage. If he finds out about us tonight, I don't know what he'll do. I tried to call your house, to warn you not to come over, but I couldn't get through."

Lane fixed his attention on her lips. Their movements shaped syllables that had become hard for him to grasp.

"Sweetheart," she said. "Did you hear me?"

"They cut our lines," he heard himself say.

"They what?"

"Cut our phone lines. The FBI arrested my father. Took boxes full of our things."

She covered the base of her neck with her hand. "But—why?"

The image of his dad being driven away, handcuffed like a criminal, came charging back. The insanity of it all beat like a fist behind his forehead. "They said they needed him for more questioning. They're wasting time. I'm telling you, he had nothing to do with it."

"Of course he didn't," Maddie said in natural agreement.

Lane raked his hand through his hair. Why did he feel the need to present her with his case?

"Oh, honey, you'll figure this out. You always do." Her eyes shone with belief, a deepened trust that he could conquer any obstacle. But rather than it fortifying him, for the first time ever, he felt afraid of failing her.

"How is Emma?" she asked. "And your mom?"

"They're all right. Or they will be, once my dad is back." By morning. That's what the agent had said. If not, Lane would find a way to bring him home. He had to. "I'll come by as soon as I know more."

"Why don't I stop over instead? At your house sometime tomorrow?"

The house. Shredded to pieces.

"We'll see."

In the awkward silence, she glanced at the neighboring home. Was she nervous about their being seen together? Lane had grown accustomed to keeping their relationship under wraps, but he'd presumed that would change after their vows.

"I've gotta go." He started to duck into the car.

"Just a minute." She clutched his hand on the rim of the door. "I wanted to say that—no matter what—I hope you know that . . ." She trailed off, enwrapped him with her arms. Against his cheek, she finished in a heartfelt whisper, "I love you, Lane. I love you so much."

His eyelids lowered, blocking out all but the warmth of her breath, the softness of her hair and body. They were again in that hotel suite, curled up under the oblivion of the sheets. A complimentary bowl of nuts and fruit adorned the bureau. It could have sustained them for at least another day. Why, in God's name, did he ever let them leave that room?

Maddie yanked herself from his hold, and the illusion followed her.

"Tomo, you're here," TJ called to him, rounding the corner. "What's going on?"

This was Lane's cue for quick thinking—but nothing came. His excuses had run dry.

"Tomo?"

Maddie jumped in. "Where did you go, TJ? Where are the others?"

He looked at Lane curiously. "Just had a meeting. They drove back to their place afterward. I walked from there."

She snuck Lane a glance, a plea for him to act natural. "So, the meeting. What was that about?"

TJ's attention traveled between him and Maddie in calculating progression. "Shooting the enemy," he replied, distracted. A struggle between denial and the obvious escalated in his eyes. His shoulders lifted an inch.

In light of all that was happening, Lane couldn't do this anymore. They needed to protect one another. And that couldn't happen until he fessed up.

"Lane was actually just leaving," Maddie said. "He has to see about his family. Isn't that right?"

A beat dragged past before Lane could push out the words. "TJ, I think we need to talk."

"Lane," Maddie breathed. "Please."

TJ's gaze lowered, sharply halting at the ring on Lane's finger. His jaw visibly tightened. "What have you done?"

Something plummeted and landed hard in Lane's chest. "We should go inside."

"No," he said. "You tell me now."

Maddie's arms closed over her chest, her neck drawn. She appeared ready for an earthquake. Clearly she had forgotten, as had Lane until this moment, that he and TJ were blood brothers. Two pricks of a sewing needle had sealed their bond in the storage room of Mr. Kern's shop. They were eight, but their pact held no expiration. Nothing could divide them.

Not even this.

Lane closed the car door. He faced TJ before speaking. "Months ago, Maddie and I, we started dating. We were afraid how you might feel about that, really about her dating anyone. So, we thought it'd be better not to say anything—just at first, though."

TJ broke in with a slow, raw voice: "Did. You. Marry her?"

No amount of padding would cushion the truth. Lane took a weary breath and answered. "Yes."

Disappointment carved its way into TJ's face. It was then that Lane imagined how it would feel, down the road, if some guy ran off and married Emma. Let alone his best pal.

Maddie attempted a voice of reason, which TJ shut down by trudging toward the house.

"Hold on." Lane followed him. "I know it looks terrible. And I'm sorry, honest I am. But you have to let me explain."

The air turned electric as TJ reached the stairs. A single spark could set off an explosion. Still, Lane couldn't let him think the worst.

"Buddy, listen to me," he said, catching TJ's elbow.

In an instant, TJ swung around and grabbed him by the shirt, cinched it up under Lane's chin. "I'm not listening to anything from you! I ought to kill you, you piece of shit!"

"*Stop it,*" Maddie shrieked. She worked to restrain her brother, his right arm poised for a punch.

"Go on," Lane yelled back. "Hit me." And he meant it, wanted the redemption found in a rightful punishment. "Do it!"

"That's enough," Maddie said.

TJ's fist quavered, as did his reddened face. Releasing his grip, he shoved Lane back several feet. "You were supposed to be my friend."

Lane's hand rose to his gathered collar. "I *am* your friend."

"No, you're not. You're a filthy liar," he seethed. "Paul was right. You're just another dirty yellow Jap."

Maddie protectively held Lane's arm. "TJ, you don't mean that."

Whether he did or not, the result was the same. The floor in Lane's gut had dropped out, leaving him hollowed. A shell unable to move.

"Get back in the house," he told his sister.

"*No.*"

"I told you to get back inside!"

"Or what? You're going to hit me too?"

Something pulled TJ's head up. Lane followed his gaze to find neighbors in their entries, watching the show. When he returned his focus to TJ, the emotion in the guy's eyes launched a chill over Lane's skin. Disappointment had dissolved into hatred.

"Get the hell off our property. I don't ever want to see you again." With that, TJ went into the house.

Maddie stared after her brother as their audience ebbed away. "I should've told him from the beginning. This is all my fault."

"No," Lane contended. "I'm just as much to blame." Tough as it was to face, he could have confessed at any time. Yet he hadn't. Not just because Maddie had asked him to wait, but because he'd been willing to sacrifice anything to ensure they stayed together.

Drained of words, they moved to the driver's side of the car. As he squeezed the door handle, Maddie clasped his hand. "Let me come stay with you."

On any other day, he would have rejoiced over living with her. But for now, aside from a guaranteed objection from his mother—undoubtedly heightened by the situation—the FBI could return without notice, interrogating anyone with links to his family. The last thing he'd do was subject Maddie to that treatment.

"Believe me, I wish you could."

"I just need to grab my things," she said. "My luggage is still packed."

"Not yet, sweetheart."

"When, then?"

"I . . . don't know. When I head back to school, I suppose."

School. Finals. Would they continue as scheduled, or be put on hold with the rest of his life?

"I don't want to be without you," she said, her bottom lip trembling.

He shook his head and offered in assurance, "You won't have to." He brought her into his arms. "This is only for now. Till things settle, it's safer for you here. Understand?"

She said nothing, but gave a reluctant nod.

"I'll call the shop and come see you when I can." He kissed her on the forehead, then the lips. Her face conveyed a craving, a need for security he couldn't deny. "Don't you worry," he told her. "Everything will work out."

When she nodded again, he got into the car and drove away, half regretting what he'd said. For what was intended as a promise felt like yet another lie.

PART TWO

月に叢雲 花に嵐

Meaning of Japanese proverb:
Like clouds over the moon and storm over blossoms,
misfortune often strikes during times of happiness.

17

Two days and still no word from him.

Maddie had arrived at the shop early that morning in search of a second letter from Lane. He had hand-delivered the first one through the mail slot on the door. Wrinkles from frequent readings covered the pages already imprinted in her memory.

My dearest Maddie,

I imagine this isn't the honeymoon you were hoping for. It certainly isn't the one I'd had in mind. At least when it comes to my arranged marriage, I won't have to find a way of letting the woman down gently. I think it's safe to assume the matchmaker has taken me out of the running. (That's supposed to make you laugh.)

On a more serious note, despite my efforts I haven't been able to locate my father. The sole explanation I've received is that they're holding him because of his position at the bank. Since the Sumitomo headquarters are in Tokyo and funds are constantly transferred back and forth, the Justice Department is investigating him thoroughly. Of course, he's not the only one. Japanese leaders and teachers are also being held. Even Christian ministers, if you can believe it.

That's what I've pieced together, anyhow, from what little the authorities will share. I've left several messages for Congressman Egan in hopes that he can speed up my father's release. I guess my dad's long-overdue bank promotion turned out to be a curse.

As for the rest, the last few days have been a blur. Between maintaining things at home and helping our Japanese neighbors turn in "contraband" (as if eighty-year-old Mrs. Kubota was going to use her RCA radio to coordinate a massive assault), I've barely had time to sit. Since the banks froze all Japanese accounts, we had to let our housekeeper go. On the upside, it's forced me and my sister to take up cooking. Most of the meals have even been edible. A husband who's handy in the kitchen. Who would've guessed?

Once things ease up, as I know they're bound to, we'll have a working phone again and I can call to hear your voice. Better still, you and I will have time to ourselves in person. In case I don't see you when I deliver this, please know I carry you always in my heart.

All my love,
Lane

Although he had brightened the letter with his usual touch of humor, Maddie could surmise the toll such hardships had to be taking on his family. To top it off, curfews were now imposed on the Japanese community, further reducing her opportunities to see Lane. Forces seemed intent on keeping them apart. Her brother most of all.

TJ had actually demanded she file for divorce, or an annulment if possible, to reverse her "mistake." A mistake! Like she'd simply mistuned her violin or forgotten an appointment.

She stamped out the thought as she worked.

At her sewing machine, she guided the pumping needle over the dress draped across her lap. The tangerine fabric, with its grid of yellow lines, could cause a traffic jam from the glare. Not to mention the maddening chore of shrinking the garb by five full sizes.

"Sugar," Bea drawled, returning from the back room, "would you watch the store for a bit?" She set a package wrapped in tan paper on the reception counter and retrieved her purse from a drawer.

"I'd be happy to," Maddie said, though Bea's errand seemed curious. Drop-offs for regular customers happened on occasion, but typically after closing hours, not in the middle of the day. "Are you making a special delivery?" she asked.

"It's for Mrs. Duchovny."

Ah, yes . . . her son's shirt. The one with blue pinstripes that needed a button replaced. His mother had brought it here the day Lane had proposed at the beach. And to think, Maddie had gone there with the notion they were going to break up.

As Bea shrugged into her pink knit sweater, Maddie said, "If you'd like, I could drop those off on my way home. Save you the trip." The Duchovnys lived only a couple blocks from Maddie's house. Besides, the complimentary service seemed the least she could do to show gratitude for her benefactress. "Or, I could go now if they need the clothes earlier."

Bea ran her fingers across the package, her coral lips pursed. Sunlight through the window reflected off the sides of her silvery bun. "I suppose there's no real rush. Since hearing the news, I just feel awful that some of his belongings aren't where they ought to be." The sullenness in her tone struck Maddie's ears like an off-key chord.

"What do you mean? What news?"

"Oh, sugar. I thought—well, I assumed you'd heard, what with your ties to the family and all."

Maddie clenched her wedding band, which hung on a necklace beneath her blouse. There it raised fewer questions, while providing strength when needed.

"I'm afraid it's not good, dear," Bea explained. "I'm so sorry to be the one to tell you, but . . . when the *Arizona* sank"—she paused—"Donnie was on it."

A sharp exhale slipped out before Maddie could cover her

mouth. Donnie Duchovny. He'd been a classmate of hers since grade school. A nice boy—one who blended. He used to weave his pencil over his knuckles during tests. She had forgotten that. Forgotten about his naval station. How was that possible, after listening to his mother's boasting since the day he'd enlisted, no subtler than her matchmaking hints for Maddie?

"That poor family," Bea sighed. "Bless her heart, Mrs. Duchovny was so excited about their boy coming home for Christmas too. And those bookshelves his daddy made for him . . ." Bea angled her face away to discreetly dab the corners of her eyes. It was the first time Maddie had seen her shed a tear. "Gracious, would you look at me. I'd better pull myself together. They certainly don't need me adding to their woes."

"I'll take it."

At Bea's startle, Maddie considered what she had just volunteered. It wasn't too late to retract the offer. Nonetheless, delivering the parcel herself would be the right thing to do. Not only had the Duchovnys promised financial help with Juilliard, soon after her father moved into the rest home, but Donnie's shirt had remained at the shop because of Maddie.

"Oh, sugar," Bea said, "I didn't mean to imply you needed to take on the job."

"You did nothing of the sort. I'd just like to do it, if you wouldn't mind."

Bea gave this some thought. Then she passed the wrapped garments over with reverent care.

Maddie nodded and headed for the streetcar. Only upon settling into her seat did she register the incongruent weight of the package. It felt much too light to be carrying the memory of a person's soul.

Two sets of light knocks on the door failed to summon an answer. Maddie couldn't bring herself to pound. Although tempted to leave the bundle beside the planter box, as she'd done in the past, she knew the situation called for a personal delivery. No question, her father would have demanded it, even done this himself if still capable. She could imagine him verbalizing as much, clear as the concertos stored in her head.

While visiting him yesterday, updating him on all that had happened with Lane and TJ, she'd received the usual static response. On her way out, though, she swore she'd heard a whisper, an urging that she and her brother make up, that they tear down their barricade of silence.

It was merely her conscience speaking.

Maddie resorted to pressing the doorbell, and heard the ring inside. Not the frazzled buzz of her own house, but an elegant *ding-dong* to match the two-story, powder-blue Victorian home. Aside from the faint rattling of a car, the area had become devoid of sound. As though the death of a resident had triggered a mute switch in the neighborhood.

She tried the bell once more. Still no answer. A service flag hung in the window. Donnie's single blue star would soon be gold, a symbol of his sacrifice. Boys scarcely of age were enlisting in droves. Estimates claimed the war would be over in months. But how many gold stars would accumulate before then?

Troubled by the notion, at the recollection of mourning, Maddie decided to come back later. She pivoted to leave—just as the door yawned open. There stood a portly woman in a bathrobe. The scarf enveloping her hair was knotted at the top behind a frizzy lock. No rouge on her cheeks, no color on her lips. Puffy bags lined her eyes.

Maddie almost didn't recognize the customer she'd known since childhood.

"What do you want?" she ground out.

"I'm sorry to bother you." Maddie grappled for words. "It was rude of me not to call first."

Mrs. Duchovny watched her dully. A painful quiet passed back and forth.

Maddie lifted the parcel. "I thought—that is, Beatrice suggested you might want these." Mrs. Duchovny didn't extend her hands, prompting Maddie to clarify. "Your jacket is done. The lovely green one." She took a breath. "And the shirt."

The woman made no reply at first. Then a soft, "Donnie's."

Maddie raised the package higher as a means of affirmation.

Hesitant at first, Mrs. Duchovny took the bundle and hugged it to her middle. The paper crackled from the pressure.

Maddie staved off her emotions by rushing through their parting. "I'm terribly sorry for your loss. Please let me know if there's anything we can do." Not expecting a response, she dipped her head and started for the rock path that edged the manicured lawn.

"Is it true?"

The question rooted Maddie's shoes. Over her shoulder, she asked, "Pardon?"

"I said, *Is it true?*" More than irritation powered the huskiness of her tone. Alarm, perhaps. Desperation.

Maddie stepped closer, racking her brain for context. Was Mrs. Duchovny asking if her son was actually dead, versus purely a rumor?

Newspapers had detailed the attack in which nearly three thousand perished. There would be no body for confirmation, Maddie realized, if Donnie had drowned while trapped in the ship. The same went for those burned beyond recognition.

How ever was she to answer?

"Mrs. Duchovny . . . ," she began.

"I want to know. Is it true what your neighbors are saying?" The woman's intensity rose. "Tell me you didn't marry a Jap. Tell me you didn't devote yourself, before the eyes of God, to a man whose people murdered my only child."

Just like that, the air turned to glass; shards scraped Maddie's throat with every breath. A reply had no chance of passing through, leaving silence to confirm the truth.

And for this, Mrs. Duchovny's face, usually warm and doughy, petrified with disgust. Her eyes glinted like steel, cool as the hidden ring dangling from Maddie's neck.

"Madeline Kern. You ought to be thankful your parents aren't here to see this day. The shame would be unbearable."

When the door slammed, Maddie winced, letting loose a tear. It blazed down her cheek and vanished on the worsted mat.

∽18∽

TJ lost all awareness of his surroundings until someone gripped his arm. He spun around.

"Easy there, slugger." Jo laughed with a start.

He relaxed his fist, dropped it to his side. "Hey, Jo."

"You know, for a second there, I was thinking you were ignoring me," she teased. "I was in the window and you walked right by. I must've hollered your name half a dozen times."

TJ glanced past her. A block down, white letters appeared on the glass pane. *Allister's Hardware.* He'd ridden the bus home from campus entrenched in thought, and evidently gotten off two stops early.

"Been studying hard?" She motioned to the canvas satchel on his shoulder.

With Maddie's situation playing havoc with his concentration, the afternoon he'd just spent at the library had been a waste. "Finals are next week, so I gotta buckle down. See you around, though, all right?"

He was about to walk away when she said, "I just clocked out for the day, and I'm dying for a Coke. You thirsty?"

Definitely sounded better than hitting the books. But, he reminded himself, a scholarship hung in the balance. "Believe me, wish I could."

As two Navy men strolled past them, he half expected Jo's eyes to follow—all the girls seemed to have gone ape over the uniforms—but her attention didn't stray. It was only her expression that changed. More serious now.

"You can talk to me, if you want. 'Bout what happened with Lane." Her eyes penetrated him with a look of understanding, same as from the night on the baseball mound.

"Maddie told you."

She shrugged.

"Dandy," he muttered.

"So, how about it?" Jo produced a small wad of greenbacks from a pocket of her work uniform. "First one's on me."

Tempted by her company, he checked his watch. His sister would be returning from work soon. Their mutual silence aside, he was still obligated to keep an eye on her.

Jo jabbed him playfully in the ribs. "Come on, it's fuel for the brain. A tall glass of Coke, *fizz-fizz-fizz*. Cherry syrup stirred in. Crispy fries, maybe? Mm-mm."

Given that Maddie made a point of cooking only for one these days, a basket of fries did sound appetizing. "Fine, you got me. But I can't stay long."

"Deal."

"And just so we're clear, I'm picking up the bill." He couldn't let a girl pay.

"For a second, I was worried you weren't gonna offer."

He laughed in spite of himself.

"Ooh, just remembered. I gotta tell Gramps about a toolbox on special order. Don't move a muscle." She jogged off to the store, bound hair swinging, her energy infectious.

TJ shook his head. Who'd have predicted that Jo Allister, his kid sister's friend all these years, would turn out to be a pal of his too? It was nice, finding a gal who was so easy to chat with. Surprisingly, they had a good deal in common, from their family losses to sports to . . .

The thought stirred a memory from weeks ago—Jo yakking him

up right before Lane showed at the house, the night they all went to the jazz club. He'd viewed her rambling about the World Series as an attempt to improve his mood. The real reason didn't become clear until now: Lane had come over to see Maddie, not him. Jo had known, and she'd let him play the idiot.

"Sorry about that," Jo said, returning. "You ready?"

TJ didn't move. "Did you know about Lane and Maddie? That they'd planned to get hitched?"

Jo flinched, a double take. "Well—no. I had no idea they were gonna run off and do that."

"You knew they were dating, though."

"Yeah," she admitted, "I knew, but . . . Maddie promised she was going to tell you. And I think she really was, except then—"

"Save it." He pierced her with a glare before striding away.

"TJ. Wait."

He continued down the sidewalk and across the street, not acknowledging a car that hit the brakes for his passage. The driver honked.

"Would you have reacted any different," Jo called out, "if you'd known earlier?"

Oh yeah he would have. He would have stopped it from ever happening in the first place.

He just wished he could convince Maddie it wasn't too late to salvage her future. The arguments he'd presented had gotten them nowhere. She'd refuted them all until there was nothing left to say.

Maybe he'd been appealing to the wrong person. If he alone couldn't open her eyes, he could think of the one person who could.

❦ 19 ❧

As Lane entered his house, the smell of smoke greeted him like an intruder. His internal alarm blasted in his ears, along with his father's words.

From now on, you are responsible for the family.

"Emma," he yelled, charging toward the kitchen. "*Okāsan!*" Visions arose of a greased pan on fire, its orange and yellow flames climbing the walls. But once he got there, he discovered the kitchen in its normal state. Dishes were drying on the rack from breakfast. The Frigidaire buzzed long and low.

Smoke, not suggestive of food, continued to pave an invisible trail. And the faintest hint of gasoline. Was someone trying to run them out, a person who hated them enough to burn down their house—with or without his family inside?

"Emma!" he shouted, panic rising. He'd witnessed the crime in his dreams.

"I'm right here." Emma's voice whipped him around.

"Where's the smoke coming from?"

In a rust-red jumper, she toted a box half her size, a trove of personal keepsakes. Sadness rimmed her eyes. "It's *Okāsan*. She's in back, burning all the Japanese papers and other stuff we still had left."

Lane mentally chided himself for assuming the worst. He'd forgotten that many other "Issei" were doing the same. The immigrants had been destroying their letters and diaries, no matter how mundane; photographs of their youth spent in Japan, of their babies dressed in kimonos. A history erased as a show of loyalty.

"Do I really have to give her my school pictures?" Emma asked tightly. "Can't I at least save the notes from my friends?"

He patted her braids, uneven and puckering from weaving them herself. "You're not giving up a thing. Go put these back in your room, and let me talk to Mother."

"But . . . she said I had to."

"She won't mind, I promise. You go up and play now. Throw a tea party with Sarah Mae."

Emma glanced at her rescued box, and a sparkle returned to her Betty Boop eyes. "Will you come too?"

"You get everything ready, and I'll join you soon."

When she shuffled toward the stairs, Lane headed for the door off the laundry room to stop his mother from this foolishness. Through the screen door he could see her. On the concrete patio, she sat primly on a wrought-iron chair. Black plumes swayed from a metal pail at her slippered feet. She lifted an envelope from the shoebox resting on her lap. Yet instead of adding it to the smoldering pile, she held the post to her chest and squeezed her eyes shut. The emotion crumpling her face glued Lane's grip to the door handle. He leaned back onto his heels, causing the screen door to squeak.

Her eyelids flew open. Again, she was a statue. "*Otōsan no kotode nanika kīta?*" Her tone remained flat, even while inquiring about news of her husband's arrest.

In response, Lane followed a longtime urge to enforce a change. "We shouldn't speak Japanese anymore. We're Americans. We should act like it."

"*Demo, watakushi no eigo—*"

"Your English is fine. I've heard you use it at stores when you have to."

Her fingers tightened on the shoebox. Her deceptively dainty jaw lifted. "*Wakatta wa.*" She agreed in her native language, no doubt to make a point. Then she snatched a photo from the box and flung it into the pail.

Lane reached out, unable to save the memento in time. "Mother, you don't have to do that."

She watched the flames devour the corners with greedy bites. It was her wedding portrait, a picture he hadn't seen since boyhood. Heat animated their kimonos by bubbling the black-and-white image. Their stately pose gained a semblance of celebration it had never appeared to have. But then her headdress recoiled. Oval holes grew as if spurred by drops of acid, wiping away the bride's youth.

On occasion, Lane would recall a trace of the innocence she'd once had. How she used to smile with a warmth that reached her eyes—like on the Mother's Day he had proudly given her a lop-sided clay pot; or the morning his father had first launched a toy glider, after a month of painstaking assembly, only to have the plane crushed by a passing truck. His wife had burst into such unbridled giggles, she'd forgotten the cultural female habit of covering her mouth.

What had happened over the years to both thaw and return her to ice?

The sound of his name sliced through his pondering. His mother's impatience indicated she was repeating herself. She pointed to their house, where a doorbell rang. He could sense her desire for protection, despite an exhibition of strength.

"I'll get it." Probably another junk dealer. Lane had shooed off two of the vultures this week. In cheap suits and tonic-saturated hair, they'd had the audacity to come here, citing reports of an impending Japanese American evacuation, offering to buy up belongings for half their worth. *Those* were the types of people who should be locked up by authorities.

He divulged none of this as he turned to go inside. While entering he glanced back, and a sight brought him pause. Something peeked out from his mother's sweater pocket. An envelope. The same one, he would guess, that he had caught her embracing. A family letter? He found it improbable, and not just because she was an only child.

Like most Issei, his parents' connections to kin in Japan essentially ended the minute they boarded the boat for a new life. Only in rare instances would he catch a relative's name tossed out, like a puff at a dandelion. Then, bound to its seeds, Lane's interest would just as soon drift away.

A double ring of the bell reminded him of the caller. He hastened toward the foyer and swung open the door. For a moment, he just stared.

On his porch was TJ Kern.

From beneath the curved lid of a baseball cap, TJ spoke first. "Hey," he said.

"Hi."

A grueling quiet. "So, I heard about your dad."

The intent unclear, Lane found himself on the defense. "They're just questioning him as a formality, because he worked at the bank."

TJ shifted his weight, his hands jammed into the front pockets of his jeans. He nodded slowly, as if organizing his words. "Listen, there were a lot of things said between us. But what's done is done. All that's important is how we move forward."

Lane became aware, right then, how much he had been hoping for this conversation. Admittedly, TJ's words had left a bruise that continued to throb. But the fact was, the guy had made an effort by coming here.

Lane stepped out onto the porch. Beneath their shoes were the same planks they had sanded and repainted as kids, when their carved designs from TJ's new pocketknife weren't a hit with Lane's mom. They'd screwed up; they'd learned. They'd repaired the damage.

"I want you to know," Lane said, "that I *am* sorry. I shouldn't have kept it all from you, but you have to understand why."

"Maddie told me."

Lane blinked at this. Last he'd heard, she and her brother

weren't on speaking terms. "She explained—about the arranged marriage?"

"She told me enough," he said. "Besides, none of that matters. All I care about is how to square away this mess."

Relaxing, Lane nodded. "Believe me, I'd love to get back the way things were between you and me—"

"Lane, I'm not talking about you and me." More jarring than the frustration in TJ's reply was the use of "Lane" rather than "Tomo."

"Then what *are* we talking about?"

"Maybe you two did have a chance at making it. Maybe you actually thought through your finances, and job, and her schooling. Even where you were gonna live. But you've gotta see that the situation's changed."

"It doesn't change how I feel about her."

"I didn't say it did."

"So what are you suggesting? That I walk away because things are tough right now?" Lane cringed at the idea of living without her. Seeing Maddie only twice over the past week had been hard enough. "They're not going to stay this way. It'll all settle down."

"Are you kidding?"

"Just hear me out—"

"We're in a goddamned war! With Japan, for Christ's sake. It's not fair what you're doing to her and you know it!"

Fair? The concept had become laughable. Lane's volume rose to the challenge. "My family's being treated like criminals, and for what? Huh? What's fair about that?"

Their eyes held, a silent standoff.

How did they come to this?

What's more, how could Lane possibly do what TJ was asking?

Since the car accident, he understood TJ's protectiveness. But he also understood that Maddie had grown up without her brother noticing. Now Lane wanted to be the one to protect her, as a husband who cared for her as much as TJ. Maybe more.

"I love Maddie," Lane told him. "You have to know, I love her more than anything."

Without pause, not even a humoring of consideration, TJ's answer came low and firm. "Prove it, then. If you really love her, do what's best for her—by letting her go."

The words sank in layer after layer. They reached down to the bruise inside, reviving a throb as TJ turned to leave.

When Lane finally went for the door, he found his mother in the entry. Darkness raged in her eyes. Lane waited for a rebuke, but none came. She simply gathered her anger and walked away.

❦ 20 ❦

Impossible hand positions on stubborn strings nearly drove Maddie to fling her bow out her bedroom window. Through sixty-four phrases of a repetitive bass line, the notes marched in twos, then threes and fours. They waded through each maddening section of Bach's Chaconne, a fifteen-minute marathon of advanced arpeggios and chord progressions.

It had been two long months since America declared war. Yet her armor of melodies, until today, had managed to keep her emotions in check. Behind their shields, she could temporarily forget the empty visits with her father, even the resentment between her and TJ, masked by what had progressed to civil exchanges.

Perhaps Bach's partita itself was the problem. This movement had, after all, been their wedding processional. Now each measure of its three-beat bars reminded her of the perfect future she'd glimpsed with Lane, only to have it swiped clean from her fingers. Stolen by strangers.

But what else should she spend her time playing? Without the Duchovnys as benefactors, Juilliard was no longer an option. Thus, maintaining mastery of Mazas's Thirty-Sixth Opus or Viotti's Twenty-Second Concerto was pointless when auditioning would merely taunt her with what she couldn't have.

And so, she persisted in tackling the Chaconne, until her back ached and fingers whined. She obsessed over stumbled trills and missed double-stops. As if conquering the piece could close the gap forming between her and Lane. She could feel the void gaining mass every time they met. It stalked them at Hollenbeck Park, straining their conversations. It hovered in Lane's car as their bodies joined in the backseat, failed attempts to re-create the intimacy they'd once found.

She wanted to scream, to yell until the world came to its senses.

Instead, she trained her vision on the sheet music propped on the metal stand. Or at least she tried. An image in the lid of her violin case competed for her focus: a small copy of her wedding photo, taken by the minister's wife. There it was, nestled in a spot previously reserved for Mozart.

Common sense told her to shut the lid, but she couldn't. She needed to keep those memories alive. She reached out and traced Lane's smile, her mother's bouquet. Relationships, like spiderwebs, required such care in the beauty of their weaving—only to be severed by a single rain. There had to be something Maddie could do to prevent her marriage from meeting the same fate.

She glanced around the room, at belongings now bearing little value—the perfume bottles and figurines, the posters of classical performances. From the thought, a solution materialized. While no umbrella existed large enough to protect them, somewhere out there the skies shone clear.

On the Moritomos' front porch, Maddie crossed her arms, unwilling to yield. "Give me one reason why."

"I can give you a dozen," Lane argued.

"I'm not talking about leaving forever. Just a month or two. Until things calm down, like you said."

"Forget about what I said. Haven't you read the papers?"

She hadn't because she didn't have to. She'd overheard enough from customers in the shop—of suspected spies and espionage labeled "Fifth Column" activity. From the Hearst and McClatchy newsies to coastal farmers and fishermen, anyone harboring anti-

Oriental sentiments had been handed a long-awaited excuse to vent in the open.

If nothing else, her family's misfortune had taught her to recognize inflated dramatics for what they were. Gossip that would gradually lose its luster. Which was why her plan made sense.

"All of this is going to pass," she persisted. "Things will get better."

"Or," he said, "they'll get even worse." He spoke with a resignation that scared her.

"Lane, that can't be the case *everywhere.*"

"So you just want to pack up and run off?"

"We did it before, didn't we?"

"That was different."

"How?" she challenged.

"Because I have my family to think about now."

Maddie hadn't fully considered what it would be like to travel with his mother, a woman whose brittle silence spelled out displeasure over their marriage like the bold letters of a marquee.

"And what about your brother?" Lane added. "Don't you think he's going to have something to say?"

"It isn't his decision. This is about you and me."

"But it's not, Maddie. Not anymore." He rubbed his temple as if fending off a headache.

Something else was troubling him. His father, maybe. They still hadn't heard from the man. Since his transfer to New Mexico—a detention center in Santa Fe—Lane had penned inquiries to more than a dozen officials, including the President.

"Have you received a reply," she ventured carefully, "from any of the letters you sent about your dad?"

"Nobody's answered," he said. "Well—except for one."

"Oh? Who was it from?"

"Congressman Egan's office."

The gentleman knew Lane personally. Of course he would be helpful.

"What did he say?"

"His secretary sent a letter. Said I should take up my concerns with the Department of Justice directly. And oh, by the way, with restructuring due to the war, they won't be in need of my services, after all."

Maddie remembered the elation in Lane's voice the day they had offered him the job. She longed to hear that voice again.

He crossed the porch, gripped the rail with both hands, and stared into the muddled afternoon sky. She could see the light inside him dimming. Striving to keep it aglow, she followed him over and laid her hand on his back. He was wearing the maroon sweater-vest she had made him for Christmas. The annual holiday had grown grimmer—as would all the days if they stayed.

"I can imagine how horrible you must feel. But if you think about it, this is one more thing not keeping you here."

"And what about your dad?" he said without looking at her.

"My dad?"

"Your visits. Don't you need to be there, to play for him every week?"

She almost replied that her father wouldn't notice. But then she saw a vision of him waiting by his window, even vaguely aware that his daughter had abandoned him, and her stomach turned cold.

"Besides," Lane said, "what would we live on? My parents' cash savings won't last forever, and who knows if we'll ever see our money from the bank. Then there's school to think about." He shook his head and faced her. "Just because I'm not going back doesn't mean you shouldn't follow your plans for New York."

Although the timing wasn't ideal, she had to tell him. She'd been keeping it from him too long. "I'm not going," she interjected.

He looked at her as though she'd lost her marbles.

"With the war, it doesn't seem right," she said. "One more year isn't going to make a difference."

"That's ridiculous. You have someone willing to pay your way. You can't turn that down."

She wanted to avoid explaining. She'd lie if she could, yet his eyes forced out the truth. "The Duchovnys have changed their minds. But it's all right. With all that's happening—"

"Why would they do that?"

The question conveyed more disbelief than bewilderment. Despite the challenge, she replied quietly, hoping to soften the impact. "Their son. He died at Pearl Harbor."

Layers of comprehension unfolded over Lane's face, followed by something more. His unjust, indirect responsibility in the matter. The revelation deepened the lines in his forehead he had only recently gained. "How much is tuition?"

Maddie suspected where this was leading. "It doesn't matter."

"Just tell me."

"It's too much, for either of us right now."

"What's the amount?" he insisted.

"Fine. It's three hundred, but that's just for classes. Room and board is at least four hundred more, another two hundred for lunches and incidentals. So you see? It's an outrageous amount for anyone, especially now. We're all supposed to be saving."

He opened his mouth as if to protest, then closed it and again turned away. Maddie went to reassure him, but felt an added presence. She swiveled toward the window. Centered between the swooped drapes, Mrs. Moritomo stood behind a white veil of gossamer curtain. The woman threw a glare before stepping out of view.

Perhaps fleeing with his family wasn't the wisest choice. Though what else could Maddie do to keep him close? There had to be another option.

Unable to think of one, she confessed to the greatest reason behind her proposal. "Lane, I'm just so afraid of losing you."

After a moment, he connected with her eyes. Only a tinge of sadness appeared in his soft smile. Gently, he pulled her into his arms. "I'm sorry, Maddie," he told her. It was all he needed to say.

She rested her head on his shoulder and inhaled the scent of his skin, like leaves after an autumn rain. She had missed this smell, this feeling, even more than she realized.

"Em!" Lane called suddenly, and broke their hold. "Emma, what is it?"

Stifling sobs, she sprinted onto the porch. She clung to her schoolbooks as she disappeared into the house.

Lane sighed. "Probably just another kid teasing her. You stay here, I'll be back in a minute." He brushed Maddie's lips with a kiss, then headed inside.

Left alone, she perched on a rail. All her life she'd lived only minutes from here, yet this was the nearest she had ever been to Lane's front door. She wondered about his room. What color was his bedspread? Which treasures had he kept since childhood? What decorations adorned his walls? Assuming his mother permitted any.

At last, Lane reemerged.

"Is Emma all right?"

He held up a crinkled flyer. Sketched in the middle was a buck-toothed boy with squinty eyes mounted on a plaque, like the head of a deer, topped with a banner of neatly penned cursive. *Jap Hunting License. Open Season. No Limit.*

"Where did she get that?" Maddie said, aghast.

"A kid from school gave it to her, thought it was funny." His tone made clear what he wanted to do with that kid, given the chance.

Maddie was searching for something to say when a cannon of slurs pelted them from the street.

"*Get out, you traitors!*"

"*Go home, Jap rats!*"

Maddie turned and spotted a red object being slung toward the house. A brick! Lane pushed her down, covered her body with his. The window shattered into a downpour. Tiny shards sprinted down her arms as she breathed against the porch floor.

Victorious whoops and whistles overlapped, then quickly waned.

Lane raised his head toward the attackers. "They're gone," he assured her. He helped her up, brushing off her arms. "Are you hurt?"

She shook her head tightly. Her heart was beating at a humming-bird's pace.

Around a distant corner, the gang of boys jetted away on their bikes. No older than twelve, they had already learned to hate.

Lane continued to stare after them, long after they vanished. When Maddie clutched his hand, he dropped his gaze to her fingers. "You'd better go," he said.

She wanted to object, but his mother had made clear Maddie was far from welcome in their home.

Neck still trembling, she kissed him on the cheek and whispered good-bye. Although the impulse to run for safety itched at her, she maintained a steady pace through the neighborhood.

Seeing her house brought a wave of relief, which ended at another sight. Her left hand. Bare of a wedding ring!

She had forgotten to move it from her necklace to her finger, as she'd always done before their visits. She told herself Lane hadn't noticed, distracted by their discussion and the vandals and Emma— but deep inside, she knew he had seen.

～21～

What a load of bull!

TJ marched out of the locker room. He continued across Bovard Field to reach Coach Barry, intent on putting the rumor to bed.

Around him the USC players were stretching and warming up beneath the buttery tarp of sun, readying for the scrimmage. This used to be TJ's favorite time of year. Spring training. He'd loved the promise found in the scent of fresh-cut grass, the feel of tight seams on a new ball, like a clean slate in his grip. Sanded bats would whoosh in effortless arcs, his spikes would find balance in the leveled dirt, and he knew he was home.

Of course, that home was now withering. In absence of his passion for the game, the banisters dangled and stairs creaked. The pipes were leaking, warping the floors. But so long as the support beam remained, the house would stand.

That's why word about his coach's plans couldn't be true. Besides, look at the guy. He was a middle-aged family man, juggling three sports for the school. No way he was leaving all that behind.

"Coach," TJ said, "got a minute?"

Coach Barry held a pencil in one hand, team roster in the other.

"What's on your mind, son?" He scribbled notes in the margins as TJ debated on his approach, decided to keep it light.

"Just thought you'd get a kick out of hearing the latest, is all. Some of the guys, they're saying you up and enlisted." He forced out a small laugh to punctuate the lunacy of the idea. Only way TJ himself would be serving was through the draft. No point in volunteering for a war due to end in a year. "Bunch of hot air, right?"

Coach Barry stopped writing. He eased his head upward. The motion carried a reluctance that leveled TJ's smile. "News sure spreads fast around here, doesn't it?"

TJ twisted his glove, trying to squeeze sense out of what he was hearing. "You're not saying you actually joined the Navy?"

"Never been one for the sidelines," he said. "And with so many students joining up, figured I could at least do my bit by helping with training. I was planning to tell everyone after practice today."

Within earshot, Paul Lamont was playing second base. He smirked at TJ, as though reveling in the news.

"Not to worry, though," Coach Barry added. "Coach Dedeaux's gonna take real good care of you boys while I'm gone. You just keep your eye on that diploma and give this season your all." He patted TJ on the back. "Go on, son. You're up now. Show Essick your best stuff."

Sent on his way, mind reeling, TJ trudged toward the mound. Sure enough, seated in the stands amid scouts for the Red Sox and Dodgers was Bill Essick. The famed scout for the Yankees had discovered the likes of Joltin' Joe and Lefty Gomez. Good ol' "Vinegar Bill." TJ hadn't done much to impress the guy during winter league. Starting today, though, he could show all of them what he had. He could prove himself the gem they first caught a glimmer of two years ago.

Unfortunately, his arm had turned to rubber, weakened from the blow of Coach Barry's news. The more he pondered his coach deserting them—the last constant in his life—the more his feeling of betrayal swelled.

Pitching would be his vent.

Once ready, he scuffed at the mound, sidled his foot up to the rubber. Greenery draped the surrounding fence leading to a scoreboard. No numbers on it today, this being practice, but today every pitch would count.

The catcher signed a screwball. TJ cleared his head as best he could. He aimed for a look of cool and collected, then let the first one fly.

A strike. With it came no satisfaction, just the compulsion to do it again. So that's what he did. Gaining focus, he hurled one after the other. Knucklers, four-seamers, splitters, sinkers. What he lacked in control today, he made up for in power. Hard and determined he threw. His shoulder burned from exertion. His eyes stung from dust and disappointment. He didn't listen for the song inside, the one he'd lost. It wouldn't be coming back.

And who needed it? Who needed anyone, really?

Another of his teammates stepped up to bat, a new hotshot scholarship pitcher. He wiggled his spikes in place, gave a practice swing, and muttered something resembling a challenge. On another day, TJ would take the needling in stride, all part of the game. But right now, his mood demanded he stuff that cockiness back where it came from.

Fittingly, the catcher called for a slurve. When executed right, the experimental slide-curve combo created a nice weapon. An unexpected pitch to throw the guy off.

TJ channeled all of his emotions into the ball trapped in his glove. He didn't bother to visualize the path, just the rookie's humbled expression. Breath held, TJ drew back and unleashed the slurve full force. The ball swung wide, too wide, before it broke—*wham* into the hitter. His lower spine.

Shit.

Coach Barry rushed to the plate. Several players from the dugout did the same. Slowly, the batter rose from the huddle. They walked him off the field, not a single eye in TJ's direction.

"Nice one, Kern." Paul closed in with an ugly grin.

"Get back to your base."

"That your new strategy? Wipe out the competition?"

TJ's fingers clawed the interior of his glove as he tried like hell to ignore the weasel.

"Guess I don't blame ya. With Coach Barry gone soon, you'll be pulling slivers out of your ass from riding that bench." Paul smacked his chewing gum around, a sound that grated on TJ's nerves like sandpaper. "Or, you could just drop out now. Maybe join your Jap friend when they clear 'em out of the area. Hell, out of the whole country if we're lucky." More smacking as he turned for his base.

What happened next passed in a blur. TJ didn't register his own actions until Paul was lying on the ground. The jerk scrambled to his feet and flung off his baseball cap, charged forward shouting. "You gonna shove me from behind, asshole?"

Other infielders interceded, keeping them apart.

"Come on, you coward! I dare you to try it again!" Paul reached through the nest of limbs and grabbed TJ's sleeve. By the time TJ wrestled the grip loose, Coach Barry stepped up to mediate.

"Break it up, the both of you," he barked. "Lamont, go cool off in the dugout."

Paul's wriggling stopped, but his glare remained on TJ.

"Now, Lamont!"

Conceding, Paul jerked away from his teammates' restraining hands.

Coach Barry addressed TJ. "What was that all about?"

It wasn't Paul's potshots that had pushed TJ over the edge. It was the fact that the guy had seen the romance between Maddie and Lane first. And worse yet, that he'd embedded digs about Japs into TJ's mind—about being liars and yellow and filthy—making the words far too easy to spit out.

"It was nothing," TJ muttered, and straightened his cap with a tug.

Coach Barry glanced over at home plate. He shook his head helplessly. "Better call it a day," he said.

TJ didn't argue. And this time, he didn't bother to gauge Essick's reaction. He just tossed away his glove and walked off the field—with no intention of returning.

≈22≈

The unfathomable had become reality. President Roosevelt had signed an executive order, allowing the removal of any persons from any area the military saw fit. That area was turning out to be the entire West Coast; and the people, those with Japanese ancestry.

They started with Terminal Island. Gave them forty-eight hours to evacuate. How does an entire community pack up and move in forty-eight hours? Their families and houses, their livelihoods.

For months, Lane had hidden daily newspapers from his mother. There had been no need to rattle her further. History courses had taught him that journalists with extreme viewpoints tended to represent a vocal minority. Fanaticism and fear, over evidence and reason, sold papers. When the *Los Angeles Times* had printed declarations of vipers being vipers no matter where they were hatched, he'd dismissed his budding of anger. Paranoia would run its short course, and the typewriters would shift to accurately reflect the overall sentiment of the country.

But through FDR's order, the country had spoken.

And Lane had been ruled a viper.

* * *

Seated in a far corner booth at Tilly's Diner, Lane reviewed these thoughts to gather his courage. The manila envelope lay front-side down on the table. He told himself he was making the right decision; that he was giving Maddie the needed out she would never ask for.

Still, he regretted arriving so early, allowing too much time to think. He should have chosen another place to meet. At a diner, she would be expecting a casual, lingering date.

Too late to make a change. Maddie had just arrived.

She approached the table smiling, radiant in her peach dress. He'd known her too many years not to recognize when she had put special effort into her appearance. Her hair hung long, pinned neatly at her temples. Rouge and lipstick brightened her face, spurring his urge to kiss her.

"Have you been here long?"

He shook his head. To his relief, she slid into the seat across from him; the division of the table hindered him from acting on impulse.

"I don't know about you, but I'm starving," she said, setting aside her pocketbook.

Hamburger sizzled and scented the air. From a corner of the room, a jukebox projected "Embraceable You" to a sparse early-lunch crowd. Autographed portraits of movie stars hung in frames on the wall. He noted all of this, not wanting to forget the place in which he and his friends—namely TJ—had spent countless hours over the years.

"Let me guess." Maddie smiled. "Strawberry malt with extra whipped cream."

He was about to agree, when he recalled the purpose of their meeting, and his gut churned. "Not today."

Her eyes widened in exaggerated astoundment. "Are you sure you're feeling all right?"

"Maddie," he began, "I need to tell you something."

Gradually she sat back, as if becoming aware of the tension.

He cleared the resistance from his throat. But before he could continue, a navy-blue form swam into his periphery. Ruth stood at their table in her diner dress, a pencil behind her ear. She held her order pad to her chest.

Expecting her predictable greeting—*The usual, Lane?*—he interjected, "We need a few minutes, please."

The waitress didn't move. Her motherly features looked distraught. "I'm real sorry, sweetie. But we have a new manager, and, well, he thinks you'd be more *comfortable* eating somewhere else. I told him you probably just missed the sign, and you weren't trying to make trouble."

Lane lifted his eyes and discovered the back of a small poster taped to the window. He could imagine what it read without seeing the front. *No Japs Allowed.* There were plenty of the same around town, at markets and barbershops, but it hadn't occurred to him that a place he'd grown up in would subscribe to the insanity.

"I'm real sorry," Ruth repeated with genuine care, then left their booth, exposing a view of customers' glares and whispers. Apparently he'd been too preoccupied to notice them.

"Come on, Lane." Maddie clutched her pocketbook. "We'll just go." She slid from the seat and waited for him to respond.

Against the weight of humiliation he managed to rise.

Outside, they walked without speaking. They were halfway down the block, in search of an alternate spot, when Lane stopped her. There was no reason to delay the inevitable, and the gentle approach he'd planned had been whittled away.

"This is for you."

Accepting the envelope, she said, "What is it?"

"Us being together," he stated simply, "it isn't going to work."

Her face darkened, as he'd expected. But then she discarded his claim with a shake of her head. "We'll be fine. I told you, we can move wherever we want to go."

"We made a mistake." The phrase felt like metal shavings in his mouth, each syllable a tiny razor. "It's time we faced the truth."

"Wh-what do you mean?"

"We made a mistake," he forced out again.

"Stop saying that!" Her eyes lit with moisture, her skin flushed.

He restrained his arms from enfolding her. "The papers are already filled out. There's a pen inside. Please just sign them." He angled his head away. He could hear her slide the packet out, the gasp from her mouth.

"Divorce papers?"

After an infinite pause, no pages rustling, he glanced up to confirm she was reading. Rather, she was staring at him. From the devastation in her eyes, he felt a ripping in his chest, the severing of his heart.

"Lane, please don't do this." Her voice strained through her tears. She touched his cheek, and a slow burn moved over his skin. "You're the only person I have left."

He clasped her fingers, harnessing truth that would only destroy her in the end. And from behind his facade, he peered at her. "I'm sorry, Maddie. But I don't love you anymore."

Before his resolve could buckle, he turned and let her go.

❧ 23 ❧

"C'mon. Just try a little." Maddie heard the words through the pillow covering the back of her head. "It's a cinnamon roll, your favorite." Jo's gentle coaxing dwindled with her patience. "For Pete's sake, you gotta eat somethin'. It's dang near three o'clock."

"I'm not hungry," Maddie mumbled into the mattress. In fact, she doubted her appetite would ever return.

A soft clink indicated Jo had placed the silverware and plate on the nightstand, where the divorce packet remained. Since receiving it yesterday, Maddie couldn't bear to open the envelope again.

The bed dipped as Jo took a seat. "You know, Maddie, could be this is for the best. Maybe it's like that opera you told me about. Where the girl and guy are keen for each other, but they meet at the wrong time, and their worlds are just too different."

Suddenly Maddie regretted that she'd relayed the premise of *Aida*. She needed someone to convince her that life could end happily. Like a snappy Broadway musical, not a tragic opera. Lane used to be that person for her.

Jo knew that. How could she suggest they'd be better off apart?

Lifting her head, Maddie squinted against the sunlight. "We're *not* too different. Lane and I are supposed to be together, regardless of what others might think."

Sure, their backgrounds varied, from finances to heritage. But they, as individuals, were the same. Their tastes in food and films were identical. During *Amos 'n' Andy* radio shows, they were always the first two to laugh. And when it came to beliefs and values, they were a perfect match.

"Okay, you're two peas in a pod." Jo agreed so naturally, it was clear Maddie had fallen right into her trap. "So, why don't you just go over and talk to him? Straighten all this out?"

"Because—it's not that simple."

"Oh. Oh, yeah, I see your point. You would, after all, have to stop feeling sorry for yourself long enough to change your clothes. How long you been in this outfit anyway?"

"I am *not* feeling sorry for myself."

"Could've fooled me."

Maddie groaned, retreating into the pillow. She should have known better than to call on Jo for sympathy. Raised in a household of boys, the girl hadn't exactly mastered the art of coddling.

"Ah, Maddie. Forget the baloney he told ya. I mean, jeez Louise, if I ever had a fella look at me like that . . . well. He loves you for sure. You know he's only doing this to protect you. Boys are cavemen. They guard their clan. Granted, often in ways that make no sense whatsoever. And they almost always say the opposite of how they feel."

In general, the explanation rang true, TJ being a prime example. The way he'd hold in his emotions, express them in an infuriating fashion. But Lane was an exception. He'd always been a straightforward guy. It was one of his greatest traits.

Although, given the current circumstances, anyone could act out of character, she supposed.

Maddie turned back toward Jo. Her eyes felt swollen from tears. "Do you really think he still loves me?" She searched her friend's face for the truth.

"Yes," Jo said with absolute certainty. "What's just as important, though, is do you love *him?*"

Faced with the probability of losing Lane, her feelings were never clearer. "Oh, Jo. I love him so much, I can't imagine living without him."

"So fight for him."

The suggestion sounded like the most obvious solution in the world. Perhaps it was. Again and again, Lane had fought for her, fought for them. If she didn't return the favor, and soon, she stood to lose him forever. But how?

She ran a finger along the side of the manila envelope. The document to end their marriage awaited her consent. What if she refused? He couldn't divorce her unless she signed the papers, could he?

This was her decision to make too.

Mouth set with determination, Maddie kicked off the covers. She'd had her fill of being guided by others, based on what they felt best suited her. It was high time she took hold of her own future. She began by sifting through her closet and grabbed the mint-green sundress. The color of spring, to reflect a fresh start.

"What do you think?" she asked, holding the garment up to her body.

Jo's lips curved into an approving smile. "I think he's going to love it."

Answer, answer, answer . . .

Maddie stood at the Moritomos' front door. With each of her steps to reach their house, her strength had gained volume and momentum. Her energy filled the porch. She felt ten feet tall.

About to knock again, she opted for the bell. She rang it twice and with purpose. Today, she had the confidence to persist even if Mrs. Moritomo opened the door. Maddie was prepared to wait for hours until Lane arrived should he be out—the cinnamon roll was enough to tide her over.

"Somebody answer," she urged quietly.

Still no one.

She rose up on her toes to peek through the arched glass in the door. The foggy pane distorted her view. Lane had mentioned that his mother scarcely left since his father's arrest. Maybe the woman had spotted Maddie through the peephole and was pretending not to be home. Or . . .

Could the FBI have returned? Taken the whole family in for questioning?

It was a ridiculous thought—Emma being eight.

Then Maddie noticed a paper taped to the window, covering the hole from a thrown brick, reminding her that anything was possible.

Anxiety rising, she strained to see through a narrow opening between the closed drapes. She could make out a mere sliver of the floor. No movement. Below the patched hole, she discovered a wider view. Her hand cleared a circle on the dusty glass. The couch was gone. And the coffee table. The whole formal room appeared empty.

At the shop, she'd heard mortifying tales of people walking straight into Japanese American homes and taking what they pleased, knowing the families were too afraid to call the police. Had the Moritomos, too, been robbed?

"Hello! It's Maddie. Hello!" She tried the knob. Unlike most houses, it was locked. Sifting through possibilities of what had happened, she rushed to the next-door neighbor's. She pounded on the door with her fist.

A plump Mexican woman poked her head out. "Yes?"

"I'm sorry to bother you, ma'am, but I think burglars may have broken into the Moritomo home. All of their things—we need to call the police."

To Maddie's dismay, the woman didn't dash to the phone. Her features simply drooped, their sullenness explained through words that cracked the sky.

"The family moved away."

⟡ 24 ⟡

How was it possible? Plenty of food in the pantry and yet TJ couldn't find a single thing to eat. This always seemed the case anymore. Reaching for things he couldn't have. An appetite for what he couldn't see, couldn't identify.

Flicking the last cupboard closed, he heard footsteps in a rapid climb of the stairs. He hollered up, "Maddie? Have you seen the tomato soup I bought?" Quick and easy, it was better than nothing. He hadn't eaten anything since his breakfast of stale Butter Horns on campus.

"Maddie?" he yelled again. A door upstairs slammed.

Oh, boy. Now what?

Given their cordial exchanges over the week, he couldn't imagine being the cause of today's annoyance. In fact, he hadn't talked to her since yesterday morning on his way out.

He went upstairs, rapped on her door. The sound of dresser drawers opening and closing projected from inside. Concern drew him into the room.

He watched his sister skitter about. Her hair hung haphazardly from her twisted-up do. Dried tears streaked her powdered face. She snagged blouses from her bureau and tossed them into a suitcase on her bed.

"Where are you going?"

At the closet, she tore through the hangers. She was moving on a different plane, where no one else existed. Garments slipped off and landed in puddles of fabric. She grabbed two skirts and a dress, added them to the chaos of her luggage.

"Maddie, stop." He raised his voice to break through, then closed his hand around her wrist. After a reflexive tug, she stilled. Her eyes raised, brimmed with pain. Before he dared to ask what had happened, she fell into his arms.

"He's gone," she said. "Lane's family. They sold everything and . . . just left."

The news hit like a spitball to the chest. It's what TJ had wanted—what he'd asked for, even—but somehow he didn't see it coming.

He rubbed his sister's back. "It'll be all right," he repeated over and over. Each time he tried to sound more convincing. Her fresh tears soaked through his T-shirt, though it was guilt that stung his skin.

"Where could they have gone?" she said as if to herself, which explained her packing frenzy.

"Maddie, you can't go off chasing them around the country. They could be anywhere. If it's meant to work out with you and Lane, it will. After the war maybe." He couldn't believe what he was suggesting.

"They couldn't have gone far," she concluded as she straightened. She was solving, not listening. "His father. How could Lane leave with his father still away?"

"His dad'll be fine," TJ insisted. "Lane said it was only a formality. I'm sure he'll be back with his family soon."

"But how will he know where . . ." As her question trailed off, she took a step back. "When did Lane tell you that?"

"When did—what?" he stammered, catching himself too late.

"You talked to him," she realized.

TJ avoided her eyes. Nonetheless, he could sense her viewing his memories; his confrontation with Lane was replaying like a scene in a picture show.

"It was you," she said.

"Maddie . . ."

"*You* did this."

"Now, just hold on. Listen to me." He reached out, but she jerked away.

He anticipated a furious outburst. Instead, her reply came slow and molten. "Get . . . out." The two words screamed with finality.

Then she turned toward the window, arms hugging her middle, and stared with the bearing of a stranger.

"Another one!" a drunkard yelled from the other end of the bar from TJ.

The bartender took the liberty of pouring the man a coffee, told him it was spiked with booze and on the house. He then stopped in front of TJ. "Problem with the drink, pal?"

Ordering a shot of whiskey had seemed a fresh solution, to drown his troubles, if only for a night. Everything else had failed. Since the accident, he'd steered clear of anything except an occasional beer. But why? Drink or not, he'd be damned if he became his father.

"The whiskey's fine." To prove it, TJ threw back the shot. Liquid heat hurtled down his throat and flamed his chest. "The same," he rasped.

Towel slung over his shoulder, the bartender refilled the glass. TJ didn't waffle over this one. He had no reason to. For the first time since he was a youngster, he had no coach demanding he keep his nose clean, no parents setting the rules. Just a sister who believed he was ruining her life. Which maybe he was.

The alcohol swished around in his stomach. Without food in there for padding, he already felt a light sway of his barstool. He envisioned himself on a raft, air seeping from a hole. He was scrambling to plug the leak, but another puncture appeared, and another. The holes expanded until he realized he'd been patching them with a knife, and nothing would keep him from sinking.

"Can I settle the check?" a guy nearby asked the bartender. In response, the man nodded and started tabulating on his order pad.

"Kern, right?"

TJ turned to the customer. Tall and skinny. Looked familiar.

"Eugene Russell," he said, indicating himself. "We have Management class together. Or had, I should say."

"Why, you drop the course?" TJ's question stemmed not from interest in his classmate, but from a desire to do just that. Way things were going, he'd have to work like a hound to skim by with a passing grade.

"My buddies and I are enlisting today. Just stopped here for a bite to eat on the way." Across the room, a group of three preppy college boys rose from their table, putting on their jackets.

"Good for you." TJ returned to his empty glass, ready for a refill.

"Six-fifty," the bartender announced.

The tall kid produced seven crisp bills from his wallet. "Keep the change," he offered with pride, then said to TJ, "Take it easy. Oh, and good luck with the season."

Yeah. The season.

"Thanks."

The guy rejoined his friends by the table. Smiles plastered their faces, a sign of purpose gleaming their eyes. How nice to have a purpose, to get out of this city and start over. Someplace where your history, your mistakes, weren't hunkered around every corner prepared to pounce.

TJ motioned to the bartender for another shot, though it was the last thing his stomach wanted. What *did* he want? He wished he knew. Those guys heading for the door, they knew what they were after. Had a future ahead guaranteeing respect. Parades. Medals. Gold stars and glory in death. He could almost hear the regal notes of "Taps" playing on a horn, could see the pomp of a folded flag.

The scene suddenly had appeal.

"Russell, wait." His voice flew out, swinging the kid around. Before TJ could think twice, he let the next words fall. "I'm coming too."

PART THREE

A sparrow flew in amongst a group of happily
playing quiet waterfowl and disturbed the peace.
For the sake of the pond's peace
the young sparrow will leave and fly away.

—Okumura Hirofumi
excerpt from a farewell letter to his lover

25

Rolling onto the graveled lot, the Buick digested its last sip of fuel and choked to a stop. Lane gripped the steering wheel, palms sweating from dreaded awareness: The dusty filling station in front of him, eight miles from their latest motel, was his family's final option. His hunt for gasoline had stretched past noon, winding him through the small Texan town planted south of the New Mexico border.

With his unpolished shoes, he brushed aside Hershey's wrappers on the floorboard—remnants from Emma's snacks during their cross-country drive—and stepped out of the car. The tang of diesel struck harder than the untrusting eyes of a middle-aged couple seated in their pickup truck. A shotgun hung on the back window of their cab.

Lane made his way toward the station attendant. The freckled teen, skin blotched from the May sunlight, was swiping his forehead with a rag when he froze.

"My tank's empty." Lane gestured to his car, which appeared as worn as he felt. "I'd like to fill it up if I could."

The kid didn't respond at first, stuck in deep fascination, as if a Martian had just landed and asked to refuel his ship. "I—uh, sure—awright."

It wasn't until Lane absorbed the words, and balked at the guy's agreement, that he realized how little hope he had sustained. "Thank you," he said. He stopped himself from volunteering the number of times he'd been refused gas during their trek from L.A. to Santa Fe. Now en route to the detention center in Crystal City, supposedly his father's most recent transfer, their luck hadn't been much better. Maybe things were turning around.

"Would you mind giving me a hand to bring it closer?" Though wary of asking for too much, Lane would need help rolling the vehicle over to the pump.

"Yessir." The kid followed him, then spread his hands on the rear of the Buick.

Lane opened the driver's side and prepared to push while steering. "Ready?"

A man's holler interrupted. "What're you doing there, Junior?"

"Just movin' this car over, Pa." The kid righted himself, his shoulders still hunched. "Fella's outta gas."

"You leave it alone now," his father ordered. Streaks of oil stained his mechanic's jumper. Beside him, the customer from the truck stood with hands hitched on his trousers, watching. "You heard me, Junior. Go on, now."

As the kid stepped away, Lane felt a bubbling of emotion. "Please," he said to the mechanic, "just give me some gas and I'll happily leave." While intended as a plea, the words came out with a gruffness he didn't intend.

"Sorry, can't help ya here." The man sounded anything but apologetic. "Have to take your business elsewhere."

Lane spoke as calmly as he could through gritted teeth. "How am I supposed to take my car anywhere? Tank's completely empty."

"Reckon that's your problem to solve, now, ain't it?"

The customer at the man's side slid a glance to his gun rack. Inside the pickup, the woman gripped the dashboard. Fret filled her eyes. In that look, Lane saw it all. Through a distorted lens of fear, implanted from Pearl Harbor, his crime was unforgivable. Even worse than murder, he had stolen their security. And eliminating the thief was a sure way to recoup that loss.

Lane showed them his palms, a sign of surrendering. He walked backward several paces, the tension waning with distance. At the border of the lot, he turned and started the long walk toward the motel.

"Hey, fella," the kid called after him. "Don't you want your keys?"

He gave the single response they all wanted from him.

His silence.

"*Onīsan!*" Emma threw her arms around Lane the minute he returned. "Where have you been? You were gone so long."

He hugged her back, and for a moment, any troubles that existed outside their dingy rented room scattered beyond care. "Sorry, Em. It just took a bit longer than I thought."

"*Onaka ga—*" His mother spoke from a corner chair, then began again. "We hungry." Her tone verged on a scolding, but Lane felt no offense. The worry that creased the edges of her eyes betrayed her veneer.

He pulled on a smile. As head of the family, the solution was his to find. "Let me clean up and we'll go get some food." He crossed the room, the bedding as threadbare as the mud-colored carpet. An odor resembling an old attic stretched into the bathroom, where unseen mold heaved its mildewy breaths.

Door closed, he splashed water on his face. Rust ringed the sink. He let the drops trail off as he stared into the mirror. His face had aged five years. A whorl of hair fanned upward, confused by the absence of Brylcreem. His white buttoned-down shirt was tinted with dust from passing cars; that, and more than two months of rotating through the same suitcase of clothing.

He went to the toilet, its sound of running water a nuisance, and retrieved his Mason jar from the tank. Coins tumbled against a thinning cushion of dollar bills. Their cash savings wouldn't last forever. That's what he'd told Maddie when she had proposed they run away.

At the thought of her, a string of memories rose into view. He could see the two of them at an aquarium, laughing as they fed the barking seals. He saw a folded note stamped with a lipstick mark that she'd slipped into his coat: *Missing you.* He had found it while on his train ride to Stanford at the start of fall. That's what the season had been—a steady fall from the life he'd known. One Maddie didn't need to suffer.

"You made the right decision," he said firmly to his reflection.

He almost believed it.

Glancing around at the chipped tiles, the window too small to escape through, he reassessed their mission. Hunting for their father served no purpose other than to keep them moving. Even if the man was indeed in Crystal City when they arrived, then what? Seeing him would be out of the question. A receptionist at the Santa Fe detention center had explained that repeatedly, encouraged them not to waste the effort.

And how would they get there—by bus? How many more motels would refuse them rooms? How long before they were denied passage? Residents at several state borders were said to be blocking eastbound Japanese attempting to resettle voluntarily.

No state wanted to be California's dumping ground, a columnist had reported.

Lane rotated the jar in his hands. *Clink, clink, clink.* Bargain hunters had bought their appliances and furnishings for five cents on the dollar. *Clink, clink, clink.* A green portrait of Thomas Jefferson peered from a two-dollar bill. Lincoln's profile shone bright in bronze. These were the faces that represented the America he knew, the men who fought for freedom and equality. The very values that defied racial internment.

Still, under their leadership, their worthy causes had required sacrifice. Maybe Lane ought to accept his own duty, no matter how wrong it all seemed. Besides, what else could he do? Evacuation of the West Coast's Japanese was in full swing, and jobs would undoubtedly run scarce for a man with slanted eyes. Highlights of the relocation centers, on the other hand, included occupations and newly built housing, recreational activities and schools.

Emma needed to be in school. She needed to be with other kids. According to a spokesman, ten camps had been established to protect, not punish, more than a hundred thousand of Japanese heritage. Lane had discounted the claim as a guise, but perhaps truth lay within the propaganda.

God, he missed his father. Nobu Moritomo would know what to do.

A knock on the door turned him. "*Onīsan,* I'm staaarving."

He clutched the jar and opened the door. Emma looked up at him with eager eyes. He tenderly squeezed her chin, praying he was about to do the right thing. "We'll get something to eat," he promised her, "right after we pack."

"I thought we weren't going to Crystal City till tomorrow."

"We're not going to Crystal City anymore."

"Then, where are we going?"

Lane met his mother's puzzled gaze before he answered. "Back home."

❧ 26 ❧

From the urgency of Bea's entrance, Maddie tensed for disastrous news.

"Lordy, Maddie. You won't believe it. You simply won't." Bea panted as she closed the shop's door. "Oh, sugar, watch the iron."

Maddie lifted the appliance from a customer's pleated skirt in the nick of time.

"Just let me catch my breath." Bea fanned herself with an envelope from the counter. An intentional delay, it seemed. What could have gone so wrong to give her second thoughts about relaying her discovery?

Oh, no—TJ. He must have been wounded. Could word travel faster through conversation than a telegram? He was still only in training with the Army Air Corps, but accidents occurred all the time. He could have been shot in a misfire at gunnery school.

Maddie had told him she agreed with his enlistment, after her initial jolt. Told him that giving each other space would be good for them both. But she hadn't expected how hollow the house would feel, amplifying worries over his safety. Nor how challenging it would be to maintain a cool distance in their letters, which she suddenly regretted.

"Tell me what happened," Maddie said to Bea. *Get it over with.*

'It's Mrs. Valentine. She was at the nursing home today visiting her aunt. I just happened to bump into her outside my husband's office while I was droppin' off his lunch. You remember Mrs. Valentine, don't you? She used to make those Christmas wreaths your daddy always bought to raise money for the Girl Scouts."

Maddie shook her head *no*.

This couldn't be about TJ. Regardless, she was hesitant to relax.

"Well, we got to chatting about the shop and what have you. Turns out, she'd heard all about your playing the violin for your daddy, and about your not going to Juilliard on account of—well, due to the war."

A gentle way to put it.

Maddie almost asked how Mrs. Valentine had caught news about her financial and marital predicament, but then, who in Boyle Heights hadn't?

"So then," Bea said, moving closer, "she tells me how her brother-in-law plays for the symphony up in San Francisco, and how he owed her a favor for something or other. Naturally, I told her you'd be grateful if there were anything he could do. And much to my surprise, she marched straight over to the phone and dialed him up. O' course, she didn't go into a whole lotta detail with him—men get all flustered from too much information—and well, he tells her there should definitely be entrance scholarships available from the school."

Maddie was well aware of that option. What she didn't know was how to respond without drizzling on Bea's parade. Maddie had never heard the woman carry on with such excitement, her pace contending with that of Mrs. Duchovny. Or rather, the Mrs. Duchovny people more fondly remembered.

"He's right," Maddie gingerly affirmed. "They don't give out more than a handful, though. And once you're accepted, you have to audition for the scholarship in person, in New York, just days before the term begins."

The scenario seemed unendurable: scraping together money for application fees and travel fare, while towing a year's worth of clothing in an oversized trunk, only to be informed she couldn't attend.

"Yes, yes," Bea said. "But apparently, it helps to have a faculty member's recommendation. He says that if the person listens to you play and speaks on your behalf, presuming you're good enough—which heaven knows you are—your chances of a scholarship increase by leaps and bounds."

This still did nothing to help Maddie's situation, or her somberness. For weeks, she had been distracting herself with extended hours at the shop. As if sewing shears could trim away the jaggedness of Lane's departure and the frays of her father's dream.

"Bea, it's splendid of you to do this for me. I'm terribly grateful. But I don't know a single person on the Juilliard staff, and I don't suspect I'll be meeting one anytime soon."

"You, my dear, have a month."

A month . . . "For what exactly?"

"To practice. You see, it just so happens that Benjamin, Mrs. Valentine's brother-in-law, is an old acquaintance of Mish—Mishnauff," Bea stammered. "Oh, bother, how did she say it?"

Recognition bristled Maddie's posture. "Mischa Mischakoff?"

"Ah, good! You know of him."

Maddie had heard the Ukrainian violinist play a recital years ago, and the magnificence of his performance, the tonality he controlled as it flowed from his Stradivarius, still reverberated in her ears.

"Here's the thing, sugar," Bea continued. "He has a trip planned to San Francisco. Benjamin will be hosting his visit, and is sure the man would be delighted to give you a private audition. As Benjamin's guest, he could hardly say no, now could he?"

Assembling the swirling pieces, Maddie asked, "Mischakoff is teaching at Juilliard?"

"Newly added, I believe they said."

"But how did—Benjamin couldn't have spoken to him yet."

"No, but he gives his word, and Mrs. Valentine claims that's good as gold. You just need to mosey on up there, prepared to show your stuff."

An audition for Mischa Mischakoff. Was it possible?

Maddie's hands flew to her cheeks, pulled by an urge to keep her grin from floating to the ceiling.

Then she considered the time line.

"Did you say a month?" Four weeks never seemed so short.

The grin that slipped off Maddie's face had transferred onto Bea's. "I'd say you'd best get busy."

"But, a month . . . I haven't been keeping up like I should have."

"Then I suggest you stop lollygagging and get to work."

Audition pieces swam through Maddie's mind as Bea handed over a sweater and purse, and shooed her out of the store. Maddie turned around, remembering. "Are you sure? There's a pile of alterations waiting, and more ironing to be done."

Bea shook her head, fists on her hips. "Seeing where your head's at, you'll be useless to me anyway. Hems going this way and that. Iron burning holes clear through. Now, go."

Maddie threw her arms around the woman before following the order. "Your father would be so proud," she thought she heard Bea say. Then she realized, yet again, the words had come from within.

As the bus rumbled toward home, Maddie didn't feel a single bump. Her body levitated over the seat, her surge of joy like a magic potion. She couldn't wait to share the news with TJ and Jo and her father—whether her dad showed outward signs of hearing didn't matter today. But most of all, she was dying to tell Lane!

Seized by reality, her heart plunged into a free fall. Too late she recalled the danger of permitting happiness to raise her spirit to such heights. The higher the jump, the more destructive the landing. She brushed the thought away, and froze at the sight. An Oriental woman was seating herself six rows ahead.

Maddie would swear the passenger was—

Mrs. Moritomo?

From the back, the woman's figure appeared identical. Familiar pearls encircled her dainty neck. A comb adorned with sparrows, Kumiko's favorite bird according to Lane, secured a smooth black chignon.

Nonsense. She couldn't be Lane's mother. They were gone. Across the country by now.

Yet Maddie watched her, unable to move. The bus paused at one stop, then another. Passengers got off, got on. They rocked in unison, tilted around corners. Finally the woman rose—for the approaching stop that used to be Lane's—bolstering Maddie's excitement.

When the vehicle squeaked to a halt, Maddie joined the line to exit. Her gaze clung to Kumiko, the key to locating Lane. Could his family be staying in their old place? Changed their minds, turned the car around? Twice Maddie had gone to their house, just to be sure, and found it vacant. A sign on the door: *For Lease.*

Treatment in other towns might have been worse. Their father could have been released, prompting their return. . . .

Possibilities multiplied until the Japanese woman turned to deboard. Her profile revealed her age to be thirty at most. With a narrower face than Kumiko's, rosier cheeks, and a higher bridge of the nose, she looked Chinese, not Japanese. Assuming *Time* magazine's comparative illustrations held any validity.

Either way, she wasn't Mrs. Moritomo.

Maddie sank into the nearest seat, her hopes kicked out from under her. The bus rolled onward, as did her thoughts until settling on Juilliard. She pictured the application, its signature line as black, solid, and blank as the one for her divorce. Countless times she had stared at Lane's petition, even hovered a pen over the pages. But a thin thread of faith had kept her from signing. A thread that now fully unraveled.

The instant Maddie entered her house, she headed for the document she could no longer avoid. She refused to mull over what she couldn't change, no matter how much she'd always love Lane. Instead, with divorce papers in hand, she said good-bye through a sting of tears. And she signed her name.

❦ 27 ❦

TJ waited for the target with his finger on the trigger. He braced his hip against the circular rail mounted on the bed of a pickup, the butt of the twelve-gauge snug into his shoulder. The truck bumped and rattled beneath his boots as it rounded the track. Behind him sat two privates who'd finished their turns. Now they were tasked with keeping score and feeding ammo.

Another clay pigeon soared from the trap. TJ followed its arc and fired, bursting the disk into fragments.

In his mind, that one was Paul Lamont.

A few guys here at gunnery school had asked TJ for the secret to his accuracy, his hits being unusually high. His answer was truthfully simple. "Picture the enemy." He just never elaborated with specifics. Better to let them assume he was referring to Nips or Krauts, not enemies closer to home. Paul had easily become his favorite target, followed closely by his father and Lane. Sometimes TJ himself.

The vehicle slowed after the final curve. TJ wasn't quite ready to give up the relief of moving air, nor the activity that passed the hours, but what choice did he have?

He relaxed his grip, lowering the shotgun. Thanks to the Vegas sun, the metal barrel could cook a Western omelet. Man, an omelet sounded like paradise compared to the mutton stew they served for chow. Between the sorry meals and sweat marathons, he hadn't been this lean since junior high.

With a rag from his uniform trousers, he mopped his neck and forehead. "Dry heat, my foot," he muttered.

No one deserved to be stationed in a barren wasteland like this. But at least he'd left the humidity of Keesler Field far behind. Basic training in Mississippi had ended not a day too soon.

The truck pulled over to the entrance, where the gunnery sergeant coordinated skeet shooting. "Gotta take a leak," Sarge told the driver, and strode away.

A small cluster of Air Corps privates waited to board. As always, Vince Ranieri stood at the helm. He wore his Italian smile like his black wavy hair, slick and suave. His magnetic confidence drew in just about everyone—except TJ.

"Save any ammo for us this time?" the guy scoffed.

TJ set down his weapon, though he suddenly found it tempting to hold on to, and climbed down with the others. He headed for the barracks without responding.

"C'mon, Kern. Don't tell me you're still sore over me tanning your hide."

Muffled snickers leaked out from the group, slowing TJ's feet. Consistently, when it came to the top spots, he and Ranieri had been neck and neck since first arriving at the airfield. From aircraft recognition to turret maneuvering to air-to-ground firing.

In the machine-gun drills, however—disassembling a .50-caliber and putting it back together—TJ had yet to have his time bettered by a classmate. Till this morning.

"I wouldn't celebrate too much," he flung over his shoulder. "Even a busted watch is right twice a day." More snickers from the bystanders.

"Ahh, so it was sheer luck," Ranieri said. "You sure about that?"

The whole scene felt too much like a repeat of TJ's last scuffle at the baseball field.

"'Cause if you're sure, real sure, maybe you'd like to put some money on it."

TJ told himself to keep walking, to ignore the dope. A few swings and they'd be tossed into the greasy pits of KP duty.

"What do you think, fellas? Surfer boy lost his stuff?"

Whether it was the excess of heat and testosterone in the air or being challenged before an audience, TJ's patience evaporated. He swung back around and caught eager anticipation on the other gunners' faces. In the middle of the desert, it didn't take much to constitute entertainment.

"So what'll it be, Kern?" Ranieri pressed. "Ten bucks on tomorrow's drill?"

TJ leveled his gaze at the smirking Italian and shrugged. "Why wait?"

Remarkable how fast news could spread about a pissing contest. That's basically what the hoopla amounted to, a stupid kids' game, but TJ's competitive streak made it impossible to back down.

In a training building, stocked with machine guns, he and Ranieri prepared for battle. They stood at opposite ends of a waist-high table, their M2 Brownings poised before them. A circle of three dozen airmen created a makeshift arena; all traded shouts of numbers, a mix of odds and dollars, with the gusto of a title fight at Madison Square Garden.

Next came blindfolds. TJ imprinted a fresh image of the machine gun in his brain. When the cloth blackened his vision, he released a long exhale. He pumped the stiffness from his hands and wrestled down the possibility of losing. With equal effort, he pushed away the ever-present thought of *What the hell am I doing here?* For a whiskey-glazed minute, enlisting had seemed the best way to care for Maddie. In spite of her recent assurances, he still questioned his own judgment.

Especially now.

"Pipe down," a guy bellowed at the room. "Let's get on with it. You boys know the rules. No shortcuts, no cheating, and the fifty-cals gotta fire to count. On your mark . . . get set . . . go!"

TJ was off, starting with the barrel group. One piece at a time, riding the border between speed and precision, he worked to disassemble the weapon. He removed the backplate. Pulled out the driving spring assembly. Took the bolt from the receiver and proceeded without a hitch.

Once he'd completed disassembly—halfway there!—he immediately charged into reversing the steps. A cough from someone off to the side reminded him he wasn't alone. The whole air base seemed to be holding its breath.

Concentrating, he replaced the barrel buffer assembly. He paused only to swipe his palm on his shirt. Collective body heat was intensifying his sweat. With the notch joined on the shank, he aligned the breech lock depressors. He snapped the spring lock and secured the parts and told himself not to rush. He was picturing the clearance hole when the bolt stud slipped from his fingers. *Damn it!* Blindly he fumbled for the piece. Following the sound of rolling metal, he recovered it next to the drive spring.

He couldn't panic. Just had to get back on track. He continued through the steps and heard Ranieri struggling with the retracting slide handle. TJ still had a chance. He unscrewed the barrel two clicks. The finishing line within grasp, he removed the link, closed the cover, and declared his win with a—

"Done!" Ranieri shouted.

A throng of cheering voices sucked the air from TJ's chest. Nothing like having your pride walloped in a public forum. Exactly what he needed, a demonstration of another shortfall.

TJ ripped off his blindfold as the ringleader shushed the mob and said, "All right, Ranieri. Let's see it."

With an arrogant grin, the guy replied, "My pleasure." He laced his fingers and cracked his knuckles to gear up for the formality. After all, he had yet to fail a function check.

TJ turned away, itching to scat before salt could hit the wound, just as Ranieri went to pull the trigger.

But it didn't click.

His face fell as he yanked harder.

Still no sound.

Half the room burst into celebration.

"Now, let's not get ahead of ourselves," the announcer warned. "Gotta make sure yours is in working order, Kern."

Ranieri stared at his machine gun, clearly stumped by where he'd gone wrong.

TJ felt the jolt and dip of a mental roller coaster. He readied his weapon for the test. Bolt latch released, he rode the bolt forward and placed his finger on the trigger. *Please work, please work.* And he pulled.

Click. The tiny sound was as beautiful as an ump yelling, "You're out!" at an opposing runner, sealing a win.

In the hustle and bustle, greenbacks transferred pockets. TJ stepped away from the table, almost giddy from the trivial upset, and found himself face-to-face with the competitor. Grimness had replaced the Italian's boastful glee from only moments before. Was he looking to go to blows?

TJ rolled his hands into discreet fists. But instead of a punch, he received two folded five spots. A nice surprise. He had to give the fellow credit. Ranieri was a far better loser than he himself would have been.

As TJ started away, Ranieri piped up. "So you gonna sport me a beer at least?" His signature grin had returned in full force. TJ couldn't help but smile back.

"I thought you meatball types only drank wine."

"Wine on Sundays, my friend. Beer every other day of the week." He offered a handshake, which TJ accepted, and by the third round that evening, in different ways it seemed both of them had triumphed.

～ 28 ～

Lane didn't know what he'd been expecting, but it wasn't this. He walked through the eerie stillness, his tweed cap pulled low, and turned from San Pedro Street onto First. Shadows spread over the block like an almighty hand. The hustle and bustle of pedestrians, the scent of udon broth, the ringing of bicycles and hollers of beckoning vendors—all were gone. Little Tokyo had been gutted.

Signs on building exteriors and in every window told a story. *Going out of business. Everything half price. For sale. Sold. Closed. We hope to serve you again. I am an American.*

For as long as Lane could remember, he had preferred to shop elsewhere. He'd chosen Sid's Drugstore over Nippon Pharmacy, Leaders Barbershop over Nakamura's. He had compiled reasons for the superiority of each. But perhaps the real basis of his favoritism had stemmed from nothing more than the quality implied by their "all-American" names.

Judging by the streets around him, a ghost town of his heritage, his view hadn't been unique. Thankfully, his father wasn't here to see this.

Just then, a silhouette moved in Ginza Market. Lane looked closer. Nobody there. A mere reflection from the retreating sun. Where would he find a snack for Emma?

He had ventured out of the Buddhist temple, his family's temporary shelter, on an errand for his sister. Her eyes had told him she wanted to tag along but understood that remaining with their mother took priority.

Mochi cakes, Emma had requested. Aoyagi Confectionery made her favorite of the glutinous rice balls filled with sweet red beans. He'd agreed, wanting to distract her from concerns over their destination, some camp in the state's eastern desert. Rumors of the place had circled like mosquitoes, nipping away, swelling fears of deportations and forced farm labor. They described roving coyotes and scorpion infestations, families separated and traded for American POWs. Mass executions if Japan invaded the mainland. All preposterous.

Or not.

Propelled by the promise to his sister, he continued down the empty street. He stepped on scraps from wooden crates. He followed the trail of crinkled flyers. The same proclamations were posted on utility poles.

INSTRUCTIONS TO ALL PERSONS OF JAPANESE ANCESTRY

Forcing the exodus of an entire race from an area had become disturbingly efficient. The pages detailed where and when to report, what they were and weren't permitted to pack.

At least Lane's family didn't have to worry about the limitation of bringing only what they could carry; that's all they had left. Little more than essentials remained after shedding items for their long bus ride back to California. Sunny Southern Cal, with its sandy beaches and lush palm trees. Where imagination bloomed and hope streamed in the sunlight.

Of course, none of these could be found in the confines of the temple's basement. In a time not so far back, Lane's mother would have griped plenty over their creaky squeezed-in cots, the mix of body odors from strangers varied in caste. But not now. And her silence, outside of one- or two-word answers, bothered him more than her complaining ever could.

Lane paused to review his surroundings. His feet had steered him to the last place he would have chosen. Kitty-corner from Kern's Tailoring. Miles of aimless walking hadn't been aimless after all. He wasn't wearing his watch—he'd hawked that too—but was certain the lights inside were shining for Bea. Maddie would be home, making supper for herself and TJ. Meat loaf and creamed corn, or a chicken casserole with Green Goddess Salad. Those were the dishes she had made when Lane used to join them.

At her absence now, disappointment flowed through him, but also relief. Seeing her would only make matters worse. Only tempt him to retract the lie he had told her.

"Holy Toledo. I don't believe my eyes!"

The familiar voice swung Lane around. In a khaki Army uniform, Dewey Owens was exiting Canter Brother's Deli. The last contact from the guy had been a brief but supportive note. He'd mailed it with Lane's belongings from the dorm.

"Good to see you." Lane smiled and accepted an outstretched hand. A friendly face was never so welcome.

"I can't believe you're in town. Thought you and your family were zooming around the country." Dewey made it sound as though they had been off on a whirlwind vacation, a road trip on a whim.

Lane was trying for a simplified answer when two GIs emerged from the restaurant. They looked on with unreadable expressions.

"Fellas! Let me introduce you." Dewey sped through their names, and all exchanged handshakes and nice-to-meet-yous. Then the two soldiers backed up a few paces, lighting their Lucky Strikes. Lane would like to think they were merely giving the old roommates space to catch up, but who knew anymore?

"What're you doing out here tonight?" Dewey asked.

"I was just looking in on a friend." Lane's chin inadvertently motioned toward the tailor shop, causing Dewey's eyes to follow. No chance taking the gesture back. He tried distracting with small talk, but the guy wasn't listening.

"So *that's* the dream girl. . . ." Dewey grinned, sly as an alley cat.

Leave it to him to make a crack about ogling Beatrice. Lane went to sling a retort—the guy's colorful love life had produced an ample amount of dirt—until he glimpsed the store window. There, Maddie appeared inside. She was hanging garments on a wall hook, balancing the fabric, picking off lint. His breath hitched at the sway of her auburn hair, the memory of feeling the silky strands on his skin.

But then he recalled what had happened since, that those times were over, and . . . that he'd never told Dewey about their courtship.

"How did you know?"

"About Maddie?"

Lane nodded.

"I was your roommate for almost four years, buddy. You think I'm *that* oblivious?" He gave Lane's upper arm a pat. "Do I get to meet her or what?"

Lane peered at the woman behind the glass. "She doesn't know I'm in town," he said. "It's better that way." Slowly, he tore his focus from her. "So you're an Army man, huh?"

Dewey shrugged. "Put me in Intelligence, if you can believe it."

"And they still expect us to win?"

"Guess they were smart enough not to give me live ammo."

Lane smiled, and for an instant, he envisioned himself in the same uniform—but only an instant. Even if the U.S. military weren't turning away Nisei, his patriotism had depleted too much to volunteer.

"Owens, we're gonna split," said one of the soldiers, flicking his cigarette butt onto the sidewalk.

"I'm coming." Dewey turned to Lane. "We're hitting some bars on Wilshire. Come out with us."

Lane considered the invitation. He appreciated any enticement to draw him from the temptation across the street. Then he spied a policeman in the distance meandering in their direction, and the invisible bars of curfew and travel restrictions returned.

"Actually, I'd better get back. We have to report to St. Timothy's by nine in the morning for evacuation. So . . ."

Dewey's face tightened, a mixture of sympathy and wanting to beat a fistful of sense into someone. But he simply said, "Take care of yourself."

"You too," Lane offered with equal sincerity.

They shook hands good-bye, then Dewey followed his friends around the bend.

Lane slid his hands into his jacket pockets. He glanced at the storefront once more, just as Maddie clicked off the first set of lights. Closing time. Before she turned off the second, he raised his collar around his ears and headed toward the temple. Empty-handed, nothing for Emma. Another promise broken.

❦ 29 ❧

Engines awoke in the distance, a stagger of roars that cinched Maddie's throat with panic. Her pace doubled in speed. Her leather heels clicked a staccato rhythm on the city sidewalk. She forced air in and out, in and out, against the burn crawling up the walls of her lungs.

Nine o'clock, that's what Lane's roommate had said when the operator connected his call that morning. Told her that his conscience wouldn't let him ship off without at least telling her Lane was in town, but if she wanted to see him, she had until nine o'clock.

She'd raced out the door. No time to think.

At last, she was almost there. . . .

A young soldier stood up ahead. He hugged his bayonet-fixed rifle across his chest, his stance undoubtedly fresh from Army basic. He stared hard into the sky, as if reading his mission etched in the ribbon of clouds. *The enemy, have to protect our country from the enemy.*

The thought curled Maddie's fingers.

In a glance briefer than a blink, the GI sized her up, her ivory skin an armor of presumed innocence. She swerved around him, not missing a beat. To her left, personal effects awaited transit in a snaking queue. Cribs and ironing boards, labeled trunks and boxes. Their tags dangled in the spring sun.

Around the corner, evacuees were amassed before the steepled church. Red Cross volunteers handed out coffee.

"Lane! Where are you?" Her words died in the bedlam, smothered by a baby's cry, a rumbling jeep, a little girl's hysterics.

"But I don't want to go," the girl shrieked, face stained red. "Mommy, I want to stay with *you!*" Tears streamed from the slanted eyes that cursed the child, dripping trails down the puffy sleeves of her lilac dress. Two nuns pried her fingers from the Caucasian woman's arms and guided the youngster toward the bus.

"Everything will be fine, pumpkin," the mother choked out against a sob. "Mommy and Daddy will come see you soon." A suited man beside her added, "You be a good girl, now." His Anglo features contorted in despair as he limply waved.

A reporter snapped a photo.

Who knew a piece of paper could carry so much power? One presidential order and an orphan could lose another family; one signed petition and marriage vows could be unsaid. Thank God she hadn't mailed the papers yet. Stamped and sealed, but not mailed.

Maddie scanned the faces around her, their features similar to Lane's, but none as flawless. None bearing the deep beauty of his eyes, his smile.

"Lane!" she shouted louder. The trio of chartered buses was filling. Within minutes, he would be gone.

"Excuse me, miss. May I help you?" A priest touched her arm. His wrinkled face exuded warmth that penetrated the morning chill.

"Moritomos—I have to find them." Exhaust fumes invaded the air, causing her to cough.

He patted her back. "Now, now, dear. Let's see what we can do." They wove through the crowd, her gaze zipping from one figure to the next. Beige identity tags hung from lapels, around buttons. Branded in their Sunday best like a herd of cattle.

"Sergeant," the priest called out. He stepped up to a bulky

Army man in the midst of lecturing two privates. "Sergeant," he tried again, "I hate to interrupt, but . . ."

"Hold your water," the guy barked, before turning and noting the source. His shoulders lowered. "Sorry, Father. What is it you need?"

"This young lady, here, she's trying to locate a particular family."

"The Moritomos," Maddie cut in.

The sergeant sighed heavily as he lifted his clipboard. He flipped forward several pages and began his search through the list. With the top of his pen, he scratched his head beneath his helmet. He blew out another sigh.

This was taking too long.

Maddie leaned in, trying to see the smudged names herself. *Maeda . . . Matsuda . . . Minami . . . Miyamoto . . .*

The sergeant turned to the next page and looked up. "What's that name again?"

She fought to keep her composure. "Moritomo. Lane Moritomo."

A loud hiss shot from behind. The first bus was pulling away, followed by the next. Another hiss and the doors slammed closed on the last Greyhound in line. The crowd launched into waves of farewells and see-you-soons, whenever, wherever that might be.

"Maddie." A muffled voice barely met her ears. It came again, stronger. "Maddie, over here!" Someone yanked open a dusty windowpane on the remaining bus. It was Lane, reaching across seated passengers to see her.

She wasn't too late!

Calling his name, she bumped through elbows to get to the blue-and-white striped transport. She scrambled for his hand until their grips linked, his skin soft as a glove. When a smile slid across his face, all else paled to a haze. Time reversed, back to happier days, before the ground had crumbled on a fault line, dividing their world in two.

"I didn't mean what I said," he implored, "at the diner. . . ."

"I know," she assured him, for it was a truth she had carried inside. Still, her heart warmed from the confirmation in his eyes.

Then the bus began to move.

"No matter what happens, Maddie, know that I'll always love you."

She tightened her grasp, refusing to let go. "I'll be waiting. However long it takes."

On the balls of her feet she hastened her stride. She struggled to keep up, but the wheels were spinning too fast. Against her silent pleas, their connection wouldn't hold and his fingers slipped beyond reach.

30

Entering the room was even harder than TJ had expected, and the sight more alarming.

Hunched in a ladder-back chair, the robed man stared distantly out the window. His profile resembled little of the father TJ remembered. Graying scruff lined his jaw. Wrinkles created a road map of time and tragedy.

TJ dropped his duffel bag on the rest home floor. Garrison cap in hand, he took a step forward, then another. The clicking of his polished shoes on tile didn't prompt a reaction. His father's blue eyes held on a summer sky of the same shade.

TJ reached for an adjacent chair, but changed his mind. He wouldn't be staying long.

"Dad, it's me."

Nothing. Just staring.

He tried again, louder. "I said, it's me. TJ."

On the train ride home that morning, he had contemplated this moment. The "delay in route" supplied his last chance to confront his father before deployment. If nothing else, he ought to say good-bye. In case.

"I know you probably can't hear me, but . . ." He cleared the rasp from his throat and straightened in his uniform. The shiny gunner's wings surely would have made his old man proud. Not that TJ cared. Why would he anymore?

"I just came to tell you that I'm shipping out soon, and I thought . . . I thought that . . ."

He rubbed a hand over his buzz cut, running low on words but heavy on memories. Snippets of his past assembled in a collage: his mother's seven-bean stew that once won a ribbon at a local fair; little Maddie following him everywhere, close as Peter Pan's shadow; his parents cheering from the stands after TJ's first no-hitter; and at the center of the images, his last camping trip with his father before college began. They'd lounged around the campfire, sipping their pungent coffee. Croaking frogs and chirping crickets had provided a backdrop to their comfortable silence.

So many moments. Now all irrelevant.

Here, in this structured enclosure, nature's sounds gave way to the squeaking of rubber soles and rolling carts, the clinking of metal trays. Each sound depicted movement with purpose. Of passersby in the hallway driven by the needs of others.

Faced by the contrast of his father's world, one of mere existence, TJ felt sympathy form low in his chest. It expanded like a bubble as he studied the room. The framed dime-store prints, the narrow bed, its solitude folded into Army-tight corners.

Then a thought returned. He'd sworn he would never forgive his father. Sworn it with everything in him. From that recollection, the sphere of sympathy popped, pricked by a needle of blame.

"Mr. Kern," a nurse said, entering. "Time for—oh, pardon me. I didn't mean to interrupt."

"I was just leaving," TJ told her, to which she gave a reassuring wave.

"There's no hurry, dear. I was fetching him for his afternoon walk. Are you a friend of the family?"

"No," TJ said, before adding, "He's . . . my father."

"Oh, I didn't realize he had a—" She stopped herself and smiled uncomfortably. "How silly of me. I should've seen the resemblance. Well. Feel free to take your time. I'll swing by later."

"No need, ma'am. I have to go anyway." He turned to his father, and without meeting his eyes, he bid a quick good-bye.

* * *

TJ recognized the tune but not the voice.

He set his duffel and tunic in the entry of his house, and followed the lyrics of "Boogie Woogie Bugle Boy" toward the kitchen. August had warmed the hall by a good fifteen degrees since the day he'd left, yet more than the temperature felt different.

The scent of a baking dessert piqued his curiosity, pushing out reflections on his father, and drew TJ closer to the singer. In the kitchen, she stood with her back to him.

Jo Allister . . . he should have guessed. She belted out an off-key high note that made him smile rather than cringe.

Arms folded, he leaned a shoulder against the doorframe. Her bound hair bobbed like a buoy as she diddel'd and yada'd about a Chicago trumpet man playing reveille. She sponged the tiled counter in a circular motion that matched the beat of her swaying hips. Nice sway actually. *And* nice hips. Her typical outfits were hand-me-downs from her brothers, hiding what now appeared to be an attractive figure. Her tan pedal pushers hinted to as much, even if her baggy button-down shirt, knotted at the waist, didn't. Which was a real shame, since—

TJ bridled the rest. This was Jo, the equivalent of another sister. Not to mention Maddie's best friend. Striking up more than friendship would verge on hypocrisy, considering his view of Lane. Besides, at this point, nothing good could come of a romance with anyone.

"You're home," Jo exclaimed in mid-turn. Her bronze eyes lit with delight, before the spark blew out. He could see her recalling their last encounter, the full bucket of anger he'd dumped on her. "Maddie said you weren't comin' till tomorrow." Her altered tone implied she had planned to be somewhere else. Anywhere else.

"I was released from the base earlier than I thought."

"Mm."

She gave his uniform a quick glance that showed no sign of being impressed, then retreated to the sink. Heat from the oven radiated through the room.

Setting his hat aside, he wiped his forehead with his sleeve. "So how've you been?"

She scrubbed her hands with soap, hard, not addressing the question. "Maddie should be back soon. She's delivering clothes to a neighbor on Fairmount, for the stamps she got."

"Stamps?"

Jo sighed, annoyed. "They made a trade. Maddie mended some trousers for ration coupons, 'cause she didn't have enough sugar. And she wanted to bake you a cake." Under her breath, she added, "Though only God knows why."

Boy oh boy, Jo was a tough nut. Oddly, though, he found her even more likable after seeing her in a huff. "So, what kind of cake you got there?"

"*Devil's* Food," she said after a pause.

"Ah, yeah? My favorite."

"Yeah, I know—" The sentence caught. She grabbed a plaid dish towel and dried her hands. "Since you're here now, *you* can keep an eye on the baking. Just pull it out when the bell goes off. It's flour-less, so it'll be denser than usual." She set the towel on the counter and walked past him.

"Come on," he said. "Don't rush off."

"Got stuff to do."

"Jo . . ." He trailed her toward the entry, led by a growing need to keep her there. He hadn't realized how much he'd missed their talks, or just being with her, till now. "Jo," he said again.

But she flat-out ignored him. Her hand made it to the door handle when he blurted, "I saw my dad today."

It was enough to halt her.

Slowly, cautiously, Jo faced him. She waited for him to continue.

"Figured I should . . . with me shipping out on Sunday."

She nodded, disdain dropping away. "How'd it go?"

"Fine, I guess. Doubtful he heard anything, but I said what I needed to."

A shadow of a smile lifted the corners of her lips. "That's good."

In the quiet stretch between them, it dawned on him that she'd never had the chance to say good-bye to her own dad.

"Well, I'd better get," she said. "Your sister's gonna want some time with you."

"Jo, listen. Before you go . . ."

She waited again.

If he couldn't right things with his father, he should at least make the effort elsewhere. "I wanted to say that . . . that I'm sorry, for blaming you about Lane and Maddie. I was angry, and, well, it wouldn't have been right for you to stick your nose in. So . . . I'm sorry for putting you in the middle."

Jo arched a brow. "Wow. Two sorrys in a single day," she mused. "How'd those feel coming out of your mouth, airman?"

"Rough enough to chip a tooth."

"In that case, apology accepted." When she grinned, he couldn't help but laugh.

"Seriously," he told her, "why don't you stay. If you helped bake the thing, you ought to enjoy a piece."

"What makes you so sure I helped bake anything for you?"

The smudge of cake batter on her cheek gave her up. He walked over and gently swiped the evidence with his thumb. He meant to withdraw his fingers, but to his surprise, found he couldn't. The softness of her skin held them in place. He looked into her eyes, and a feverish charge shot through him, sending a bead of sweat down his spine. His mind said to step back, but his body acted on its own. He watched his hand venture to her neck and her mouth slightly open. Her breath smelled of cocoa, her hair of lemon. He leaned several inches closer, wanting to taste the sweetness dusting her lips, when he heard a click.

The front door.

He shifted away with the speed of a rifle drill. "Maddie," he said.

His sister's eyes widened—from his return, he hoped, not the scene. "TJ, you got in early! You should have wired me. I would've met you at the station."

"I—wanted to surprise you."

Maddie returned his smile. But then her lips relaxed as she glanced at Jo, whose skin had gained a shade of pink. Maddie's attention bounced back to him with an air of suspicion. "Am I interrupting . . . ?"

"What, us?" He scrunched his face, motioning to himself and Jo. *She's one of the guys,* he said without saying it. "I was only walking her out." An uneasy pause.

"Yeah," Jo said coolly. "I was just leaving."

Unable to meet Jo's eyes, he tossed her a "see ya," and headed for the kitchen.

What the heck was he doing? Months of training with an assigned bomber group would do this to any fella, right? Too much time spent in the barracks. Too many postcards of pinup gals or chats about one broad or another. With the amount of testosterone packed into their B-17, it was a miracle they'd made it off the tarmac.

At the sink, TJ downed a glass of water that wasn't nearly cold enough. He refilled it as Maddie entered the room. Dodging an inquiry, he gestured to his uniform. "Whaddya think of the getup? Not too shabby, huh?"

She shook her head at him. A skeptical look, he assumed, until she spoke. "I can't believe you made corporal already." Her face warmed with pride.

Too bad the pride was unwarranted. In his view, he hadn't earned the rank more than any other private. "Don't let the stripes fool you. Just luck of the draw."

"Oh, I highly doubt that."

He didn't respond, simply drank his water. Why dim her glowing opinion?

"So . . . ," she said, a prompt that dangled. With nowhere to go from there, the conversation hovered over unwritten words in their letters.

TJ preferred to concentrate on what had actually appeared on those pages. Six months of postal exchanges had helped fill the cracks in their relationship.

"So," he parroted as his sister checked on the oven. "Give me the dope. What's the latest round here?"

Maddie tucked her pageboy hair behind her ears and leaned back against the counter. "Well," she said, thinking. "I did receive a nice note from Professor Mischakoff. He invited me to play for him again, once I get to New York. Sort of a final polish before going in front of the panel."

"Does that mean you got confirmation from the school, that they've given you an audition slot?"

"They did."

"And what about the application for the scholarship?"

"It's taken care of."

"Filling it out, or mailing it?"

"TJ." She reached over and touched his sleeve. "I've got it handled. Really, I'm not a little girl anymore."

Despite the maturity she'd gained while he'd been away—more definition in her cheeks, more curves to her sundress—she was still his baby sister. Always would be.

Skirting a debate over the point, he charged on. "And what about the shop? Business picked up any?"

"A little. Lately most of the alterations are just to make old clothes last. But it's all for the war effort, so we can hardly complain."

He was going to ask about managing the store, since they'd both be away soon, but then Maddie added, "Bea has assured me over and over she'll have everything under control. Combined with your Army pay, the bills are covered. And Jo will be checking on the house."

Had his nagging become that predictable?

TJ grinned in spite of himself. Tension inside him loosened, a settling into the familiar.

In a casual tone, Maddie continued, "Lane's family is doing all right, by the way, in case you're wondering."

The run-in with Jo had thrown him off. Otherwise, he'd have been better prepared for this subject. He would have noticed, before now, the wedding band on his sister's finger that solidified her stance.

"I'm glad to hear that," he said, a reflexive reply he immediately regretted. He didn't mean to cause the flicker of hope in her eyes.

"I'm planning to go see them soon," she said. "By train, it's only about five hours away. I keep asking in my letters, but Lane told me they don't allow visitors yet." She paused and lifted a shoulder. "I was thinking, if you're back here on furlough sometime, maybe . . ."

These, he recognized, were the unwritten words. He knew what she wanted in response, but as much as he loved his sister, he couldn't give it to her.

In the wake of his silence, she dropped her gaze to the counter. As she scraped her thumbnail at a dried spot of batter, he realized she might have the wrong idea.

"I want you to know," he told her, "I don't necessarily agree with what's been done. Driving the Japanese from their homes, putting them into camps. Just because I can't forgive Lane doesn't mean I think it's right."

She raised her head. "But, why *can't* you forgive him? You've forgiven me, haven't you?"

"That's different."

"How?"

"You're my sister."

"And he was a brother to you."

"Maddie, stop." He rubbed the back of his neck in agitation. But soon, calming himself, he forced out a sigh. What harm would there be in giving her an inch? "Listen. When the war's over and he comes back, and if you do end up staying together"—which hopefully wouldn't be the case—"we'll sort through everything then." He finished gently, "Till that happens, let's enjoy the time we've got before I ship out. Deal?"

With a thoughtful nod, she offered a smile. "Deal."

The cooking timer rang, a welcomed interruption. Maddie clicked off the dial, and TJ handed her a potholder. He breathed in the heavenly wafts of chocolate as she retrieved the metal pan from the oven. His mouth salivated, starved for better food than Army chow.

"Damn—I mean, dang, that looks good." Again, too many hours with airmen and no ladies present. "Let's dig in."

"Hold your horses. We have to let it cool first."

"No way. I ain't waiting."

"But you'll burn your tongue."

"A small price," he said, pulling a fork from the drawer.

"TJ Kern, don't you dare eat out of the pan." After a roll of her eyes, she conceded by reaching into the cupboard for plates. "Some things never change," she muttered with a small laugh.

Though TJ kept it to himself, he disagreed.

Everything was changing.

❧ 31 ❧

"You don't know what you're talking about!" The guy shot up from his wooden bench at the mess hall meeting. Lane recognized him as a kitchen worker. A Nisei in his late twenties, he wore a thin mustache, a rarity among their community at the Manzanar camp.

"Then why don't you tell us what's happening to our block's sugar?" another fellow demanded. The roomful of seated Japanese men murmured their agreement. "You saying our supply's been walking away on its own two feet?"

"I'm saying you better think again before you accuse our crew of stealing."

Listeners fanned themselves with magazines, sheets of paper. The evening temperature sweltered. Lane had to consciously contain his urge to speak, his collegiate council days over. No good would come of intervening here, he'd learned. After ratcheting up, the meeting would land on its circular tracks. A repeat of arguments would roll out from every corner.

The War Relocation Authority thought it a favor to allow self-government, but achieving cohesion was no simpler than finding a needle in a sack of rice. From immigrants' dialects to cultural diversity, residents of the fourteen-barrack block differed in every way save one: the ancestry that had sentenced them to this desert wasteland.

Tonight, as usual, it didn't take long for the guys from Terminal Island—with their shogun-like attitudes and rough fisherman's language—to make their opinions known. They wanted better meals and higher pay for jobs, improved medical treatment in the understaffed, undersupplied camp hospital. And they wanted someone to blame.

"I say we get the whole camp to boycott meals," one guy announced.

"That's genius," a man behind him sneered. "Let's starve ourselves. I'm sure the *hakujin* officials will come running."

"You got a better idea?"

"Yeah. How about you JACL'ers learn to shut your mouths for a change? You're the reason we all got sent here in the first place."

More *here-we-go-again* grumbles. More guys brought to their feet. After two months of these gatherings, Lane wasn't quite sure why he attended at all. Except, he hated to admit, for the slim possibility of making a difference.

A lean kid with glasses stood up, a seasoned debater. "The JACL," he said, "has done nothing but defend us as loyal Americans. What would it have said if we'd protested? Everyone in the country is doing their part. And when the war's over we'll have erased any doubt of us being the enemy."

That was as far as he got into his spiel, delivered as a devout member of the Japanese American Citizens League, before his opposition chimed in. Once more, they revived the tired dispute of the organization being in cahoots with the FBI, even prior to the attack on Pearl Harbor.

The block manager started tapping his gavel. He didn't cease until the group quieted. At the semblance of order, he called upon an elder at the end of Lane's row, who rose to impart reasoning.

"*Shokun, sukoshi kikinasai,*" he began, but a Nisei interrupted.

"Speak English, old man. You know that Japanese isn't allowed at meetings."

The suited gentleman was taken aback. Although he carried a humble, dignified countenance—not unlike Lane's father—he clearly wasn't accustomed to taking orders from one so much younger. And frankly, Lane wasn't accustomed to watching it. Filial piety, values embedded since birth, dictated respectfulness that propelled Lane now from his seat.

"*Shikata ga nai.*" He hadn't planned to spout his father's phrase, but it flew out all the same. *Shikata ga nai. It can't be helped.* One couldn't walk past four barracks without hearing an Issei recite the saying. Same for their reminder of the reason to quietly persevere. *Kodomo no tame ni.*

For the sake of the children.

"Regardless of what brought us here," Lane told the room, "we're in this together. We need to stop wasting time by fighting. We need to find solutions."

The sea of men's heads nodded in agreement, reigniting a familiar flame, though small, in Lane's chest. He faced the rows behind him, gaining momentum. "If the kitchen crew says they're not taking the sugar, then I for one believe them. We have to trust each other. If we want to solve the problem, we should take the matter up with Director Nash. Maybe start with beefing up patrols at the warehouse."

"*Kuso!*" The word *bullshit* boomed from the doorway, where three members of the Black Dragon gang glared with arms crossed. These particular Kibei, Japanese Americans who'd spent much of their lives in Japan, had channeled their anger over internment into a mission: to promote loyalty to the Emperor, through violence if need be.

Lane turned away from them and continued. "What I'm saying is, we'll make more progress if we organize our approach. Remember, this was how we succeeded at the net factory. Last month, when we asked for—"

"No!" shouted one of the Dragons. A small scar cut through his left eyebrow. "Only way to make *hakujin* listen—this!" He smacked a fist into his other hand. "You want know who steal sugar? *Hakujin* who work camp. White people. They take warehouse food and sell on black market. And *inu* helping them!"

Whispers through the mess hall grew like static. Paper fans fluttered faster.

"*Inu* like you maybe?" The same gang member pointed at the JACL defender. "Or *you.*" His finger angled at Lane, who gritted his teeth at the accusation.

Being called an *informant*, a traitor to his own kind, topped the list of insults. His father remained in a detention center for the simple fact that he wasn't a rat—for either side. He was a loyal American, as was Lane. And the real *bullshit* lay in every syllable vomited from these lunkheads' mouths.

Lane couldn't hold back, his honor at stake. He moved toward the Dragons, all three now descending upon the room. They incited feuds with challengers, mainly the fishermen with no qualms about going to blows.

Then a hand touched Lane's chest. It was the elderly man in his row, warning him with a shake of his head. Without speaking, he communicated the reason for restraint.

Kodomo no tame ni.

For the sake of Emma, for the sake of his family. To keep them safe.

Lane took this in, unclenched his fingers. His duty came first. Once more he tucked away his pride, and forced himself to turn around. Voices rose as the gavel rapped, and Lane ducked out of the room.

On the bumpy dirt road, gravel crunched beneath his scuffed shoes. The ever-present wind whipped off the Sierra Nevada, howling along with unseen coyotes. He raised the collar of his shirt against the flying sand and blinding searchlight. The beam followed him as he made his way toward the paltry unit that had become his family's home. Each "block" contained matching tarpaper barracks and a full set of community buildings. Latrines, laundry, recreation and mess halls. Clever residents gave their barracks names like "Little Tokyo Hilton" and "The Dust Devil Inn."

Come to think of it, Lane was wrong. Manzanar evacuees had more in common than bloodline; they had the alkaline dust. It invaded their food, their hair, their clothes. Warping of unseasoned lumber caused knotholes and cracks that invited inches of the blessed stuff into their "apartments." Like every conversation, every cough or baby's cry, it traveled through their dividing walls and raised flooring. It moved like a ghost, left trails thick as lies.

The one saving grace? Complaining about the dust meant not talking about the guards. It meant avoiding acknowledgment of the barbed wire that framed their one square mile of existence, or the machine guns perched on sentry posts, their barrels facing into the camp, not out.

Of these things, naturally he would make no mention to Maddie. For while he didn't regret calling out to her on evacuation day, he would continue to shield her from his ugly new world. In letters, he would tell her about camp baseball games and gardeners planting flowers and Emma learning to twirl a baton. He would write about getting his mother to try a painting class, a great feat after weeks of her stubborn solitude. And only on occasion, to explain grime on his stationery, would he mention the dust.

At the entry stoop, Lane glanced through the window of his family's unit, a twelve-by-twenty with the barest of essentials. No carpet on the planks. No Sheetrock on the walls. A single lightbulb hung from a splintery beam. When they'd first moved in, he told his family, "Think of it as camping, but in a wooden tent."

Emma had agreed. His mother said nothing.

Those attitudes hadn't changed, illustrated now by the usual scene. Emma knelt on her cot, playing jacks with their assigned roommates, a mother and a daughter who was roughly Emma's age. Lane's mom sat on her mattress, striped ticking stuffed with straw. Though she stared into her open Bible, the look in her eyes placed her somewhere far away. A place of lavish comfort. No doubt, in an ancient city across the ocean.

For the first time in his life, Lane understood the appeal.

❧ 32 ❧

L ife was becoming an endless requiem of good-byes.

Maddie had chosen to trade parting words with TJ at the house, rather than at Union Station. Watching his train pull away that morning would have been too much to bear.

It was the thought of losing yet another loved one that now brought her to the rest home. She treaded her standard path, down the tiled hall. She held her violin case to her chest. Her emotions were jumbled and in need of order, and who better to tame them than Johann Sebastian Bach.

"Sugar, aren't you gonna say hello?" A voice from behind.

In a staff uniform, pushing a cart around the corner, was Beatrice Lovell.

"Sorry, I didn't see you," Maddie said. "Are you working here on Sundays now?"

"Just for the day. Laverne's replacement couldn't start till tomorrow, so my husband asked if I'd lend a hand." Bea laughed, adding, "I suppose he was scared he'd have to launder the sheets himself."

Maddie smiled as they continued walking together, until news of the staffing change sank in. A stranger tending to her father's private needs made for an unsettling thought. "Will Laverne be coming back here?" She prayed Bea meant to say "substitute," not "replacement."

"So long as we got a spot available, I imagine it'd be hers. All depends on when she's done at the camp, I'd say."

Right then, a tall man approached Bea, identifying himself as the nephew of a resident. While they discussed a medication, Maddie's mind seized hold of the word *camp*. No longer did it refer merely to Girl Scout outings, or family weekend adventures by a creek.

Once the man left, Maddie asked, "By camp, do you mean . . . ?"

Bea nodded wistfully. "The one up in Wyoming. Not where your husband's family is staying, I'm afraid. Otherwise, sure as rain, I'd ask her to report back with an update."

"But what is she doing there?"

"Don't know specifics. Just that it's a hospital job at the relocation center."

A hospital job . . . for a white woman . . .

The information began weaving into a curious shape, one with promise. Visitors weren't allowed at Manzanar, but they might be hiring. "Do you know if the camps are filling other kinds of positions?"

Bea replied as they resumed their walk, "I've heard about them needing teachers. For high schoolers, I do believe." She stopped. Lips pursed, she peered at Maddie. "Sugar, I know how anxious you are to see Lane and his family, how worried you must be. But I gotta think, at least for now, music school is where you belong."

Not at an internment camp for Japanese. While unspoken, the implication was there.

"You'll have to make up your own mind, I suppose, without your folks having their say." Bea patted Maddie's shoulder. "Just give good thought to whatever you do, is all I ask."

With that, she left Maddie alone—at her father's door.

So far, nothing about their encounter surpassed the norm. As Maddie prepared her instrument, her father's attention remained on the window. Today's visit, however, was destined to end differently. At long last, she would present the Chaconne. It was the one favorite of his she'd neglected to learn—until Lane revived the piece in her memory. She could still smell the bouquet, could feel his hand holding hers as they exchanged promises of forever.

Maddie hastened to raise the bow. Months of drilling the composition, of perfecting her phrasing, had led to this moment. She wouldn't let emotions sabotage her efforts.

Tick. Tick. Tick. The reliable metronome obliged in her head. Shutting out all but the goal, she played in simple triple time. Ingrained notes promenaded through their basic harmonic scheme. Slowly she dealt them out, too slow. The image of Lane's smile slipped in between the measures. She pushed him away and focused on the melodic lines, the shifts between soprano and offbeat bass.

Yet more memories persisted: Lane lying beside her, their limbs tangled in the sheets; his eyes darkening and disappearing as the blue bus drove away. She attacked the strings with ferocious intensity, determined to override the past. But the visuals kept coming, of life and death, happiness and despair. She saw Emma and TJ, her mother and father.

Bach's chords slurred in her head and the metronome lost its pace. A sound trumped the movement. A sob. The sound had come from *her.* Arms too weak to continue, she lowered her bow and sealed her lips. Deep inside, the cries sang on. Salty moisture reached her mouth as she collapsed onto her knees.

Her father scarcely blinked.

She had come here bearing the Chaconne, a last hope to reach him through the wordless language of music. For hours upon hours she had practiced the movement, played long after her fingers had begged her to stop.

Now, what she had envisioned to be her greatest triumph had been unmasked as a failure. Not for the unfinished performance, but the undeniable futility. No matter which concerto she perfected—she could master each and every one—still he would not hear her. He had traveled too far to reach. Just like Lane. . . .

No, she thought suddenly.

Not like Lane. For him, it wasn't too late.

She gazed up at her father, and the dullness in his eyes sealed her decision. She would not stand by again, merely waiting for the return of someone she cherished. Even if, in the end, Lane didn't come back, at least he wouldn't go it alone.

❧ 33 ❧

Clock ticking, a twinge of dread set in. TJ knelt on the platform of Union Station, rummaging through his duffel bag.

"All aboard!" the conductor hollered as gruff and loud as a baseball coach.

While getting his shoes shined, a final touch to his pressed uniform, TJ had tossed his ticket into the bag. It couldn't have fallen out, could it? Doggone it all, he had to find the thing. With the long lines in the station, no way could he get a replacement in time. And the next train to San Fran wouldn't depart for several hours. He scrambled his hand in and out of his packed khakis.

Passengers continued to board, thinning the crowd. Through open windows on the locomotive, servicemen and sweethearts exchanged farewells. Mothers blew kisses and waved their handkerchiefs. Children twirled little flags like holiday sparklers. It was a scene from a parade on the Fourth of July, featuring a float TJ was about to miss.

"Blast it," he said, and dug deeper. Rowdy flirtations streamed from a gaggle of sailors inside the train. They sliced through his concentration. But then his fingers brushed the corner of something. He yanked out a small paper. His ticket!

He issued a sigh, cut short by the sight in front of him. A pair of legs rivaling the slenderness of any pinup's. His gaze traced the woman's stockings, from the red heels to a matching dress. Its snugness showed off her shapely curves and explained the persistent catcalls.

"Lose something, Corporal?"

Sunlight created a halo around her short-brimmed hat. Steam from the steel transport floated around her. She'd pass as angelic if not for the devilish temptation of that red-wrapped figure.

"Sure thought I did, miss," he answered, rising. The remainder of his thought vanished at her familiar features. Not with the rouged cheeks and cherry-glossed lips. Not with the hair draped long with the scent of styling lotion. But past all that, he would have sworn she was . . .

"Jo?" he said.

She confirmed his guess with a smile.

"Wh-what are you doing here?"

She placed a white-gloved hand on her hip, as if in a practiced pose. "I came to see you off, silly. Why else?" Her voice had gained the sultry tone of Gene Tierney. In fact, everything about her now resembled the starlet.

"But, you look so . . . different." He tried to keep his eyes on her face, yet the shock of her firecracker figure fought for priority.

"All aboard!" The conductor's warning boomed, followed by encouragement from the sailors.

"*Plant a smooch on her!*"

"*Don't be a schmuck!*"

"*Give her something to remember you by!*"

Jo blushed, same shade as when he'd nearly kissed her at the house. More than a few times since, he'd caught himself envisioning that moment play out. Now was his chance.

He could see her waiting. The train was waiting. Their audience was waiting.

Succumbing to the pressure, he leaned toward her. Her eyelids lowered in acceptance. But something—nerves, uncertainty—veered his lips from hers and onto her cheek. "Bye, Jo."

He snagged his duffel and swung toward the train, an attempt to avoid any hurt in her eyes. And he succeeded.

At the coach's entry, however, a rush of emotion stalled his foot from boarding.

"Hey, airman." Drawn by Jo's voice, he turned to find her a breath away. "You forgot something."

Swifter than a blazing fastball, she placed her mouth on his. The act stunned him in place. He couldn't break away even if he wanted to, which he didn't. His eyes closed and his arms wrapped around her waist. The Navy men cheered wildly as her fingers laced behind his neck. He pulled her in closer. Warmth from her body, from those curves of hers, coated every inch of his skin. He kissed her deeper. The electrical current he'd felt at the house paled in comparison to the charge now shooting through his body.

Finally, he came up for air. It was then, peering into Jo's eyes, that he saw the girl beneath the rouge, the one in overalls with a nice pitching arm. The one who knew how to push his buttons and to make him think.

The girl he had fallen for.

Powered by the revelation, he went to kiss her some more when she stopped him with two words. "Your train."

He struggled to decipher her meaning. The syllables seemed foreign.

"TJ, your train," she stressed.

The locomotive was slowly chugging away. Servicemen onboard laughed from their open windows, yelling at him to move his ass. Instantly sobered, he gave her a final peck, then took off in a sprint. He extended his arm and grabbed hold of a handlebar. Following a heave of his bag, he leapt onto the step.

He leaned out, once secure, and raised a hand toward Jo. She didn't wave back, but he could see her grinning long after the station became a tiny dot.

TJ rode the high of their parting for five full stops. Then, as it always did, fear crept in, implanting thoughts he couldn't dismiss. Thoughts like, if fate stayed on its usual path, what chance would they have at happiness? And, most important, could either of them handle losing more than they already had?

34

Maddie's entire future hinged on this performance. She rehearsed the appeal in her head, feeling pressure akin to taking the stage. The buzzing over her skin, the restlessness of her fingers.

Seated in the reception area of the Civil Control Station, she started to cross her legs, then thought better of it. She had to look her best today and couldn't risk smearing the makeup-drawn seams down the back of her legs. Granted, she was all for rationing—particularly when nylon was used for airmen's parachutes—but that didn't stop her from missing her last pair of good stockings.

A man two chairs away grumbled as he flipped through the *Examiner*. Headline after headline, all about the war. Allied ships torpedoed by U-boats, a RAF night raid on Düsseldorf, an Eighth Army victory against Rommel's forces in Egypt. It was difficult to remember what had filled those articles before America's day of infamy.

Again, Maddie regarded the clock on the wall. She layered her hands over the pocketbook on her lap to still her fidgeting. She noticed the shortness of her nails and hard-won calluses. They were the marks of a musician, unfeminine traits she had never been fond of until this instant. Today they just might work to her advantage. Testament to her experience.

"Mrs. Moritomo, please." The receptionist surveyed the room. "Mrs. Moritomo?"

It took Maddie a moment to recall the name was hers. "Oh, yes." She jumped to her feet. "That's me."

The thickness of the woman's glasses magnified her surprise.

Maddie found the look disquieting, then reminded herself the reaction would soon be customary. If, of course, the impending meeting went as planned.

"I'm afraid Mr. Sanborn has had a family emergency," the gal reported. "So he won't be able to meet with you. I'd be happy to reschedule your appointment for the sixteenth, however, if you're available."

Sixteenth? That was two weeks away! The very thought was unbearable.

"I can't," Maddie blurted.

"I see. Well, I won't have another opening until—"

"Please," Maddie pleaded. "Is there any other supervisor I could speak with? It's regarding . . . a family emergency of our own."

The receptionist's gaze held on Maddie's face, studying her, clearly intrigued. Finally, she said, "Very well."

Maddie sighed. "Thank you."

Following the woman through the bustling office, Maddie smoothed her suit jacket and adjusted the belt. Ringing phones and tapping typewriters crowded her ears. Her eyes darted from stenciled doors to a large U.S. map. Colorful triangles hung from several states. Relocation centers.

The gal paused at an office door and poked her head in. After a brief mumbled exchange, she turned to Maddie. "Go on in."

Stretched to her full height, Maddie proceeded into the room.

A stout gentleman stood before an electric fan set on the metal secretary. Warm air from the open window flailed his loosely hanging tie. He lit the pipe between his teeth. His wreath of hair was blacker than shoe polish.

"Good afternoon, sir. I'm Madeline Mori—"

"Have a seat, have a seat." Genially, he flicked his hand toward the visitors' chairs. He puffed musty-smelling plumes into the confines of his office.

Maddie sat down. She clasped her ring finger for inspiration, and waited anxiously to continue. The man moved in slow motion. He wiped his forehead and neck with a rolled rag like a person of eighty rather than forty.

"Jiminy Cricket," he groaned, "this heat's for the birds." He twisted his head toward her. "I was born and raised in Washington. The state, not the capital. Rains so much up there, when the sun comes out people think it's an alien ship."

She proffered a smile. The second he perched on the edge of his desk, forcing her gaze upward, she restarted. "Sir, as I was saying . . ."

"Please. Call me Dale."

"Madeline," she replied in turn. His friendliness struck her as rather informal for a first meeting, particularly with an administrator at a government agency. But she needed him on her side. "Sir—or Dale, rather—I've come to ask about applying for a position."

His eyebrows popped up. "Is that so? And what sort of experience do you have? Shorthand? Typing, I presume."

Realizing his assumption, she clarified. "Not for the office here. I'm a violinist. Since I've heard the camps are hiring teachers, I wanted to offer my services as a music instructor. Specifically, I'd like to work at Manzanar." Wary of coming across too bold, she added, "If at all possible, that is."

"Manzanar, huh?" He sounded befuddled she had even heard of the place. He took another pull from his pipe.

Perhaps her credentials would help.

"I've been professionally trained for more than ten years. Naturally, I'd be happy to play for someone to prove my qualifications." She should have brought her violin along. Why hadn't she thought of that?

He shook his head, mopped his neck. "That won't be necessary."

Worried by what that meant, she pressed her case. "I have people I care about there, which is why I'd like to lend a hand. So if a music teacher isn't needed, I'm more than willing to help in any other area."

After a thoughtful pause, he leaned an elbow on his knee and grinned down at her. A sign of progress. "I can see you've got the best of intentions, miss, and—"

"Madeline," she corrected him, and smiled.

The redness in his cheeks seemed to spread. "It's an admirable gesture you're making, *Madeline*. And I'm sure your friends there would be awfully touched. But I have to tell you, Manzanar isn't the type of place for a sweet, pretty lady like yourself."

Yet it *was* a place for a sweet, pretty child like Emma?

This wasn't going the way Maddie had hoped. A dead end lay ahead. She would have to switch tactics, no matter how risky.

"Pardon my saying so, Dale"—she spoke with a cordial naivety—"but if the conditions are acceptable for residents of Japanese descent, surely they're just fine for me. Unless, of course, you're implying that the living standards, per your organization, aren't up to par."

His teeth clenched around his pipe and his eyes hardened.

The point was made.

"You fill out an application at the reception desk," he told her, "and we'll get back to you once an appropriate spot opens up."

"When?"

In the midst of rising, he huffed a sigh. She knew she was pushing it, but what choice did she have?

"In two weeks. Maybe three. Now, if you'll excuse me." Grabbing documents from his desk, he returned to the fan. He flipped through the pages, a bald suggestion she leave.

But she didn't. She couldn't. Something told her that if she left this chair, this office today, without her request fulfilled, she'd never see Lane again.

Images of their last exchange shuffled through her mind. She saw the rows of cribs and ironing boards, the Japanese girl being ripped from her adoptive family. What possible threat could the youngster have posed to national security? One-sixteenth of Japanese blood was all it took for exclusion. One-sixteenth. A drop in a filled bucket.

And therein lay her solution.

"Miss," Dale addressed her, irritated. "Unless there's something else . . ."

"Actually," she said, "there is. You see, I forgot to mention one important detail."

"Oh? And what would that be?"

She steeled herself—there would be no going back—and through a tightened jaw, she pushed out the lie. "I'm pregnant," she said. "With a Japanese baby."

PART FOUR

I am for the immediate removal of every Japanese on the West Coast to a point deep in the interior. . . . Herd 'em up, pack 'em off and give 'em the inside room in the badlands.

Let 'em be pinched, hurt, hungry and dead up against it. . . .

Personally I hate the Japanese. And that goes for all of them.

—Syndicated columnist Henry McLemore

～ 35 ～

Aside from missing Maddie, hunger was all Lane could think about. Not even the stench of burlap and camo-net dye, compounded with body odor in the factory, could curb his stomach grumbles. Behind the mask covering his mouth, he licked his lips at the memory of shrimp tempura and pickled vegetables. He tasted fresh abalone salad and seaweed-wrapped rice balls.

Things were clearly getting desperate for him to be daydreaming about Japanese staples rather than good ol' American burgers.

Unfortunately, all that awaited today were more impetus for the "Manzanar Runs": Canned hash and sauerkraut, boiled potatoes too hard to eat. "Slop suey" that spoiled from refrigeration failures. Evacuees acting as cooks, with little knowledge of cooking.

It was the same routine for every meal. People in line for the mess halls would stare in through the windows. Their famished eyes spurred those inside to rush. Mess tins and forks had replaced elegant bowls and chopsticks. Kids would eat with their friends, same for the parents. Table manners and family meals were things of the past.

Lane's constant appetite, however, sadly remained.

"Hey, Lane," said the worker next to him. A Burbank native, he used to be an encyclopedia salesman. "We missed you at the block meeting again."

"Yeah," Lane said simply.

The guy nodded in understanding. Together, beneath the twenty-foot ceiling, they used a pulley to raise another net for weaving. Dyed white, it would camouflage tanks in the snow.

"You going to the picture show tonight?" he asked Lane, adjusting his rolled-up sleeves.

Although Lane was willing to do just about anything to break up the monotony—even watch a fuzzy projection on a white sheet in a sandy firebreak—the last film had ruined any allure. *The Hunchback of Notre Dame.* If he'd wanted to see people scorning a love-starved outcast from society, he could have replayed his own memories. "I don't think so."

"You sure?"

Lane was about to confirm his answer when he noticed a rash forming on the guy's arms. He'd seen it before, a reaction to the dyes. "You'd better go see the doc," he said, pointing to the swollen skin.

"Ah, great."

The fellow left the factory without seeking permission. Army engineers were there to supervise, but still this was "voluntary" work. Sixteen bucks a month for eight-hour days, six days a week. The scenario teetered on the brink of comical. Here they were, unjustly imprisoned by their own country, contributing to the fight for freedom and democracy.

The thought, if nothing else, suppressed Lane's appetite.

"Moritomo-*san!*" A civilian patrolman peeked in from the doorway. "You got someone here to see you."

"Who is it?" he hollered back, muffled through his mask.

The man left.

Lane groaned. It had better not be another person trying to convince him to run for block leader. He'd had his fill of government. From Congressman Egan to FDR, they were nothing but performers on a stage—ventriloquists—giving lip service for audience approval.

Shucking off his gloves, Lane threaded his way through workers and equipment to step outside. A low sun scorched the valley and a wave of dust brushed over his eyes. He blinked hard to clear the grit as a throng of schoolgirls strolled past. In their arms, they toted preparations for the annual festivities. Paper lanterns and dragon kites, bright obi to belt their kimonos. Even barbed wire couldn't hinder Obon, a tribute to the dead, an ancestral prayer for good fortune.

For the Moritomo family, of course, it would be just another August day. Lane's mother had discouraged their involvement in the celebration since he was a kid. He couldn't recall why. Evidently mingling with ghosts violated a superstition.

"Somebody here want to see me?" he said over the commotion, and yanked down his mask. No one spoke up. He squeezed his gloves with impatience. Then a hat-covered woman angled toward him, and the sight snagged his breath.

It was Maddie. Here. In front of him.

A smile spread over her lips. Her hair caught a drift of wind, lifting it from the collar of her traveling suit. He knew this outfit, the burgundy number she wore on the train to Seattle. He'd never seen her so beautiful.

Could his mind be playing tricks on him? The heat and desert could do that to a person. So could three months of loneliness.

Tentatively he moved toward her, afraid she was a mirage. "Maddie?"

Her smile widened, losing none of its sensuality.

He risked breaking the moment by touching her face. She layered her hand over his. The feel of her creamy skin, like satin to his roughened fingers, eliminated any doubt. She indeed was real.

In a reenactment of a scene straight from his dreams, he brushed strands of hair from her neck. Then slowly, to savor the moment, he leaned in for a kiss.

Clang, clang, clang.

The iron triangle announced lunchtime and entrapped him back in Manzanar. His heart twisted like *mochi,* a glutinous mass formed from stretching and pounding. Maddie was never supposed to see him in this godforsaken place.

"Come with me." He seized her upper arm. He felt her wince, but marched onward to the rec building.

"Honey, what's the matter?"

He gave no explanation upon entering. In a back corner, he released her, though he didn't speak until stragglers sprinted for the bell. "What are you doing here? I told you not to come. Why didn't you listen?"

Looking confused, Maddie rubbed her arm, where he'd left a handprint of factory dust on her sleeve. The last thing he ever wanted to do was hurt her.

Again, though, that's what he had done.

"I'm sorry," he said. "I didn't mean to grab you like that."

"It's okay . . . it's just tender from the shot."

The shot?

For typhoid, he concluded in near disbelief. "So they're making visitors get shots now too? What is that, some new policy because we're so filthy?"

All evacuees had endured a multitude of vaccinations. Emma, like most kids, had taken days for the effects of fever and vomiting to subside. Yet after all that, they weren't considered clean enough.

Maddie stared, a new reaction in her eyes. "How long has the camp allowed visitors? When you wrote to me, you said . . ."

He knew very well what he had said. White lies flowed easier through a pen.

He crossed over to the window. Work gloves in his grip, he rested a hand on the sill. His reflection in the glass—a dusty, sweaty, blue-collared laborer—confirmed his cause for reservation. This wasn't the man she had married.

"Lane, please. Tell me what's going on."

He averted his gaze to an American flag flapping in the distance. Alkali stained its white stripes, sunlight bleached the red. How many gusts would it take before the stars simply blew away?

Maddie's shoes clacked on the wooden floor. He didn't know which direction he wished they were moving.

"Sweetheart, listen to me," she said, close behind him. "Just like your father, you haven't done anything wrong. You've got nothing to be ashamed of."

From the words, or her hand on his shoulder, something cracked. An internal shell that had formed without his awareness.

Hesitant, he twisted to face her.

"Don't shut me out," she told him. It wasn't a plea, but a command. Her eyes, though glowing with warmth, had acquired a newfound strength, powerful enough to override his fear.

After months of separation, pride had no business tainting their reunion.

Lane reached out, as he should have the second he spotted her, and reclaimed her in his arms. The ache in his gut faded away, dissolved by a memory of hope. A reminder of the reward that waited at the end.

He rested his cheek on Maddie's, and whispered in her ear, "How much time have we got, before visiting hours are over?"

Although he dreaded the answer, there was one thing he knew for certain. The less time she spent here, the better. For her own sake.

"Well," she said, "the truth of it is . . ." She drew her head back and her mouth curved upward. "I'm not exactly visiting."

❧ 36 ❧

Beverly Hills. That's what they called the segregated living area for Manzanar's managing staff, all of the buildings fittingly painted white. Facilities were upgraded, barracks were pristine. Japanese gardeners manicured the grounds.

Maddie wondered how else their conditions differed as she trekked back from the laundry troughs. Trying not to dwell, she focused on the afternoon air rippling above the heated sand. She kept her eyes there while passing two teenage Japanese boys. She had nothing against them in particular. She avoided contact with anyone she didn't know at camp—which, even after several weeks, included everyone but Lane's family.

What good would come of reading in strangers' faces how much she didn't belong? She received enough of that from Kumiko.

Left arm tiring, Maddie adjusted the apple crate of laundered clothing on her hip. She'd folded and ironed each article exactly as her mother had taught her. The woman used to whistle show tunes while pressing her husband's shirts. Maddie would stifle giggles, watching her father sneak in to hug his wife's slender waist.

Would a day ever pass when missing them didn't hurt?

Just then, the wind whipped back a corner of the towel draping the crate. Dust assaulted the exposed garments. Her right hand raised the flattened Oxydol box, a four-foot shield. The carton would be her best peace offering yet, if it didn't soar away before reaching the barrack.

At the intersection, elderly men played Go on a handmade table. Their black and white stones battled in strategy on their gridded game board. A young girl nearby squealed over a hopscotch victory.

Distracted, Maddie stumbled on the bumpy road, but prevented a disastrous fall. In her relief, she glanced up. A mistake. An armed guard in a high wooden tower peered at her from the observation platform. He blew cigarette smoke out the corner of his mouth. Had they been alerted to keep an eye on her, to decide if she were a traitor? Did they suspect she wasn't pregnant?

She imagined an array of consequences. Jail time, a monetary fine, a media frenzy.

Hurrying off, she used the Oxydol box to conceal her waistline. She'd already untucked her blouse as a precaution. If, as she feared, the war crossed the threshold of 1943, a pillow wedged into her skirt could buy a little more time. While her actually conceiving would be ideal, lack of privacy greatly reduced that possibility.

Beside the entry of her barrack, a man paused while trimming his garden. He looked to be in his fifties, wore a Japanese wraparound shirt and straw sandals. According to Lane, he'd started his own flower nursery after serving in the Great War, even earned a Purple Heart while fighting for America.

She opened her mouth to say hello, just as she spotted his left hand. The pinkie and half of his fourth finger were missing. Irrational guilt overcame her. He sent her an amiable look and bowed. Then he returned to his plot, a tidy design of plants and rocks that would help reduce the dust.

She awkwardly tipped her head in kind, though he didn't see her, and she continued inside. There, a pleasant surprise awaited. Lane stood by his cot, fastening the buttons on his jean pants. A sheen of perspiration graced his bare torso. The V of his shoulders had gained definition from long hours at the factory.

When he turned to face her, she felt her skin flush from being caught gawking. Intimacy felt less natural in daylight.

"What are you doing home so early?" she asked, and busied herself with closing the door. She used her foot for lack of a free hand.

"Some meathead spilled dye on me, so I had to change my clothes. Here, I'll help you."

Maddie let him take both the crate and the cardboard.

"What's this for?" He held up the collapsed Oxydol box before propping it next to the laundry stack.

"It's a little something for your mom."

His forehead scrunched a question.

"I thought she could use it in the restroom as a divider." Portable makeshift walls were in high demand for the latrines, all un-partitioned like the showers. Hopefully, the gift would earn Maddie a few points.

Lane bent over and grabbed a clean shirt from the crate. With Kumiko at a painting class and Emma running around with friends, finally Maddie was alone with him. She couldn't recall when that had occurred last, and hated that even this would be short lived.

A yearning propelled her hand to touch his back. "Can't you stay a little longer?" Her request, without planning, came out breathy and swung him around. A sudden spark in his gaze said he misinterpreted her intentions. She went to clarify, but it dawned on her how much she meant exactly what he'd heard.

As he leaned in, she closed her eyes to welcome his kiss. His mouth joined hers in a motion that fueled desire. Then his lips broke away and his tongue traced the side of her neck. She explored the landscape of his chest and stomach with her fingers. His muscles hardened beneath her touch. He laid her down on his mattress and heat shot through her body.

Only an oil stove separated their cots, yet since her arrival at Manzanar something about him felt unreachable. His initial reaction to her moving here hadn't been the elation she'd expected; he'd mostly voiced concerns over her schooling, her safety.

But any reservations seemed to now burn away in the fire rekindled between them.

Lane's hand traveled under her skirt and up and down her thigh, taking time they normally weren't afforded. For the sake of hot water and crowd avoidance, three A.M. had become Kumiko's regular bathing hour, her absence providing their sole opportunities for romance. Well, as romantic as a couple could get in the span of twelve to fifteen minutes, and with Emma sleeping on the other side of an Army blanket tacked to a beam. No wonder their lovemaking had felt groggy and shameful and rushed. The exact opposite of this moment.

She ran her fingers through his hair. The scent of burning orange peels, meant to drive away mosquitoes, drifted from a neighboring apartment. Wind rattled soup-can lids nailed over knotholes. She grew heady from the certainty of his wanting, his abandon.

Perhaps he had been cautious of getting too comfortable. The uncovering of her charade, just like before, could threaten their reunion.

With her mind rotating on the axis of this revelation, it took her a minute to comprehend that Lane had stopped moving. His breaths fell heavily on her neck. Voices of a married couple resounded off the peaked roof. Their volume was increasing in a standard argument. Once more, the man was accusing her of making eyes at another fellow.

Lane slid away and rose to his feet, the magic dispelled. They weren't alone, after all, and this was no place for abandon. Maddie sat up while tugging her blouse into place. Emma could have walked in at any time. How careless to forget to lock the door.

"I gotta get back to work," Lane said, pulling on a clean shirt.

She agreed through her discomfort. "I'll . . . see you at supper, then?"

He answered with a smile, the kind reserved for putting a person at ease, though it only reinstated a maddening sense of distance. He flew out the door without another word.

Pushing down her frustrations, Maddie sought an activity. Any activity. She could always reread her latest letters—reports from Jo on Maddie's house, and Bea about the shop. But those just made her miss her old life more than she already did, and writing them back would mean crafting another glossed-over update. Responding to her brother's post, a demand she return home, wasn't any more appealing. Nor was playing her violin. Musical memories of her father would scarcely lighten her mood.

Her attention shifted to the window. Fingers of a breeze ruffled the polka-dotted apricot curtains. They offered a touch of home, with the practical benefit of blocking nighttime searchlights. She had purchased the material through a Sears, Roebuck catalog, the sewing supplies from the camp's co-op general store. With nervous zeal, she'd presented the accessories to Kumiko, who barely gave them a glance.

To win her approval, Maddie would need to do something drastic. Something Kumiko couldn't ignore.

She rose up on her elbows, her gaze wandering and calculating. The mother and daughter who'd been assigned to their quarters had relocated to Poston, a relocation camp in Arizona, to be with their family. The vacancies would allow more spaciousness, given a little scooting of the furniture. That's what Maddie could do—a rearrangement to improve their days together. Maybe they'd all be happier if they weren't literally living on top of one another.

Reenergized, she stood up.

Time to redecorate.

Forty-five minutes later, the job was done. Their beds sat in a new direction, clearing an area that could pass for a parlor. The square table and pair of chairs Lane had made from spare lumber created an invitation for visitors, should they have any, and the hanging blanket now gave Kumiko privacy.

Best of all, the gap between Lane's and Maddie's cots no longer existed.

After dusting the room—a perpetual need with the cracked planks—a single task remained. Find a good spot for Kumiko's paintings. The woman had accumulated a hefty stack, her specialty being sparrows. Never in flight, always alone, they perched on branches and rocks and rooftops. Maddie was curious about the bird's significance, but her relationship with Kumiko hadn't ripened enough to ask.

Careful not to crease the pictures, Maddie placed them in the Oxydol box and tucked the casing under Kumiko's bed. A temporary solution. The minute Lane returned from his job, she would ask him to build a storage shelf. They could now accommodate more furnishings.

As she stepped back to admire her work, she heard the door open behind her. Emma bounded in, a twinkle in her gaze.

"Hiya, pretty girl," Maddie exclaimed, eager to unveil her work.

"Close your eyes," Emma urged. Not yet noticing the room, she held her hands behind her back. "Go on, close them."

"All right. But then I have a surprise for you too."

Emma nodded, and Maddie followed the order. "Now, put your hands out."

Maddie raised her cupped palms, praying it wouldn't be a reptile or insect. Thankfully, the object felt inanimate.

"Okay, open them."

It was an arrowhead the length of her thumb. The black stone—obsidian, Maddie guessed—glistened as she flipped it over. She rubbed the grooves, saddened by the similarities between the Japanese Americans and Paiute Indians. Their people were once exiled from this very desert. "Emma, this is amazing. Where did you find it?"

"By the old apple orchard." She accepted the artifact back and studied it in awe. "Some of the old guys here are collecting them. Hana said I could get fifty cents for it. *Fifty cents!*"

Maddie smiled. "You could get a lot of Tootsie Rolls for fifty cents."

"Or," Emma said, looking up, "I could buy some new fabric for a dress."

"That's true, you could. But . . . are you sure your mother won't mind?"

"She only told me I couldn't use my brother's pay to get new clothes. She didn't say anything about my own money."

Maddie mulled this over. "I suppose you're right."

"Would you make it for me? We could pick out a pattern in a catalog," she suggested. "Golly, Maddie, it would be sooo nice to wear something new. Even Hana's mom let her buy a new hat for church. Please, please, please?"

How could anyone say no to that?

"Well, all right. But we can only pick out a style your mother would approve of."

"Thank you, thank you! You're the best." Emma beamed with a smile that had been gradually fading. After an exuberant hug, she asked, "Didn't you say you have a surprise for me too?"

The apartment.

Maddie had nearly forgotten. She angled her body out of the way, flinging a hand out to display her creation. "Ta-da! A whole new house. What do you think?"

Emma glanced around and shook her head. "We really should move it back." Her voice was heavy with concern—perhaps at the prospect of another change in her life.

"Oh, Em, I know it'll take some getting used to. But look how nice it is." Maddie stepped into the parlor and stretched her arms. "There's so much space, we could put on a circus act. Sell tickets at the door. And hey, just think of all the fabric we could buy from *that* money."

"We need to put the beds back," Emma said with growing urgency. "We have to, before Mother comes home. It's *kita makura.*"

"I—don't understand."

"*Kita makura.* Our heads can't be to the north. It's bad luck. They only do that for funerals. She'll be furious. We have to hurry." Emma was already grabbing the foot of Kumiko's cot.

Though stunned, Maddie assisted her. She gained momentum while comprehending the potential backfire of her gesture. She strove to recall each item's original placement. One chair below the window, the other in the corner with the table. The laundry crate got in the way more than once, and the dust they kicked up now blanketed the formerly clean clothes.

They were over halfway done when Emma froze, her hands on the far end of Lane's bed.

"*Nani o shiteruno?*" Kumiko said in a horrified rasp. She stood in the doorway, clutching a small box of painting supplies.

Before Maddie could say a word, Emma launched into Japanese. She inserted Maddie's name twice during what seemed a diplomatic explanation.

Kumiko didn't respond. She just stared at the room, lips sealed, her chest heaving as though preparing to breathe fire.

"Maddie, come on," Emma whispered, seeking help to place Lane's bed in its cramped corner. Maddie wanted to smooth the situation over herself, but not knowing the extent of Kumiko's English, she continued with their task.

Only when every furnishing had been returned did Kumiko set aside her supplies. From the entry, she walked straight to the folded Oxydol carton leaned up against a wall. She laid it on the table and studied the partition.

At least Maddie had done one thing right.

Kumiko's fingers closed in on her paintings, their corners peeking from the box. She guided them out and a deep red stained her face.

Oh, no. She thought Maddie planned to discard them, along with the empty carton.

"I can explain," she said to Kumiko, then addressed Emma. "Please tell her, I was just trying to protect them."

Emma started to translate, but Kumiko cut her off. Her words flew like darts, fast and pointed, and her fingers flicked toward Maddie.

"But, *Okāsan . . . ,*" Emma said repeatedly, not being heard.

Maddie moved forward. "Mrs. Moritomo, this is my fault, not Emma's. I didn't mean to offend you. I was only trying to help."

Kumiko's palm shot up, a universal sign for *stop*. Her eyes skewered Maddie for a stretch of several seconds before she hissed a final phrase at Emma. The air became colder than a December night as she inspected her paintings for damage.

Emma stood there, lip quivering and tears welling. Maddie started to reach for her, to console her and apologize, when Emma pitched the arrowhead across the room.

"*Okāsan nanka daikirai!*" she shouted at her mother, then ran out the door.

Though Maddie didn't understand the language, she recognized the tone.

It was that of a spirit being broken.

37

"**P**ut a sock in it, 'Ravioli,'" TJ grumbled from his seat in the rec hall. If the barracks were cooler, he'd have stayed in there. In which case, he could have written ten letters by now. "You sound like a blasted cat in heat."

Unfazed, Ranieri kept right on singing and hula dancing for an audience of airmen. A ground crewman, with just as little talent, strummed a ukulele. As part of some dare for a couple packs of smokes, Ranieri swayed his grass skirt over rolled-up khakis. He swatted at hands groping his coconut-shell brassiere, padded by his curly-haired chest. Throw in a long black wig and he could almost pass as Hula Hattie, the Hawaiian beauty painted on the nose of their B-17.

A disturbing thought, actually.

Even so, when the numskull broke into a Tahitian shimmy, TJ couldn't hold down a smile. Although grateful they'd been assigned to the same crew, based in tropical paradise—whether by sheer luck or the Italian's doings—TJ did wonder how much more peaceful Kahuku Air Base would be without the guy. Boring maybe, but more peaceful.

TJ tore his attention from the tune, so off-key it would have disintegrated Maddie's eardrums, and returned to the letter on the table. He breathed in plumeria on the salty breeze, cleared his head. Pen in hand, he reviewed the last words he'd written to Jo.

> *Not a whole lot of goings-on here, just the usual practice bombing runs, dull lectures, air raid drills, and whatnot. Vince (that's Ravioli's real name, by the way) and I are going to hitch a ride down to Honolulu this afternoon to catch a double feature. Supposed to be a new one starring Gene Tierney. Even though you've got the girl beat in every way, at least seeing her will remind me of that morning at the station. Boy oh boy, what it does to me just thinking about that whopper of a kiss. All I can hope is that one day we can pick up from where we left off.*
>
>   *Better close now or I'll need a cold shower from more than the island humidity! Take good care, Jo. Keeping you always in my thoughts.*
>
>   *TJ*

He sealed the pages in an envelope marked solely with her name. He never bothered with an address, although he knew the hardware store's by heart. Her posts, after all, wouldn't be leaving his footlocker.

Some might consider it strange, penning notes he had no intention of mailing. But a sense of freedom came with spilling anything he wanted to on paper, a freedom no way he'd feel if his messages were going to be shared. It was like scribbling in a diary, minus the surety of jabs or questions or curious peeks from the fellas. Nobody thought twice about TJ writing letters home, and addressing them to Jo only upped his comfort.

"Aloha, *haole*," Ranieri sang out. An unlit cigarette peeked from behind one of his ears, a red hibiscus flower from the other. He dropped an orchid lei around TJ's neck. "About time we got you laid."

"You need some serious help, pal."

Ranieri exaggerated a gasp, covering his mouth like a dame.

"And to think, I saved a letter for you at mail call. But now? You can forget it."

A letter.

Jo Allister.

Had she taken initiative once more? Finally written the first note?

"So hand it over," TJ said, a little too strong. He yearned to hear from her as much as he feared it.

Ranieri reached into his grass skirt. When he pulled out an envelope, TJ leaned back in his chair. "Please tell me that was only in your pocket."

The guy grinned and tossed over the mail—from Maddie, it was only from Maddie.

A good thing, TJ reminded himself. He was doing Jo a favor, leaving her be.

"Better read it lickety-split," Ranieri told him. "Kaleo promised us free drinks at his bar if we get to Waikiki early enough." Maybe due to his dark, Hawaiian-like features, but Ranieri had befriended just about every native on the island.

"Yeah, well, I wasn't the one putting on a vaudeville act," TJ pointed out. "And don't think I'm going anywhere with you till you take off those ridiculous coconuts."

Ranieri studied the shells. "What, too small for you?" He massaged them in circles and used the pidgin dialect from the locals. "Handful mo' bettah, brah. Only lolo buggah want humungous bobbi."

TJ laughed. What other response could he possibly give?

"Be back in ten." Ranieri sauntered away, presumably to change clothes.

With time to spare, TJ opened his sister's letter. He anticipated her usual updates woven with nudges about Lane, some more subtle than others. He made it through three sentences before his eyes jumped back to the opening.

> *Dear TJ,*
> *I know that what I am about to tell you will surely disappoint you, but please understand I must follow my*

*heart. I have given my decision a great deal of thought.
Even if you were here, rest assured I would have done
this regardless.*

Suspense from the disclaimers spurred him to skim. Two-thirds
down the page he discovered what she'd done.

"The hell you're not!"

Faces turned in his direction.

He didn't finish. He'd read enough. Grabbing the pages, he
stormed off, dead set on getting Maddie home.

Lieutenant Colonel Stone sat at his desk, flipping through
paperwork that had nothing to do with TJ's request. He spoke
without looking up. "Afraid I can't help you, Corporal, unless you
fill me in."

"The emergency involves my sister's safety, sir."

"And what *precisely* would that emergency be?"

In the center of the office, TJ gripped his wrist behind his back,
wanting direly to strangle something. Or someone. "Sir, it's a—
personal matter."

The squadron commander chuckled as if entertained by an inside joke. Gray smoke wended upward from a cigarette on the
man's overflowing ashtray. Finally he raised his eyes. "See, now,
that's the beauty of belonging to the Army. We're one big happy
family, which means there *are* no personal matters. At least not
until you add a few more stripes to your sleeve." His lips flattened
below his thick mustache.

The joke was over.

"Way I see it," he went on, "you either tell me what's got your
drawers in a bunch, or you can pack up your furlough request and
get your butt out of my office. I got work to do."

With TJ's usual chains of command out on training flights for
the day, he needed the man's approval to get clearance off the island. Minus that and he'd be facing a court-martial. He'd be no
good to his sister from a jail cell.

TJ tried not to cringe as he shoved out the explanation. "Our parents are deceased." In essence, the truth. "And my sister has followed her husband, a Japanese American, to live in a relocation center on the mainland. That's why I just need long enough to travel there and move her back home. I'm sure I don't have to tell you that her life's in danger." That was it. All the essentials—except for one: "Sir."

Gradually, Stone reclined in his chair. "Well, that's not one I hear every day." He peaked a thick brow. "I don't suppose this is some cockamamie excuse for wanting to buzz back and see your sweetheart?"

"I wish it were."

The officer exhaled through his nose, contemplating. "I've got a sister myself. She's working as a riveter in some aircraft factory. Didn't listen to a dang thing I said about those dangerous jobs being for others. So, Corporal, I do understand where you're comin' from."

"Thank you, sir." TJ managed a level tone, concealing his relief. He could already see himself on a train, riding back to L.A. with Maddie. Maybe now, after actually living in the camp, she wouldn't be hard to persuade.

Then Stone said, "That's why I'm real sorry I can't help you."

A sucker punch to the gut.

"We've got special missions coming up, and I won't be able to spare a single one of ya. Definitely not for that long. And no chaplain I know is going to override this one, if that's what you're thinking."

"But, sir—"

"You want her home? You help us win this war and that's exactly where she'll end up. In the meantime, you just write her the best letter you can, and above all, keep her in your prayers." The commander paused before slapping on a "Dismissed," then huddled over his documents.

TJ remained in place, anchored by defeat. Finally he gathered the strength to move toward the exit.

"And just so you know," Stone added, "I think it's a shame."

TJ's grip stopped on the door handle. He didn't need his embarrassment stoked over the matter. Solely for protocol, he glanced back.

"My parents' best friends are living in one of them camps," Stone said. "The Ishinoyas. Decent, hardworking people. Don't deserve what they're gettin'." He shook his head. "Like I said, a real ugly shame."

❧ 38 ❧

In the doorway of his apartment, Lane scowled at the awaiting welcome. A Nisei man stood in a brown and tan uniform, nightstick in his belt, white *POLICE* band around his arm. As the guy attempted to communicate with Lane's mother—his Japanese sounded broken—Emma sat on her cot. She sent her Mary Janes a look of boredom, scuffing the leather toes on an inch-wide crack in the floor.

Nothing pointed to an emergency. No FBI raid or arrest. Just another wrist-slapping for his sister.

Still, Lane didn't need this today. A colicky infant in their barrack had been robbing him of what little sleep he could finagle. And more than tired, he was hungry after a long day of monotonous work.

"What's she done this time?" he muttered.

The civilian officer looked over. His face, shaped like an eggplant, showed relief at Lane's arrival.

"Has she been skipping more classes?"

"Afraid that's only part of our problem."

Lane shot a glance at his sister, whose shoulders suddenly drooped. Truth be told, he couldn't blame her for avoiding school here. Lessons were held in a rec building, as short on teachers as they were supplies. But her education had been a major lure to the camp, which meant she sure as heck better show up.

"As I was trying to tell your mother here," the officer said, gesturing toward the table where she now sat, "it's about your sister and some kids from San Pedro—a pretty rowdy group, I might add. Seems they've all been mess-hall hopping again. Three or four times a meal, according to my reports."

Lane asked Emma, "Is this true?"

She hesitated, shrugged.

"Emma, for crying out loud. We've talked about this. You're not supposed to eat anywhere but in our block."

"And I would," she said, "if ours didn't taste like doggie doo." A roll of her eyes made clear just how much her demeanor had soured, and not just tonight. "You know our cook used to be a barber, don't you? He can't even make rice the right way."

Not a bit of her statement rang false, but pressure from his mother's gaze, along with the policeman's, called for Lane's sternness. "You eat the food you're given or you won't eat at all. I don't care if the meals taste like dirt. You're lucky to have them. Understand?"

"Fine. Then I'll starve."

The challenge at first shook him, then pricked him with anger. The loss of control in all parts of his life was enough to drive his fist through their tarpaper wall.

"Is everything all right?" Maddie's voice entered.

He didn't turn toward her. This was a private affair, a moment of familial embarrassment. He'd never invited her to see any of this.

"There's one more thing," the officer said. "We don't have a name, but we believe a kid in your sister's gang is responsible for an incident yesterday. It involved the ladies' showers in block ten. A couple lizards were tossed into the stall. Caused quite a ruckus."

The visual of screaming women jumping around in the showers, all to avoid a pair of harmless reptiles, would have struck Lane as comical a few months back. But humor had since escaped him.

"It won't happen again." The graveness of his pledge appeased the officer, who traded small bows with Lane's mother.

"Have a good evening, ma'am," the guy said to Maddie, and closed the door behind him.

The perfect ending to a perfect day.

Lane stepped toward Emma. "You're grounded. From now on, Maddie will walk you to and from school. You'll eat with no one but your family. Other than the showers and bathroom, you don't leave this barrack."

Emma stood up, devastated. "But I didn't have anything to do with the lizards. Cross my heart, I really didn't."

From the look on her face and plea in her tone, he believed her. Yet that didn't matter. With their father under suspicion, it wouldn't take much to further tarnish the family's standing. A man's name, as their mother always said, was no less precious than skin to a tiger. To reestablish their worth, the Moritomos needed to act better than everyone else.

"It was that dummy with the spiky hair," Emma went on explaining. "When he brought up the idea, I told him not to."

"I don't want to hear it," Lane ground out.

"But at least let me tell you—"

"Urusai!" He'd heard enough.

Hurt sprang into her round face. He'd always listened when she asked, never treated her like a baby.

All that was before.

Gently, Maddie touched his forearm. "Honey, please. She deserves a chance to tell her side."

Deserve? The word had lost any value. No one in this family deserved to be here, yet here they were.

"Emma doesn't *deserve* anything. She's a kid. She needs to do what she's told."

"Lane," she said, "you're her brother." *Not her father,* he could hear her thinking.

He felt his chest stretch in defiance. "Well, in case you haven't noticed, our father isn't exactly around."

As he spoke, doubts planted deep inside shot up like weeds. Doubts he didn't even know were there: Why *wasn't* the man here?

Other detainees had been released and rejoined their families at Manzanar. All that their own family received were periodic letters from their father, idle talk censored with black markers or scissors. What words had been cut out? If Nobu Moritomo was innocent, wouldn't the Justice Department have let him go by now?

Emma dropped hard onto her cot. She snatched her Sarah Mae doll into her arms. "You're acting so *bōtchie,*" she grumbled at Lane.

Japanesey. That's what she'd called him, as if the rest of them were actually something else. The only real exception was Maddie, whose very presence made him feel more Japanese than ever.

"I wish Papa were here," Emma said to her doll, each word a puncture to Lane's soul. A flood of emotion burst through him.

"Oh, yeah?" he said. "Well, Papa's never coming back, so you'd better get used to me being in charge."

"Takeshi!" His mother jumped to her feet. It was her first sign of passion about anything in months.

Emma glared at him, sharp with fear. "That's a lie. Take it back."

He opened his mouth to soften the impact, but couldn't. His declaration, he realized, could very well be the truth.

At his silence, a whimper leaked from Emma's throat, a heart-wrenching sound. Mother started to reach for her, then pulled back. She gave way for Maddie to sit on the bed and hug the girl to her side.

That used to be Lane's role. The comforter. Now he was the bad guy. What other significance did he have?

TJ, Dewey . . . heck, half the guys from Lane's old neighborhood were serving in the military. Fighting back, making a difference. And here he was, coloring nets for a living. At sixteen bucks a month, he was a mindless volunteer, a husband pretending to provide. He couldn't even be intimate with his wife as a real man should.

The thoughts grew smothering. The walls were closing in.

Needing to breathe, he left the room.

* * *

Above the mountain range, grayness mottled the October sky. The makings of a daily thunderstorm. Five lines of barbed wire ran parallel to Lane's path, each connecting wooden posts in the ground. Nearly two feet spanned each opening. Guided by an urge, he angled his walk, edged a bit closer to the perimeter that screamed with a sign.

EVACUEES
STAY 10 FT. AWAY FROM FENCE

The closest guard tower sat a good hundred yards away. No older than eighteen, the GI held his rifle in the tedious, clumsy manner of a city kid manning a hoe. Would he actually have the gumption to shoot if a prisoner made a run for it?

"Where are you going?" Maddie demanded, catching up to him. Displeasure burned in her eyes.

"Maddie, please stay out of this."

"You need to talk to your sister. To tell her you didn't mean what you said."

"This is between me and my family, all right?"

She narrowed her eyes. "And I'm not part of your family?"

"That isn't what I—" Frustration brewed inside, tightening his jaw. "You just don't understand our culture."

They stared through a tense pause. Then she took a step back, looking equally stern and hurt. "You're right. I don't understand all of it. But more than that, I don't understand *you.*"

She tramped away, headed for their barrack. A pathetic excuse of a home. If he'd been more truthful in his letters to her, described the real conditions at camp, would she still have been willing to come? To make the sacrifices she had?

Those with Japanese heritage didn't have a choice of being incarcerated. Maddie did.

Your wife sure must love you, guys at the factory had told him. Although meant as a compliment, a sign of acceptance, the remark further tipped the scales of his unbalanced marriage. What did he possibly have left to offer her?

A cattle call for supper rang through the desert, launching another meal session for a crowd of ten thousand. Lane wandered away from the growing mass, his appetite lost to a dose of irony: In the confines of but one square mile, he was losing everyone he loved, as well as himself.

❧ 39 ❧

Maddie had been in line at the post office that morning—at Manzanar half their days were spent in lines—when a white woman extended an invitation. A job at the garment factory. News of Maddie's tailoring background, she'd explained, had traveled through the grapevine. By their conversation's end, a startling fact became clear. The woman was an evacuee.

Maddie had seen her before and presumed she belonged to the staff; rather, she was a spouse who refused to be separated from her Nisei husband and their "half-breed" son. And yet, Maddie's greatest revelation wasn't the similarity of what had brought her and Elaine to the camp. It was that she and Elaine had the right to stay—or leave—by their own choosing.

Once more, Maddie could tuck in her blouses, free of her deception. Given her blowout with Lane, however, still lingering from days ago, questions formed and gathered. In a bundle of doubt, they lodged on her shoulder. *Was moving here a mistake? Was her staying only making things worse for them all?*

To drown out their incessant whispers, Maddie turned to a trusted friend.

* * *

At a far side of camp, near the chicken ranch, Maddie found a vacant spot behind a storage shed. A trace of apples and pears from the old orchard rode the autumn breeze, touched with the scent of sage. Distant cheers indicated a scoring run between the Aces and Yogores. Their weekend games always drew a large crowd.

Maddie opened her case on the ground. Her hand slid down the fingerboard, over the length of the strings. A feeling of coming home after a long trip washed over her, an odd sensation of reuniting with something familiar yet, due to time apart, seemingly new.

Since her move to Manzanar, Lane had often inquired about her not playing. She'd blamed the scarcity of privacy. How could she focus on her music with curious eyes staring, ears around every corner? Her goal was to blend—the same goal of the Japanese before the evacuation.

At this, they had failed equally.

Today, though, her desire for order outweighed any concern. Eighth notes, quarter notes, rests, repeats. To Maddie, the best-written pieces gave little room for interpretation. A musician could thereby play the same combo of notes hundreds of years after initial transcription, and still it could sound the same, or at least very close.

Such consistency would soon bring her reprieve, witnessed by the audience of a setting sun. Patches of clouds joined in a quilted stage, stitched by threads of a purple and orange sky. A lovely if unsettling scene. For with the majestic rise of Mt. Williamson to one side, and the desolate low of Death Valley to the other, she felt insignificance in a tangible form.

Too windy for sheet music, she would play by memory.

The Chaconne, for her father.

With rosined bow she began her tuning, and tried not to think about the dust scouring her violin's varnish. She started with A. The note, as expected, emerged off-key. She twisted the corresponding peg and tested the note again. Repeated adjustments improved the sound, but its vocal cords had changed. Resisting panic, she went on to D, then G and E with open fifths. A garbled tone raked the tunnels of her ears. She shook dust from the F-holes on its wooden body, willing to try anything.

Then the answer hit her: the climate. The dry air and dramatic heat had choked the voice from her precious violin. Was the gift from her father ruined, her only connection to him lost?

In the desert, no amount of cold cream could replenish her parched skin. What did she think would happen to a wooden instrument? The most basic fiddler would have taken precautions.

Maddie folded onto her knees, scorning herself. Moisture filled her eyes as tumbleweeds rolled past. Now thorny withered flowers detached from their roots, they continued aimlessly on their solitary paths.

She stored her violin and bow, ushered her emotions into the velvety coffin. About to close the lid, she glanced at her wedding picture. She studied Lane's face, then hers, their temples touching. When it came to physicality, the racial differences were obvious—the shape of their eyes, tint of their skin—but she had genuinely believed that beneath all that, they were the same. Always she'd thought of Lane as just another American. Perhaps, in reality, he was an immigrant's son who *strove* to be American.

And how would he achieve this? By stomping on tradition, by marrying a girl whose heritage and complexion could complete that evolution.

A tear broke free.

"Maybe you were right, after all," she whispered to the adjacent photo, a military portrait of her brother. She suddenly missed the guidance she'd spent so much time resenting.

"What wrong, *hakujin?*" asked a male voice. Derision in the word *foreigner* made her wary to make eye contact. "You not play for us?"

As she swiped her cheek dry, the guy leered, dressed in all black, a scar through one eyebrow. To his side, another fellow in black spat at the ground; chewing tobacco lumped his cheek.

Maddie knew about them from Lane's warnings. The Black Dragons were troublemakers whom even the administrators were reluctant to punish. Their fanatical allegiance lay with the Emperor.

Now this close to them, she could feel their hatred toward her kind.

She hurried to close the latches on the case.

"We want music. You play," the scarred one told her. Orochi was his name. How could she forget the namesake of a mythological eight-headed serpent?

Rising, she went to leave, but their firm stances implied a blockade. Her pulse pumped like a captured prey's. The closest watchtower was out of sight, far from reach. She shouldn't have come out here alone.

"Really, I'd love to." She strained for casualness. "But I'm afraid I can't. It's broken. From the heat." She motioned to the sun, unsure how much he understood. "Maybe after it's fixed, though. Another day."

"No." Orochi stepped closer. "Now."

Every fiber in her body quaked beneath his roving gaze. She squeezed the case to her chest, clutched the handle even tighter. The crowd roared again. Would a guard mistake her screams for cheering?

She produced a smile, stalling for a plan. "Okay. I'll play for you. But just one song." She bent over a bit, as if to open her case on her thigh. A vision of being dragged into the shed firmed her resolve. She had to make a break for it.

As Orochi angled his face back, her defenses kicked in. She slammed her case across his jaw, knocking him aside. The second guy grappled for her arms.

"Get away!" she yelled, and caught him in the ear with a shorter swing, then took off running. She'd made it around the corner of the shed when a hand grasped the back of her skirt. Her body flew forward, knees and palms skidding across gravel. Her violin case landed open and out of reach.

Lane, she thought, her only thought, before a grip closed around her arm, pulling her to her feet. The second guy hadn't gone down.

"*Bakamono!*" a voice growled, a new voice. "*Nani o yatterunda?*" Not ten yards away, the veteran from her barrack set down a pail of chicken feed and fisted his hands at his sides. His eyes shone with the combative instinct of a warrior. The soft wrinkles of a gardener were nowhere to be found. He said something else in his language, fiercely low and cool. Maddie found herself hypnotized by the controlled power of his voice. Until now, she had never heard him speak.

Orochi arrived from behind the shed. He scowled at the sprinkling of evacuees who had appeared on the scene. The baseball game had ended. He grumbled a word and tapped his lackey, who released Maddie's arm, and the two strutted off down the street, heads held high.

In an instant, a flock of Nisei women encircled her.

"Are you okay?"

"Did those creeps hurt you?"

"Do you need the police?"

Maddie shook her head, stunned by their concern. "No. It's not necessary, but . . . thank you." Suddenly remembering her rescuer, she looked over to express her gratitude. Yet he'd drifted into the growing crowd, drawn back into his humble shell.

"Your knee—does it hurt?" one gal asked. "Do you need a bandage?"

Maddie glanced down to find blood surfacing on an ugly scrape. Oddly, she didn't feel anything but kindness and compassion. "I'm all right," she assured them, and at that moment, she recalled how it felt to belong.

The sting set in soon after. Treatment at the hospital had cleansed Maddie's wounds, but the long trek to her barrack caused a throbbing in her leg. She refused to rest regardless. She was too anxious to reunite with Lane.

As she pushed toward the net factory, smiles from genial strangers gave her pause. They couldn't *all* know about the incident. Maybe they had always been this welcoming. Perhaps she'd needed only to raise her eyes and see them.

"Maddie!" She made out Lane's voice through a cluster of kids. School had just let out for the day and many young girls had gathered tightly around him. "Wait up," he hollered.

A resonance of urgency told her the news had already reached him. Was that the reason for the children's overlapping chatter? Good grief. She hoped the version he'd heard hadn't been exaggerated from gossipy momentum. If anyone could master the art of stretching tales it was kids.

Lane strode away from the group. As he approached, Maddie felt an overwhelming desire for the comfort of his arms.

Surprisingly, his features weren't taut with concern or anger. Rather, he boasted a wide and wonderful smile. The sight, like seeing the sun after a yearlong winter, blinded her mind against any other thought.

From a high-pitched squeak, she traced the source of his mood. In Lane's arms lay a puppy with enormous black eyes. Its narrow pink tongue draped to the side as if an inch too long for its mouth. No wonder the children had swarmed around. They were likely missing their own pets they'd been forced to leave behind.

"Who's this?" Maddie asked him.

"Townspeople have been dropping off strays at the edge of camp. Guys at the factory say this one's been snooping around for the past week. He's a little skittish, but I fed him some bread, and now I can't get rid of him."

She ran her hand over the length of his white fur, all of it needing a wash and trim. His rib cage displayed a need for more regular meals. "Hiya, sweet stuff," she said to him. "You hungry for lunch?"

The dog whimpered twice, a presumed yes.

Maddie grinned. "What kind is he?"

"Some kind of terrier, I think." He massaged behind the animal's ears, causing the pup to lean into Lane's chest for more. The sight reminded Maddie why she and TJ had always wanted a pet growing up. Their schedules, packed with sports and music and school, hadn't allowed the luxury.

"Has anyone given him a name?" she asked.

"Not yet. I thought Emma should do it, since the dog's going to be hers."

Maddie could already see the girl's face beaming from her gift.

Reconciliation with her brother would be instantaneous. "Oh, Lane, that's grand. She'll absolutely love him."

"For years she's talked about wanting one. But Mother didn't want anything shedding in the house, chewing on the furniture, that kind of thing. Now, though, with the place we're living in"— he shrugged—"I figured there's nothing a dog can ruin."

A refreshing upside of their abode.

"So does this mean Emma's off restriction?"

"Oh—that's right," he said, remembering, making Maddie wish she hadn't brought up the topic. Then he shook his head. "You know, I think a pet might be just the thing to keep Em out of trouble. Don't you think?"

Maddie smiled. "Definitely."

Although Lane's eyes looked weary and reddened from the wind, his skin rough and speckled with dye, Maddie detected the youthful, carefree man she loved.

"Here," he said, "why don't you go give him to Emma." When he began passing the dog over, Maddie gently refused.

"He's *your* gift. You should be the one to give it."

Lane peered down at the pup, and he nodded.

Together they all set off for their barrack. With school out, under orders, Emma would be headed straight there.

"What happened to your leg?" Lane stopped, his gaze on Maddie's bandage. Her limp had given her away.

She geared up for a recap, but swiftly changed course. Why ruin the resulting grace of this day? She'd learned her lesson well: not to wander off solo, and best of all—given all those she had befriended—that she wouldn't have to. Besides, nothing horrendous had taken place. And if the administrators weren't going to act anyway, what good would it do to rile Lane up?

"Did you trip on something?" Lane pressed for an answer.

Maddie gripped the handle of her scratched violin case, formulating an honest reply. "These uneven roads, they weren't made for clumsy girls." She motioned her chin toward their home. "Come on. Our new buddy here needs some food."

The puppy contributed two whimpers of agreement, aiding Maddie's cause. She loved this dog more every minute.

Lane placed a free arm around her back to support her walk. Truthfully, she didn't need the help, but she wouldn't dream of letting him know. Her heart, like her skin, warmed from his tender touch.

Near the entry of the barrack, the gentleman who'd saved her was in his garden, weeding. When he glanced up, Maddie worried he might give Lane a report. Instead, he merely bowed. This time, she made sure he saw her bow in return.

The dog snipped off a tiny bark as they reached the door. Maddie turned around to quietly shush him; she wanted the full effect of Emma's surprise. But then a figure caught her eye. A man in black was watching from a distance. Before she could make out his face, he disappeared into the firebreak.

❧ 40 ❧

Follow orders, do his time, get the hell home. That was the plan. Only then could TJ retrieve his sister, who refused to move back to Boyle Heights.

Until then, at least the world at a few thousand feet wasn't looking too shabby. Through the Plexiglas of the B-17's tail section, his eyes feasted on the beauty of the Hawaiian Islands. It was a tropical buffet of banana groves and sugarcane fields, trees lush with mangoes, guavas, papayas. His mouth watered at the memory of the pineapple he'd split with Ranieri that morning. The slices were so sweet you'd think they'd been marinated in honey.

To the droning tune of the bomber's engines, palm trees swayed lazily over white sandy beaches, and clear blue water sparkled like crystals. It was on the distant shores of this very ocean, on the California beaches, that he and Lane had spent every free moment during summers in high school. With tidal strength, the waves had drawn in swimsuit-clad girls and clusters of food stands. Those were the days, all right. Nothing like a ride on the Giant Dipper on the Venice Pier to get cozy with a foxy stranger. A pocketful of pennies at any arcade was worth an hour of laughs.

Then, on occasions when TJ's dad let them borrow the car, they'd cruise the coastline out to Malibu, join a volleyball game or a bonfire at Zuma Beach. That spot had been Lane's favorite, even after he'd almost drowned there, yanked under by a vicious riptide. Once TJ had realized the guy wasn't fooling, he'd jumped in after him, searched frantically through a screen of swirling sand. Not until a lifeguard later commented on the dangerous rescue—about TJ being either really brave or really stupid—had his own safety occurred to him. The act had been a mere reflex. After all, as he'd explained in reply, Lane was family.

"All right, gentlemen, keep your eyes peeled." The voice of First Lieutenant Hank Cabot filtered through TJ's headset as they reduced altitude. Known as "Cabbie," a fitting nickname given his duty of taxiing his crew up and down the Pacific, he was a decent pick as pilots went. Fairly quiet, but a straight shooter. Got the job done, didn't take unnecessary risks. Being the father of young twins would do that to a guy. That style, unlike the old days, suited TJ just fine.

"Think I got something," the navigator reported over the intercom. "On those big rocks, eleven o'clo—" He stopped. "Ah, strike that. Just a couple of seals."

Ranieri whistled from the waist section. "Hoo boy. Looks like the one on top's getting frisky," he said. "Hey, Tack!"

The ball turret gunner—a mustard-haired kid, no bigger than a thumbtack—answered, "Yeah, what?"

"Might wanna take some notes. Even the sea animals here are gettin' more action than you are."

TJ chuckled along with the others.

"Real funny, wise-ass," the guy retorted. "Too bad the last dame you banged had more whiskers than a seal."

The pilot broke in firmly. "Enough clowning. We got some of our guys down there, so pay attention."

Yeah, TJ thought, *in the unlikely event any were alive.* The two other search missions they'd handled—stepping in when the Navy was shorthanded—had been nothing more than a "milk run." A trip smooth as cream from takeoff to landing. Since TJ rarely mingled with any airmen outside his crew, a couple more empty seats at chowtime was no skin off his nose.

But he obeyed the order anyhow. What else was he going to do up here?

He shifted himself on what resembled a bicycle seat, and scanned the vast water. With his height of five-ten, the cramped tail section wasn't the ideal station. He should have left the poker table the second Ranieri added the crummy position to the betting pot.

One of these days he'd learn.

TJ held on as the plane bumped from side to side. Trade winds were picking up. He blinked away imaginary dots from the sun, then returned his attention to the ocean. The night before last, a B-24 had hit the drink on an anti-sub patrol between Hickam and Midway. Water landings had a tendency to smash those bulky bombers and all onboard to smithereens, one of several reasons they were known as "Flying Coffins"—which was why right now TJ didn't trust his eyes. He strained his vision to confirm what appeared to be movement coming from a raft.

"Six o'clock low," he announced, tentative. Cresting waves could be deceiving from this far above. "Might be nothing, but—I think I see hands waving."

"Roger that," Cabbie told him. "Coming back around." He angled *Hula Hattie*'s wings for a second pass, dropping altitude for a closer look.

"Well, I'll be . . . ," Ranieri murmured.

Excitement tightened the bombardier's voice. "Sure thing, got two standing in a raft, flailing their oars around."

"Yep, got 'em," Cabbie said. "Attaboy, Kern. I'll call it in, let the Navy get these boys home."

TJ couldn't help smiling. The recognition was nice, he couldn't deny that. Imagining the elation of the guys below, though . . . that was the real McCoy. A son or husband or father might actually make it home. The feeling was a good one. Although it had taken time, he'd accepted the fact that he couldn't have saved his mother—but he'd done this. This offering. This first step in reconciling his past. Too often he had let others down, been let down by those he loved.

That run of losses, he decided, was over.

Again the pair came into view. As described, the men were on their feet. Their oars were jumping all about, but not in celebration. Something was wrong. Beneath the water, the coral was moving. The guys were banging away at the side of the raft. A fin. It was a shark's fin! That wasn't coral down there. It was a swarm.

"Lieutenant," TJ cried out, "they got sharks attacking! We can't wait. We gotta find a way to get 'em out!"

Cabbie's response faded into the roar in TJ's head, louder than all four Cyclone engines. TJ splayed his hands on the window as one survivor disappeared from the raft. The other fell backward and into the sea. Outstretched limbs and yellow rubber—their Mae West life preservers—flapped through the torrent of splashes. TJ could hear their screams of terror in his mind. Could see a tinge of red at the surface.

And then . . .

Nothing.

❧ 41 ❧

Lane moved slowly through his day, aware that every face he saw, every barrack he passed, would soon be a memory. The cold November breeze had waned by sunset, but his skin remained chilled over his decision.

He hesitated to imagine the reactions of his mother and sister upon hearing his plans. But Maddie's he dreaded most of all. Little in life would be harder than saying good-bye to her yet again.

At last, gearing up, he entered their apartment, where he discovered only his mother. She sat on her bed with the Bible open on her lap. Loose pages in her hands absorbed her full attention. He recognized the letter, less from its yellowed paper and Japanese scrawling than from the glistening it caused in his mother's eyes. Indeed she had brought the memento from home, saved it from the flames she'd fed with their family's history.

He should have guessed this mystery of her past had escorted them all the way here.

"What are you reading, Mother?"

She fumbled with the letter, tucked it into her Holy Book. *"Betsuni."*

Obviously the token amounted to more than "nothing."

Lane strode over the freshly installed linoleum, ready to press the point. Then he recalled his plans, and the interrogation fell away. They had so little time left together; why waste it on attempts to pry loose a confession that might be better left withheld?

He shifted to a more pertinent topic. "Where's Emma and Maddie?"

"At garment factory," she intoned.

He'd forgotten. Maddie had mentioned working late. Emma must have volunteered to help, given the high demand for clothing at the Children's Village. The camp's orphanage needed all the supplies they could get, and Maddie had gladly offered her services. He just wished those services weren't being used tonight. He had hoped to tell all three of them at once.

On the other hand, maybe this was the way it should be—telling his mother first. The woman had brought him into this world, and it was the stony strength she had passed along that he'd be counting on to survive.

"Mother," he began, and took a breath. The oil stove clanked.

She glanced into his eyes, registered a confrontation awaited, and briskly threw on her winter coat. The letter. She didn't want to talk about the letter. But that wasn't the issue at hand.

"I have to speak with you," he told her.

"*Chambara* playing tonight. I must go."

A decent excuse. She had always been a fan of the old ninja and samurai flicks. In Little Tokyo, Lane used to join her on occasion when he was a kid. Then, over the years, for some reason he'd stopped.

"Mother, wait."

She paused at the doorway, a sadness clinging to her lowered gaze.

Lane tried to continue, but he couldn't. Not like this.

"I'll go with you," he found himself saying. He half expected her to refuse. Rather she nodded, showing no trace of the surprise she surely felt.

They walked in quiet. A searchlight paved their path.

Inside the rec building, Manzanites bustled around them, talking and laughing with new and old friends. Many wore surplus uniforms from the Great War, the administration's answer to a shortage of winter wear. Their fabrics smelled of mothballs. Actually, the whole scene resembled a children's skit. On Japanese bodies, nearly everything hung oversized. Khaki wool trousers and canvas leggings, jodhpurs and olive-drab knit caps. The one stylish attraction was a scattering of peacoats Maddie had converted into capes, a popular trend among the girls.

"Lane, over here!" A man from the net factory waved Lane and his mother to two open spots beside the aisle. When the lights went black, the room's chatter dropped off as though connected to a switch. A worn projector clickety-clacked from behind, splashing black-and-white images across a white sheet.

Seated in the front row, a *benshi* commenced his performance. A candle illuminated the script on his lap. He used a range of voices to match the actors' lips that moved silently on the screen. As samurai warriors sparred with swords, the gray-haired *benshi* obliged with cymbals and clappers. It was a marvel, really, a unique art form with roots so purely Japanese. Which, no doubt, was the reason Lane had lost interest as a kid.

The battle ended and the victors rode horseback out of the village. Their sleek hair in a *chonmage,* the samurai's traditional top-knot, bounced with each gallop. Soon an elderly woman in a kimono shimmied onto the screen. Behind her, the sun descended upon a towering pagoda. When the *benshi* vocalized her voice, warbling like a sheep, the audience broke into giggles.

It was then that Lane glimpsed his mother's expression. Without turning, he watched a smile play over her lips. Light from the projector erased years from her face, all hardness from her eyes. Her warmth glowed like a thousand moons.

This, he decided, was how he would remember her. A lunar radiance in a room full of darkness.

❦ 42 ❧

Searchlights swept the grounds. Barbed wire winked from the nearest fencepost as Maddie awaited the signal. She crouched behind a pair of trees in the Block 12 Garden. Her body trembled as much from the cold as from fear. The beam made another regular nightly pass before Lane tapped her arm.

"Let's go, let's go," he whispered, and took off for the fence. In the dark, with his tweed cap and duffel bag, he looked like a hobo racing for a train car. Maddie followed his hunched form, shielding her eyes from the winter wind. A flurry of dirt pelted her face.

For most of her life, she had been anything but a rule breaker. In fact, she'd prided herself on living between lines set by parents and teachers and society as a whole. Yet here she was, not just pushing those boundaries this time, but literally busting through them.

"Go on," he told her, and lifted a string of wire. His foot pressed down on the one below.

A mass of nerves rose to her throat. She glanced over her shoulder. The closest guard had taken shelter inside his tower. His silhouette moved behind the pitted windows.

"Maddie, hurry."

Carefully, she hurdled the enclosure. Lane joined right behind, but then his hat flew off and landed in the perimeter. A clue of their escape. He reached through the fence, his fingertips barely brushing the cap. The searchlight was closing in.

"Come on," she rasped. "We have to go."

"I almost—have it. . . ."

"Lane, please. Just leave it."

He stretched a bit more. Finally, he snagged the cap's bill with two fingers. "Got it."

Grabbing her hand, he dashed toward the snowcapped mountains. He clicked on a flashlight once they were far enough away.

Adrenaline warmed Maddie's body for a good stretch of their hike. Only from the sound of the creek beside them did she catch an occasional shiver. High above, air whistled through treetops that filtered a path of moonlight.

"Are you sure they won't find us here?" she asked.

"In the summer, guys snuck out before dawn all the time. Spent the whole day fishing. No one's had a problem yet." Lane guided her over an icy puddle. "If I can find the spot Kiyoshi described, we should be safe all night."

Safe. In all its complex simplicity, *safe* had become one of Maddie's favorite words. During innings when her brother used to pitch, she'd dreaded the umpire's call of that single syllable. Now, meandering through woods thick with nighttime noises, she clung to the cushion of its four letters.

Lane paused to assess the area. "Stay here for a second," he said, and headed toward a massive wall of rock.

Chills crept over her from standing still. She hugged her arms and rubbed her woolen coat sleeves. If they were to lose their way, would anyone ever find them? Would they freeze first, or starve? It was the first of December. They had to be *kichigai* to go camping now. Flat-out nuts.

"Here it is," he declared, unveiling a cave half hidden by a bush.

Maddie followed and stooped to enter. A ways in, the ceiling swept upward, high enough for them to fully stand. While Lane foraged for branches to build a fire, Maddie laid out the blanket he had packed. Soon they settled before the mounting orange flames.

"Are you hungry?" he asked. When she nodded, he produced a

box of crackers, a small block of cheese, and two bottles of Coca-Cola from the camp's canteen. He topped it off with jarred apple-sauce, its fruit from the nearby evacuee-run farm. The meal was perfect for the outing she had agreed to, admittedly, with reserva-tion.

Although delighted by his proposal of a private overnight date, she'd worried—as she always worried—about the risks: the conse-quences from authorities, the potential rumors from those she had only recently befriended. Yes, she and Lane were married, but his culture was particularly conservative.

She now regretted any reluctance. The wonderment of being alone with him, really alone, had never been greater. An air of en-chantment exuded from the glowing fire that sent soft ripples over his skin. "Lane, I've missed you so much."

"Sweetheart," he said, "I . . . I just . . ."

She leaned forward, nudging his words aside. Their lips met with a tenderness that swiftly gave in to hunger. Passion flared from her knees to her thighs and crawled upward to her chest. Desire became a razor's edge, sharp and dangerous. His hands roamed over her curves, under her coat and shirt, arching her back. His tongue trailed from the valley of her neck. Shadows danced on the ceiling, swaying in time to her escalating pulse.

From the heat of Lane's breath, she released a moan, and an image replayed in her mind: Emma's balloon from the beach, a red dot drifting toward the clouds, an indescribable pressure leading to an implosion. This was the sensation ruling her body. It swelled with the scent of burning wood, the textures of the cave. A primi-tive force overtook her. An African drumbeat filled her ears.

She pulled off Lane's shirt and trousers with hasty hands. His expression displayed pleasant bewilderment. Their garments dis-solved one by one. As she explored the contours of his body, a raw gasp slipped from his mouth. She rose to him, pressed her bare chest against his, savored the salty taste of his shoulder. Surrender-ing to her instincts, she guided Lane onto his back. The air turned electric around them, and at the brink of their fulfillment, she swore, for that tenuous moment, they had sampled the true essence of freedom.

* * *

Maddie awoke to find she was alone.

The remnants of the fire simmered with a memory of warmth. She called Lane's name. His clothes were gone. Surely he would have woken her before heading back to camp. Maybe he was fetching firewood for their breakfast.

She cocooned her body with both blankets. With shoes on, she headed out of the cave in search of her husband. Dawn was approaching in a foggy frost.

To her relief, she soon spotted Lane seated at the edge of the creek. He stared into the current, elbows on his knees, chin atop laced fingers. She touched his shoulder, startling him.

"Good morning," she said groggily.

"Morning." He didn't smile.

"How long have you been up?"

"A while."

In order to sneak into camp with ease, they would need to beat the sun. Logic told her this. Her heart told her they should never return.

"I ought to get ready to go, I suppose." She dragged her words, somehow hoping he would argue. Wanting him to suggest they prolong the bliss of their hideaway.

He merely pitched a pebble into the water.

Confused by his change of mood, she flashed back to their night together. Had he viewed her behavior as too brazen? Her bareness, even now, left her vulnerable. She tightened her wrap of blankets.

When she turned for the cave, a small tug halted her, Lane's hand on the fabric.

"Please, don't go yet. There's something I need to tell you." The foreboding in his tone sent a shudder down her back.

Reluctant, she lowered onto a large rock at his side.

He shifted to face her, though his gaze remained on her lap. "Army recruiters came through the other day," he said. "Some of the factory guys wanted to go over. I just went with them to find out more. When I got there . . . well, they handed me a test. Most of the guys failed, but apparently I aced mine. So they asked me to stay."

Maddie warned herself not to jump to conclusions, not to panic. "What did they want?"

After a moment, he raised his eyes. "They swore me in, Maddie. I thought I'd have more time, but they're busing us out tomorrow night."

Army? He'd joined the *Army?*

The news taking hold, she questioned if she were dreaming. This had to be a nightmare. With American casualties steadily rising, having a brother *and* a husband in the war was unfathomable. Enlistment wasn't even supposed to be possible for Lane.

"Japanese Americans aren't allowed to serve," she insisted. "You said so yourself."

"That's how it's been—until now. It's a secret branch in Intelligence. They won't tell me much. Just that I'll be putting my language skills to good use."

"No. . . ." She shook her head, and repeated with vehemence, "No. You can't do that."

"Honey, I have to."

"The only thing you *have* to do is stay with me."

He rested a hand on her covered knee and said, "Don't you see, Maddie? I'll be helping our country win. Then everyone can go home—to our real homes." He gave her a smile, the kind that took effort. She found his reasoning even less convincing.

"That country, if you recall, is the one that locked your family up in the middle of nowhere."

"And that," he said, "is exactly why I'm doing this. It's the only way I'll ever prove our loyalty."

"How? By spilling your blood?" When Maddie bit off a laugh, his eyes firmed.

"If that's the only way, then yes."

She stared in disbelief. This couldn't be happening. They'd sacrificed too much to lose each other now.

Then she remembered his father. The man's predicament could selfishly prove a blessing. "Do they know about your dad? That he's still being detained?"

Lane sat back. His gaze slid toward the water. "They didn't ask, and I don't plan to bring it up. If it becomes an issue . . . what's the worst they can do? Send me back to camp?"

Exactly right.

"In that case, I'll make sure they know, so I can save you the trip." She returned to her feet.

"Maddie, don't." He rose, grabbing her elbow. "Please, don't do that."

The plea in his eyes reached out and closed snugly around her. There was no room for debate. He'd made up his mind—without her.

God, how she wanted to hate him.

"Just try to understand." He relaxed his hold but moved closer. "I'm doing this for you too. You shouldn't be living in a prison. And I know you won't leave as long as I'm here. I talked to the administration already, about getting you out."

"You made plans for me?" she said, stunned.

"Of course I did. I wouldn't go without doing that first."

"What about talking to your own *wife* first? Don't you think—" She stopped, pulled her arm away. "Never mind. I'll go if that's what you want. In fact, you should have just told me from the beginning, since you've clearly wanted that all along." She stormed off and, in the cave, started throwing on her clothes.

He trailed her inside. "Sweetheart, listen to me. There's another reason I joined up."

She continued to button her blouse, avoiding his eyes.

"For months now, I've felt like I was losing myself." He leaned against a rock wall, let out a breath. "Maybe I've never really known who I was. But if I'm ever going to find out, I have to do this. And not just for me, for us."

Maddie heard what he was saying, though she didn't want to. She knelt on the ground to collect their picnic supplies.

Lane squatted down and gingerly grasped her wrist, rendering her motionless. "Do you think I'd leave you again, ever, if I thought there was any other way?"

The sound of his struggle, the truth of his words, forced her into quiet defeat. He was leaving tomorrow.

Tomorrow . . .

"But what about Emma?" she asked, recalling the girl who finally resembled her old self. "If I go home, she'll only have your mother."

"She'll have Yuki too," he assured her.

The puppy, a model companion, had claimed a daily spot outside the grade school. There he waited until Emma bounded out of class. Even in terrible weather, he never neglected his post.

"My sister's strong, like you. I know she'll be all right." He raised Maddie's chin and peered into her eyes. "With you to come back to, so will I."

These final words ripped through her, shredding all doubts about their history, their bond. A single tear rolled down her cheek.

He offered his arms, and she folded against his chest. Aware they'd soon have to let go, she stored this moment away. She'd hold the vividness in her mind, like a talisman to keep her strong. In times of fear she would rely upon these: The comfort of Lane's body, the melody of a creek. The chill of coming snow. The fading scent of ashes.

43

TJ threw back another gulp of beer, avoiding the thief who'd just plopped down on the next stool.

"You can't seriously still be steamed," Ranieri said in a snickering tone. Liquor wafted from his breath and cigarette smoke from his khakis. "If you got a look at those dames, you wouldn't blame me a bit."

TJ gripped his bottle on the bar. Ignore the guy and he just might go away.

A pack of sailors chucked laughter across the open-aired tavern, rising above the static of waves pounding the beach. Flirtatious girls added their giggles to the gratingly happy clamor.

TJ took another drink, the one and only reason he'd gone out tonight. He certainly hadn't come to Kanoa's for company. Or to listen to anyone's excuses.

"Ah, don't be such a sorehead, Kern. Said I was sorry. Let bygones be bygones, whaddya say?"

In a mirror behind the racked liquor, TJ could see Ranieri's trademark grin, slick and smooth as ever. He should have trusted his instincts from when they first met at gunnery school.

"Here, let me buy you a shot. Make it up to you." Ranieri

turned to the bartender. "Hey, Kanoa! Need some whiskey over here."

The Hawaiian covered in tribal tattoos poured two shots. If not for his husky build, he could have been any one of General Tojo's soldiers. A third of the population, after all, was Japanese. The fact that few had been detained could give anyone with common sense a headache.

Following Ranieri's request, the bartender left them the bottle. *"Salute,"* Ranieri toasted, raising his glass to TJ. No doubt, the guy believed a couple shared drinks could solve the world's problems.

TJ snubbed the offer. He'd even lost his desire for the beer. He threw a crinkled dollar onto the bar.

"You gotta be kiddin' me. All this over a lousy chute?"

It was more than that.

Ranieri didn't make for a real friend. And not just because he'd given TJ's parachute to some broads, so they could sew slips and pajamas from the coveted fabric. Not for the hassle TJ had endured with the supply sergeant upon discovering it missing. Truthfully, the swindle was pretty impressive; he would have otherwise thought it damn near impossible to smuggle a pack from the personal equipment shack. But the jerk should have come clean on his own, rather than bragging to others about his deed.

Better to cut him off before any real damage could be done.

"Lighten up, will ya?" Ranieri set down his shot glass. "If they'd charged you for a replacement, you know I would've covered it."

TJ stood up to leave.

"Kern."

When he didn't stop, Ranieri clamped a grip on TJ's arm—and that finally did it. An ancient anger burst free.

"Get your paws off!" he roared.

Ranieri backed up, showing his palms. Disgust creased his face. "Fine by me," he muttered as TJ turned away from him. "Besides, who needs a pal who only gives a shit about himself. No wonder your sister ran for the hills."

On reflex, TJ spun around and grabbed Ranieri by the shirt, shoving him against the bar. Stools tipped, a bottle crashed. TJ raised his fist, about to clean the guy's clock, when a memory returned. The night he'd gripped Lane the same way. The night TJ lost a brother.

No other betrayal could compete.

He sharply released his hold while Ranieri pushed himself free. A table of sailors looked eager to join in.

"Take it outside," the bartender growled, holding a wooden club.

TJ shook his head and replied through clenched teeth. "He ain't worth the trouble." Then, tossing out a couple more bucks, he snagged the whiskey bottle and left their friendship behind.

Sunlight pierced TJ's brain like an ice pick. Eyes slowly adjusting, he assembled pieces of reality. Air Corps. Hawaii. War. Booze.

Thankfully he'd woken up on his own cot. He tried to recover moisture on his tongue. His mouth tasted like a bin of dirty cotton.

"Rise and shine!" A guy entered the barrack. Short. Yellow hair. Through groggy vision, he looked like Tack. "You missed chow, buddy. Too bad. Powdered eggs and Spam actually tasted good today."

The mention of food curled TJ's stomach. "Not hungry."

"Yeah, you're lookin' a little green." Tack blew out a breath, amused, and rustled through his footlocker. Every noise blared in the halls of TJ's mind. "Gotta say, though, serves you right for waking me up last night. I was smack in the middle of making it with Rita Hayworth."

TJ rolled over onto his side and smothered his ear with the pillow. He had only a vague recollection of returning from the beach. That's right . . . it was a beach where he'd emptied the bottle. What had it been—half full? Ah, Christ. He could still feel the liquor swishing around like the waves he'd watched roll in. Couples had strolled by in the moonlight, shoes dangling from their fingers. TJ had kept to himself. Invisible in the shadows, he'd stared into the sky, searching for Jo's stars.

"Better get up soon," Tack warned. "Cabbie's gonna chew you out if you're late for the practice run. Oh, and I handed off those letters to him. Don't know what was so urgent, but they're gone like you asked."

TJ's mind spun with nauseating visions of aerial maneuvers. "What're you talking about?" he rasped. "What letters?"

"To your girl. Jo Allie-whatever." Tack hitched his hands on his hips. "What, you don't remember that either? Sheesh. How much you drink anyway?"

Letters . . . to Jo . . .

Letters to Jo?

Panic propelled TJ's body to sit upright, the alcohol sloshing. His dog tags clanked together as he reached into his footlocker. He lifted stuff up, shoved it around. They weren't there. Each page he'd written—never intended for her eyes—was missing.

Then he realized: "They didn't have her address."

"Not till you rattled it off," Tack said. "Some hardware store in California. And don't forget you owe me two weeks of cigarettes."

The soul-baring confessions TJ had poured onto those pages came rushing back. Strung together, the words did a loop-the-loop and skid landed in his gut. "Holy crap."

TJ worked to throw on his uniform.

"Where in the Sam Hill you goin'?"

Cabbie, as first lieutenant, censored all the crew's outgoing mail. TJ had to stop him from sending out those posts. Jo couldn't read those posts!

He was still buttoning his shirt as he raced outside. Finally he located Cabbie on the hardstand. In the midst of a preflight inspection, the pilot stopped to give TJ an earful over his appearance. Only then did TJ get an answer to his pressing question.

The letters to Jo Allister were already en route.

There was no way to get them back.

❧❧ 44 ❧❧

At the main gate, surrounded by MPs, Maddie and Emma waved good-bye to Lane. To avoid conflict with those opposed to enlistment—the Black Dragons, in particular—the Army smuggled out Nisei soldiers in the frosty black of night.

"Kiotsukete" was Kumiko's single bid to Lane before he turned for the bus. Even Maddie understood the phrase: *Take care.* His mother's face had remained stoic all the while, but the slight quiver in her voice had betrayed her.

As Lane boarded the steps, Maddie pondered the keepsakes he'd claimed would bring him home. Packed in his travel bag was a photo of Maddie, a paper crane Emma had once given him—a symbol of a thousand cranes for luck—and a *senninbari* from his mother. Kumiko had recruited a thousand residents to each sew a red stitch into the white waistband that would, in wartime, protect her son.

A thousand stitches, a thousand cranes. A thousand years, it seemed, until Maddie would see him again.

Four days later, the eruption began.

Fred Tayama, rumored to be an FBI "stool pigeon," had just returned from the national JACL convention in Salt Lake City. Representing Manzanar, he'd reportedly spoken there in favor of a Nisei draft. Not all camp residents shared his stance. Six masked men beat him severely. An investigation led to the arrest of the kitchen union leader, a popular Kibei who'd recently charged two administrators with stealing food supplies to sell on the black market.

Maddie knew none of this until today. She had gone to the Administration Building, in anticipation of her release papers, when she discovered a protesting mob. Obscenities in Japanese and English flew at a barricade of soldiers armed with mounted machine guns. Eventually, negotiators reached a compromise and the crowd dispersed.

Rumors about the incident, however, were only getting started. Even Emma had plenty to share. Seated on a cot, beside Maddie's half-packed suitcase, she continued her rambling.

"Hana says they moved the guy back to camp—the one they arrested. His name's Harry something. But they're still keeping him in jail. And some other guys are gonna try and break him out."

"So your friend knows all this for a fact?" Maddie challenged, trying to shut down the topic.

"She says there's a lot more of *us* than them. So really, what could the guards do? If we took over the camp, they'd have to let us go. Right?"

In that "us" versus "them" equation, Maddie herself resided on a vague border between both. She folded a skirt, added it to the pile. "Em, that's not really how it works."

Emma shrugged. "Either way, there's bound to be a whole lot more fights and stuff." She fingered a sachet Maddie had set out for packing.

All afternoon, the girl had been carrying on about potential disasters, a thinly veiled attempt to keep Maddie from leaving. Kumiko, in contrast, had exuded a silent triumph; yet not even this was boosting Maddie's confidence over her decision.

"Did you hear about the fella getting beat up?" Emma asked.

Maddie didn't respond, not wanting to know.

"They say he was sleeping in his bed when it happened. And now the police can arrest anyone they want."

Anxiety climbed, hastening Maddie's folding.

"According to Hana's brother, the guys who did it are even madder now. So when Tayama-*san* gets out of the hospital, they're gonna hurt him again. Maybe even *kill* him."

"That's enough," Maddie snapped.

Emma's face clouded and her gaze dropped. On the floor, Yuki rested his head on her Mary Janes and peered up. A show of defense for a girl who wasn't to blame.

Maddie took a leveling breath, then sat down next to Emma. "I'm sorry, sweetie. But gossip like that is dangerous. Besides," she said, "everything's going to be fine."

"Everything's *not* gonna be fine." Emma's finality squashed any debate.

Oh, why wasn't Lane here? He would know what to say; with charm in effect, he could coax a mama bear from its cub. Now, the role had fallen to Maddie. For so long, she'd taken for granted the luxury of being the sibling cared for, and not the reverse.

Emma turned to her with those eyes—those big brown, heart-rending eyes. "Why can't I go with you?"

Summoning her strength, Maddie answered cheerfully. "Because you have to take care of Yuki. Where else would he have this much space to run around?"

Emma pursed her lips as if to prevent a surge of tears.

"You know, we'll only be apart for a little while. The war will be over before long." By saying that enough times, maybe they could all make it true. "Until then, I won't have a clue what's happening here. So I'll need a letter from you at least once a week, to keep me in the loop. Just like you do for your dad. Will you do that for me?"

After a beat, Emma issued a small nod.

"Thanks, pretty girl. I knew I could count on you." Maddie smiled, smoothing Emma's hair. Goodness, it nearly reached her collar. The length was more noticeable since a wide ribbon had replaced her pigtails. How much older would she appear when they saw each other next?

To cast off the thought, Maddie concentrated on her packing. She would leave out her travel clothes, plus an extra outfit and toiletries.

Emma started to put the sachet into the suitcase—the girl had always admired its crocheted covering and rosy scent—but Maddie stopped her. "Nope. You keep it." Anything to battle the smell of alkaline dust should stay in this room. "On one condition. You have to return it when your whole family moves back to Boyle Heights."

A gradual smile found Emma's lips. She nodded again, with more perk. Her eyes shone with hope of reclaiming an old life. It was a hope they shared, though Maddie tried not to dwell. With both TJ and Lane away, and her own father showing no progress, she feared nothing about home would feel right.

"Say, I have an idea," Maddie said. If one thing kept a mood light, it was a sugary treat—a decadence Kumiko discouraged. Luckily the woman was off meeting about New Year's festivities. "How about a soda and some penny candy at the canteen? Maybe some of that *mushi* you like to eat."

Emma giggled. "You mean *mochi*," she corrected. "*Mushi* are mosquitoes."

Maddie waved her hand dismissively. "Oh, tomato, tomahto." When it dawned on her that *tomahto* was in fact the Japanese pronunciation, she too couldn't help but laugh.

The camp roads were disturbingly empty.

Maddie glanced around. The last dinner shift wasn't over yet. People should have been milling about the mess halls, either coming or going.

"Where is everybody?" Emma asked.

"Maybe the cold's keeping them in." Maddie tightened her scarf around her neck and discarded an impulse to turn back. The glee club could be putting on another performance. "Let's get to the store before we freeze."

Around the next barrack, three teenage boys marched past with purpose. Hana's brother led the group. Since his family seemed to be in the know, Maddie called out to him.

"Excuse me! Is there a special event going on tonight?"

He spoke over his shoulder, not stopping. "A big meeting in Block Twenty-two. About freeing Harry Ueno."

Emma tugged at Maddie's sleeve. "Can we go see?" Before Maddie could refuse, she added, "Please, *Onēsan?* Just for a minute?"

The respectful address of *Older Sister* snagged a thread around Maddie's heart, and a reason for agreement slipped in. Dispelling morbid rumors would mean she could depart from Manzanar with fewer concerns.

"All right," she said. "But not for long. Your mother will be home soon."

In a zealous motion, Emma grabbed Maddie's hand to charge at a rapid clip.

More and more evacuees came into view as they neared the mess hall of the twenty-second block. A male voice projected over a speaker, his words indiscernible from afar. Drawn by his speech, Maddie and Emma entered the dusty firebreak. The sheer number of people was astounding. Three, maybe four thousand. The man screamed in Japanese. His face burned with anger. His eyes were as menacing as the crossbones flag beside him. He appeared to be the Black Dragons' leader. As he rattled on, a slew of listeners shouted their support. He was speaking so fast, Maddie couldn't understand a single thing.

Then she heard a word she recognized. "Moritomo."

Another phrase came and went before he said it again—*Moritomo*—this time with more disgust. As if the very combination of syllables deserved to be spat on.

Maddie forced a breath. No need to panic. For all she knew, the surname could be as common as Jones or Smith. Rationale told her that nobody in Lane's family had been involved in the scandals. Not with the sugar theft, or the FBI or JACL. Then again, who could say when it came to his father? She'd heard so little about him, and even Lane, in passing frustration, had questioned the grounds behind his detainment.

She turned to Emma. "What are they talking about?"

The girl stared at the gang leader in a frightful trance. Maddie crouched before her, shook her arms. "Emma, tell me what they're saying."

Emma barely moved her mouth as she answered. "They're giving the names of *inu.* They're saying Lane is one of the traitors. That anyone who joined the American Army is an enemy."

Maddie grappled with the translation. The Dragons were in fact talking about her husband. Oh, thank God he'd left Manzanar when he did.

She hugged Emma tight. "They can't do anything to your brother. He's at a base far away, in Minnesota, where he's going to be safe."

"But, there's more. . . ." Her voice cracked and Maddie couldn't tell if it was Emma's body shaking or her own. Leaning back to listen, Maddie encouraged her to finish.

"That man," Emma said, pointing a finger, "he says there's a death list. If they can't get those traitors, then they'll kill their families instead."

No . . . no, that couldn't be. Emma must have misunderstood.

In search of reassurance, Maddie focused on the ranting leader. A few feet beside him stood another Black Dragon. *Orochi.* When his eyes connected with hers, he blew a kiss and a sneer curled his mouth.

Maddie urged in an undertone, "Emma, let's go. *Now.*" She snatched the girl's hand and strode from the crowd in a restrained sprint. Weapons glinted in the hands of those she passed. Hammers, hatchets, screwdrivers, knives. Maddie lowered her face into her scarf, hiding her white skin. Gaining attention could be a fatal mistake.

Once in the next block, they broke into a run. She didn't release Emma until they were safely in their apartment. Maddie bolted the locks and scanned the room, needing to create a barrier.

A sound came from the door. The knob jiggled. Someone was trying to get in. Maddie's heart thrashed about, then Yuki whimpered.

"Shh," Maddie commanded. Emma quieted the dog, and they all waited in silence.

Until the person knocked. A hard, impatient pound.

She imagined Orochi smiling crudely as he prepared to break the door in.

That's when the caller spoke. "Emma-*chan! Naka ni iru no?*"

Kumiko's voice. Never had Maddie thought she would welcome that sound.

Emma raced to open the door. *"Okāsan,"* she cried in relief.

Kumiko tsked. *"Naze kagi o kaketetano?"* She peered at Maddie with a look of suspicion, a question of what they had been up to behind a locked door.

An explanation would have to wait.

"Get her in here," Maddie ordered. Emma ushered her mother from the doorway so that Maddie could reseal them inside. Then the girl helped Maddie shove a table across the room. It scraped over linoleum until slamming into the door.

Kumiko stared as if they'd gone insane. Emma started to respond, but Kumiko interrupted, indignant over a situation she didn't understand. She sputtered a few phrases before an object shot through the apricot curtains. The window shattered. They dropped to the ground, hands covering their heads. A fist-sized rock rolled through the scattered shards.

In a flash of a memory, Maddie was back on Lane's old porch, assaulted by a downpour of hatred and glass. "Stay down," she whispered.

Cautiously she peeked out the window frame. Three men wielding baseball bats and an axe had created a protective line against a pair of Black Dragons. Orochi hollered gruffly at them in Japanese. The human blockades—two of them Lane's coworkers from the factory—didn't surrender an inch.

Maddie crawled around the glass, in search of weapons as backup. She found a shovel near the stove, nothing else. From her directive, Emma guided her mother onto a cot in the corner. The two huddled together, eyes on Maddie, who took up a post beside the front door. She squeezed the wooden handle, posing its grimy spade overhead.

Yuki volunteered to help. He stood in front of the door and simmered a growl.

Finally, the shouting stopped. Quiet reigned until a man poked his head through the window, and Maddie gasped. The net worker told her of the news traveling through camp, about a "death list" that confirmed Emma's translation, and gave assurance that he and his buddies would keep watch all night. The Dragons were gone, but Maddie knew they could be back. Next time, in larger numbers.

She glanced at Emma and Kumiko, the apprehension clear in their faces. The family couldn't stay here. Yet where could they go?

If the rumors were true, about a planned siege on the jail, the police station would be in equal danger. The Administration Building would be their best option. Maddie decided this before another report arrived: A riot had exploded on the administrators' doorstep.

The verifying sounds gained volume. Boisterous Japanese songs and yells of *"Banzai!"* soared on the night air.

An hour crept by, every second wrangling Maddie's nerves.

Then gunshots tripped a wire of shrieks. What was happening out there? Had evacuees taken over the camp?

After that came silence. Just breathing and hunger and silence.

The announcement of death, a universal sound, came in the tolling of bells. Their metallic mourning rang from the mess halls.

Word trickled in of an unmanned truck being pushed into armed soldiers, of ignored warnings by the enraged crowd, of tear gas and bullets flying in a panicked blur, and MPs regaining control. Among the eleven evacuees shot, the one killed was a teenager evidently on his way to work. Cries over his death echoed off the jagged mountains, joining a chorus created by Paiutes who'd once wept on the same desert floor.

Maddie, too, wallowed in the tragedy, embittered by its senselessness, until the thought of revenge seized her. Not her own revenge, but of those who might seek it out with heightened motivation.

"We have to go." She unblocked the apartment door. Exhausted though fully alert, she stepped outside and informed their defenders of her intentions. One of the men offered to escort them, yet Maddie wouldn't have it. Tonight, women and children traveling alone would garner safer passage from nervous sentries.

Kumiko made only a small fuss over heading out. Maddie's ultimatum—*Come with us or stay here by yourself*—managed to do the trick. With a shovel in Maddie's hands and the puppy at Emma's heels, they navigated their way toward First Street. At the intersection, they swung around the rec hall, where a shadowy man appeared.

"Halt!" The deep voice straightened Maddie's spine. He wore a helmet; he was a soldier.

Maddie grabbed hold of Kumiko's wrist to communicate the order. A searchlight draped them in white.

"Drop your weapon!" he yelled.

Maddie released the shovel, let it clink against the ground.

"What're y'all doin' out here?" he demanded, approaching them. "Get back to your apartment."

Maddie squinted against the beam. "There's some men coming, and we might be in danger. . . ."

"You a staff member?"

She shook her head, allowing him to formulate the rest.

"In that case, you're a hell of a lot safer in your barracks. So go back where you came from." He used the barrel of his Tommy gun to indicate the road behind them.

Maddie's first instinct was to comply, to abide by the rules. Then she glimpsed Emma, reminding her of the stakes. "No," she told him, "we can't. Our lives are in danger and we have to reach the Admin Building."

"Little lady," he said, "maybe you didn't hear me the first time, but martial law's been declared here. For your own good, I suggest you hightail it back—"

"I said *no*." She stepped forward, prompting him to lift his gun. Sweat beaded at the base of her scalp. She couldn't back down. "You can either shoot us all or you can take us to the director, where we'll be his problem, not yours."

After an infinite pause, he blew out a ragged sigh. He signaled to a guard tower. In the midst of striding away, he turned around. "You comin' or not?"

The women scrambled to follow. At the next barrack, he passed them on to another GI. This continued, a rescue brigade from post to post, until they reached the door of their destination. Lights glowed in the windows. The smell of tear gas floated above the bloodstained dirt.

Once granted entry, they discovered other families inside, solemnly gathered for the same reason. All were refugees robbed of yet another home, but at least they were in this together. Relief eased through Maddie. She leaned her back against a wall and rubbed her eyes.

"Maddie," Emma said, her voice tight, "have you seen him?"

Maddie's mind was a haze. "Who?"

"Yuki. Have you seen him anywhere?"

"Oh, sweetie. I'm sure he's around here." The front door opened, giving sanctuary to another family. "After all the excitement, he's probably curled up taking a nap. Maybe off in a corner, so he won't get stepped on."

"I don't remember him coming in with us, though. I think we lost him on the way." Her chin crinkled from emotion. "I should've been watching him, but I was so scared. . . ."

Maddie squatted down and squeezed the girl's shoulders. "We'll find him, okay? You go check the hallways, and I'll try the offices."

They parted in opposite directions, whistling and calling the pup's name. Maddie looked under chairs and desks, behind doors, inside closets. Her worry grew with every elimination. She had to remind herself that Yuki was a pet, that even if he were out wandering, chances were slim that revenge on the family would extend to their dog.

Or would it?

Dread from the possibility brewed, interrupted by a sound. A bark. Yuki's bark.

"Thank heavens," she sighed, before realizing the bark came from outside. A problem, but easily solved. One of the soldiers was sure to have a soft spot for animals. He could retrieve Yuki once the area was deemed safe.

Maddie hurried in and out of rooms, past folks huddled in conversations, to tell Emma so. Yet the girl was nowhere to be found.

Beside the fireplace, Kumiko sat alone. Maddie went over to ask the woman—though why would she suddenly have an inkling of her daughter's whereabouts? The rest of the people offered better odds.

She called out, "Has anyone seen Emma Moritomo? A little girl, about this high. Wearing a white ribbon."

A man by the window pointed outside, toward the barking. "She's out there. Just got past the MPs."

Maddie darted over to catch the view. A small, moving form faded into the blackness.

"*Kocchi ni kinasai!*" Kumiko, apparently understanding, had opened the front door. She waved her hand frantically toward herself, demanding her daughter's return. "Emma-*chan! Dame yo!*"

A guard at the entry stopped Kumiko from following. It was clear Maddie wouldn't have any more success.

How did Emma sneak out? Had she found a back door?

Questions whirled in Maddie's head as she tracked down the new project director. He'd taken over the position just a week earlier, and was probably regretting his acceptance right about now.

She located him seated at his office desk. "Mr. Merritt," she broke into his discussion. He and another man looked up. "There's a nine-year-old girl. She's supposed to be here, but she ran back for her dog. I need your soldiers to let me get her."

Merritt rubbed his temples, as if trying to solve a problem on the fumes of thoughts. "We'll get her back here, but you stay where you are." His tone was firm as concrete. Arguing would only cause a delay.

Conceding, Maddie volunteered vital details. Emma's name, what she was wearing. Her block, barrack, and apartment numbers.

He faced the other fellow. "You heard all that, Campbell. Now, send out an MP to find her."

Maddie accompanied the second gentleman to the door, where Kumiko still stood, arms at her sides. "Don't worry," Maddie told her, "they're going to find her."

Slowly Kumiko returned to her chair by the hearth.

"Mrs. Moritomo?" Maddie fought to keep her voice calm.

The woman just stared into the flames, the laxness in her face resembling . . . resignation.

Propelled by fear, Maddie's memories tunneled up in a rage: The coldness Kumiko directed at her daughter. The disapproval, the indifference.

"What kind of mother are you?" Maddie blurted.

Before she could say anything more damaging, she marched off to wait by the window.

The moon continued to rise behind a scattering of clouds. Maddie gripped the windowsill as a jeep finally pulled up to the building. Shadows outlined what appeared to be a young person in the passenger seat.

Overcome with relief, Maddie yanked open the front door and found Yuki there, offering a yippy greeting. "Hey, troublemaker." She bent down, gave his head a mere pat. Despite her delight over their safety, a lecture would be in order.

When she rose, she caught eyes with the GI marching closer. His graveness led her gaze to the limp body draped over his arms. A young girl. With a white ribbon.

"Oh, my God." She ran to meet them. The entry guard didn't bother stopping her. "Emma, no," she whispered, commanding, pleading.

Dust covered Emma's cheeks and blouse. Blood streaked in thin lines from a gouge on the side of her forehead.

"She's just unconscious," the soldier offered in assurance.

Maddie released a breath. She walked with them to the couch, where he laid Emma down.

All went silent as Kumiko emerged from the crowd. She took one tentative step after another, both hands over her mouth. Kneeling beside Maddie, she looked at Emma with anything but resignation.

"Is there a doctor here?" someone asked.

"I was a nurse cadet," a gal replied, entering the room. She called for a bowl of water and a washcloth. She checked Emma's pulse, her wounds.

The GI explained, "Looked like some kids were tossing the dog around. Right when I drove up, they'd slingshotted rocks that made her fall. Banged her head on a woodpile."

Kumiko lifted her eyes to the nurse. Her hands and voice trembled. "My daughter . . . she go hospital?"

Hovering close by, the director supplied the answer. "I'm afraid that's too dangerous. There's a mob surrounding the place."

Fred Tayama. That's who they were after. Maddie could guess without being told.

"But the minute we settle that problem," Merritt said, "we'll bring Dr. Goto over to care for your daughter."

According to the nurse, there was nothing to do. Nothing but wait and see.

Emma had been right—about the avengers and people getting hurt. As her older sister, her *onēsan,* Maddie should have listened. She'd underestimated the power and insight from a single voice. She went to embrace Emma, to tell her she was sorry, but an unexpected act halted her. Kumiko leaned down and rested her cheek on Emma's waist. She grasped her daughter's fingers and rocked to a silent lullaby.

Maddie's emotions bubbled over, along with her tears. Unable to resist, she dared to lay her hand on Kumiko's shoulder. The woman didn't pull away; she continued to sway, back and forth, whispering what sounded like a prayer. Only when Maddie leaned closer did she make out the Japanese words, repeated over and over like a chant.

"Please, not again. . . . please, not again. . . ."

❦ 45 ❧

They were on a secret, two-plane recon mission with a bonus of
dropping a payload. Since his crew's reassignment to the 5th
Air Force in New Guinea, TJ had grown to miss the luxuries of his
old base. Granted, from the air, the islands they'd been bombing
for the past month could easily pass as Hawaii. Palm trees split up
by mountain ranges. Beaches and rain forests dotting an endless
supply of water. Ironic that whoever did the most damage got to
claim the territory. Congratulations, you blew it to hell. Enjoy your
prize.

Closing in on the targets at last, the airmen moved to their sta-
tions. Before the shark episode, TJ had been pretty fond of their
gatherings in the radio room, a nice place to keep warm. On return
stretches the gunners would sit in there, listening to tunes like
"Take the 'A' Train" and "Don't Fence Me In" on Armed Forces
Radio. Aircrews became like family, against the regulations of military pecking order, and TJ's was no different. Except now, he chose
to be the token black sheep. In spite of the cramped quarters, he
parked himself in the tail as often as possible. He'd rediscovered
the comfort of solitude. Once more, he was on the mound. Like
hand signs during a game, nothing but voices crackling over the intercom connected him to his team.

That's how it should have stayed all along.

Oxygen mask on, a requirement at over ten thousand feet, TJ manned his guns. He scanned the Philippine skies for enemy aircraft. The B-17s were known as Flying Fortresses, and for good reason. That's exactly how they felt. Sturdy and safe. But this, like so much of life, was an illusion. Just last week, those fortresses had escorted three crews from their base to the Promised Land. One plane had cracked up on landing, another exploded mid-air. A third flew through "soup" hiding the broadside of a mountain. Here today, gone tomorrow.

This was the inescapable reality that had guided TJ to mail Jo a short note before his transfer from Kahuku. Several combat missions later—destroying convoys, warships, cargo vessels, and subs—and that blasted letter still clung to his thoughts.

> *Dear Jo,*
> *By now, I'm guessing you've received a stack of letters from me. Please do me this favor—rip them up, burn them to ashes, throw them out. They were just the ramblings of a tired airman who wasn't thinking straight. Truth of it is, they were only sent out by mistake. You're a sweet gal and you deserve to be happy, but with another guy. As harsh as it might sound, I don't care about you enough to have you wait for me. I'm sorry if this hurts you. Just wouldn't be fair to keep leading you on.*
> *TJ*

Imagining her reaction to the cold message had tempted TJ to pitch the page into the trash. He was wild about that girl, no two ways about it.

But then, that was precisely the reason he had to let her go.

"They're rolling out the welcome mat, fellas," Tack warned. "Hold on tight."

Adrenaline heightened TJ's awareness. Antiaircraft guns on Samar Island were peppering the sky with flak. Those impact-bursting shells were every bomber's nightmare.

Cabbie yawed the plane, evading, but one exploded near the port wing. The concussion gave their ship a violent shake. Thick smoke smudged the view. TJ squinted, searching for Zeroes, the notorious Japanese fighter planes. Sweat trailed the inside of his flight suit. A second burst knocked him to the side. Their fuselage was taking a pounding.

He regained his grip on his weapon, heart contracted in his chest. Their lead plane, another B-17, dropped back into his sights; fire blazed in an orange ball from its right inboard engine. Its whole body seemed to pause, suspended like black smoke from flak, before dropping off sideways.

Two . . . three . . . four parachutes plumped into white mushrooms.

"They're shooting at the flyers," Tack yelled. "The bastards are shootin' 'em!" Fury in his voice swept straight into the tail section, where it gripped TJ's body. The airmen drifting downward should have been seen as surrendering. Evidently, Japs respected the Geneva Conventions no more than the fleet they'd decimated at Pearl Harbor.

"Bombs away," the bombardier hollered. Their ship lurched upward upon releasing the demolitions: fragmentation clusters and 100-pound GPs. An airstrip lit up. A fuel-supply depot heaved fire and smoke at the sky. "Bomb-bay doors closing," he announced after the radio operator had verified all bombs were clear. The noise and shaking dimmed. "Let's get our asses home."

Mission completed.

TJ sat back on his seat. Their sleek ol' bird had survived another run. Typically, after nerves settled, this would be chow time. K rations that hadn't frozen from the altitude. Hard candies as backup. Today, though, no food sounded appealing. All TJ could think about were those floating mushrooms being raked with lead.

He let out a breath, one he sucked right back in at the sight of red taillights. "Got Zeroes—two Zeroes—at eight o'clock level!" TJ laid on the trigger, short bursts of .50-cal slugs. The first of the pair peeled to the right. "One's coming around!"

"I see it," Ranieri yelled. Bullets whizzed between the planes.

Focus, TJ told himself. Without the buffer of a squadron's formation, he'd have to focus. Circling a track in the rear of a pickup, while shooting disks that didn't fire back, might not have been the most effective training for combat. Still, he could do this. If he didn't panic, he could do this.

He went after the rear fighter with another spray of gunfire. *Hula Hattie* rocked and shuddered.

"Hang in there, girl," he said, just seconds before the Zero disappeared behind a cloud.

TJ ordered his nerves to take the bench. There wasn't room enough in the tail section for anything but confidence. He'd been here before—down three runs in the ninth inning, full count. All he needed was one good strike, straight into the catcher's mitt. His dad had taught him that; concentrate on one pitch at a time.

The Zero sprang up from its cover. It unloaded machine-gun fire on *Hattie,* piercing a small hole in the skin of her tail. TJ swore the goggled pilot was smirking, and that's all the incentive he needed. Leading the target, TJ opened up with a string of purposeful shots. Soon billowing smoke sailed from the nose, and the little white plane sputtered and dove toward the sea. The bright red dot beneath its wing shrank on descent. Another rising sun had set.

TJ declared the kill over the intercom, then swiveled in his seat, ready to pick off the other Zero. But Ranieri got him first.

Cabbie called out for a status check. Shrapnel had ripped through the navigator's flight pants, yet merely grazed his leg. Somehow, everyone had made it through in one piece.

Once below ten thousand feet, TJ pulled off his mask. Nobody spurted words of celebration. Maybe they were reflecting on the crew that wouldn't be coming back. Maybe, like TJ, they just wanted to go home.

Daylight waned as they soared over a long runway of ocean. All that water was making TJ thirsty. He unplugged his heated flight suit so he could go fetch a drink. Chest-pack parachute in hand, he went to unhook his headset when the co-pilot spoke. Their number-four engine had up and quit. TJ stayed in the tail, waiting to hear all was clear.

Cabbie summoned the engineer to feather the props. Angling the blades would at least cut back air resistance. Three engines could get them through, but four was ideal, and they still had a ways to go.

"Damn gremlins," the co-pilot muttered. The invisible elflike creatures were often blamed for mechanical troubles on warplanes. For the sake of the Allies, TJ hoped gremlins didn't pick sides.

From the cockpit, the pilots and flight engineer traded suggestions, experimented to restart the engine. Then the ship's usual drone quieted a bit. Not in a peaceful way.

"Number three's out!" the engineer reported. The whole wing was dead.

Hattie groaned into a straight plummet. TJ braced his hands against the walls. A boost in the throttle tilted the port wing up and drove them into a sharp circle. Restrained yells ricocheted back and forth on the flight deck—about lowering the RPMs to level them out. Nothing worked. They were losing altitude and speed, two things you didn't want to be short on while in flight.

Do something, TJ thought, even though he himself had no piloting skills. All he had were remnants of wishful thinking, which fled the moment someone shouted, "Prepare to ditch!"

A mix of screams and orders and prayers had to have traveled over the intercom. But strangely, TJ heard nothing in his headset. Instead, an utter calm enveloped him. This was the end. They were falling too fast, being tossed too much, for a clean bailout. They were trapped in their own Fortress, yet somehow, TJ felt indescribable relief.

"I'll see you soon," he whispered to his mother.

And he closed his eyes.

PART FIVE

Look upon the wrath of the enemy.
If thou knowest only what it is to conquer,
and knowest not what it is to be defeated,
woe unto thee.

—Tokugawa Ieyasu, Edo shogun

⤜⤛46⤜⤛

Lane didn't dare touch her. The expression on her face emitted a sheer sense of peace. Though still tanned from the desert sun, Maddie resembled an angel as she slept beside him, oblivious to morning's light filling the bedroom. A quilt rested low on her bare back, her muscles toned since moving to the Illinois farm.

After the incidents at Manzanar, families in jeopardy had been relocated to Cow Creek, a former civilian conservation camp in Death Valley. From newspapers, he'd learned about the protest and the Black Dragons. Maddie's letters added accounts of nurses who'd saved Fred Tayama by hiding him under a bed, and factory workers who had bravely guarded the Moritomos' apartment.

Nothing, however, shocked Lane more than the description of his mother embracing Emma for hours, of the woman's tears spilling when her daughter regained consciousness.

The protected evacuees, sixty-five total, had apparently rallied together to make the abandoned camp livable. Within a few months, the American Friends Committee had helped place them in jobs and homes free of barbed wire, almost entirely in Midwestern states. Until then, everyone—refugees, soldiers, WRA staff—had shared facilities. The same showers, same meal tables. A crisis had torn down the walls between them, proving his father's old saying: *After the rain, the earth hardens.*

Now, after spending two days of his furlough on the farm, Lane had to agree. When it came to the ladies in his family, the ground had become more solid after the storm they'd survived. As had their resolve.

He had seen it in Maddie's eyes last night. Never straying from each other's gaze, they'd made love slowly, as if moving underwater. Newly gained maturity and assuredness had flowed from the woman in his arms. Even her hair seemed to divide over her shoulder in thicker locks. Her sheer beauty could make any soldier in his right mind go AWOL.

What if he did just that—never returned for his orders? By enlisting, he had put his family in jeopardy. Obviously they needed him more than the Army. He wasn't an officer or a skilled combatant. He'd had only the barest bones of basic training. How much difference would he really make in the MIS? Permitting Nisei any vital roles in the Military Intelligence Service would contradict the government's stance of distrust. And one missing Jap GI would hardly constitute a nationwide search.

Why not stay here? He could help out in the fields, wake up beside Maddie every day. . . .

Breaking from the thought, Lane forced himself from the covers. The temptation would be too great if he shared her bed a minute longer.

Quietly he slid into his khaki trousers and white undershirt. On the way to the door, he leaned over to grab his shoes. Noise from his swinging dog tags caused Maddie to stir. He froze and waited, and found relief when she continued to sleep.

He needed her to dream enough for them both.

An enticing aroma led Lane to the kitchen. Crisp-fried bacon wafted from two plates left on the table. Clean dishes on the drying rack indicated he and Maddie were the last to rise. His hunger fully awoken, he shoveled down his meal in record time. Eggs from the chicken coop, butter freshly creamed, muffins so soft he imagined himself eating a cloud made of corn bread.

To wash it all down, he poured a tall cup of joe. He had never been a fan of the stuff until moving to Camp Savage, where hot beverages were a staple. The Minnesota winter had been absurdly cold. And without heavy doses of caffeine, how could he have survived all those grueling exams on military vocabulary? Lessons on an ancient Japanese script had required all-night cramming sessions in the latrine, a study spot exempt from lights-out. He could still see the flash cards flipping.

All of that faded now as he stepped out onto the wraparound porch. The traditional white farmhouse was weathered but warm. He sipped the strong black coffee to keep himself alert. He couldn't afford to get too comfortable.

"Morning, soldier." Mr. Garrett paused while in passing. The farmer's medium paunch matched the roundness of his face, stubbled with salt-and-pepper at age forty. He had on a red checked shirt that showed as much wear as his cowboy hat. "Catch some good shut-eye?" he asked.

"I did, sir. Thank you."

"You find your breakfast okay?" He gestured his shovel toward the screen door. Over his other shoulder, he balanced a dirt-crusted hoe.

"It was delicious," Lane replied. "You're definitely a better cook than the ones in the Army."

"Well, the grits yesterday were mine. But can't take credit for the tasty spread this morning. That was all your ma's doin'."

Deep sleep must have plugged Lane's ears. No way could she have whipped up a meal like that—not only edible, but full of all-American standards. "My mother?" he said.

"Sure as mud." Mr. Garrett scratched his nose with the work glove on his hand and laughed a little. "The gal couldn't make toast or fry an egg when she first got here. Just goes to show ya. Amazing what a person can do when they set their mind to it."

Lane agreed, "It's amazing all right."

"Your sis, actually, is teaching her how to milk a cow today. Might want to pull up a seat. Should be an interesting show." He grinned broadly, the bottom teeth a little crooked.

Lane tried to envision the outlandish scene, but Mr. Garrett's manner struck it right down. Something wasn't sitting well. The guy was being . . . too nice. He'd welcomed in Lane's family, offered to provide room and board in addition to small pay. He even drove Emma to and from school. What did he have to gain? Anymore, white folks in America weren't this generous to Japanese, not without an ulterior motive.

"Well, gotta get back at it," the farmer said. "Only so many hours the Lord grants you in a day. If you need anything, give me a holler."

"You bet." Lane pushed up a smile, which fell as Mr. Garrett turned for the toolshed. Detouring suspicion, Lane centered his thoughts on the meadow, the scents of early spring. When he took another drink, a cynical reflection swayed on the surface. Maybe Mr. Garrett really was a Good Samaritan, a kind widower who'd accepted the female crew to help with cooking and chores, allowing him to better supervise his seasonal field hands.

Given that Lane was due back at the base tomorrow, he certainly hoped that was the case. Just as he hoped Maddie truly enjoyed living here, as she claimed. His aspirations had never included his wife doing manual labor, yet it was a concept he'd have to accept.

As for his mother working a farm, the thought was pretty amusing.

He finished off his mug before journeying into the barn. In a far corner, with their backs to him, Emma and his mother sat beside a cow. They perched on low wooden stools, straw beneath their shoes. The Mahjong socialites in Little Tokyo would have keeled over from the sight.

"See that? You just get in a rhythm," Emma was instructing. "Mr. Garrett says you always sit on the same side. And once the stream gets going, you use all your fingers, like this." Shots alternating from two pink teats rattled the metal pail.

Yuki barked from excitement.

Startled, the cow mooed and shuffled backward, causing milk to squirt at Lane's mother. She gasped and jumped to her feet, hands blocking her face.

"I'm so sorry," Emma said, frantic with regret.

Milk trailed down their mother's shirt, a casual button-down, presumably from the late Mrs. Garrett. Brow creased, she brushed away the drops that hadn't yet soaked in. Ruining another's belongings could provoke shame in their culture.

"Do you want a towel?" Emma asked. Her shoulders hunched the way they always did before a verbal lashing.

Out of habit Lane went to intervene, stopped by his mother's response. Not her words specifically. Her tone—as calming as a sunset.

"*Daijōbu yo,*" she said to the girl, an assurance that all was fine. The lines on her forehead softened with her tendering of a smile. Then she reclaimed her stool and patted her daughter on the back. It was a single touch that lasted a mere instant. Emma's heart, however, melted from the gesture.

Lane knew this for a fact because his did too.

Suddenly, as though sensing his presence, Emma spun around. "*Onīsan,* you're awake!" Her cherubic cheeks had thinned, stretched by time that refused to slow. "And it just so happens that today's your lucky day," she said.

"Oh? How you figure that?"

" 'Cause I'm giving milking lessons for free. Tomorrow I start charging."

"Well, as your brother, I hope I'll at least get a special rate."

"You will." She grinned. "For family, it'll cost you double."

Their mother covered a second smile. She seemed to suppress a giggle as she looked at them both. From that look, a feeling of affection swept through the barn, rising past the rafters. When it settled, Lane found a surety of one thing.

For his father to see her now—to view their family like this—he would have paid any amount in the world.

Gravel crunched out a reminder as Lane exited the barn, of the many thousands who remained imprisoned. Overlooking roads just like these, armed guards continued to survey the communities. Self-contained and trapped. A human ant farm. All Lane could do was hope his military service would help set them free.

"A delivery just came for your wife." Mr. Garrett approached without a smile. He held a sealed envelope marked *Western Union*. "Wasn't sure if you wanted to wake her."

Lane accepted the cable and the farmer walked away, a clear gift of privacy. The luxury had become such a rarity; Lane felt the space around him like a cold spot in a summer pond. So much so, a chill covered his arms.

Or was it from anticipation of the message?

Images of TJ snapped into his mind, followed by Maddie's father.

To protect her, Lane would need to read it first—whether to buffer a tragedy or save her from fretting. Telegrams also brought good news on occasion.

Warily, he opened the envelope. He read the note to the end. Then he read it through again, slower, begging the words to change.

"You should've woken me up," Maddie said sweetly, embracing him from behind. "Unless you're planning to sweep out the horse stalls, in which case I'll gladly keep sleeping."

Lane hesitated in facing her. He wanted to shield her from the pain that would follow. But the news wasn't his to keep.

He gingerly broke from her arms and wheeled around. In denim coveralls, hair gathered for a day of work, she'd never looked happier.

"What's wrong?" she asked.

Before he could answer, she caught sight of the cable. She reached forward a few inches then pulled back, as though touching the page would burn her skin.

"It's . . . about TJ." Lane's explanation ground to a halt, impeded by his own dread and worry. Yet not until he pushed out the rest did he discover how deeply it would cut. "He's missing in action."

ᔄᔄ 47 ᔄᔄ

The rice was moving.

Protein, TJ told himself. He carried his mess kit from the slop line and sat on the dirt. The huge April sun beat down and baked his gruel. Get hungry enough and a guy can force down just about anything. At least today they threw in a piece of steamed sweet potato. Like a cherry on a sundae at Tilly's Diner.

Using two fingers, he scooped the watery meal into his mouth, mixed with tiny pebbles, maggots, and God knew what else. And he did it without complaint. From POWs crazy enough to protest about their measly rations he'd learned to keep his head down and mouth shut. In the middle of an island jungle, it was a wonder the camp cooks could scrounge up any food at all.

"Mm-mm, lookee what I got today," Tack declared. He limped over to his usual spot on the ground. His knee was still healing from the crash three months ago. "Pumpkin pie with a big glob of vanilla ice cream." Flies circled his rice like buzzards in the humid air.

Ever competitive, Ranieri sat next to him and said, "You're getting cheated, pal. I got my mama's world-famous Spaghetti Bolognese. On the side here is a soft chunk of garlic bread, dripping with butter, hot from the oven. And to wash it down, a whole bottle of Chianti." He licked his fingers.

TJ's stomach grumbled thanks to the numskull's description. If not for the body aches from their bamboo sleeping bays, pains that wriggled through his joints like the bedbugs and rodents through their barracks each night, TJ would have moved out of earshot. Instead, he buried his nose in his food and tried to ignore the dopes.

"You know what I miss the most?" Tack slurped from his bowl. "Creamed corn and honey biscuits. What I wouldn't do for a basket of honey biscuits."

"You buggers can keep the lot of it." A British airman closed his eyes and smiled dreamily. His grimy uniform hung like oversized rags on his thinning, barefooted frame, same as most prisoners. Dirt stained his skin, same as *every* prisoner. "All I need," he said, "is a big plate of blood pudding like my mum makes it."

"Blood pudding?" Ranieri looked disgusted. "You Limeys all vampires, or what?"

"It's a sausage," the guy clarified.

"No," Ranieri told him, "it's repulsive."

"Ah, you Yanks don't know what you're missing."

Tack turned to TJ. "How about you, Kern?"

"Don't bother," Ranieri muttered to Tack, who continued regardless.

"Tell us what you got there for dinner."

TJ's mumbled reply didn't vary from any other day. "Rice."

Ranieri shook his head. "What'd I tell ya." He smacked a mosquito on his arm. "A waste of breath every time."

TJ hated anything that proved the guy right, but not enough to participate in group bonding. Caring about another fellow only meant setting up for a fall. After the plane crash, seeing half their crew floating dead among burning debris, TJ should have remembered that. But their crisis had interfered, and he'd found himself working as a team with those who'd made it into the raft. He'd even given a good amount of his water rations to the injured bombardier—for little point. The guy didn't last two days.

When the remaining four crawled onto the shore of some Philippine island, they'd deliriously traded congratulations and shoulder pats, only to be captured minutes later by occupying Japs. On his knees, TJ had watched Cabbie, the father of young twins, beheaded for his officer's rank. For a culture that viewed the Emperor as a god and valued honor above all, those who surrendered as "cowards" and worshipped the Lord Almighty were an abomination.

Yet they kept the inmates alive. Who knew why? For duty maybe. For kicks. So they could bat them around like catnip whenever the mood struck. TJ's crew had passed through two other prison camps before settling here, and nothing was different. POWs at each of them, to lessen the frequency of being pounced on, made a habit of studying their captors. TJ didn't bother with anything past the basics. He despised them all equally.

"Happy ain't lookin' too good." Tack motioned his chin toward the pudgy guard. Among those dubbed Tojo's Seven Dwarfs—wielding samurai swords rather than pickaxes—this one was known for his permanent grin.

"It's that moonshine he drinks," the Brit said. "Could topple a bull from the smell of it."

"It's not moonshine," Tack explained. "It's *sake*." He'd learned this from giving the jovial guard discreet English lessons. Payment was cigarettes and bits of food, which Tack always shared with others.

Ranieri suddenly grinned. "Two smokes says Happy loses his lunch out here in the open."

"You're on." A redheaded GI beside him perked. "Guy drinks like my old man. No way it's coming back up."

Curiosity prodded TJ to glance at the guard, who did look more green than yellow. Last night's talent show must have given him cause to indulge. He and the other guards had watched the POWs recite jokes, impersonate stars like Bogey and Jimmy Durante, belt out songs—only one cut short by booing—and put on a Three Stooges number. TJ was amazed the camp commander had permitted the prisoners any relief from their reality.

But then, that's why they called him "Looney." Not for being a crackpot. For being unpredictable.

At that moment, as though conjured from TJ's thoughts, the

regal-looking commander strode into the roll call area. His angular features appeared etched in stone. An interpreter called for the four-hundred-some prisoners to stand and bow.

Grumpy was on the ready with his bamboo stick. Above his toothbrush mustache, pleasure filled the guard's expression as he pummeled POWs who took too long. TJ hustled to his feet, glued his gaze to the ground. Eye contact with Looney would lose you a head. Eye contact with Grumpy would earn a beating so brutal, death would be a treat.

Shined to a perfect gloss, Grumpy's black boots approached. The closer they stomped, the more TJ's left shoulder blade throbbed, as if his muscles were reliving the last daily whupping from the jackass.

"Hayaku, hayaku!" Grumpy shrilled nearby. He kicked a mess kit away from a skeletal inmate, who reached for the spilled rice. A reflex, no doubt. Just like the sharp twinge of TJ's instant fist— which instantly drew the guard over. A potential challenge must have offered more appeal than the pitiful crouching prisoner.

TJ dropped his fingers with head bent, trying to remain one of the numbers, though still expecting a pounding. But Grumpy just stood there, a blatant dare to glance up. And TJ wanted to. God, how he wanted to push back with a hateful glare, right before throwing an uppercut at that sadistic face.

It was a tempting idea. If nothing else, just to see the guy's initial surprise. . . .

Another pair of boots appeared. They belonged to Dopey, the seemingly mute guard. He stopped next to Grumpy. A bad sign. TJ doubted his current ability to take them both on.

A needless worry, as it turned out. Dopey simply tapped Grumpy on the arm and pointed toward the small wooden stage. Their commander was ascending the steps. The two guards dispersed to their assigned spots at the end of the row. TJ didn't know whether to feel relieved or shortchanged.

Over the faint trill of tropical birds, the commander shouted an order in Japanese. Two Marines were marched along the barbed-wire fence and into the arena. Blood trailed down their faces, their torn dungarees. Guards tied their hands up and pulled out thick bamboo clubs. The Marine with an eye swollen shut struggled to break free; the other stared, unseeing, having lost his will to fight.

Looney's translated words were forebodingly simple. "Try to escape, and *this* will be you."

For the infinite minutes that spanned their beatings, TJ's mind looped the first song that came to him. "Take Me Out to the Ball Game." He replaced the sounds of screaming and bones breaking with verses of peanuts and Cracker Jack, the memory of a bat smacking a ball.

When there was nothing left but limp shells of men, Looney ordered them cut down.

And then they were shot.

The POWs bowed to the exiting commander. As the corpses were dragged to a mass grave, the audience returned to their seats on the dirt. Tentative murmurs gradually grew, like a sprinkling toward a drizzle, until the horror seemed never to have happened.

TJ picked up his mess kit. He held the sweet potato he'd saved for last, unable to eat. His stomach twisted into vicious knots—not just from revulsion that this had become normalcy, but over his shameful gratitude for being alive.

∞48∞

In the barn, Maddie yelled through the wire mesh, "Throw out a handful!"

Kumiko hugged the bucket to her chest and shrieked for help. *"Chotto tasukete!"* Feathers flew as chickens pecked for grain around her shuffling shoes.

When Emma started for the coop, Maddie stopped her. "It's okay. Let her do it." Then she told Kumiko, "They don't want to hurt you. Just stay calm." She spoke more sternly. "Toss the feed *away* from you."

The lesson sank in at last. Kumiko began to fling the cracked corn, causing the chickens to scatter. She grabbed another fistful and spread out their meal. Confidence eased into her face, lifted her chin. This was the Kumiko Moritomo that Maddie recognized. Though with a softened edge.

"That's enough now," Maddie called to her. Kumiko appeared to be enjoying the activity a little too much. "Really, that's enough. You don't want them to pop!"

Reluctantly, Kumiko exited the coop.

Maddie held out her hand to take the pail. She wondered if she would have to pry it from the woman's grip. "I'll let you feed them tomorrow, I swear."

As Kumiko surrendered the bucket, Emma snorted a giggle. Surprisingly, her mother joined in with a soft laugh. It was a lovely sound, a braid of happiness Maddie used to weave with her own family, with her brother.

At the recollection of TJ's disappearance, her smile slipped away.

The Army had sent additional letters, but their investigations failed to produce any updates good or bad. Thus, Maddie relied upon nightly prayers and faith that intuitively she would sense any devastating loss—about Lane, too, whose deployment came sooner than expected. Something told her she would know, in her heart, if either of them were gone.

"Mr. Garrett's back," Emma exclaimed.

Maddie listened and barely caught the rumbling of his truck traversing the long driveway past the cornfields. Impressive that the girl had heard it. But then, Emma always did have an ability to hear what others didn't.

"Mother, can I ride the tractor with him? Please, can I?"

Kumiko only hesitated a moment before nodding. "*Demo,* be careful, *ne?*" she hollered after Emma, who was already leading Yuki in a dash from the barn.

"How about we start on supper?" Maddie suggested.

Kumiko answered with a smile, which fell at the sound of Emma's yell.

"Maddie, come quick!"

The dog's frantic barking magnified the pull that brought Maddie outside. "What is it?"

Emma pointed toward three pickup trucks snaking up the drive, clouds of dust billowing like fear. Things had been calm on the farm since their family's arrival. No protests, no visitors. Maddie, however, wasn't naïve enough to believe the Midwest was immune to racism. If the West Coast wanted Japanese residents out—even neighbors they had grown up with—why would people in Illinois be any different? Separated by vast acres of farmland, perhaps hatred just took longer here to gain momentum.

"Get in the barn," Maddie said. With Mr. Garrett in town and no field hands in sight, the three of them were on their own. "Stay there till I say," she commanded.

Emma ushered Yuki and her mother inside, and Maddie took off running for the house. She retrieved the remaining shotgun from the rack above the fireplace. The barrel felt cold, the weapon heavy. Swallowing her nerves, she shook out casings from a box stored in a nearby drawer. She loaded the shells as Mr. Garrett had shown her—lessons meant for fending off coyotes. Then she emerged from the house to find the trucks still approaching. In the lead pickup rode two men—one older, one younger—with a shotgun racked behind their heads.

Maddie clenched her weapon diagonally across her chest, hoping to God she wouldn't have to use it. The trucks rolled to a stop on the graveled road, just as Kumiko reappeared. The woman held a rusty hoe, all too reminiscent of the shovel Maddie had carried during the riot.

Go hide, Maddie was about to insist, but Kumiko's expression said an objection would be pointless. Besides, Maddie had to admit, she felt stronger with the woman standing so clearly on her side.

The driver of the first truck stepped out from his door. More than six feet tall with a mountain man's build, he gripped the hips of his overalls.

"Something I can do for you?" Maddie kept the tremble from her voice.

He didn't look the least bit intimidated. Why should he be? Between him and the teenage boy, plus two other couples, they far outnumbered Maddie's gang. "I gather we heard right," he said, referencing Kumiko with his chin. "That the Garrett farm is housing a couple Japanese from the camps."

Maddie edged her finger toward the trigger, and gave a single nod.

"Well, then," he said. "We've come to welcome them to the neighborhood."

An old newspaper article passed through her mind. Below the photo of a burning cross, the caption had read: *A Southern lynch mob welcomed their new neighbors.*

Just then, one of the gals moved closer. Middle-aged, she wore a faded shirt and trousers, her hair sleeked into a ponytail. Her eyes shone soft and warm, like the afternoon sunlight filtering through the fields. "If it's a bad time, we could certainly come back. Or if you'd rather, we could just leave the goodies Jean here brought for ya."

The other woman, more proper in a long skirt and blouse, held up a basket of food.

Maddie sighed inside. With a hint of embarrassment, she relaxed her grasp on the gun. "Sorry. You can never be too careful."

"Oh, we understand." The first woman dismissed the concerns with a flick of her hand. "These parts are brimming with crazies. I ought to know. Been raised here all my life."

Maddie smiled and patted Kumiko's arm, a sign they were safe. But as it turned out, her mother-in-law didn't need reassurance.

"Please," Kumiko told the group with a slight bow of her head, gesturing to the house. "Please, come."

The post-supper chatter had just died down when Mr. Garrett uncorked his homebrewed liquor. Ida, the ponytailed spitfire, poured a glass for Kumiko, who sat with her on the couch. Maddie could sense a struggle between propriety and courtesy before Kumiko ultimately accepted.

"To our new neighbors," Ida said, lifting her glass. "May the Lord watch over you and keep you in His care."

Kumiko stifled a choke on the first swallow, then drank another sip that went down smoother. Maddie let the jug pass on by, her body a bit tired and unsettled from the day's yo-yoing excitement. But nothing kept her from enjoying Mr. Garrett's tunes on the harmonica. She clapped in time with the others while he puffed away. Occasionally he misplaced a note or rushed a phrase, but tonight all that mattered was the joy the melodies evoked. Even Jean and Merle, the quiet couple from Belknap—who Ida claimed had never quite recovered from the drowning of their little boy two decades ago—began to sing along, swept away by the festivities and laughter. By music that flowed from Mr. Garrett's soul.

Music had that power, Maddie now recalled. It could bring back memories or, for the bliss of a moment, make you forget.

When Kumiko came to her feet, Ida's nephew let out a whoop. "Looks like someone's got a song for us."

Kumiko raised a palm to decline and tried to explain she was only getting some water. By the gentle sway of her legs, she appeared to need a tall glass, having had her fill of Mr. Garrett's concoction.

"Aw, don't be shy," Ida urged.

Kumiko shook her head. "I know only Japanese song," she said bashfully. "My voice—no good."

"We're no opera stars ourselves," Ida pressed. "C'mon. We'd love to hear anything at all."

"Mother, sing for us." Emma glimmered with hope, and in no time, the rest of the room joined in on the appeal. They didn't stop until Kumiko relented.

It went so quiet that Maddie could hear the prelude of crickets through the closed windows.

Slowly, Kumiko closed her eyes. Then from her mouth came a Japanese folk tune that drifted out in a sullen tone. The lyrics grew steadily in volume, as did the grace of her syllables.

Emma whispered the translation to Maddie, seated on the rug beside her. She related verses of standing on a temple's bridge: during Momiji, the season of viewing leaves, the trees in Kyoto blaze red and gold; their youthful green is gone, changed with no choice; the branch yearns to hold on, but a cold wind blows and the last leaf falls; a mere reflection on water remains, a memory of red and gold.

After a long beat of stillness, Kumiko opened her eyes. Looking startled by her surroundings, she wiped her moistened cheeks. The audience didn't clap or speak, nothing to disturb the transcendence she'd formed over them like a dome.

Maddie glanced around, in awe that hers weren't the only eyes welling. Songs of such sadness evidently needed no translation.

Kumiko bent her head and rasped, "I am sorry," and with that, she fled the room.

* * *

Maddie debated on allowing Kumiko her space. Japanese people, she had learned, preferred to deal with issues in private. Yet so had Maddie's father and brother, and both had ended up out of reach.

So she searched the house and porch, the barn and the shed. Finally she spotted her by a crooked fence bordering the freshly planted field. Maddie approached with caution and rested her elbows, just like Kumiko's, on the top rail.

For several minutes, they stared wordlessly at the luminescent moon. The fact that the woman didn't tell her to leave seemed an invitation to stay.

"I was arranged to marry—when fourteen year old." Kumiko spoke softly, her gaze straight ahead. "Kensho Demura was true love for me. He write letter, say, *We go away, you not marry Nobu.* But in Japan, family first. Family always first."

Maddie concentrated on the story, rather than the shock of how many English words Kumiko actually knew.

"Nobu get work in America, so I go. Wife always go. No ask question," she said. "Later, my heart begin to forget Kensho. When I have Takeshi—Lane, *ne?*—I try be happy, have good family. We have new baby . . . here." She gestured to her stomach.

At the pregnancy reference, Maddie's mind went to Emma. Then she recalled Kumiko's mysterious phrase, from the night her daughter lay unconscious at Manzanar—*please, not again*—and Maddie braced herself for more.

"To make good luck for baby, must wear *hara-obi.* White belt for mother. Always start to wear on 'dog day' in fifth month. Dog have puppy very easy, healthy, so must be 'dog day.' *Demo* . . . I so tired, I forget. Next day, I hurry, put on belt. Doctor say, inside me baby good. But I have much worry. We go doctor many time. Always he tell me, '*Daijōbu,* everything fine.'

"*Sorekara* . . . one night very late, I not feel baby move. I tell Nobu, 'We go doctor.' He say, 'Kumiko, baby just sleeping. We wait for morning.' I want to be good wife. I say, '*Hai*—okay.' In morning, I wake up, but . . ." Her voice strained and lowered. "*Demo,* too late. Baby die."

Maddie gripped the rail as she watched Kumiko's mouth go taut, an attempt to retain her composure.

"Nobu very sorry. He say we have more baby. But I say *no*. He try to make better, say one day we go back Kyoto. But work at Sumitomo very busy, too busy for us to go." Kumiko paused briefly before continuing. "Many years pass, and I have baby inside. Very hard I try. I think, *Everything be okay*. Then . . . she born *kugatsu yokka*. Fourth day, ninth month."

"Emma," Maddie realized. The girl's birthday was September fourth.

"In Japan, kanji—writing of four and nine—this bad luck. Very bad. It mean death, and pain."

The sum of four and nine, unlucky thirteen in America, wasn't lost on Maddie. Nor was the cause of Kumiko's initial resistance to Emma. "You were afraid something would happen to her," Maddie concluded, "even after she was born healthy."

Kumiko gave an almost imperceptible nod. "Many year I think, Kamisama make mistake, soon He take her back to heaven. Many year I blame Nobu for baby, for leaving Japan. For life without Kensho. *Demo atode . . .* I see Takeshi and you. I see you marry. I think, *Why I not more strong? Why I not follow heart?* I see you and I have anger. Not because my husband is Nobu. Nobu very good man. Always give much for me, for children. No. I blame only Kumiko. For weakness." She angled her face toward Maddie and asked, *"Wakatta?"*

Maddie meant to nod yes, that she understood. However, taken aback by the confession, all she could do was stare.

Kumiko looked away before Maddie found her voice.

"You, Mrs. Moritomo, are *not* weak. In fact, you're one of the strongest people I've ever met. Think about what you've been through. Moving to some country thousands of miles away, to a life so different from what you'd known."

Kumiko shifted her weight, a suggestion of leaving, and Maddie bristled. She didn't want her to go. Yet she couldn't think of anything to keep the woman there—except a confession of her own.

In comparison, Maddie's burden now seemed minor. Nonetheless, she forced it out swiftly so as not to lose her courage. "When I auditioned for Juilliard last year, I failed. Halfway through a piece, my hands just stopped. It can happen to even the best students, from the pressure.

"What nobody knows is that I did it on purpose. I was afraid of leaving my family and home. I was afraid that . . . that I might lose myself by letting them go." Reflecting on the riots and Black Dragons, the challenge of fitting in, the opposition from Lane's mother, Maddie was struck by the irony of just how far away she had landed.

Kumiko said nothing in reply. In the silence, Maddie wondered if she had divulged too much. But then their eyes met, and from the exchange came a flicker of warmth that spread through Maddie's chest.

"We go back," Kumiko said gently. "Company waiting."

Maddie nodded, agreeing with a smile.

As they walked together, toward the glowing windows of the house, an owl called out to the moon. The sound channeled Maddie's thoughts to a bird of another kind. Featured in Kumiko's paintings, most of which camp officials had salvaged, were sparrows whose symbolism now became clear. Alone and grounded, they were creatures with wings that had forgotten how to fly.

They were pictures of Kumiko.

They were Maddie.

❦ 49 ❧

The only good Jap is a dead Jap.

Since arriving on the Aleutian Islands, just off the Alaskan coast, Lane had heard the phrase muttered by plenty of guys in the 7th Infantry Division. It was no wonder so few enemies were delivered to the team of ten Nisei linguists for interrogation. Assuming TJ was alive, hopefully his Japanese captors found more value in gathering prisoners.

The possibility to the contrary, however, ravaged Lane's sleep for yet another night.

On his cot, he wrestled with his wool blankets in search of a comfortable position. Alternating snores from eight of his roommates—the ninth was posted on a nearby ship, intercepting radio transmissions—wasn't helping.

Sure, the pain Maddie would suffer from losing more of her family troubled him. But in truth, that wasn't the core of his unrest. It was the realization that his last talk with TJ, packed with bitterness and spite, might have been their final one.

He flipped over and back before giving up. Insomnia won the battle.

Wrapped in his blankets, he clicked on his flashlight and padded across the Quonset hut. The damp, bone-chilling weather had made their three weeks here feel like three months. Or maybe it was the boredom, inherent in being stuck in the rear echelon.

He sat down, thumbed through a fresh stack of *LIFE* magazines sent by a linguist's mother. The covers spoke for themselves. *VICTORY OF BISMARCK SEA. SOLDIER'S FAREWELL,* featuring the added bonus of a lieutenant kissing his sweetheart good-bye.

Lane tossed that issue aside. As if he needed a reminder of leaving loved ones behind, just so others could achieve victories he'd personally never see.

If your mom really wants to keep our morale up, one of the fellas had said about the magazines, *she'd mail us some pinups next time.*

Lane had laughed along at the remark. What he'd actually been thinking was that no pinup could hold a candle to Maddie. Even now, his pulse picked up at the memory of holding her, of sharing a bed on his last night at the farm. Perhaps he should have stayed. . . .

Second-guessing made for a pointless pastime. He opted for stationery and a pencil. As he did every other day without fail, he penned his wife a letter, ever careful with his wording. Treading the line between his doubts and honesty was a slippery task.

May 29, 1943

My dearest Maddie,

 Not much to say tonight except that I miss you terribly. I reread your latest batch of letters after chow this morning. You'd think they'd help me miss you less, but I have to admit they do just the opposite. That said, don't you dare think about sending any fewer! With the bleak tundra here, the sun never in sight, a post at mail call is the best source of brightness a guy could hope for.

 Thanks for the update about my mother and sister. I'm sure glad to know Ida and Mr. Garrett are treating you all so kindly. Please tell them I'm grateful. Also, tell Em to keep up with her letter writing to Papa, no matter how short or censored his replies may be. Hearing from family, a sign you haven't been forgotten, means more than she could ever know.

 I received another letter from Dewey. He doesn't

have anything to share about TJ yet, but said he'll keep
nosing around. Like you said, we have plenty of reasons
to keep our hopes up. Regardless of what's happened
between your brother and me, please know I'm praying
daily for his safe return.
Best close now. Morning will be here before long.
Sending my love to all of you.
Yours forever,
Lane

On the envelope he jotted her address and set the post aside for censoring. Just writing to Maddie made him feel better.

He rose from his chair, knocking something to the ground. One of his roommates rolled over, but all kept snoozing. Lane directed his flashlight downward and onto the splayed book. A diary awaiting translation. Journals from fallen Japanese soldiers made up the extent of his assignments. Those, and harmless letters confiscated from an island resident with relatives in Kyushu. If any significant documents were floating around out there, the GIs were ignorantly pilfering them for souvenirs.

Lane retrieved the diary, its front cover smeared with blood. A dried cherry blossom peeked from inside. A wife's gift, he guessed. A reminder that the soldier once had family and friends, a home and a life. Japanese scrawling filled the pages, a sample of Lane's ancestry. If his mother had gotten her wish of remaining in Kyoto, this keepsake could have been his.

He shut the book tight and shoved it beneath the magazine pile. The deeper he buried the connection, the better.

As he turned for his cot, a muffled yell caught his ear. He went still, instinctively listening for sounds of battle. A silly notion. Although the Japanese were ferociously defending Attu, territory they'd occupied for close to a year, being vastly outnumbered by the Americans limited their movement.

"What's going on out there?" a roommate grumbled.

Another voice boomed from outside. It couldn't be later than 0400. Were they running a nighttime drill?

Lane peeked out to investigate. A wall of cold met his face, but the shiver that ran through him came from the sight. Guys were emerging from their tents in a frenzy. Engineers, clerks. An NCO was distributing rifles to them all.

"Grab a weapon!" someone yelled. "It's a banzai attack!"

It took Lane a few seconds to comprehend. The claim meant Japanese soldiers were charging en masse.

"How far are they?" he shouted to anyone who might answer, then grabbed the arm of a skinny cook hastening past. "I said, how far?"

The guy looked scattered. "Cap'n says—he says they're past the Ridge, closing in on our hill." To reach Engineer Hill, the Japanese would first be plowing through the hospital tents below.

As the cook tore away, a GI appeared at the hut entrance. He was one of their group's bodyguards. "Everyone up! We gotta get you fellas outta here."

Lane spun around to find most of his roommates already rising from their sleeping bags. Their assigned guard didn't waste time explaining, using clipped words to usher them from the command post.

"What about the patients?" Lane demanded in stride, throwing on his overcoat and helmet.

"My job's to get you guys to safety. Now, move it." His statement wasn't heartless; the treachery of what could happen to a captured Japanese American GI was no secret. *Save a bullet for yourself* went as the unspoken rule. Of course, more relevant to the Army was the linguists' potential value. They could prove to be priceless weapons if given a real chance.

But would that chance ever come?

Could that moment have arrived?

Lane fell back, discreetly, to the rear of the fleeing huddle. They were koi swimming upstream against the current of soldiers creating a defensive line. Thick fog aided Lane's goal of dissolving into the shadows. From a snow patch on the ground, he snagged a rifle—he'd forgotten his own—and confirmed it was loaded. He pulled his helmet low to hide his face and ran.

As he approached the hospital clearing station, screams layered the night air. Shots were blasting inside the first pyramidal tent. All three were boldly marked with the Red Cross symbol, but patients were clearly being attacked. Wounded GIs, lying helpless in their beds.

Terror coated Lane's throat, his mind. He crouched behind a withered tree. A wave of Japanese soldiers snaked toward the second tent. Lane took aim, and he fired.

No discharge.

He tried again—the M1 was jammed!

The men disappeared into the tent. More screams, more shots. Lane squeezed the weapon's barrel to his chest. An urge for survival bit down on him, yet he summoned his strength, battled the instinct to race away. He had to do something before they killed them all.

A Japanese soldier materialized through the mist. He was marching toward the last ward. Lane ducked as additional enemy flew from the other tents. They rushed past and swarmed up the hill. But the lone soldier continued on his path, and through the door.

Defying all rational thought, Lane launched himself forward. "Get out here, you bastard! You coward! You filthy rat!" He yelled in English, in Japanese, anything to draw him into the open. Lane was two yards from the entrance when the soldier resurfaced.

With the butt of his M1, Lane took a swing. The man blocked him with his bayonet, a mere blade fastened to a rock, and immediately jabbed back. Pain sliced through Lane's forearm as he dropped his rifle. Adrenaline thrust him onto the guy, a tackle to the hardened ground. The bayonet fell free as they scrambled for control.

Finally Lane's hands reached the soldier's throat and fastened like a vise. Tighter, tighter, he had to squeeze tighter. The man fought against the trembling grip, fought for a breath—until something blinded Lane. A handful of dirt. He blinked fast and hard, but the stinging loosened his grasp just enough for the guy to slip free and punch Lane in the face.

Toppling over, Lane felt his helmet fly off. In an instant, the soldier regained his spear; he hollered, drawing back to strike, before their gazes caught hold. The man froze. Lane could see the confusion in his eyes, a sudden recognition: The GI he was about to kill reflected his own image.

But the scare didn't last. When the guy lifted his blade again, Lane's arms rose in defense. Then a shot pierced the air, ripped through the soldier's chest. His body wavered for a moment and collapsed onto Lane. The weight of death pressed down like a mountain.

Lane worked to wriggle free. Strengthened by panic, he succeeded in shoving him off.

"You okay?" asked an approaching sergeant.

Lane managed a nod.

A couple of GIs hurried into the wards. Lane rose slowly and followed into the third tent. Motionless mounds covered the beds. No wisps of breaths, no sign of hope. Had he somehow been too late?

The sergeant spoke to the room, announced that all the Japs were battling up on the hill. Gradually the patients came to life. A doc lit a candle. Below the lineup of cots, several other GIs rolled out from hiding. To stay alive, they had pretended to be dead.

Lane stepped forward and his boot hit a bump. A patient lay sprawled on the floor. Leaning down, Lane tapped the guy's shoulder. He offered assurance that it was safe to rise, just as he spotted a small hole in the fellow's temple. A rivulet dripped from the opening.

The captain paused beside him. "Stray bullet," he explained, then plunged into dealing out orders.

Though still dazed, Lane obeyed, functioning robotically. He searched the other tents for survivors, aided the wounded, scoured for salvageable supplies.

Suddenly, an explosion boomed in the distance, trailed by another, and another. A series of detonating grenades. Lane did his best to filter out the noise, the moaning from men around him.

A private soon stumbled into the tent. His eyes underscored the vacancy, the disbelief, in his voice. "They're gone. Every last one of 'em . . . . gone."

The report gripped the room. Had the Japanese wiped out the Americans' defense? Or was it the other way around?

"What happened?" The captain cracked the quiet. "Answer me, Private."

"It was the Japs, sir. When the last of them were surrounded, they stood together. Just pulled the pins and . . . blew themselves up."

Despite how much Lane knew about his heritage, such fanaticism shook his core. As did the possibility that the Allies could actually lose. How do you beat an opponent willing to do anything to win, and who isn't afraid to die? A country that fully believes that the power of their god won't allow their defeat?

"Your arm," a doctor said, pointing to the cut on Lane's sleeve. Blood soaked the fabric. "You'd better get a wrap on that."

Lane had forgotten about his wound and only now felt it throbbing. As he waited for a bandage, he gazed down at his jacket, at the mixture of blood—from himself and the Japanese soldier—that would forever mar his uniform.

With dread he realized: He wasn't sure which blood was his, and which was the enemy's.

TJ stared out the open-air window, every nerve bundled. "What're they waiting for?"

"Shuddup, will ya?" a soldier in their barrack shouted in a hush.

"You're gonna get us all killed," said another. "Go to sleep."

It was at least an hour past curfew. The Jap guards executed POWs all the time without cause, but they preferred a reason. Felt more justified maybe.

TJ had been trying for shut-eye. For the past few nights, he'd actually caught some decent if fractured hours. Tonight, though, he couldn't lower his lids without visualizing Vince Ranieri. The guy had been caught stealing soap. Not a whole bar, just a lousy sliver. He'd been beaten, then rope-tied to a pole, left to face the heat without water, the swarms of mosquitoes eager to poison his blood.

During mealtimes and roll call, prisoners had pretended not to notice him hanging like a wind sock. TJ too had kept his gaze down. Ranieri had asked for it, hadn't he? Besides, it could have been worse. In three days' time, Grumpy was supposed to cut him down. That had been the announcement Commander Looney made to the camp. Yet dusk had fallen on day four, and still Ranieri remained on display.

The guy wasn't a buddy anymore. TJ reminded himself of this as he willed his body to lie on his cot. Rain poured over the thatched roof. He trained his mind to block out all but the jungle's rustling leaves. His memory lapsed back to his mother knitting a scarf, to summer barbecues and playing tenpins at Jensen Rec. He jumped to another day, saw Maddie and his father at the dinner table, laughing over some semi-clean joke TJ had learned in the dugout. And of course he saw Jo, the peach of a girl he still wrote letters to in his mind. The one he'd lied to by saying he didn't care.

Pain poked through the thoughts. A sore had formed near TJ's hip from his bamboo bed. Its deep sting returned him to their reeking hellhole. He twisted to find comfort as the sailor above him ground out a moan. Another prisoner scratched incessantly at fleas. A series of *tick-tick-ticks* sounded from a rat scrambling for traction.

Again, TJ tried to retreat into his past, but an image yanked him back. Ranieri. Without looking, he could see the shadowed figure bound in the rain. Something told him the airman wouldn't last out there till morning. He couldn't say why exactly. He just knew, and that knowledge would eat at him all night—maybe forever—if he didn't act.

"Damn it."

TJ jumped to his feet. He reached below the Brit's cot and snagged the sharpened rock hidden away. The guy started to object, but TJ was already halfway down the stilted barrack. POWs sat up, tapping each other awake. Free entertainment.

He stormed into the rain and splashed through the mud. Didn't so much as peek at a raised guard tower. When he got to Ranieri, he went straight to sawing the ropes. Thick and damp, they took all the strength his worn body could muster. Ranieri raised his head a fraction, his lip split and blistered. The night's darkness concealed most of the damage he'd endured. Maybe he'd still die tomorrow, or the day after that. But he wasn't going to die like this.

"Yamenasai!" The far-off voice alerted TJ that he'd been spotted, yet he didn't stop. Just one rope to go. He continued as though he were invincible, a ghost. You couldn't kill a ghost.

The last threads fought him until giving way. TJ reached for Ranieri, the bundle of bones that was once a larger-than-life Italian gunner, and barely caught his torso. Through the guy's rib cage, TJ could feel a heartbeat clinging to its slow, stubborn rhythm.

"You're gonna be all right," TJ told him, wanting to believe it.

Ranieri blinked heavily as raindrops washed his face, soaked his rags. He opened his mouth to speak, but the conversation died with a blow to TJ's head. It was like something exploded in the back of his brain. When he opened his eyes, he was staring into a vertical pool of muddy water. Drizzle bounced from left to right. The world had tipped onto its side.

A black boot came into view. It connected with his gut, stealing his air. In a haze, he found himself being dragged by two guards flanking his arms. Then they righted his body, ordering him to stand. He strained to recognize the building in front of him. The camp commander's barrack.

There was only one way this was going to end.

Minutes later, Looney stepped outside, escorted by Dopey holding up an umbrella. The commander wore a kimono, light-weight with a knotted belt. His pajamas. He was like a nun caught without a habit. And this, more than the imminent punishment, captivated TJ. So much so, he nearly forgot to bow.

Although why bother? Whether TJ would be off'd or not wasn't in question. It was a sure thing, which oddly made it refreshing.

Yeah, fear was there; it was always there. Yet the feeling of nearing a finish line was stronger. A restful reward just steps away.

Grumpy rambled on to the commander, no doubt a recap of TJ's stupidity. Once Grumpy was finished, a whisk of metal sounded through the rain. A samurai sword being unsheathed.

Two hands shoved TJ onto his knees. His neck tensed, his eyes closed. His trousers drank up the water as he prepared for Cabbie's fate. Images darted through his mind. Portrait drawings from a high school textbook, of Anne Boleyn and Marie Antoinette. Both were beheaded, just like TJ soon would be. A royal death wasn't such a bad way to go.

He held his breath, gripped the sides of his trousers. At least it would be quick. He waited for the impact . . . that . . .

Never came.

Cracking an eyelid, he discovered the commander, a sword in

one hand, speaking quietly to Dopey. Miraculously, the mute guard had something to say.

What could they possibly be yakking about? Taking bets on how many swings it would take?

Then Looney declared an order and handed off his weapon. Two guards lifted TJ by his underarms, marching him away. Relief fluttered inside as a reflex, promptly trampled by terror. Death was a welcome visitor—not torture.

"What are you gonna do?" TJ yelled, struggling uselessly against their grips. Eyes glinted from the windows of barracks. A sea of men watched him go. "Where are you taking me?" He screamed loud enough for the entire island to hear.

Nobody answered.

∽51∽

The blur of her surroundings gradually sharpened into walls, a ceiling. Maddie tried to sit up, but nausea rolled over her and flattened her down.

"Take it easy," a woman said. "Here, have some water."

Maddie felt a hand behind her head and a glass touching her bottom lip. She sipped the cool liquid, then sank into the cushioned surface. She was on a couch, but not in her house. Mr. Garrett's farm, she remembered. And perched on the coffee table beside her was her dearest friend.

"Jo, you're here. . . ." Memories of the gal surprising her with a visit came floating through the mist of her mind. "What happened?"

"You fainted on the porch. Guess my news about going pro was too much to handle," she said with a smile.

Going pro?

Oh, yes . . . . baseball. A girls' baseball league. "You were telling me about tryouts—in Chicago," Maddie recalled. "About you playing for the . . . the . . ."

"Kenosha Comets."

"Right. Kenosha." The puzzle was reassembling. "How long can you stay?"

"Only till tonight. We're up against Rockford tomorrow, but with you so close, I couldn't pass up a chance to see ya."

"My gosh, a major leaguer." Maddie sighed. "I'm so proud of you." As she edged herself up, Jo touched her arm.

"Don't push it now. Mr. Garrett is out getting the doc."

"Doctor? That's silly, I'm fine. It's this summer humidity. Plus, I've been fighting a stomach bug."

"Well, he's gonna swing by all the same." Jo handed her the glass of water.

Maddie obliged by finishing it off despite her discomfort of being fussed over. "So what's with the new getup?" she asked, diverting.

Jo glanced down and replied with a sneer. "Charm school. Mr. Wrigley's got it in his head that ticket sales depend on us looking like debutantes. Heaven forbid we don't raise our pinkies high enough when wiggling a bat." She blew out a puff of air. "I guarantee they never made Ted Williams walk around balancing a book on his head. And don't get me started on the dresses we have to wear while actually playing."

Maddie pursed her lips to contain her laugh, but a portion leaked through. "Anyway, you look lovely." Although she meant it, the sight would take some getting used to. She'd rarely seen Jo's hair down, much less in fancy finger waves. Her red-painted lips were a perfect match to the rounded collar and polka dots on her white belted dress. Maybe she would have always appeared this way if she'd been raised with a mother.

"So tell me." Jo leaned forward. "What's the latest scoop with Lane's mom? Any good knockdown drag-outs lately?" A devilish glimmer shone in her eyes, a trademark of the Jo Allister that Maddie knew.

"Nothing to report that I can think of."

"Aw, tell the truth. She's out hanging laundry with Emma. I swear she can't hear us."

"No, really. It's actually been . . . nice."

Jo arched a brow, skeptical at first, then impressed. "Wow."

Considering where Maddie and Kumiko had started, *wow* was an understatement.

"In that case," she said, moving on, "what about Lane? Anything new?"

Maddie shrugged. "Not much. He's still traveling with a Marine unit in the South Pacific. I wish he could tell me more, but the darn censors . . ." Then again, it was probably best she didn't know what risks he took on a daily basis.

Jo countered the notion. "No matter what he's up to, I'm sure he's being careful. The fella has lots to come home for."

Grateful for the offering, Maddie smiled. But it turned heavy when Jo's gaze dipped to her polka-dotted lap. She fidgeted with a loose thread, balled it between her fingers. Something else was on her mind.

Maddie thought to inquire about her brothers, three of them Army men, when Jo asked, "Any word about TJ?"

Ah, yes. Maddie should have guessed.

"All they say is that they're still searching," she said, then added with certainty, "He's going to make it through fine though. I know he will. . . . After all, TJ has a lot to come back for too."

The pointed remark, naming Jo among those incentives, raised the gal's eyes. For a second, she looked like she might deny the connection—which Maddie had sensed even before he'd come home on leave. Any boy and girl *that* annoyed with each other were destined to be a couple.

Jo's body suddenly slumped. "TJ sent me a bundle of letters," she admitted. "All of 'em came at once. Before I could write back, I got one more. Told me to take a hike. Not that it matters. We're completely wrong for each other anyway." The phrase sounded worn, as if used repeatedly on herself.

Maddie's agreement would be no less convincing. Instead, she cited a universal truth learned from Jo. "Boys are imbeciles."

"Dumbbells," Jo muttered.

"Morons."

"Pinheads who think burps and farts are the funniest things on the planet."

A brief pause, and they both giggled. Maddie welcomed the release until meeting a fresh surge of nausea. She grabbed her middle to slow its flip-flopping and lay back down.

"How long have you been sick for?"

"I don't know. A week or two."

Jo crinkled her nose and said, "Maddie, this is probably a silly question, but—you wouldn't be pregnant, would you?"

"What? Gosh, no."

"You sure?"

"Of course I'm sure. Lane hasn't even been around since . . ." As she leafed through her mental calendar, it occurred to her that her monthly cycles hadn't resumed. They'd first waned then disappeared at Manzanar, which a doctor had attributed to her stress and change of food. But three months of farm life had proven calming. With weight regained from hearty country meals, her body should have settled by now.

Unless her waistline, like her appetite, had been increasing for another reason—

"My God," she said. "I *am* pregnant."

A broad grin overtook Jo's face. "Holy mackerel!"

Maddie's hand went to her stomach. Could this be happening?

If the assumption was right, she would soon have a family of her own. Although they were separated for now, she had a husband she adored. From a perfect night together, they'd conceived a baby. A tangible, undeniable symbol of their love. It was an enormous step toward regaining what Maddie had lost and obtaining what she had always wanted.

So why, instead of joy, did she feel only a cold rush of dread?

52

After an hour of Lane's pleas over the loudspeaker, the Japanese holed up in the cave had yet to surrender. They were surrounded by Marines, in a dense island jungle, with nowhere to go. Their stubbornness would end only one way if Lane didn't succeed.

Sweat dripped from his helmet and slid down his back. He breathed against the humidity and launched into another appeal.

"Enough," Captain Berlow barked, marching onto the scene. Daylight polished his bald head to a shine. A full cigar, squeezed between his teeth, remained unlit as always. "Sergeant Schober!"

"Yes, Cap'n."

"Do what you need to do."

With a hint of reluctance, the NCO acknowledged the order.

Lane strode over to meet Berlow. "Please, Captain, just give me a little more time. I'm sure I can get them to come out if—"

"They had their chance." His gruffness hadn't let up since Lane's arrival to the Solomon Islands. It was clear Berlow wasn't the one who'd requested a Nisei interpreter to be attached to his unit. And he afforded the same value to diplomatic talks.

"Sir, I'm asking you to reconsider."

The man gazed toward the cave, gnawing on the end of his cigar. Not in a contemplative way, more like an irritated grind.

Assigned by Sergeant Schober, two riflemen and a flamethrower gathered their gear. They headed toward the cave bored into the steep mountain. In his memory, Lane could still smell the acrid stench of burning flesh, the result from his last failed attempt. He could see the pair of Japanese soldiers rooted out of hiding, their uniforms aflame.

"I'll go in." Lane's words tumbled out before he could stop them—as he surely should have. Cave flushing was a treacherous task for anyone, much less for men viewed as "traitors" by those dwelling inside.

Berlow turned slowly to face Lane, and the suggestion of a smile rounded his cigar. The possibility that Lane wouldn't return appeared an enticing thought. "Hang on, boys," he shouted without breaking from Lane's eyes. "Let's . . . give them one more chance."

Lane snagged a flashlight while weeding out sprouts of regret, and treaded up the rocky slope. For protection, he took only a knife, aside from the thousand-stitch belt he wore daily beneath his shirt. His mother's gift likely had nothing to do with his surviving the banzai attack, but carrying a charm couldn't hurt.

As he scaled the mountain to reach the cave, he yelled upward to announce his peaceful approach. There was no reply, no indication he wouldn't be shot on sight. He glanced over his shoulder. A dozen Marines watched with interest. Though most had been civil to Lane, some even friendly, their air of uncertainty was as constant as the tropical heat.

If he pulled this off, he just might save lives on both sides, and gain a little trust.

At last, he reached for the lower lip of the cave. With caution, he hoisted himself up and onto his knees. The barrel of a pistol, just as he'd expected, waited to greet him.

"My commander," Lane began, then amended, "our shogun has sent me to speak with your superior." He chose his Japanese words with purpose, kept his gaze considerably low. For the first time ever, he was thankful for his mother's insistence that he speak her language properly.

After a torturous silence, a Japanese order shot out from the shadows. "Let him in."

The soldier jerked his weapon twice, signaling Lane to move. Inside, the man who had spoken sat cross-legged on the floor. His army insignia marked him as a *sōchō,* the equivalent of sergeant major.

Lane realized his oversight. He should have borrowed an officer's bars. Rank was everything to the Japanese, ingrained by centuries of feudalism. Lane's T4 grade, a lowly technician, hardly commanded respect.

Too late to turn back.

He compensated by bowing deeply from the waist. He stayed there until the *sōchō* waved for him to sit. Once settled, vision adjusting to the darkened space, Lane made out forty, maybe fifty civilians in the background. Faces worn, clothes raggedy, they huddled in nervous quiet. The handful of Imperial soldiers appeared to be in no better shape.

Christ . . . how long had they all been living here?

"You are Nisei," the commander observed in Japanese.

Lane affirmed with a nod.

"Hm." A sound of intrigue—or perhaps disdain. "So you fight for America?" Not a question. An invitation into a minefield. The wrong answer and the world could explode.

As a precaution, Lane secretly hovered his hand over his knife. "I serve humbly," he said, "the country of my birth." He tipped his head down. "As do you, *Sōchō.*"

The man pondered this for a long moment. Then, to the closest soldier, he said, "Get him some rice."

Lane breathed a little easier as he accepted a small wooden bowl. Given the circumstances, it was the best rice he'd ever had. A burger couldn't have tasted better.

For at least an hour, sharing a lemon soda, they discussed Japan and MacArthur and the tragedy of war. A father of three girls, the *sōchō* had been raised in the Kyoto Prefecture, where propaganda evidently ran rampant. American soldiers were believed to torture and execute POWs, abuse captured women, roast and eat enemy babies.

No wonder the Japanese would rather commit hara-kiri than surrender to alleged monsters.

Falling back on his Kyoto dialect, Lane worked to dispel the rumors. Only when the commander appeared reasonably convinced did Lane broach negotiations. He just hoped a mood shift in the cave didn't result in him becoming a hostage.

"*Sōchō,* the reason I am here is . . ." Enabling the commander to save face would be a must. "I was ordered to extend to you a proposal. Out of acknowledgment of your valor, and that of your men, my leader is offering a peaceful solution."

The casualness of the man's expression shut down. "Surrender."

Carefully, Lane replied, "Yes."

Shows of interest from the other Japanese soldiers intensified.

"The area is surrounded by the Allies," Lane explained. "With your meager resources, you will all soon perish. If you choose to come out, each person will receive rations and clothing. Medical attention will be given to the sick."

"And what of shame?" A cool challenge. "What remedy can you provide for presenting oneself a coward?"

A baby broke into a liquidy cough, drawing Lane's attention to the natives. The lives of women and children rested in this conversation. More specifically, in his next reply.

"A coward," Lane maintained, "doesn't sacrifice his own worth for the well-being of others. According to the Bushido, the act is a noble one."

At the reference, the commander's eyes displayed marginal surprise. The warrior's ancient code, as detailed by Lane's father, called for benevolence. Among its other seven virtues were respect and honesty.

"Should you surrender, you will all be treated with the same regard."

Tension turned the space stifling. Not just from the man's silence, his unreadable face, but from the thought of the flamethrowers Berlow was apt to send in at any moment.

"I shall leave you in private now, as you have only an hour to consider a great deal." Lane went to stand, spurring a soldier to lift his pistol. The *sōchō* jerked his chin an inch, a sign to let him go, or permission to shoot.

Banking on the former, Lane pivoted around and embarked on the longest walk of his life. The light waiting outside too closely resembled heaven.

He reached the opening and raised his hand, signaling Schober to hold their fire. Before descending, however, Lane braved a final note to the commander. "One day, perhaps we will make sense of this war. But may that day come when we are safely home with our families."

Still, the *sōchō* said nothing.

The captain checked his watch. "They got ten minutes," he warned Lane. The deadline for surrender was rapidly closing in. "They go so much as one minute past, and we get 'em out my way."

Sweat drenched Lane's entire shirt. He stared hard into the slanted opening of the cave, willing faces to appear.

Five minutes . . .

He glanced at the audience. More Marines had gathered for the impending outcome. A few had taken bets.

Four minutes . . .

Come out, damn it.

Three minutes . . .

Two . . .

"Well, that was lovely," Captain Berlow said. "Sergeant, let's do what we should've done from the start."

"Hey, look," someone yelled. "They're coming out!"

Lane snapped his head up to find civilians surfacing from the cave. They crawled down one by one, aided by Marines at the base of the slope. Japanese soldiers came out next, hands held high. But no sign of their commander.

Thoughts rushed at Lane in a flurry: the lack of protest his father put up when arrested without grounds; the seemingly docile acceptance of Japanese Americans when ordered from their homes.

All this time, Lane had attributed those actions to a cultural weakness. Yet it wasn't that they were weak. They were simply willing to do anything, even at the cost of their pride, to avoid a display of shame.

"Got one more, Cap'n," Schober reported.

At the edge of the cave stood the *sōchō*. His gaze connected with Lane's. As it held, the man slowly raised his hand toward his head. The pistol, Lane remembered. It was too far away to see, but he envisioned the man pulling the trigger and diving to his death. An antidote for dishonor.

Lane ran forward to scream, *Nooo!* But the *sōchō* opened his hand. There was no weapon inside. He was merely angling a salute. Then he turned around and started down the mountain.

Reeling from relief, Lane bit out a laugh.

Kishi kaisei. The old adage came to mind: Wake from death and return to life. From even a desperate situation, a person can wholly return.

As the prisoners were searched for weapons, a slew of Marines encircled Lane, congratulating him on the achievement. There would be no reward from the captain, no gesture of approval; the guy had already left the scene.

What Lane got instead was a feeling of camaraderie. And for today, that was enough.

❧ 53 ❧

By day four, TJ chose talking as the activity that would prevent him from going nuts. Not talking to himself. That actually *would* be crazy. He spoke instead to Dopey, who'd been awarded nightly guard duty for whatever he'd said to the commander that landed TJ in the cage.

Dopey, of course, never contributed to the chats—which was why he'd become the perfect companion on nights like this, while the rest of the island slept.

It remained a mystery to TJ why he'd been spared. So far, punishment entailed no worse than being locked in an isolated bamboo cell in an open corner of camp. But then, there was no telling how long they planned to leave him there. Maybe keeping him alive in solitary forever, anxiety-ridden over tomorrow's fate, was a form of torture in itself.

"Now, what was I saying?" he continued as Dopey paced nearby. A rifle hung from the guard's shoulder strap. "Oh, yeah. DiMaggio's hitting streak. A total of fifty-six consecutive games. Enough to make you speechless, isn't it?" TJ considered his company and laughed to himself. He straightened his legs out in front of him on the dirt, his knees popping from the needed stretch. His bare feet could almost touch the cell's other side.

"Rumor has it, if Joltin' Joe had hit just one more, the Heinz company would've given him ten thousand buckaroos. All for smacking a tiny white ball." Realizing Dopey wouldn't understand the logic, he explained, "It's on account of the sauce they make. Called Heinz 57. Supposed to have fifty-seven ingredients in it, though I wouldn't take that for gospel. I mean, can you actually think of fifty-seven different ingredients that would fit into a little glass bottle?"

In the moon's dim glow, Dopey rubbed his eyes below the lid of his military cap.

"Probably hard to imagine," TJ said, "since you seem like a simple kinda guy. Just splash some soy sauce on everything, right? I've tasted the stuff before, by the way. Lane—the guy I told you about, the one who looks sort of like you—well, his real name's Takeshi. Moritomo's his last name. Maybe you've heard of him?"

Dopey sat down, his back against a large rock.

"Yeah, well, you never know. Small world." TJ scratched his developing beard. "Point is, he bet me I wouldn't try some octopus with that black sauce on it. Tasted like salt water on a piece of rubber. Nasty stuff if you ask me." He shuddered as his taste buds relived the event. "Was worth it though. Got myself a Babe Ruth baseball card out of the deal."

The timing of the win had been perfect. TJ had ruined his own copy when he'd accidentally dropped it into a puddle during recess weeks before then. He still couldn't believe Lane had been dumb enough to gamble that card. After all, the Bambino had been Lane's favorite. . . .

At that moment it dawned on him. Lane had given it away intentionally.

Flicking away the notion, TJ studied a bamboo bar with vertical lettering, carved by either a rock or a fingernail. *KILROY WAS HERE.* Nobody seemed to know who Kilroy was, or if he actually existed. It had become a game U.S. servicemen played, being the first to write the phrase in every foreign town they reached. Even in war, guys would find amusing ways to pass the time.

"So you must have been the youngest in your family, huh? Had to fight to get a word in?"

Dopey produced a bundled handkerchief from the pocket of his uniform trousers. He unwrapped the same kind of snack he'd eaten every night since TJ had been put in here. A black strip of dried seaweed looped the packed triangle of rice. Thankfully, since Dopey didn't seem the sharing type, nothing about it struck TJ as appetizing.

Didn't these people ever get a craving for something better? Like a nice juicy steak? A bacon lettuce sandwich, a side of crispy fries? A platter of Spaghetti Bolognese from Ranieri's mom?

TJ tried not to think about whether or not Vince had survived. There had been no sight of him, and other POWs weren't allowed to make contact with TJ, much less provide an update. Regardless, oddly enough, cutting Ranieri free that night didn't feel like a waste.

"You got radio shows in Japan?" he asked Dopey, whose mouth stretched in a long yawn between bites. "I don't mean those dumb Tokyo Rose propaganda reports. Something more like *Easy Aces.* Or *The Burns and Allen Show.* Those two were a stitch together, especially Gracie." TJ continued listing his favorites, as far back as childhood. The detective dramas, the *Superman* episodes. He was recapping the Man of Steel's special skills when the guard began to snore.

It was startling to see a Japanese soldier do anything remotely human. So much about them seemed robotic. Even their features hardly varied, with their slanted eyes and black hair, yellow skin. Resembling demented men of steel, they marched and killed without question or emotion. Well, besides hatred. And they followed orders to the letter, or faced the consequences.

TJ wondered what punishment they might earn for falling asleep on post. A beating or beheading? Eagerness poured through him as he imagined causing any one of them misery.

He scanned the area through the bars. The trick would be to snag a supervisor's attention without waking Dopey first.

Then he realized . . . they'd just replace the guy. With the way TJ's luck had been going, he'd get someone like Grumpy, who wouldn't hesitate in beating TJ to a pulp to shut him up. Probably better to leave things alone.

TJ tipped his head to the side and gazed at the stars. Once again, he penned Jo an imaginary letter.

Dear Jo,

I'm still in this dang cage, but at least it's not raining tonight. Sleeping in the mud is no picnic, trust me. I wish I were tired. With the heat and humidity, I took too many naps today and now I can't fall asleep. So I'll just look up at your stars instead until counting them wears out my eyes.

It's a clear night, so it's not too hard to imagine lying on the baseball mound with you again. Remember how you liked the idea of someone on the other side of the world admiring the very same stars? Bet you didn't think that person would be me. I haven't seen Orion and his buddies lately. In my mind, though, I can see his belt and sword just fine. Above those is Taurus. And then there's the brightest one—I think you called it "Seerus." Makes you think of your father watching over you, right? I wonder if your dad was the person who nicknamed you Jo. Funny that after all these years, I don't know your real name. Josephine doesn't seem to fit. Neither does Joanne. I should have asked you that before I left. I should have asked you a lot of things.

What I regret most, of course, is sending you that last letter. Odds are high I won't be making it home—guys die here daily by the dozen. I was just so afraid of hurting you, maybe even more of getting hurt myself. But now what pains me more than anything is that you'll never know how much I care. And all because—

A voice interrupted him. It was a mumbled whisper, but in English. The lazy English of an American. Some POW had made it out here!

TJ pressed his face between the bars, straining to search in the shadows. Could it be Ranieri coming to return the favor?

"Ranieri," he shouted quietly. "That you?" He waited, hearing only the clicks and coos of the jungle. "Ranieri."

Vince had been trying to concoct an escape plan since they'd arrived here six months ago. Had he figured out a way to sneak out? If not, he was taking the same risk as TJ had, and they could both wind up wishing the sharks had gotten to them first.

"Where are you?" TJ pressed.

Several seconds passed before the voice returned, at a higher volume. "I can't go. I told them. . . ."

"Shhh," TJ ordered. What was he thinking? Did he want to wake up Dopey?

"I wanted to . . . I wanted to . . ."

"Wanted to what?" he demanded in a hush.

"You can go . . . he's here and—so I can't . . ."

The phrases didn't make sense. Was some delirious prisoner skulking around?

TJ's gaze darted back and forth, hunting for the guy. He needed to confirm his own sanity, that the voices weren't imaginary. He was about to call out once more when he spotted the source of the gibberish.

It couldn't be possible. Had to be a dream.

He pinched himself, twice. Then the person spoke again. And there was no question it was real.

"Ho. Lee. Crap," TJ breathed.

The visitor wasn't Ranieri, or another POW. He was Dopey, the mute prison guard, rambling in his sleep.

✖54✖

The best way to handle her predicament, Maddie had decided, was not to dwell on "what ifs." She could drive herself mad with an endless list of potential disasters. *What if Lane didn't come home? What if she had to raise their child alone? In four months, when their "half-breed" baby was due, what if the hospital turned her away?*

And among the worst she could imagine: *What if the combined races prevented their child from ever fitting in?*

"Worry no good for baby," Kumiko had insisted while first tying a *hara-obi,* the white maternity sash, around Maddie's waist. The advice had come without Maddie uttering a single concern. Maybe Kumiko had read her expressions. Maybe she'd simply been pondering her own regrets. It had, after all, been the time of Obon. No different from the August before, Kumiko had grown sullen until the festival dates ended. Against cultural tradition, according to Emma, Kumiko had again neglected to pay tribute to the departed. Only this time, Maddie understood the reason.

"Now, why didn't you *say* you played the fiddle?"

Mr. Garrett's voice snapped Maddie's attention to the doorway of her bedroom. He entered holding a medium-sized cardboard box he'd picked up from Ida. The hodgepodge of garments, collected from the local church, was meant for various stages of Maddie's widening figure.

"Bet you play a whole lot nicer," he said, "than the mess of notes I blow on my harmonica."

"That's nonsense." Maddie smiled, seated on the corner of her bed. The quilt beneath her was soft and handmade, warm in dusty pinks and yellows like the rest of the room. "I think you play beautifully."

"In that case, you might need your hearing checked." He winked. "Just be warned, now that your secret's out, you're in charge of kicking off our next sing-along." As he set the container down in the corner, Maddie's eyes dropped to her violin resting on her lap.

"Afraid I won't be of much use." She trailed her fingers over the strings that had lost the magic she used to rely on. In the wake of Obon, with thoughts of her parents surfacing anew, the draw of her touchstone had been too strong to deny. Her hands, today more than usual, had yearned to feel the grain of the wood, its pattern like veins of a heart that no longer beat. She knew better, though, than to restart its pulse. Even if awakened, its soul had changed, its voice had been altered. An old friend she didn't recognize.

"It got damaged from being in the desert," she told him.

"Ahh, I see. That's too bad."

Maddie set the instrument back into its satiny tomb.

"Looks like you got quite the album there." Mr. Garrett gestured to the lid.

Indeed, the lineup of what TJ would call "classical-composer trading cards" had gradually become a scrapbook. Even Tchaikovsky had recently given up his reign for a picture: Maddie watching a judo match with two Japanese friends from the garment factory. With cameras prohibited at Manzanar, she was grateful for the sketch sent by an evacuee.

"Some are friends, the rest are family," she explained. "And then there's Bach, of course." Her sole remaining judge on the musical panel.

"Bach . . . ," Mr. Garrett said. "He an uncle of yours?"

Maddie's throat cut off an impolite giggle. "Um—no. He's a composer. A pretty famous one."

"Any tune I might've heard?"

Good golly, where would she possibly start? She strove to enlighten him without inundating him with too much detail. "You know, I'm sure several of his pieces would sound familiar if you heard them."

Mr. Garrett threw his head back, chuckling. "I'm just pulling your leg. I'm real familiar with old Johann."

Maddie shook her head, as stunned as she was relieved, and laughed with him.

"So are you a fan of classical music?" she asked when they quieted.

"Didn't start out that way. Though it grew on me 'cause of Celia." He rarely volunteered information about his late wife.

"Did she play an instrument?"

"Played the piano as a girl. Gave it up for one reason or another. But she sure loved listening to those songs. She'd put 'em on every evening after supper, didn't miss a day."

Maddie smiled, touched by the reminiscent look in his eyes, the flickering of his mind projecting those moments together.

"Follow me," he said all of a sudden.

"What is it?"

He nodded toward the hall. "Got something to show ya."

Maddie's mind flooded with possibilities as Mr. Garrett rummaged in the attic. At the base of the pull-down ladder, she watched him descend with a wooden crate. He set the box on the floor and slid away the large brown handkerchief to reveal a collection of records.

"Seeing as we weren't blessed with children," he said, "I suppose these sorta became like kids to Celia. Bringing them out to keep us company. Letting 'em play, then tucking them into bed."

Maddie knelt beside the box. She took care in going through the sleeved disks. Schubert's "Unfinished Symphony" and Vivaldi's *Four Seasons.* Dvořák's Symphony in E minor, op. 95.

"Gramophone broke down a while back," he told her. "Otherwise, I'd let you give them a listen."

She continued flipping. As if clicking through radio channels, she heard snippets of Beethoven and Schumann and Wieniawski. "These are all lovely. Your wife had exceptional taste."

"Well, she married *me,* didn't she?"

Maddie boosted a grin, which collapsed at the discovery of the next record. A performance by Yehudi Menuhin. It was a famed rendition of Bach's Chaconne for solo violin. She touched a tattered edge of the label, and thought of her father. Was there any chance at all he had noticed her missing?

"Ah, yeah," Mr. Garrett remarked, leaning over her. "Celia liked that one an awful lot. Made her a little sad, but it didn't stop her from playing it as much as the others."

Maddie had never considered the Chaconne anything but challenging and brilliant and powerful. "What about the piece made her sad?"

"Oh, it wasn't so much the notes as the story behind it. You know, about Bach and his wife and all."

She shook her head, exposing her ignorance, inviting him to elaborate.

"Gosh, let's see. . . ." One elbow leaning on the ladder, he scratched his stubbled jaw. "As I recall, Celia got this bit from her old piano teacher. Said that Bach had been busy traveling—working for some prince, I think. When he finally made it home, come to find out his wife had passed on while he was away. Already buried too. A real misfortune, especially with seven children to raise. So they say—though don't quote me here—that he wrote that song about all the grief he was feelin'."

"I had never heard that before," Maddie said in wonder.

The man exhaled a breath, a personal mourning in its heaviness. She knew that breath. She understood the desire to awaken memories of a loved one, only to be reminded that memories were all you had left.

"Anyhow," he said, straightening. "Tractor needs some tuning up. You take your time with those. Just leave the box when you're done. I'll put it away before bed." With that, he started heading out.

"Mr. Garrett."

He stopped.

"Thank you," she said, "for sharing these."

He smiled ruefully, then continued on.

Left alone, she reviewed the Chaconne from a new perspective. It was as if she had passed by a landscape painting all her life, framed and hung in a hall, and suddenly learned that hidden beneath the strokes was the original Mona Lisa.

As she entertained the idea of emotion underlying the composition, a series of buried notes rose from the depths of her mind. A saxophonist's version of "Summertime." She'd listened to the man play at the Dunbar, his feelings rather than technique ruling every haunting phrase. For what she'd viewed as self-indulgence, her ear had found fault in his loosey-goosey style.

Now, though, the memory of that tune stirred her emotions. For it signaled the last time she, TJ, Lane, and Jo had all been together, like a necessary complement of four strings to make a whole. Replaying that night, she saw them running from the cops, hiding in an alley, teasing, laughing. Long since divided, they had entered the "bridge" of their lives. In music, that's what they called the transitional period. A time to reflect on what had passed and to prepare for a new phase.

A fluttering in her stomach trailed the thought. Her baby was moving around, as if reminding her that blessings, too, had been gained along their journey.

"You're right, sweetheart. You're right," Maddie murmured, and reclined against the wallpapered hallway. She rubbed her belly and, rocking side to side, she hummed "Summertime" for them all. A wish for tomorrow. A lullaby of hope.

～55～

By the light of the moon, Lane traced the image of her face. His fingers glided down the photo, over Maddie's shoulder and down her beautiful, rounded figure. In just a few months he would be a father. A father! The idea was overwhelming and frightening and amazing all at once.

What would the child look like? Would he be an athlete? Maybe a lawyer . . . a judge. Or would it be a girl? One smile from her and Lane would be nothing but putty.

Doggone it all. What was he doing? Hiding out in a jungle infested with as many Japanese soldiers as disease-carrying bugs wasn't the place to be thinking about the future.

He tucked Maddie's picture back into the dome of his helmet, next to Emma's crane. He needed to concentrate on why he was here, what he came to do. Not stoke fears over what he stood to lose.

"Moritomo," Sergeant Schober said quietly, approaching the Banyan tree. Lane sat amidst the protruding, interwoven roots, waiting for recon orders. "Cap'n wants you to sneak into the field. See if you can hear anything."

Lane strapped on his helmet. He followed without pause, in spite of knowing what he was in for. The prior night, he'd volunteered to crawl into the same meadow. Not surprisingly, Captain Berlow hadn't objected. For an hour, Lane had eavesdropped on Imperial soldiers discussing their unit's positions. From either ignorance or arrogance—perhaps from both—the Japanese tended to speak carelessly about such things, secure in the belief that no outsider would understand their language.

The details Lane had related helped the Marines wipe out an entire machine-gun nest. Still, the captain remained unimpressed. Translated maps, insightful interrogations. Nothing could win the guy over. All Lane received were snide remarks about being too chummy with the POWs. Berlow didn't realize that screaming to make them talk was pointless. Intimidation only clammed them up. Show them compassion and they answered every question.

The reason was simple. Japanese weren't trained to be prisoners of war; they were never supposed to be taken alive. And few of them were, in fact, until Schober had offered a reward of three Cokes for the delivery of each POW. The prisoner count had substantially risen.

Now near the edge of the field, Lane admittedly felt more fear than compassion.

Sergeant Schober gave a hand signal, directing him northeast. Lane waited for acknowledging nods from the Marines positioned close by. Being mistaken for the enemy was a major reason most MIS guys weren't stationed at the front.

On his stomach, he inched his way through the tall swaying weeds. A decent breeze helped camouflage his movement. Island noises rode the salty air, reminding him of nights spent on the California coast. Tipping back beers with TJ, cracking jokes around a bonfire.

Finally he heard a murmur of voices. He moved in on them to discern the words. Idle chatter filled most of the exchange, hunger and pitiful rations the looping topic. Nothing Lane wasn't experiencing himself. Even with his jittery nerves, he could eat a feast for ten. His belly let out a grumble at the thought. He grabbed his middle to mute the gurgle, flattening his face in the dirt.

The men continued without a break, thank God. Time to get out of here before it happened again.

Lane started to crawl backward, but then caught the word *"shūgeki."*

Assault.

He stopped and leaned forward, listened intently. Once he'd gathered ample information, he suppressed his alarm and returned to find Schober. Lane passed along what he'd heard, about the enemy forces closing in on the area. They were using tunnels for strategic movement to get a drop on the Marines. He relayed the quantity of their soldiers, far outnumbering the American outfit, and their plans to attack at dawn.

A mere flitter of concern appeared in the captain's eyes, but the urgency of his orders conveyed the weight he afforded the report.

"Captain, I have an idea," Lane interrupted. Before Berlow could dismiss his input, Lane tossed out his proposal.

The man chewed on his cigar for several seconds, then grumbled. "This don't work, you'll be the first one they shoot." A statement of the obvious.

"It'll work," Lane insisted.

If it didn't, they could be overrun by morning.

"Well then," Berlow replied, "what are we waiting for."

As the plan spread through the company of Marines, Lane took up position in the field, no more than five yards from the captain. Berlow wanted a front row seat, where he could immediately adjust if the scheme failed. Clearly he was already banking on the need for plan B.

Lane hugged his rifle, keeping low to the ground. He eyed his wristwatch. Thoughts of his wife, his family, his unborn child, crammed themselves into every trudging minute.

Finally, the anticipated hour arrived. At 0300, Berlow gave him the cue, along with a look that said, *Don't you dare screw this up.*

So much for camaraderie.

Following a quick silent prayer, Lane inhaled a lungful of air. And in a sharp commander's voice, he shouted, *"Totsugeki! Totsugeki!"*

A drove of Japanese soldiers, fooled by the order to charge, rose in the meadow. They let out hollers as they ran straight into an instant shower of ammo. Lane took a chance and repeated his yell, his prime contribution. He wasn't expected to fire unless necessary. More men appeared and fell into the weeds. It was an all-out turkey shoot.

Off to the right, Berlow fired away, cutting down the opposition. But then a dark form materialized out of his sight line. A Japanese soldier leapt straight at the captain with bayonet raised. The scene rolled out in slow motion, each frame a still life of impending death. Just in time, bullets halted the enemy, jerking his chest in rapid hits, and slammed him to the ground.

Berlow threw Lane a glance. It was only then Lane realized that he himself had pulled the trigger. A banzai shout from another soldier yanked the captain back to his duties, and before long, Lane too was firing against the other side.

Come morning, the counterattack a success—including the surrender of several dozen Japanese—Lane joined others in scouring the field. He focused on finding documents, averting his conscience from the faces of those, in one way or another, he had murdered. With purposeful steps, he hurtled the obstacle course of pockmarked bodies, and wondered how many more sacrifices it would take to bring this blessed thing to an end.

❧ 56 ❧

Amazing how a single night can entirely change how you view a person. TJ had learned this from both his father and Lane. What he hadn't expected was a Japanese guard to reinforce the theory. But back in June, that's what had happened when flawless English slipped out while the guy talked in his sleep. It took TJ threatening to report Dopey, about his snoozing on post, to uncover the shocking truth.

"I'm an American," Dopey confessed, seated on the ground against the rock where he'd nodded off. "I was born and raised in Claremont. Graduated from Berkeley in '41."

"An American?" TJ found himself stuck on the lone admission.

"After my dad died, my mom moved back to Nagoya to be with her sisters. Took my little brother with her. She understood why I wanted to stay. California was my home. But then she had a stroke." He layered his arms over his bent knees, shook his head. *"I was only planning to be there a couple weeks. Once I got there, though, it was hard to leave until I knew my mom would be okay. And my boss at the ad firm said he'd hold my job for a month. So I stayed. I mean, how was I supposed to know what was about to happen. . . ."*

"Pearl Harbor," TJ murmured.

Dopey worked his heel into the ground as he continued. "I tried everything I could. Went to the embassy, wrote officials in the States. Nothing worked. They weren't letting anyone with Japanese blood back into the country."

In the pause that followed, TJ's grip remained on the bars of his open-aired cell. His initial shock was dissipating, though not his wariness. Regardless of citizenship, the guy was a Jap soldier. "If you were such a patriot, then why the hell are you here? How can you stand to wear that uniform?"

"I was conscripted," he said gruffly. "You think I want to fight for the Imperial Army? Watch Americans being murdered every day?" He jerked his face away, yet even in the dark, with only the moon lighting their corner of camp, TJ could see emotion cross his features, his shoulders dip. He could feel the guy's guilt as distinct and binding as the seams of a ball.

"Eventually I found a way to escape," he went on. "Got papers and a travel pass through the black market. I was all set to go. But then . . . in the end, I couldn't do it."

"So you stayed by choice?" The question wasn't a challenge. TJ was sincerely perplexed.

"You wouldn't understand," Dopey muttered.

"Try me."

Though looking hesitant, he replied, "Because of my family. If I'd fled like that, abandoned my duty, I would've disgraced them. All just to serve myself."

"But—that doesn't make sense. Who would've looked down on them for that? A couple of pencil pushers in Tokyo?"

"No," he said, a statement of fact. "The whole country."

For six weeks following that exchange, TJ and Eddie—that was Dopey's real name—had spent their nights gabbing in secret.

It had been nice for TJ, having someone actually respond when he talked during his stint in the cage. And clearly Eddie had missed speaking, not just in English but in any language. At military training, his subtle but telling American accent had spurred distrust. So he'd learned to open his mouth only when needed. This was also, TJ guessed, the reason Eddie had been assigned guard duty at their prison camp. Really, how much damage could a potential spy do while entrapped by barbed wire on a remote island?

In some ways, Eddie Sato was imprisoned as much as any POW here.

"I'm sorry it's over." This served as TJ's standard reply when prisoners asked how he'd managed in solitary. Viewed as a hero for his offense, he'd received the question a whole lot. "I'm sorry it's over," he'd tell them, and they presumed he was being sarcastic, or arrogantly brave.

Truth was, he meant it.

Five months had passed since he'd been returned to his thatched barrack. He'd enjoyed reuniting with fellas like Tack and Ranieri—Ranieri had mostly regained his health by then, plus a permanent case of gratitude. The space to stroll and stretch was also a welcome change, not to mention a bath and shave. But while lying in his sleeping bay at night, he'd think of Eddie and their talks, from starlets and radio shows to meals from home. They'd traded jokes and stories, and created a game of tossing pebbles onto circles drawn in the dirt.

It wasn't until discussing the great hitter Ted Williams, though, that TJ had realized what he relished most about their chats: With features sculpted by the shadows, Eddie could have so easily been Lane. Like it or not, TJ missed his old friend. The person he could go to with family frustrations or for help with school projects, to swap advice on dating and girls. To share whoops and boos over every broadcast from the World Series, a buddy to celebrate with whenever the occasion arose.

He wished he could tell that to Lane, but the guy was about as far from reach as Bovard Field. TJ stewed on this thought for several nights. Only when it brewed into a feast of an idea—one that could deliver him to freedom—did he risk conferring with Eddie in private.

In the inky blackness, hidden behind the latrine, TJ tried not to inhale the fumes. The facility was nothing more than a walled-off slit trench. His past "honey details" had required him to scoop up bucketfuls to be used as fertilizer for Looney's garden, which was how TJ knew this was the perfect spot to meet. Aside from a few emergency runs by POWs with dysentery, the stench would deter anyone from coming out here by choice.

TJ angled toward a sound. Boot steps, coming closer. He held his breath and prayed those boots belonged to Eddie.

The footfalls stopped, then slowly rounded the corner.

"Eddie," TJ whispered, overcome with relief.

"What'd you want?" he whispered back.

TJ cringed at the cool greeting. He had to remind himself that they weren't truly friends. In daylight, they stood on opposite sides of the war. Eddie was a means to complete a mission, and that's all.

"Look, I just need to ask you something."

"Shh." Eddie threw up a palm to silence him and froze. They listened to movement in the latrine. A man grunted as he relieved himself. When he departed, Eddie shot TJ a glare. "You have ten seconds."

Refocusing, TJ answered, "I need a favor."

Eddie let out a frustrated breath. "I can't get any more quinine until supplies come in. When I get some, I'll give it to you the same way as before."

The first note TJ had passed to him had been a request for the anti-malaria pills. Two days later, a small handful of the tablets had magically appeared beneath the Air Corps jacket TJ used as a pillow and, as a result, saved Tack's life.

"That's not why I'm here."

Eddie enunciated each word. "What do you want?"

"Baseball." Eddie's expression crinkled as TJ continued. "We want to play against the guards. Sort of like an exhibition game. The commander's a sports fanatic, you said so yourself."

That, as it turned out, was the reason TJ hadn't been executed. Looney had raised his sword to hack away when Eddie intervened, claiming he'd overheard that TJ was a famous pitcher, the kind Japan—a country wild about baseball—would need after winning the war. Truthfully, Eddie had been in the stands when TJ sealed a Trojan victory against Berkeley in '39, and for some reason that even Eddie couldn't fathom, he'd recognized TJ at the prison, later confirmed by his name.

Apparently staying mute had been easier when the victim was an unknown. Now, TJ hoped the guard's compassion would come through one final time.

"In the next shipment from Japan," TJ went on, "I was thinking, maybe we could get a little equipment. Like a bat and a few balls. Heck, we could use coconuts if need be—"

"I know what this is about," Eddie broke in, his face hardening. "It's suicide for nothing."

TJ paused, briefly thrown off. "What do you mean?"

"So, what—you're gonna try to show up the guards? Put them in their place? You do that, they'll beat the shit out of all of you for disgracing them."

Actually, in this case, winning would just be a bonus. As much as TJ wanted to explain that, it was safer for them both if Eddie didn't know. "We just want to play."

"The commander isn't going to permit it."

"Why wouldn't he? He lets us have talent shows and dinnertime songs. Hell, the other night, he even allowed a Christmas Eve program."

It was while listening to the raggedy choir sing "Greensleeves" that TJ's mind hopped from "Green" to grass to a manicured baseball field, and ultimately landed on escape.

"Just hear me out," he insisted when Eddie angled to leave. "You told me you'd help if you could. Here's your chance."

Eddie didn't turn back around, but he stayed, listening.

"One lousy game could raise morale enough to pull a lot of these guys through. Once our spirit loses all hope—once that's been crushed—we're done for. I *know* you understand that."

TJ had one last argument, which could either win the guy over or push him further away. Thinking of Ranieri, who would take the gamble, he stepped closer and said, "You're not one of 'em, Eddie. No matter what uniform they make you wear."

Slowly, Eddie glanced over his shoulder. Something simmered in his eyes. Not anger or disapproval. More like . . . suspicion. "I'll talk to him," he replied flatly.

Before TJ could thank him, he marched away, leaving in question what precisely that discussion would entail.

$$\mathcal{57}$$

Maddie tried to follow orders, but ultimately found it impossible. She simply couldn't spend her day lazing in bed despite Kumiko's overprotective warnings. The holiday was making her too restless. Christmas had passed with ripples of sadness rather than tides, but New Year's Eve was a different story. Given nothing to do but dwell on the anniversary of her parents' accident would plunge her into self-pity, deep and devouring as quicksand.

In a tent of a dress, she waddled out of her room. Her belly ruffled a potted plant on a hallway table. Two weeks until her due date and still she hadn't adjusted to her expanded circumference. She wondered how women bearing twins ever fit through a doorway.

Outside the kitchen's lace-curtained window, patches of snow dotted the ground. The sun, pinned to a clear blue sky, reflected off a pair of shoveled mounds. They sparkled like polished diamonds. It was early January, yet the house smelled of lemon oil and springtime, a result of Japanese tradition.

"We call 'Osoji,' " Kumiko had explained. "Start year free of past. Old dirt we not keep. Must have clean spirit, begin new." Maddie had assumed she meant this only figuratively until she assigned a list of chores to be divided among herself, Emma, Mr.

Garrett, and even Ida, who insisted on participating to prevent Maddie from lifting a finger.

Make that a swollen finger, same as her ankles. Nevertheless, there had to be some way she could contribute; she was pregnant, not incapacitated.

"Put down the broom and step away," Ida declared.

Maddie tightened her grasp on the handle. She had barely swept two square feet below the kitchen sink. "I was just going to—"

"Nope."

"But I—"

"Hand it over." Ida extended her palm, her ponytail as sleek as her raised eyebrow. "Come on, little mama. Don't make me pry it from ya."

A standoff. Over a broom.

With a groan, Maddie gave in.

"That's more like it."

Maddie folded her arms over her bosoms—those too were swollen—and leaned back against the cutting block. "There has to be something I can do."

"Well, I can think of one thing."

Maddie perked.

"You can kick back and relax. That baby'll have you running from here to Kingdom Come. So you best enjoy the quiet time while you got it."

As Maddie blew out a sigh, a rhythmic thumping descended the stairs, along with a rustling sound. Emma appeared from around the corner dragging a bulky plastic sack. She stood up in her cuffed jeans to stretch her back while Yuki growled at the bag.

Ida rested her hands on her hips. "I hope Stanley hasn't got you clearing out dead bodies."

It took Maddie a moment to register the reference to Mr. Garrett, though the growing familiarity between him and Ida hadn't gone unnoticed.

"They're just some of his old clothes," Emma replied with a smile, "and Sunday dresses from his wife. He said your church would find a better use for them than the moths and dust mites in the attic."

"Oh," Ida said softly. "Oh, I see." She seemed to understand what it must have taken for Mr. Garrett to give up Celia's special garments.

"What should I do with them now?" Emma asked her.

"How about you separate them into piles for men and women?"

Maddie chimed in, "I can do that," and she started for the bag.

"Whoa, now," Ida said.

Maddie turned, exasperated. "For goodness' sakes, I'll do it sitting on the couch if you want." Sifting shirts and skirts wasn't going to break her.

"I suppose that's fine," Ida said finally. "So long as Kumiko agrees."

Was she kidding?

Ida answered by pointing toward the back door. "She's out hanging sheets."

"Unbelievable," Maddie muttered. She waddle-marched from the house and into the crisp winter air. Wooden clothespins secured white walls of fabric to the laundry lines. But no sight of Kumiko. Pulling her sweater closed, she called out, "Mrs. Moritomo!"

Maddie rounded the sheets and found her seated at the picnic table Mr. Garrett had built in the fall. It was the same week he'd added a tire swing to an oak tree for Emma.

With a pensive look, Kumiko held wrinkled pages in her hands. A plated candle burned atop the table. Maddie suddenly felt intrusive.

"I'm sorry, I didn't mean to interrupt." Maddie lingered for a couple seconds before turning to go back.

"Time for fresh start." Kumiko spoke just loud enough to halt her. "Say good-bye to past. We start over, *ne?*" Her gaze remained on what appeared to be a letter scrawled in intricate Japanese characters. A letter from Kensho, Maddie realized.

The letter.

At the table, Maddie sat on the damp bench. She took care to leave a cushion of respectful space. She glanced from the stationery to the flame, comprehending Kumiko's intention, the struggle of the task she faced.

"Maybe it's not about starting over," Maddie offered. "How can we really break from the past? It's what made us who we are. The people we loved, all the laughs, even the tears. Those things will always be part of us." As Kumiko's eyes rose, Maddie reflected on the evolving chords of her own life. "It's like in music. You can't just cut out the hard notes, or the piece wouldn't be whole. So, maybe what it's really about is . . . moving on."

Kumiko's attention slid back to the pages. They were tangible reminders of an alternate path that would forever remain a mystery.

Suddenly, the baby wiggled, and Maddie grabbed her side. It wiggled again and again, in a pattern of dance steps. A solo conga line.

"Baby okay?" Kumiko fretted.

"Oh, yes." Maddie laughed. "It just likes to jitterbug on my ribs." At Kumiko's befuddlement, she clarified. "The baby likes to move around a lot." Without knowing she was going to, Maddie asked, "Would you like to feel?"

What a foolish question. Kumiko wasn't one for such a personal act. But then, to Maddie's amazement, she tentatively reached out and touched her fingertips to the rounded bulge.

"Over here." Maddie guided her palm to lie flat over the usual area of movement. They waited there until the baby gave a stomp.

Kumiko gasped, covering her mouth with her free hand, and a smile spread her lips. "Same as Suzume," she said. "Always here, she *pon-pon.*" She tapped her own side, accompanying the sound effects of an internal pounding.

"Suzume?" Maddie asked. "Was that your baby's name?"

Kumiko's smile lowered but only halfway. *"Hai,"* she confirmed. "Suzume. Meaning is . . . sparrow."

Instantly, the images of Kumiko's paintings passed through Maddie's mind—a beautiful, solitary bird robbed of a chance to fly.

Now understanding, Maddie replied, "It's a lovely name."

Kumiko gave a nod. As if the mention of her child fed her strength, she angled back toward the candle and squared her shoulders. One by one she let the fire crawl over the pages until Kensho's letter had shriveled into ashes.

The scent reminded Maddie of being at the cave near Manzanar. A mix of ashes and snow. Of Lane's arms around her, and the sound of a creek, its water changing, searching, adapting. Like all of them.

Kumiko blew out the flame. Time to go inside, time to move on. When she started to stand, Maddie followed—before a pain pierced her stomach. She doubled over, felt a ripping low inside. A scream flew from her throat.

What was happening? It was too early. The baby wasn't due yet.

Kumiko held her under the arm and yelled something toward the house.

A series of cannonballs shot through Maddie's body, tossing her into a heap on the cold, stiffened grass. The sprinkling of snow had turned red—red from blood.

"I've got you." It was Mr. Garrett's voice, his arms lifting her, then carrying her inside. He unfolded her onto the couch. Beneath her, she felt the fuzzy texture of a blanket, yet she couldn't stop shivering. She concentrated on the impossible calmness of Ida's tone.

"Go fetch the doctor," the gal said, launching Mr. Garrett out the door. "Emma, gather up towels, sheets, anything of the like. I'll heat some water."

The three scurried away as Kumiko slid a throw pillow under Maddie's head. Blood continued to flow. Dark thoughts began to spin. Would her death be the cause of bringing Lane home safely? Provide the purpose in his life he was searching for?

The world grew foggy, clouding all but a single plea. "Promise me," she said as Kumiko knelt beside her. "Promise you'll take care of the baby. If I'm not here, *please* promise me. . . ."

Kumiko's eyes widened and her lips pressed together. With trembling hands, she placed a cool rag on Maddie's forehead, and she nodded.

❧ 58 ❧

Lane clenched his garrison cap at his side. He'd never been summoned to the commander's tent before. The trip felt strikingly
similar to a visit he'd once paid to the principal's office; a week of
custodial chores for sticking gum under a desk had reinforced his
illusion of justice.

"Morning, Captain," he said, stepping inside with a salute.

Berlow's shiny head didn't rise in greeting. Seated at a small
table, he continued studying a map covered in penciled arrows and
circles.

Just the kind of exchange Lane needed today. With Maddie past
her due date, he had bigger concerns to occupy his time. Like
whether they were now the parents of a beautiful boy or girl.

"You wanted to see me, sir?"

The man grunted around his unlit cigar and waved a hand to release Lane's salute, his manner as austere as ever. Since that night in
the meadow, back in October, Lane had been praised and welcomed by their entire unit. With the exception of Berlow. Not even
saving the captain's life had forged a bond.

Lane surveyed the room, looking to solve the riddle of this man.
Yet no answers lay in his personal space. Despite being stationed in

an island CP, the Marine kept a Spartan tent. You could bounce a bowling ball on his perfectly tucked cot.

"So, had a chat today with Major Paulsen," the captain said at last. Reclining in his chair, he laced his fingers over his chest.

"Yes, sir." The response seemed expected.

"Talked about you and what you've been doin' here," he said. "And about your father."

"My father?"

The topic puzzled Lane. Why would they be—

Shit. His detainment.

Lane should have anticipated this. Various organizations were known to investigate backgrounds of the MIS. The Counter Intelligence Corps, for one. Their undercover spies were rumored to be everywhere, hunting saboteurs, exaggerating offenses. After a year without being questioned, though, he figured the connection to his father had been lost in a file.

"He's still being held by the DOJ, isn't he?" Berlow's tone made the question rhetorical.

Lane confirmed with a nod, and it occurred to him that perhaps the captain had known all along, that the CIC had even put him in charge of watching Lane. And now Berlow had gathered enough info to send the "suspect" packing.

In hindsight, saving the guy might not have been the wisest move.

"My father isn't guilty," Lane began to explain.

"That, son, is none of my concern."

At the utter indifference, Lane squeezed his hat tighter. *He's no less a patriot than any man in this company,* he wanted to shout. In his gut, he'd always known the goodness of his father, the devotion to his family and country.

The thought delivered a trace of guilt from having ever doubted him.

Berlow pulled the cigar from his mouth. His fingers removed a speck of tobacco on his tongue and flicked it away. "When the major asked about you, however, I put in a good word. Don't know it'll help your pop. But there you have it."

That was what Berlow and the officer had discussed? The status of Lane's father wasn't grounds for discharge?

Considering the usual treatment by the captain, his sudden support didn't make sense.

Doubtful, tentative, Lane replied, "This is unexpected, sir."

Berlow appeared surprised by the reaction, the lack of gratitude maybe. He rolled his cigar between his fingers. "Look. I admit, I'm not a fan of anyone being assigned to my company who isn't a Marine. We're trained to think the same, act the same. Outsiders add danger to that system. My job is to protect those boys, return 'em to their mamas in as good of shape as they came." He shed a breath, shifted in his seat. "That being said . . . as Army guys go, well . . . you did all right."

Lane felt a sensation in his chest. A tingling of pride he almost didn't recognize.

"Point is," Berlow said a bit sharply, "Major says you've been ordered to HQ in Sydney. I don't know how the hell we're supposed to get anything useful out of any POWs here with no one to speak their language. But that doesn't seem to be the brass's damn concern. . . ." The rest faded into a mumble as he replaced his cigar.

A transfer back to Australia wouldn't have been arranged on a whim. With the impressive progress Allies were making in the Pacific, reams of Japanese documents would have been captured. Vital translations or officer interrogations could be waiting.

"When do I leave?" Lane asked.

"Jeep will pick you up at o-six-thirty."

Tomorrow? He'd be returning to civilization tomorrow?

Lane found his contributions here of value, but he'd had his fill of living like Tarzan.

"Thank you, Captain."

The man grunted. "Dismissed," he said, and returned to his map.

Lane ventured back to his quarters, envisioning what lay ahead. Real showers and actual mess halls. Streets and buildings, air thin enough to breathe. And Dewey, his pal and college roommate, stationed there in Intelligence. What a time they'd have catching up, shooting the breeze. Just like old times.

Then he thought of TJ, and the fact they'd still received no word. "Old times" without the guy were hard to remember, the future even harder.

Lane curbed the idea. He forbade himself from imagining the worst. This was a day of celebration, wasn't it? A day Maddie would appreciate. Although he hated to leave his new buddies behind, a handful in particular he'd gotten to know, the safety of his new station would bring her relief. That in itself brought him comfort.

He was picturing Maddie's delight as he entered his tent. The discovery of a gift on his pillow hitched his breath. A post! From Illinois! Clerk must have dropped it off. If the fella were still around, Lane would have hauled off and hugged him.

He tore into the envelope, unable to contain his excitement. He got as far as the greeting when he stopped. The handwriting wasn't Maddie's. He turned to the last page to identify the sender.

Ida. The gal from the farm. Why would she be writing to him?

Tamping his trepidation, he flipped back to the beginning. He sank onto his cot and read the woman's message. The further he got, the more his mind scattered, a reflexive defense against the razor-sharp words.

Maddie . . .
Labor . . .
Baby . . .
Complications.

59

"Let's go over it again," TJ said, crouched in the center of the small huddle. His command caused a hum of groans that echoed in their barrack. He threw a glare at Bobby the Brit and the redheaded Sully.

Repetition, drills—TJ knew from a lifetime of sports that these were the keys to success. Tonight there would be no room for failure. "A single thing goes wrong and Looney'll be slicing us up for sushi. You tired of listenin', you can stay and rot. You got that?"

The guys nodded, though TJ could tell that gathering during daylight was making them nervous. He looked over his shoulder and confirmed the room was still empty. Then he turned to Ranieri kneeling beside him. "All right, one last time. Make it quick."

Ranieri proceeded to detail the plan they had been revising and polishing for more than two months: After the game today, they would go to bed as usual. At roughly 0100 hours, Tack would send a bird trill from outside TJ's window. By then, most guards would be knocked out from exhaustion, maybe even from victory *sake*.

At the signal, TJ, Ranieri, Bobby, and Sully were to sneak out of their barrack, as if headed for the latrine, and join Tack—who was smuggling in supplies right this minute. Together they'd move from cover to cover until reaching the southeast corner of camp. There,

Happy would be catching some hefty Zs, thanks to the flask Tack would give him as a gift before lights-out. According to their Filipino aid, a sympathetic farmer in the vicinity, the moonshine spiked with sleeping powder would do its job, as would the wire cutters. A few snips to the fence and the five men would take off through the jungle.

If they got separated, there was no going back. All they could do was hope to see each other in the hull of a commercial fishing boat ready to sail at dawn. The vessel, bribed by a quiet force of island resistance, had been confirmed once the game date was finally set. Wanting a fair competition, Looney had given both teams until early March to practice. Strange that sports rules applied while wartime rules didn't. He'd actually improved rations for the POW roster, even adding raw sugar cakes, like fattening up Hansel and Gretel before the slaughter.

At the time of tryouts, TJ's goal had been twofold: wear out the guards and capture the title. This was the reason he'd handpicked players whose thirst for revenge compensated for muscle loss and malnutrition. But then, based on Eddie's advice, TJ wound up instructing his team to put on a worthwhile show that would lead to their loss. Not just any kind of loss. Lose by too much and Looney might kill every POW player. Win by anything and the guards would eventually make them pay. Sure, it would be long after TJ was gone, but he didn't need that kind of burden on his conscience.

"Ah, good. There he is." TJ sighed at the sight of Tack entering the barrack with his now subtle limp, and he was just in time. People would be gathering for the game soon. "Got the stuff?"

Tack nodded. As he drew closer, though, the flush in his face looked an awful lot like panic. "Fellas," he said, "we have a problem."

They shot to their feet, voices overlapping. "Why? What is it? What happened?"

"It's Guico, the farmer. He says the ship's leaving at eighteen hundred."

Jesus . . . evening rather than dawn. It was a challenge, but somehow they could make it work. Everything else was in place.

Ranieri shook his head. "We'll have to hide out in the boat all day long tomorrow. The Japs'll be searching high and low for us."

"Not tomorrow," Tack said, sweat dripping from his forehead. "That's eighteen hundred *today*."

Silence plowed through the room, followed by an eruption of hushed cursing. TJ raked his hands through his hair, wishing a solution could be combed from the grimy strands.

"Bloody hell," the Brit rasped over and over.

Ranieri stared off with a look bordering on terror and hopelessness. Worse than the daily beatings, strategic humiliation over the past fifteen months had worn him down. The only thing that had kept him going was the promise of escape.

"We won't make it." Sully paced the floor. "Even if we left right after the game, no way we'd make it in time."

TJ squeezed his eyes shut and breathed himself calm. Soon a solution—the only solution—appeared on the blackboard of his closed lids. In that instant it became clear what he'd been training for since childhood. The one game that actually mattered.

"What're you talkin' about?" Ranieri said, pulling TJ's gaze. "You ain't staying here."

Until then, TJ hadn't realized he'd voiced his intention. He continued consciously with the thought, his certainty solidifying. "I'm the team captain. I'm the one who asked for the game in the first place. Without me, Looney will know something's fishy."

Ranieri stammered at him, "Yeah, he'll get suspicious later. So what?"

"So I'm the pitcher, is what. Think about it. I can slow the game down all I want, give you guys extra time to get there." He turned to Tack, who stared back at him stunned. "You go and give Happy his sleep potion right now. Then once it kicks in, and the game's off and rolling, you all sneak out same as we planned. And Sully"—he swung to face him—"you tell Anderson he needs to play shortstop. That Ranieri's got a bad case of the gallops."

Bobby interjected, uncertain. "It's bloody risky. We'd be fleeing in broad daylight."

"More than half the guards will be in the game," TJ reasoned. "You might have an even better shot."

"That's bullshit," Ranieri spat with renewed vigor.

Sully and Tack mumbled their agreement.

"What's bullshit?" TJ said. "The rest of you giving up your one chance? You guys don't make it out, none of us will."

The final step of their plan had always been to inform Army headquarters of the camp's location. An American Intelligence officer, who'd recently been captured, claimed their prison was nonexistent on any map he'd seen. This confirmed the reason no POW letters went in or out, why they'd yet to glimpse a Red Cross package. If nobody knew where they were, there would be nothing to stop their captors from erasing proof of their gruesome crimes should the Allies win the war. And the Allies were going to win. They had to.

"What if they figure it out, Kern?" Ranieri's volume grew. "It wouldn't take a genius to trace it all back to you."

"But they won't—if I stay."

"What's the goddamn matter with you? Don't you wanna go home?"

At the idiocy of the question, TJ got right up to his face. He barely kept himself from gripping the guy's tattered shirt. For months that's all he'd thought about—returning to Jo, to Maddie. If the escape worked, odds were good that Looney would execute a handful of POWs as a deterrent for future breakouts.

But what option did they have? Stay and they'd all die.

TJ spoke low and firm. "We don't have time for this. Now, pipe down or you'll blow the whole thing."

Ranieri went to argue, but his words crumbled. Emotion welled in his eyes.

Bobby stepped forward and said, "He's right, old chap. He's right. . . ."

"Eh, Kern!" a voice hollered. Their first baseman, a former all-star at Boston University, entered the barrack. "Fellas are getting antsy. Time to warm up."

TJ relaxed his muscles, took a step back.

The infielder, sounding curious over the scene, asked, "What you want I should tell 'em?"

With eyes on Ranieri, TJ replied with a final request. A plea for his family back home. "Just tell them I'm here."

PART SIX

Had I not known that I was dead already
I would have mourned my loss of life.

—Death poem by samurai Ōta Dōkan

60

A single letter had changed everything.

It had been six months since Lane received the post from Ida. Six months since the news about Maddie's ordeal had woken him to the reality of his life. Nothing like nearly losing your wife and baby to set a guy's priorities straight.

Even after Maddie recovered, she never went into detail about the scare she must have had. She'd only confirm facts from Ida's account, about the placenta pulling away from the uterine wall. When bed rest hadn't stopped Maddie's hemorrhaging, and the baby's pulse slowed, the doctor performed a C-section. All had ended in a happy and healthy outcome, which Maddie continually spotlighted. She seemed to understand he'd otherwise go AWOL to make sure she and Suzie were safe.

Suzie. That was their daughter's name—short for Suzume, meaning "sparrow." It was a favorite of Lane's mother, Maddie had explained. He had fallen in love with it instantly, just as he did with his daughter from the first peek at her photo. In every letter to Maddie, he would ask, *How's our baby bird today?*

Now, in a restaurant booth, not far from his base in Sydney, Lane read his wife's latest response to that very question. The description of Suzie sitting up on her own and blowing spit bubbles made him smile. He laughed out loud, picturing the incident at supper, how she'd turned a bowl full of rice into a hat. It took two baths to loosen the sticky grains from her hair.

Then, in the next paragraph, arrived the greatest gem of all. Suzie had spoken her first word. *Da-Da,* she'd cried when Maddie held up his portrait. As Lane read this, his heart brimmed with love and pride and longing for the only thing that truly mattered. His family.

That, above everything, had become his motivation for aiding the war effort. Not his own vain aspirations. Not even to prove the loyalty of Nisei to his country, a need that continued to lessen for them all. Japanese Americans had earned back enough trust to fully qualify for U.S. military enlistment, as well as the draft, and the segregated units weren't taking the "privilege" lightly. The 100th Battalion and 442nd Regimental Combat Team were receiving as many citations from their battles in Italy as they were Purple Hearts.

Lane, on the other hand, was fine not possessing either. All he craved was a ticket home, which he appeared to have recently earned. In the midst of wading through a fresh tide of Japanese documents—maps, charts, operational plans from the Allied capture of Saipan—he had been called to his CO's office. Based on his service record, coupled with Berlow's endorsement, Lane had been recommended for Officer Candidate School.

"Nothing set in stone," the man had warned, "but if all goes well, you could be stationed at Fort Benning by New Year." Though many aspects had improved for the Nisei, MIS promotions weren't among them—unless you attended OCS.

Interesting that measurable recognition for Lane's feats came only after his drive for it had ended. Admittedly, the prospect of donning those shiny bars was still appealing. He couldn't wait to tell Maddie once the paperwork went through. In the meantime, he would celebrate with Dewey, who'd insisted on treating him to dinner.

Speaking of which, where was the guy?

Lane checked his watch. Twenty-five minutes late was unusual, even for Dewey.

"Are you ready to order, love?" An Australian waitress with a sweet smile stood beside the booth. How refreshing that Aussies saw him as a Yank, not a Jap.

"I'm actually waiting for a pal." Just then, sizzling salmon wafted from the next table. One long inhale and temptation took over. "Ah, the heck with it. The guy can fend for himself. Does the salmon come with potatoes? Or . . . just the beans?"

Instead of answering, she pointed toward the front door with her pen. "Reckon that's your mate. Looks like the soldier's in a rush."

Lane turned and spotted Dewey hurrying from the entry.

"Nice of you to show up," Lane chided.

But Dewey didn't smile, didn't take a seat. "We gotta talk," he said. "Outside."

"Are you *sure?*" Lane asked, wary of his friend's claim.

Two strangers sharing a black umbrella passed by on the sidewalk. Dewey refrained from replying until the area cleared. "That's what he said."

Lane wrestled with the news, turned it over in his brain. He shivered from rain falling in a watery curtain from the awning above. Winter in August. Everything was backward, mixed up. Nothing seemed clear anymore.

"So Maddie was right." Lane shook his head. "She swore he was alive, even after the telegram, but—deep down, I didn't believe it."

Dewey broke in gently. "Keep in mind, though, it's been weeks since these fellas escaped. There's a chance TJ's fine, not saying he isn't. But you need to know, the Jap commanders at these camps, they—well, from the stories we hear . . ." He tightened his lips before finishing. "Just saying things can get ugly for the ones left behind."

Lane heard the warnings, forced them in. It was sound advice. *Don't get your hopes up.* This was wartime, after all. The Allies were making huge strides toward victory, yet when they would reach TJ's prison was a mystery.

"I want to talk to 'em," Lane decided.

"Who, the prisoners?"

"The one who gave you the list of POWs. This . . . Ranieri guy."

Dewey slid his hands in the pockets of his Army overcoat and angled his face away, right before his cheek twitched. Lane knew that telltale twitch; meant there was a problem he wasn't disclosing.

"Just tell me where they're keeping him."

"Listen, Lane." Dewey turned back toward him, not quite meeting his eyes. "I think you should give it a little time, is all. You know, let the fella get settled. The higher-ups are working on gathering more intel, so we'll know more soon."

"I'm not going to hound him, if that's what you're worried about. Only need to make sure it's not a mistake."

"Really. I don't think it's a good idea."

"Why's that?"

Dewey sighed, hedging. What the hell was he not saying?

"Forget it, I'll find out myself," Lane bit out. "Tell me where he is."

Something in Dewey's silence struck like an invisible shove. Lane pushed back with a roar of words, "Tell me where he is!"

"The hospital," he murmured. "By the base."

Lane didn't stay for more details. He took off into the rain, charged by a sudden, desperate need to connect with TJ, in any way possible.

"He's alive," he whispered as he splashed a path through the street. "He's alive." It wasn't a fact, but a wish. One he'd been too scared to make ever since Maddie had received the last military cable. A year plus a month was the standard time line to announce the presumed death of someone missing in action. A mere formality that didn't mean a thing, Maddie had insisted.

Oh, God, please let her be right.

He's alive, he has to be alive.

The phrase looped in his mind as he entered the hospital. From a nurse's odd glance, he noticed his poor appearance, soaked from cap to shoes. He used his palm to swipe moisture from his face.

"May I help you?" the Australian woman asked.

"I'm looking for an American POW. His name's Ranaree." That wasn't right. Damn, what was it? "Or, something close to that. First name, Vince . . . I think."

Her eyes said she was still gauging Lane's intentions, and likely his sobriety. Another case of battle fatigue frying the brain. "Might I ask how you know the bloke?"

Lane considered spinning a plausible scenario, as he would have in the old days, but much had changed since then. He chose the truth, banking on faith that she would help. "He's a friend of . . ." Lane paused to gather the syllables that carried the weight of his past. "He's a friend of my brother."

After a moment of consideration, she nodded. "Follow me."

At a counter, she skimmed pages on a clipboard, then guided him through a hallway and down the length of a ward. The smell of antiseptic blended with the coppery scent of blood, the subtle reek of urine. Beds lined both sides of the room, each filled with wounded men.

On the front lines, Lane had witnessed his share of broken bodies. Yet seeing them here was somehow more unsettling. In a civilized environment—covered in fresh bandages, pajama sleeves or pant legs flattened from missing limbs—they no longer looked like warriors in the trenches. They were just men, many of them boys, who would soon return to a home that didn't recognize them.

"Over there, on the right." The nurse gestured before stepping away to answer a medical query from another nurse.

Lane scanned for features that would fit a name like Ranieri. He found a patient lying in bed, puffing on a smoke, with black hair and an olive complexion. Italian, as Lane expected. What he hadn't envisioned was the gauntness in the guy's cheeks, the dark circles cupping his eyes. Outlined by the sheet, his legs appeared starved for muscle. His arms were no better. Scars slanted over his neck and forearm. Facial scrapes and a cast-bound wrist boasted a narrow escape.

This, Lane realized, was the picture Dewey didn't want him to see, because of the natural question to follow: If this was how a survivor looked, what about those who remained imprisoned?

"Excuse me." Lane edged himself forward. "Are you the one who knew TJ? TJ Kern from Boyle Heights?"

The patient turned his sunken eyes in Lane's direction, studying him, not answering.

Lane removed his damp garrison cap and continued, "My name's—"

"Tomo," Vince finished.

The nickname gripped Lane's throat. "That's right," he said softly.

"Thought as much." Vince leveraged his weight onto his bony elbow. Then he offered his hand, and a heavy smile touched his dry lips. "It's a real pleasure. I've heard a lot about you."

❧61❧

Eyes squeezed tight, Maddie waited for the signal. She could smell the sulfuric burn of a match.

"Almost ready. . . ." Emma drew out the words. "A couple seconds, and—oops, wait, a couple more." She giggled. "Okaaay, open them!"

"Surprise," exclaimed the others.

At the kitchen table, Maddie's vision landed on the round chocolate cake. The whole group sang "Happy Birthday" with Yuki howling along. A merry occasion if not for the blazing fringe of candles.

"Good grief," Maddie moaned, "this is depressing. Twenty-two looks more like a hundred."

"Oh, hush now." Ida flicked the air. "You just wait another decade before you start complainin'. When my next birthday rolls around, we'll need to put the fire department on alert."

Mr. Garrett raised his bottled beer in the manner of a toast. "Well, I think all you ladies look youthful and lovely." His words addressed the whole room, but his gaze lingered long enough on Ida to make her blush.

"Time for a wish," the gal said abruptly, causing Maddie to smile.

Beside the counter, propped on Kumiko's hip, Suzie gurgled. Light from the flames bathed her tiny face in orange. "Ma-ma," she greeted.

Maddie couldn't resist kissing the nine-month-old's round nose. Her silky auburn hair smelled of lavender, her olive-hued skin of love and warm milk. She was a perfect blend of Maddie's and Lane's features. "What do you think, peanut? What new wish should I pick?"

She asked because, quite honestly, she wasn't sure. Her daily wish for confirmation that her brother was alive had been granted, and now she continued to pray every day that both he and Lane would return soon and safe. These were nothing new. Even her old standby didn't apply; for in this very moment, as her gaze circled the room, she discovered that the yearning for a family of her own, in an unexpected way, had come to fruition as well.

At the table, she leaned over the dancing wicks. She lowered her eyelids, inhaled a breath, and wished that she would remember this night forever—so that someday she could share the magical memory with her father.

Then she blew out the candles.

"So let's see how it tastes," Ida said.

Emma motioned toward Suzie, cringing. "I think someone's already checking that for us."

"Suzie-*chan*." Kumiko gasped.

The baby glanced up at the group. Chocolate covered her cheeks. Her little pudgy fingers were still plunged into a ceramic bowl bearing remnants of frosting. Yet her deep brown eyes seemed to say, *What? Did I do something wrong?*

Kumiko distanced Suzie from the bowl. "*Dame yo.* This no-no," she admonished in a gentle voice.

"It's okay," Maddie assured her. "She was just testing it for me. Weren't you, cutie?"

Suzie replied by slobbering on her chocolaty fists.

"So what's the verdict?" Maddie asked. "Did Emma's cake pass the test?" On cue, Suzie's eyes locked on the platter. She squealed with delight and reached with both hands.

Everyone burst into laughter, even Kumiko, whose occupied

arms prevented her from modestly covering her mouth. Her smile was charming and perfectly white, just like her son's, and Maddie found herself hoping that one day Suzie's would look identical.

"*Onēsan,* open mine first." Emma beamed, holding out a wrapped box.

Maddie removed the paper. She lifted out a turquoise flowing skirt, sewn from stitching skills she'd taught the girl. Thankfully it had an adjustable waistband. Maddie still had some pregnancy pounds to lose, and her cesarean section hadn't made it easier. She hugged Emma in gratitude, same for Ida and Mr. Garrett, who had purchased an oval-shaped jewelry box. The Viennese Waltz tinkled upon opening the lid.

And then came the last present.

After passing Suzie over to Ida, Kumiko retrieved an item from the hall closet. Eyes lowered, she handed over the blanketed painting. "This not very good, but please accept."

Maddie had learned about the customary phrase from Emma. It wasn't to be taken literally, but rather viewed as a compliment, a formal acknowledgment that the recipient was worthy of much more than any gift.

This message alone, delivered with such sincerity, tightened the area around Maddie's heart. Carefully she peeled back the blanket to reveal the depiction of a ship riding the ocean. Between the dragon-shaped helm and puffed ornate sail were seven Oriental figures clad in colorful kimonos.

"Boat is *Takarabune*—Treasure Ship," Kumiko explained. "People here, they are Seven Lucky Gods."

Emma added, "Each one stands for a different kind of fortune. That's why one is carrying fruit and another one has a spear. And that one there has a bundle of fish. The really cheerful one is Hotei. He's the god of good health."

The individual images were stunning, but their collective meaning even more so. They were a group born of optimism, traveling forward on a journey unknown, with faith they would eventually find land together.

"What about this one?" Maddie asked Emma, pointing to the

most prominent figure. The lone female in the center. In vibrant dress, she held an instrument resembling a guitar.

Kumiko supplied the answer. "That one Benzaiten. She goddess of art, beauty. Goddess of music." *Benzaiten is you,* she said without words.

Speechless, Maddie bowed her head in thanks. She had often worried that the closeness she'd shared with Kumiko following Suzie's precarious birth would dissolve as time passed. Yet here they were, two seasons later, and their bond continued to expand. The best part was, the more she learned about Kumiko, the more she understood Lane.

In the beginning, Maddie had believed she and Lane were the same; later she'd feared they were too different. All the while, they were actually somewhere in between. They were a perfect marriage of two cultures. A perfect complement of two people.

"How about a song?" Mr. Garrett declared, already fishing out his harmonica. "Who knows, maybe tonight we can even get the birthday girl to whip out her fiddle."

Maddie tossed him a playful glare. "Not likely."

High on the moment, though, she actually did feel an urge to entertain the idea.

Mr. Garrett grinned. "So what's the first request? Emma, you got one for me?"

The girl could always be counted on for suggestions.

"Emma?" he repeated.

Maddie turned to discover Emma's face glued to the window. Lines of concern etched her face, drawing Maddie over. "What is it, Em?"

Through clouds of dirt and descending sunrays, a taxi trudged up the drive. It was the kind of vehicle that often delivered telegrams. Announcements of casualties.

Maddie couldn't recall heading for the door, but in a flash she stood on the front porch. Fear drained her of the moisture needed to swallow. She only realized the whole family was beside her when Suzie whimpered an ominous cry. Maddie thought to relieve Ida of the baby, but worried the forthcoming news would turn her limbs to water.

Please make me strong, I have to be strong for Suzie.

It took the cab a million years to roll up to the house.

Finally the car stopped. Everyone watched as the door swung open, and—

Lane's father stepped out.

Relief spread through Maddie in a heated wave, reaching the tips of her ears. The urge to simultaneously laugh and cry threatened her balance. She gripped an arm of the closest person—Mr. Garrett—with both hands.

Emma dashed over and hugged her father. "Papa, Papa, Papa," she cried, as though willing his presence into permanence.

He seemed to hold his breath while Kumiko approached. Without hesitation, his wife reached out and embraced him. His eyes flared in surprise. Then tentatively, he returned the gesture and squeezed their huddle close.

They were together again, a family reunited. Even Yuki was welcomed into the center of their circle. It should have been a moment of bliss and warmth for all the people there. Yet from a revelation, a chill penetrated Maddie's skin: Despite his being Lane's father, the man was a virtual stranger, one who'd been incarcerated by her race; a father who, in fact, had chosen a different daughter-in-law.

Right or wrong, Maddie was seized by a feeling that Mr. Moritomo was about to ruin everything.

❧ 62 ❧

Nine months had passed since the breakout, yet prisoners' commentaries on the story still thrived at TJ's camp. With Christmas around the corner, fertile grounds for depression, hope was the key to survival. Ranieri's gang had provided that: hope that soon they'd all have a chance to escape themselves. The only other topic covered as frequently was the camp baseball game, one that had gifted them with a taste of both normalcy and revenge.

At the top of the sixth inning, the POWs had been up by a run, a miracle considering the sad shape they were in. TJ was rearing up for a knuckleball when a camp-wide alert cut the game short. Looney flew into a rage and a frantic search party ensued. The game never resumed. There was no prize. No winner. Well, except for TJ, who knew in his gut he'd done the right thing by staying behind.

Scuttlebutt claimed Happy was caught passed out with a flask at his post, where an incriminating hole appeared in the wire fence. Some said that while being arrested he was too drunk to walk without help. Prisoners laughed about the tale, unaware that sleeping powder had laced the man's liquor.

Two mornings later, guards escorted him to stand before the

camp. It was one of the rare times TJ had seen the guy without the jovial grin that defined him. Initially, TJ presumed Happy was being executed for being an inadvertent accomplice, but the interpreter explained otherwise. Rooted in the samurai code, the guard had been granted permission to perform *seppuku,* a penance to restore his honor. He had taken full responsibility for the crime, and this alone had prevented the commander from decapitating fifty POWs.

Happy knelt on the stage in a white robe. He sipped from a cup and ate a small plate of food with chopsticks. On the small wooden block before him, he wrote what the translator described as a death poem. Then he loosened the upper part of his robe and tucked the long sleeves beneath his knees to angle himself forward. As a "friend" stood behind him with samurai sword in hand, Happy gripped a short blade wrapped in white paper. Staring distantly at the crowd, he held the silvery tip to his bare stomach.

An irrational sense of injustice seized TJ. *You don't have to do this,* he wanted to shout. *It wasn't all your fault!*

Of course, he stayed silent, as did Happy while making a sideways cut to his own abdomen. In that split second before his merciful beheading, TJ glimpsed the look in his eyes. It wasn't fear or fanatical determination. Rather it was a deep-reaching regret, one TJ recognized from his father.

"So, Kern, when you gonna get us a rematch?" a grimy POW now asked, but TJ continued to shovel the mud, not answering.

"What're you—dense?" muttered a GI, working in a nearby trench. "Even Looney isn't nuts enough to let us do that again."

"Damare!" Grumpy marched over and slammed the butt of his rifle into the GI's shoulder. No question, the prick had turned meaner since the escape. *"Shigoto ni modoranka!"*

TJ, too, followed the command and dug faster. The hole he stood in was waist deep. His blistered hands shook from exhaustion. Brown water splashed with every scoop. Another monsoon season had come and gone, but for days rain had been soaking the jungle. Not a treat when you're literally forced to live in it.

TJ and twenty other POWs deemed well enough to work had

been ordered to this spot, a mile or so from camp. Until completing their task, they were to eat, sleep, and burrow in the mud like moles. A scattering of blue sky today provided their sole break in the monotony.

"Don't make sense to me," whispered a corporal shoveling close by.

TJ would have ignored the remark if not for one thing. The guy had learned some basic Japanese from his parents, former missionaries in Okinawa. If the airman had caught whiff of a secret, TJ wanted to know. Before replying, he glanced up and confirmed Grumpy had moved on to harass one of his own men.

"What doesn't make sense?" TJ said quietly, still plowing the ground.

"Why are we building bomb shelters for the whole camp? Why not just the Japs? They don't give two shits if we die or not. And why put them so far away? Bombs start dropping, ain't none of us making it here in time."

The thought had crossed TJ's mind.

"I've kept my ears open. None of them is saying squat. They're up to somethin'. And it ain't good, I know that much."

TJ's arms slowed. He surveyed the deepening holes scattered about. Could they be digging their own graves? If Ranieri's group had reported even a fraction of what took place here, wouldn't Allies have sent help by now?

That's assuming his buddies had reached friendly shores. . . .

A shout from behind awakened TJ to a more pressing thought. The fact that he'd dropped his shovel. He scoured the murky puddle. Found a rock, his own foot. He'd just recovered the handle when a grip yanked at his collar and slid him out of the trench. TJ reflexively shielded his face. Past his wrists, he glimpsed Eddie standing over him, rifle butt raised, an internal struggle on his face. This was the first work detail they'd shared in months.

Another guard hollered, urging him to strike. It was Grumpy, closing in with a glower.

Eddie tightened his grip and lifted the weapon.

"Please don't, Eddie!" TJ begged. Once the words came out, he registered his mistake. He shouldn't have said the name.

Eddie confirmed this with a dark glint in his eyes. Being the guard who'd requested the ball game, a suspicious act, he had even more to prove than before.

"Tate!" Eddie waved the barrel of his rifle to illustrate the command to stand.

TJ continued to shake, though now from fear, while he climbed to his feet. Eddie shoved the nose of his weapon into TJ's side. Grumpy continued to watch in judgment. Instinct told TJ to close his eyes and wait for the shot, but he couldn't break from Eddie's gaze. Somehow, regardless of the company, in that moment, he didn't want to die in the blackness all alone.

Eddie pointed the barrel at TJ's face. His grip found the trigger. After a brief pause, his finger began to flex—then he stopped and jerked his head upward. A dull roar sang from the sky.

TJ knew that sound. He knew those engines.

The revelation spread through the prisoners like a gust of wind. They scrambled out of their ditches. Between a checkering of clouds passed the most beautiful sight TJ had ever seen. An American bomber!

With the B-25 headed their way, the ragtag group jumped up and down, waving deliriously with joy. TJ couldn't help joining in their whooping. Allied bombers meant the Japs could be losing their stronghold. It meant the camp had been found.

Grumpy's shrieks did nothing to regain order. He scuttled this way and that, looking confused over what to do.

Eddie merely stared at the sky, speechless as usual, until releasing a bellow that rattled TJ's bones. Not from its volume, but from the meaning of the English words. "Get down!"

TJ's gaze shot to the sky. Bomb bay doors were splayed open. In his mind, he could hear the crew's radio announcement. *Bombs away!*

The POWs were celebrating too much to notice.

"Hit the dirt, hit the dirt!" TJ shoved one of them into a hole before diving in himself. He didn't hear the bombs whistling downward, just a series of explosions shaking the earth, punctuated by an enormous boom. They'd hit an ammo dump, from the sound of it. Trees burst into flames. Dirt hailed over TJ's body, rolled tight into fetal position in the pooled water. Screams sailed through the air—men's screams. They were being killed by their own side.

Or did sides exist anymore?

As if to answer, a B-25 zoomed overhead and dropped another payload.

❧ 63 ❧

One hundred thirty-nine American POWs—all murdered. Lane had tried to convince himself it was just propaganda, but multiple accounts from men who'd survived the Palawan Massacre verified the horrors. Only eleven had made it out alive. With the Allies gradually recapturing the Philippines, MacArthur had sent out a directive to the area's Japanese commander in chief, citing warnings of accountability for the mistreatment of prisoners.

Evidence of crimes by their captors was soon set aflame. The POWs at Palawan were ordered into air raid shelters they'd built themselves, then the structures were doused with gasoline and torched in a coordinated effort. Nearly all who broke out were bayoneted, shot, clubbed, or tortured.

Palawan wasn't TJ's prison camp, but the same could happen there any time. And Lane carried in an envelope the proof supporting his claim.

He strode into the building with a look of confidence. It had taken a dozen phone calls to secure the meeting—not to mention a furlough pass, as well as hitchhiking jaunts on four different jeeps in the roasting January heat—in order to reach Melbourne. Now all he had to do was make it through the officer's door.

"I'm here to see Major Berlow, please." Lane presented his most charming smile to the receptionist.

"And you are?"

"Sergeant Lane Moritomo, ma'am."

She pushed up her bifocals and scanned her schedule. Frank Sinatra crooned "Blue Skies" through a tabletop radio. "Ah, yes. The major will be with you shortly. Have a seat, if you will."

He thanked her and propped another smile, which she reciprocated. A good sign. He'd welcome any ally who had a connection to Berlow; the guy was his last chance. Also a last resort.

Lane had spent every day for the past several months slogging through various chains of command. He'd campaigned to politicians, brass, anyone in the upper echelons with the potential to liberate TJ's camp. He'd referred them to atrocities shared by Ranieri: appendectomies with no anesthesia, iron-club beatings for stealing a single papaya, little or no medical attention while men suffered from malaria and scurvy, beriberi and tropical ulcers.

Although listeners extended their sympathies, reports from other Japanese camps were too similar to make Lane's case stand out.

Helpless to do much more, he had thrown himself into his work. His spot at OCS had been confirmed but delayed. His goal of being home by New Year's had changed to Valentine's. He liked to visualize surprising Maddie at the station with a bouquet of peach roses, though the vision never lasted. Thoughts of TJ would crash into his mind and return him to task.

Hence, he applied tireless effort, surpassed expectations. He treated each document, each Japanese POW, as if the secret to achieving peace lay in their translated words. On occasion, he'd uncover an item of significance. He had even earned a promotion for his deeds. No doubt, the MIS's Nisei and Kibei were collectively shaving years off the war. Their translation of the Z Plan, Japan's naval counterattack strategy, enabled a major U.S. victory in the Battle of the Philippine Sea; decoding an intercepted itinerary led to the assassination of Admiral Yamamoto, mastermind of the Pearl Harbor attack; and the list went on and on.

The theory was simple: Win the war, and TJ would come home.

So long as the war didn't outlast TJ.

"Sergeant," the receptionist called. "The major will see you now."

Lane rose, overseas cap resting on his manila envelope. He followed the woman's directions toward the office in the northern corner of the building. Ringing phones competed in volume against snapping typewriters and chattering secretaries.

At the door, he heard a muffled voice. He rapped a knuckle on the glass.

"Yeah, yeah, come in!" The gruff response belonged to Berlow. A sniper's shot to the knee may have raised the man's military rank, even secured a cozy office, but obviously it had done little for his social graces.

Lane proceeded inside. Berlow sat behind his desk, his face slightly thickened. He was dictating notes to a young gal struggling to keep up. As predicted, the room was meticulously neat, not a speck of dust on the oak desk or cabinets. When the girl dared ask for clarification, he dismissed her with a grumble. She slinked from the room, head bowed.

Snapping a salute, Lane direly hoped his own encounter wouldn't end the same.

Berlow returned the greeting in a vague motion, then pulled a cigar box from his desk. Was he going to offer one for old times' sake?

"Nice to see you again, Captain—I mean—Major Berlow."

The officer chose a single cigar, for himself, and slapped the lid closed.

Lane continued as planned, laying groundwork for the scene. "Speaking of which, congratulations on your promotion. I'd only just learned you'd been transferred from the islands."

Berlow stuck the cigar into the corner of his mouth and his teeth clamped. "You come all this way to blow sunshine up my ass, Sergeant? 'Cause Colonel 'Blowhard' has decided to call a lunch meeting, giving you exactly"—he checked his watch—"ten minutes and three seconds to speak your piece. I wouldn't waste them if I were you."

Lane cleared his throat. Luckily, he'd prepared a speech.

"Sir, I'm here to inform you of a situation. I recently translated an official memo from the Japanese Ministry of War, sent to their prison camp commanders. In it are orders to execute their Allied POWs if our advancing forces are closing in on them. I'm convinced this memo set the stage for the Massacre at Palawan."

Berlow chewed on the end of his cigar, devoid of expression.

"There's also a camp on Magtulay, a small island south of Mindoro. With the Allies' recent invasion of Mindoro, and General MacArthur's return to Leyte, this camp is particularly vulnerable. Escaped POWs from there have already attested to numerous war crimes."

Remembering his envelope, Lane reached inside to retrieve a copy of the memo. "I have the document with its translation here, confirming my report."

The major threw up a hand to refuse the pages. "I'm familiar with Magtulay," he ground out. "*And* the memo. *And* the mistreatment of our POWs—in a whole lot more Jap camps than this. So what is this really about?"

Lane slowly tucked the papers away, reviewing his now barren arguments. In a single swipe, the man had stripped the effectiveness of them all.

"Well?" Berlow pressed.

Coming clean seemed the only choice left. If nothing else, perhaps Berlow would appreciate Lane's honesty, and the drive to protect his own.

"The truth of it is, sir," he began again, "an old friend has been held there for two years. By the time our forces liberate the camp, it might be too late. Given your connections and experience, I was hoping you could help get these guys out."

"Ahh," Berlow said, sitting back. "Get 'em out. Just like that."

Lane tried to expound, but the major cut in.

"Surely I don't need to remind you that every soldier, sailor, and Marine out there is someone's buddy or sweetheart. Some mother's pride and joy. So you must have a mighty good reason this pal of yours deserves more attention than the rest." A question and answer combined in one. More than that, his aloofness gave no hint that he and Lane were more than strangers. There existed no trace of their last somewhat genial exchange on the islands. No suggestion that they had served side by side in battle.

One would never know, for example, that the man behind the desk was alive because of the technical sergeant standing before him.

Lane had hoped to bypass that truth, but there was too much at stake. He straightened and replied, "It would be a favor, sir."

Berlow cocked his head, waiting, eyes narrowing.

"After everything I've . . . been through with your company." He'd inserted the pause to draw out the allusion, which he let hang there, gaining definition.

Comprehension stroked the length of Berlow's face. His features hardened as if coated in glaze. "I think we're done here."

An alarm rang in Lane's mind, a warning to backpedal. "Major, all I meant was—"

"I said, we're done."

The tactic had proven a grave mistake. Push any harder and Lane could wind up behind bars himself.

In acknowledgment of his defeat, he simply said, "Yes, sir." Then, left without choice, he headed for the door, his final solution crushed at the hands of Berlow's pride.

As he reached for the knob, he noted the major's cane, leaned against the wall beside him. At the sight, Lane's view of the room changed. It wasn't an office. It was a cage for an animal meant to run free, to hunt.

For Berlow, a man who thrived in the heat of battle and lived entirely for leading his pack, a desk job was a prison in disguise. Not all that different, perhaps, from an internment camp.

Turning back, Lane offered what he could. "I'm sorry about your leg, sir."

The major didn't respond, but the rage in his cheeks began to fade.

"Thank you for your time." Lane saluted and again went to leave. When he stepped over the threshold, he heard Berlow curse to himself.

A holler followed: "Sergeant, get your ass back here. And close the damn door."

Despite the choice of words, the order landed in the realm of civil, with the potential for pleasant. Lane obliged, hope kept in check, and returned to his chair.

From a desk drawer, Berlow snagged a small matchbox and a clean ashtray. Amazingly, he lit his cigar. He stretched out a smoky exhale, as though savoring a long-denied delight. Finally, reclining in his throne, he confided, "There's a raid in the works—on Magtulay."

Lane's whole body perked, first from elation, then from the fearful image of strafing fighter planes. "What kind of raid is it?"

"The kind that could get your buddy home safe and sound. Or, get him and everyone involved killed. Got several being planned at different camps in the area. Course, that's not for you to spread around." He continued once Lane shook his head in agreement. "There was talk about tasking our Raiders with the toughest ones, but now that Vandegrift disbanded the units, I imagine the Army'll be tackling them solo." He didn't sound pleased about the decisions.

Those weren't of Lane's concern.

"Sir, about Magtulay . . ."

"Huh? Ah, yeah. Well, it seems a Philadelphia congressman has a nephew who got himself shot down off Panay. Reports say he's being held at your pal's camp. Goal is to get him out before the Japs figure out what kind of bargaining chip just fell into their pocket."

The news was miraculous, almost too good to be true—making Lane wary. "May I ask why you're telling me this, sir?"

"G-2's waiting on some captured documents, maps and such, from Mindoro. Seeing as you have a vested interest here, you might want to be in charge of translating those papers when they come in. Make sure nothing's missed." He added stress to his next point. "With a good number of Marines in that camp, part of my duty is to bring them home."

So that was Berlow's angle. To liberate guys sharing his uniform. But what about those who weren't Marines? Or above all, any prisoner without a powerfully connected uncle?

Lane knew enough to understand that casualties would be considered a calculated cost. Also that TJ would be among those labeled expendable.

He couldn't allow that. Which made what he had to do utterly clear.

"Major, could you tell me who I should speak to about accompanying the rescue team?"

Berlow expelled a sharp gray puff. The expanse of his forehead knotted. "Oh no you don't. They don't need you jumping in and fouling up their plans. And I'm not about to take responsibility for your welfare."

"Please, sir, just consider it. On the front lines, I could contribute to the mission's success. Listening in on enemy conversations, translating on the spot." Even though Berlow hadn't praised him for those acts in the past, Lane knew he was aware of them. "I simply can't sit back and watch. Not when I know how much I could help by being there."

Berlow shifted his gaze to his ashtray. He tapped a finger on his desk, mulling over the idea. The seconds passed as if dripping from a leaky faucet. "All right," he muttered. "I can't promise anything, but I'll talk to the colonel."

Lane suppressed a smile.

"Just try not to get yourself killed for Christ's sake."

"I'll do my best, sir."

For hours, during the jeep rides back to Sydney, Lane thought about his beloved Maddie. He questioned if he were making a mistake by putting himself in danger, their future on the line. In less than a month he could be on a ship sailing home to not only her, but the daughter he'd yet to meet. Suzie, his sweet baby bird.

He longed, too, to see the rest of his family, at last reunited after his father's release. The man's innocence should have been evident from the start. And yet Lane's dad would never voice this; he would forge on with patience and endurance. Such admirable traits had apparently paid off in other ways. For, according to Emma, their parents had discovered a newfound affection. The idea still filled

Lane with wonderment—as did every cherished letter from Maddie. Her mentions of even the most mundane daily tasks seemed like paradise when he imagined completing them together.

But how could he enjoy any of that without first doing everything in his power to bring her brother back? That was a gift she deserved for the love she'd given Lane, the devotion she'd shown for him and his family, when walking away would have been easier.

No wonder TJ had been so fiercely protective of her. If Lane had been in his shoes, what's to say he wouldn't have lashed out the same way, regardless of friendships sacrificed? Maybe it was too late to make amends. Maybe what had been broken could never be fixed. But for the relationship they'd once had, if a chance of rescuing TJ remained, Lane would be there to see it through.

⤞ 64 ⤝

Suzie's piercing shriek sent Maddie racing toward the sound. She tore into the living room—a mother's curse, she'd learned, was to expect the worst—yet no catastrophe awaited. Rather she found the opposite. Nobu, on all fours, was chasing Suzie's wobbly walk around the doily-draped rocking chair. Ousted from her hiding spot, the girl bopped him lightly with raggedy Sarah Mae, then joined him in a bout of laughter.

Maddie sighed in relief, over more than her daughter's safety. Her fear of their being shunned by Lane's father, after he'd first arrived at the farm, lasted only until his wife declared Maddie and Suzie family. Behind closed doors, Kumiko may have detailed what the women had survived together, but more likely it was his wife's transformed demeanor that had persuaded him. That, and the heavenly giggles of a child who was destined to further the man's lineage.

"Nani yatten no, Papa?" Kumiko entered from the kitchen and tsked at his foolishness. Her fists pressed against the hips of her housedress. *"Mō shizukani shite kudasai."*

He gently waved her off and turned to the girl. "No listen her, Suzie-*chan*. We not too loud." Spiking his volume, he added, "*This* too loud. *Ne?"*

With a squeal, Suzie bounced in her winter jumper.

Maddie hid a smile from Kumiko, who grumbled under her breath. Before the woman swung back toward the kitchen, however, her gaze caught on Nobu's. There was power in the exchange. Like a bolt of lightning, it struck in a flash and sent visible heat through Kumiko's cheeks. Maddie knew that blush firsthand. She used to feel the same uncontainable glow every time Lane walked into a room.

Maddie resisted the memory, the onslaught of longing. "Suzie," she called out. "It's almost bath time."

The baby, already a year now, shuffled back behind the chair.

Nobu bowed his head toward Maddie, and they traded smiles. Then he returned to Suzie and broke into her favorite tune. The girl babbled along to the Japanese nursery song, about a baby bird searching for its nest.

The scenario was a fitting one. In days, they would be leaving the only home Suzie had ever known. Would uprooting the child forever rob her sense of security?

Oh, nonsense. Surely it wouldn't. Besides, better now than later. The more time spent here, the greater the loss.

Back in her room, Maddie held the cardigan to her nose. The yellow sweater, with its scalloped collar and pearly buttons, had often been her favorite for dates with Lane. She inhaled deeply now, tried again, but his scent was gone.

Resuming her task, she folded the garment and placed it in the suitcase on her bed. She continued to pack the pile beside her pillow. On top was a pale pink dress with daisy appliqués that Bea had sewn for Suzie's birthday. If Maddie had known they'd be moving home by year's end, she would have saved the woman the postage. Yet out here, being so removed from the happenings of the world, who could have guessed the government would finally regain its sanity?

The exclusion order, banning all Japanese Americans from the West Coast, had officially been lifted. At last, they could all go home.

Maddie ran her fingers over a bound pile of envelopes, set atop her nightstand. Soon, she would reunite with each of their senders: Bea, who was about to burst from eagerness over meeting Suzie; Jo, whose grandfather's stroke required her assistance with his care, cutting short her career in the pros. And of course, there was Lane. In mere weeks, he'd be traveling safely toward the States. Although eventually his stint at Fort Benning would mean their relocating again, he had assured her it would be temporary—and staying together was all that mattered.

God, she missed him. So often she dreamed of holding him close. How she yearned for Suzie to know her father, and, as always, her uncle, TJ—not separately, but as the friends, the brothers they once were.

Four years had passed since words and wounds divided them. Four years since America set out for revenge. Now, as Hitler waged desperate battles on the Western Front, the Axis powers were dwindling. Victory was within reach. Though for Maddie, only when the two men reconciled would the war truly be over.

A knock on the gaping door pulled Maddie's attention to Emma. "Hey, pretty girl. Whatcha need?"

"Got a present for you." Emma approached the bed, hands behind her back. Her movements had become as graceful as the hair that swung past her shoulders.

"Em, you shouldn't have. You gave us plenty for Christmas." No question, for Suzie, nothing could possibly top Emma's gift of Sarah Mae.

"It's not from me. It's from Ida." She handed over a photograph from Thanksgiving, a copy of the one Maddie had sent to Lane. In the image, Maddie and Suzie stood before the fireplace with Nobu, Kumiko, and Emma. A wisecrack from Mr. Garrett had caused the group to laugh just as Ida snapped the shot.

"But she's already given me this picture," Maddie said. "Is she certain she wants to spare it?"

"She told me it's to be doubly sure we remember her."

"As if we could ever forget." Maddie's aim for levity soared past its mark. She grabbed her violin case from the corner and sat beside Emma on the bed. From the lid, she removed Bach's portrait—the last of the originals—and inserted the new addition. A complete display of memories. TJ. Lane. Marriage and war. The evacuation, the riot. So much had happened in a span of four years.

Emotions rising, Maddie shut the case and gestured toward the crate on the floor. "Can you believe Mr. Garrett gave me his record collection? I told him it was too generous, but he insisted there's only one he wanted to keep. Also, his gramophone doesn't work anymore, so . . ."

Emma showed no sign of her reliable, infectious grin. She absently fingered the suitcase buckle. Her gaze low, she whispered, "I'm scared, *Onēsan*."

There was no reason to ask why. Maddie understood all too well the fear of the unknown, of losing ones you loved. The fear that a single day, an unwanted change, could permanently alter your life.

"Ah, cheer up, now." She directed this to Emma as much as herself. "Just think of all your favorite things in California that you've missed. Like feeding the ducks at Hollenbeck Park. Or eating rhubarb pie at Clifton's. The holiday parades downtown?"

"Yeah, but," Emma began, and hesitated.

"But what, sweetie? You can say it."

Emma lifted her glossy eyes. "What if nobody wants us back?"

Maddie wanted to offer an assurance. The lie, however, refused to form. Concern over treatment that awaited—for Suzie, in particular, who might not fit into either world—constantly hovered in her mind.

"Why can't we just wait until next fall?" Emma pleaded. "That's when I'll be going into junior high anyway. Why can't we do that instead?"

Nobu was determined they depart before outwearing their welcome, and Maddie did see his point. Mr. Garrett had initially signed on to house three able-bodied women for helping out with chores; not five guests to take over his house, including a tot who was hardly reducing his workload.

"Everything's going to be fine," Maddie told her. "You'll see. Once we're settled, it'll all be grand."

"How do you know?"

"Because, pretty—" She was about to say "girl," but stopped herself. Emma had grown up right before her eyes. At eleven years old, she'd gained maturity and insight beyond her years. For that reason alone, she deserved an honest answer.

"Because we're survivors," Maddie said firmly. "That's how I know."

After taking this in, Emma nodded.

"Come here, honey." Maddie welcomed her into a hug. She stroked Emma's long ebony hair to the sweet, innocent tones of Suzie's humming, which floated down the hall and into the room.

"I miss Lane," Emma said softly, her cheek on Maddie's chest.

Maddie closed her eyes and confessed, "So do I, Em. So do I. . . ."

❦ 65 ❧

The mission was running according to plan—so far. With ten soldiers in each *banca,* Lane's unit had crossed the Sulu Sea undetected, despite danger that swayed like kelp in the dark waters. Filipino guerrillas had delivered on their promise; in preparation for the stealth landing, they'd cleared Magtulay's far north shore of Japanese night patrollers.

More than once the question had scratched at Lane's mind: *What in God's name am I doing here?*

Too late to turn back. What's more, TJ was here. On this very island. By dawn, they could be sailing toward freedom together.

A hazy moon and the captain's map served as their only guides. The armed GIs snaked their way around a mangrove, then cut through an island passage to reach the barn designated their coordinating point. Along the way, they'd captured a valuable asset, a Japanese corporal with thorough knowledge of the POW camp's interior.

Using a stick, the guy sketched the officers' quarters into the dirt. Lane crouched beside him, propping a flashlight. A circle of Army Rangers looked on intently. Over the past few days, a small recon team had provided a sufficient amount of intel, but was unable to determine details that the Japanese soldier was suddenly spilling freely.

"So what'd you say to him?" the husky captain asked Lane, sounding puzzled and rightly so. Until a moment ago, the enemy corporal had firmly declared he would die before doing anything to help America.

"I told him if he didn't tell us everything, you were gonna send a message to his parents through the Red Cross. That it'd say the second we landed on the beach, he surrendered without a fight."

A smile eased onto Captain McDonough's face. "Glad someone round here understands how these monkeys think."

The comment typically would have caused Lane an internal knee jerk. But the fact was this: He did understand them; like it or not, they were part of him. The line between him and the enemy had simultaneously blurred and solidified. Somehow, while perhaps it shouldn't have, this thought provided a strange sense of peace.

"Okay, listen up," the captain announced after gathering enough details. He went through the plan one last time, utilizing the diagram on the ground. Speed and surprise were essential. Should something go awry, they were all to rush the camp, weapons firing. Two Rangers were tasked with seeking out the politician's son, referred to as the "Goddamned VIP." All other Allied prisoners were to be rescued as the situation allowed.

A runner arrived at the tail end of the recap and reported all was going smoothly. Two other Army units, making their total U.S. force just over a hundred strong, were now hunkered down by rice paddies a mile away. Thanks to their band of Filipino accomplices, a supply of makeshift stretchers, wheelbarrows, and carabao-towed carts was ready to transport debilitated POWs to the beach. There, rescue subs would meet the whole lot of them—if they pulled this off.

The minutes dragged as though soaked in tar. Seated against a barn wall, Lane removed his helmet and retrieved the photo from inside. A picture of his family that Maddie had sent. His wife's arm wrapped sweet Emma around the shoulders, and his mother beamed with an expression he recognized solely from his boyhood.

Suzie, growing like a weed, clung to Lane's father, who held the girl snugly in his arms.

For the millionth time, Lane stroked Maddie's face, little Suzie's plump cheeks. He imagined the melody of the laughter that had filled the room. Though he ached to join them, even now he didn't regret the risk he was taking. Instead, the thought of them reminded him why he was here.

Finally McDonough gave the word. Time to move out.

The men adjusted their battle gear. They secured white armbands, identification to prevent friendly fire, and they slipped out a side door. A breeze whispered warnings through the leaves of towering palm trees. Waves crashed on the distant shore.

Then came a thud.

Lane swung his rifle toward the sound. His pulse doubled in speed.

"Coconut," assured the Ranger beside him in an undertone.

Lane forced a swallow and continued on, his weapon slick in his moistening palms. In a single-file column, the soldiers trekked through the jungle over branches and rocks, fallen trees. Unseen creatures rustled like agitated ghosts.

At last the captain raised his hand, the signal to halt, then to take their positions. The unit quietly scattered as McDonough summoned Lane to the front. In a natural ditch of dried mud and giant leaves, the commander passed Lane binoculars after taking a peek himself. Lane raised them to his eyes. A dirt road, just over eighty yards ahead, divided two stilted guard towers flanking the prison entrance. To the raid's advantage, there were no searchlights to illuminate the perimeter that was now virtually surrounded.

"The *paguda* thing," McDonough said to him, "is that what I'm seeing over there? Fifty yards northeast of the flagpole?"

Lane peered through the main gate webbed with barbed wire. The flag's circle—the Emperor's red sun—fluttered, then drooped with the sigh of a drained balloon. Or perhaps a sleeping beast. From there, Lane located the decorative stone pagoda, which the Japanese corporal had described. The narrow, temple-like sculpture would serve as their reference point.

"Yeah, Captain," he confirmed. "That's the one."

"Well, looks like he was telling the truth, after all."

Lucky for the corporal. The coarse Filipino farmer who was guarding him didn't seem the lenient type.

McDonough accepted the binoculars to further study the landscape. Once more, the minutes dragged past. Morning strained blackness from the air, until less than an hour awaited before the raid.

At 0600 the majority of the prison guards were expected to begin their daily exercise. With no weapons and little clothing on, they would be slower to react. Allied casualties would be minimized during the coordinated assault.

McDonough now gave a sign. A couple of Army snipers crawled forward to take their positions in the bushes. At the prescribed hour, they were to neutralize the sentries at the gate. This would pave a path for the rescue units to swoop in with their rifles and grenades, their Tommy guns, BARs, and bazookas.

Lane was concentrating on keeping his breaths even and silent when a voice echoed through the dawn. A man's voice. Had to be Japanese. He was too far away though, too mumbled to understand.

"Damn it," the captain whispered, binoculars raised. "He's coming closer." The enemy guard spoke again, and McDonough turned to Lane. "What's he saying?"

Lane grabbed the binoculars. He'd have better luck if he could see the guy's mouth move. The Japanese soldier was yelling something back at the sentries in the towers. He was holding his rifle as though preparing to shoot—but at what?

Studying the guy's lips, Lane tried to make out the words. *Yumi . . . ma . . . so . . .* His mind scrambled to understand. Then it came to him. *Yubimasubi!*

"Possum," he alerted the commander. "He's only hunting possum."

The captain launched a hushed order of "Hold your fire, hold your fire," but before it could spread, the Japanese man discharged his weapon. Not two seconds later, a return shot leveled him to the ground. The invisible wire had been tripped, and just like that, their calculated plan exploded. Wounded, the guard screamed to his comrades. An exchange of ammo snapped and boomed.

"Let's go! Let's go!" McDonough hollered. Yet as Lane started to rise with the others, the captain commanded, "You stay put."

Lane started to argue, but McDonough was gone.

The island shook and grumbled. Lane would be smart to remain in his spot of relative safety. He was far from an elite Army Ranger trained for special missions. He'd been assigned merely to help guide them to their stationing point, which he'd done. Now he was supposed to sit tight and wait.

But how could he? The kid he'd grown up with—the one who, in fact, had once saved his life—was trapped inside that corral of barbed wire.

Ah, stuff the order!

He stormed forward and into the mouth of the roaring beast. A machine gun peppered the main watchtowers, sending a guard to his death below. The other sentry hung limply over a windowsill.

Lane took cover behind a supply hut on the prison grounds. He peeked around the corner. A Japanese soldier was charging straight in his direction. Lane pulled the trigger and cut him down in two shots.

A lineup of long thatched buildings created a backdrop to the battle. The prisoners' quarters. Breath held, heart pounding, he took off toward the closest one. Bullets zipped past his face, but he didn't stop, didn't turn back.

Inside the barrack, he found haggard POWs huddled in corners, crouched beneath sleeping bays. The smell of filth and degradation caused Lane a jolt.

"It's all right," he yelled to them. He knelt down to avoid being spotted or shot through the open-air windows. "We're Americans. We're here to bring you home!"

Half the men looked dazed, some plain terrified. For others, the realization that this was real—not the same dream they'd had every night since being captured—played across their faces.

"What do you need us to do?" asked one nearby.

"Grab anything you can use as weapons." It wasn't an official order, just the first thought Lane had. "The guys well enough to fight back ought to be in front. Are any of you strong enough to take out guards if they come inside?"

"Oh, we're strong enough," another prisoner replied. He had revenge in his voice and smile.

Lane nodded. "Till it's over, the rest of you fellas stay low and keep safe."

More and more of the dazed prisoners appeared to be reentering the present. POWs shuffled around the room, gaining momentum. Small hidden weapons—sharpened rocks, rusted blades—emerged from hiding. A sailor snapped a whittled cane over his knee, creating two jagged points.

Lane searched their faces, their hollowed eyes, hunting for the one he'd truly come for. Would he recognize his old friend even in this ghastly state?

"Listen," he called out, "does anyone here know a guy named—" A blast outside blew through the rest. He tried again, louder. "I'm looking for an airman. His name's Kern. TJ Kern. From California."

"You mean the baseball pitcher?" someone asked.

A surge bolted through Lane's veins, so strong he stammered his answer. "Yes, that's—that's him. Is he here?"

"Nah." A cough followed, and then: "He's gone."

The word *gone* halted Lane in place. A single syllable, and yet it stilled all movement in his body. With effort, he asked, "Gone where?"

The prisoner who first greeted Lane spoke up. "About a mile north." Machine guns rat-tat-tatted outside. Another explosion boomed. The guy's speech quickened. "We were almost done with the air raid shelters when Looney wanted an airstrip instead. I was helping out till I came down with a nasty fever."

"So he's alive?" Lane broke in.

The man paused before nodding. "Last I saw."

Lane's emotions raced and skidded, spun and reversed, trying to keep up. "Tell me where."

The prisoner filled him in. Then Lane jetted from the barrack and again took cover behind the hut. Scads of Japanese soldiers littered the ground. Still, a continuous stream of guards rolled in, each rippling from shots and slamming to the ground.

Lane's gaze zipped from left to right and back. He looked for the captain, for reinforcement. But there was no one free to help. At least a dozen POWs, including TJ, were bivouacked outside the camp, in equal need of rescue. More so, in fact. Sounds of the raid were surely reaching them. Made nervous enough, their supervisors might eliminate all dozen liabilities with a single spray of bullets.

Time, above all, had become Lane's greatest enemy.

He had no choice. He'd go it alone.

Ducking down, he ran out the gate. The dirt road was the fastest route there, that's what the POW had said. Hiking through the jungle would keep Lane out of sight but could take twice as long.

In the heat of his dilemma, he spotted the possum hunter, dead and sprawled on the ground. An idea bloomed.

Lane dragged the corpse into the jungle lining the road. He replaced his uniform with the Japanese guard's, though he retained his own boots—the guard's were too small—and balled his white armband into his trouser pocket. Aware the strategy could backfire, he resumed his sprint.

Birds awakened with the sun. They chirped to the beat of Lane's choppy exhales. His right boot rubbed open a blister on his heel. The Japanese rifle's weight and shape felt foreign bouncing in his hands. He'd considered keeping his own, but the M1, held at waist level, would have given him away at a glance.

At the sight of a shovel in a shallow ditch, he reined in his pace and pulled his field cap low. A wide clearing in the trees appeared fifty yards ahead. A runway in the making. The guys had to be hiding close by.

Unless Lane was too late.

An enemy soldier stepped out from the jungle and yelled in Japanese, "Private Asano! What did you discover?" Tucked below his patch of a mustache, the man's scowl looked as tight as the grip attached to his rifle. Behind him, a younger guard kept watch over a cluster of POWs seated on the ground, shoulders hunched, bare-footed and tattered.

Lane jerked his gaze back to the frowning guard; the slightest reaction to spotting TJ could blow his cover. "It's a rebellion," he announced in Japanese. "By the prisoners."

The man's eyes narrowed in suspicion. Obviously he was expecting a different messenger.

Lane pressed onward. "Commander Yamazaki has ordered me to supervise the inmates." Thankfully, the captured corporal had shared the leader's name. "Both of you have been ordered back to the camp to help subdue the uprising."

The mustached guard moved closer. He wrinkled his nose as though preparing to sniff out a stranger's identity. "I've never seen you before. What's your unit?"

Lane squeezed his elbow to the side of his borrowed tunic. Bloodstains were understandable, but the bullet hole would raise questions. "I'm with a reinforcement troop from Luzon. We arrived late last night."

Permeating with scrutiny, the man lowered his eyes—toward Lane's boots.

Shit. Lane should have forced his feet into the other pair. "The commander's waiting," he reminded the guard sternly. At the lack of response, he shouted, "Go now!"

The second guard, a lean, clean-cut guy, convinced the first to obey. Together, they jogged off down the road. Once they disappeared around the bend, Lane turned to the POWs, who stared up at him watchfully. His mind switched back to English before he spoke.

"Don't be afraid," he told them. "I'm with the U.S. Army."

That voice. TJ knew that voice. He'd recognize it anywhere, but still he struggled to believe his ears. He rose to his worn feet, and from the rear of the group, he edged his steps forward. "Tomo . . . is that you?"

Their eyes connected, confirming it was Lane. Yet how could it be?

TJ wondered if he was hallucinating, or maybe already dead, until Lane marched over and embraced him.

"Thank God," Lane breathed. "You're alive. . . ."

TJ managed to raise his arms. The fabric beneath his hands was real. His old friend before him was real.

"Hey, where we supposed to go?" another guy interjected. The anxious prisoners were all now standing.

Lane released his hold and motioned to the west. "Cut through the jungle this way. Go past the rice paddies. Stay off the road." He instructed them on how to reach the rendezvous point by the beach. "I'll give you a head start, just to be safe."

The group took off in a run.

Lane started stripping off his costume, to avoid getting hit by his own guys.

"So," TJ said, struggling to find the words. "You were in the neighborhood, I take it."

Lane's mouth quirked into a smile. "Something like that."

TJ again tried to talk, hindered by a rise of emotion.

Appearing to understand, Lane replied with all he needed to say. "Let's get the hell home."

Home. No word could have sounded better.

Lane flung off his Japanese field cap, and they turned to follow the others.

"Yamenasai!" A shot burst through the air.

TJ's hands flew up in surrender, an ingrained reflex. He told his legs to run, but they wouldn't. Two years of cowering to that voice, of being terrorized by the man and his bamboo stick, had robbed TJ of his will.

He listened as Grumpy marched up from behind. TJ's body braced to be struck down, executed at close range. Instead, once beside him, the guard aimed his rifle downward—at a form on the ground. It was Lane, grabbing his side, legs writhing; blood leaked over his hands. TJ yearned to reach for him, but his limbs remained immobile.

Grumpy spewed a scolding at Lane in Japanese, so harsh and fast TJ could understand only a few of the words that might normally register. *American. Lies. Dishonor.*

The guard's instincts must have prompted his return to investigate. Eddie strode over from the trees and confirmed that the POWs were missing. Grumpy belted out a roar and trained the barrel on Lane's forehead. Before he could pull the trigger, a tide of strength instantly gathered and swept through TJ.

"No!" he screamed, and tackled the guard to the dirt. The rifle flew out of reach. They rolled over once, twice, grappling, punching. TJ got in a hearty slug to the guy's temple, but the knock only heightened Grumpy's rage. In a flash, he was cinching TJ's neck. Fighting for air, TJ tried to shove him off. The world was graying, its lines blurring. . . .

Then two quick shots blasted, and Grumpy collapsed beside him.

Coughing and inhaling, TJ looked up and found Eddie with a rifle . . . . Eddie had killed him. He'd come through in the end.

TJ started to speak, just as the guy turned his aim onto Lane.

"Don't!" TJ scrambled over. "Don't do it." He threw his arms up into a barricade. "He's American. Just like you, Eddie. *Just like you.*"

"No . . . no, he's a traitor. Now get out of the way."

TJ shook his head. "I can't do that," he told him. "He's my family. You shoot him, you shoot us both."

Eddie adjusted his grasp, holding firm. "I don't want to kill you."

"And you don't have to. Not anymore."

At that, the weapon shuddered. Eddie's eyes swam with confusion.

"It's over now. Don't you see? It's all over." TJ let the words hang in the air.

Slowly, Eddie glanced down at his hands. He appeared startled by the revelation of what he was doing, of the stranger he was becoming. Then, to TJ's surprise, he lowered the rifle. As it hit the ground, TJ hastened to face Lane. Immediately he put pressure on the wound. Blood was seeping through their layered fingers. Lane's breaths were short and labored.

"Get some help," TJ called to Eddie. "Get a medic!"

"Wait," Lane rasped. "In my pocket."

TJ reached in and retrieved a white cloth.

"For his arm," Lane said. "It'll tell 'em . . . he's American.'"

Once TJ passed it over, Eddie stared at the wadded band, as though amazed something so simple could return his identity.

"Hurry," TJ urged. The word spurred a fresh alertness in Eddie, who took off racing down the road.

TJ yanked off his T-shirt and pressed it against the wound, just below Lane's ribs. "Rangers will be here soon. So you just hang on, all right?"

Lane nodded, despite his body's trembling. Gradually, his eyelids began to droop.

"Stay awake, buddy. You gotta stay awake."

Lane's eyes opened, yet the weight of his lids seemed to be growing.

"Don't you dare think about dying on me. You got it? You do that, and I swear I'll kick your ass."

A muted laugh puffed from Lane's mouth, morphing into a gurgled cough.

Next to this, even TJ's most horrific moments spent in this island hellhole withered in comparison.

Someone get here, please, God, please. . . .

"Tell her," Lane breathed. "Tell Maddie I love her and . . . that I'm sorry."

At the message, the goddamned resignation, TJ pushed harder on his balled undershirt. Red was devouring the fabric. "Tell her yourself."

Lane grasped TJ's wrist. "Promise me."

TJ tried to uphold a wall against his tears. He succeeded until he replied with a nod, and that wall came crashing down. Through the sheen, he saw Lane's eyes close. They closed and wouldn't open.

"Tomo, wake up. Please, don't do this. Not now."

But TJ could feel it. His friend's spirit had broken free, released from the binding ties to his body. Already, Lane was drifting away on the ocean breeze.

Stunned and weakened, TJ let the shirt drop away. He wanted to scream, to curse high heaven.

His lungs managed only a whisper. "I'm so sorry." Over and

over he said this, wishing he and Lane could trade places. "I'm so sorry, I'm so sorry. . . ." He held Lane's head to his chest and shook as he wept.

When something touched his shoulder—the hand of an Army captain—he realized help had arrived. Yet it was too late.

TJ fought to hold on, even while soldiers went to cart Lane away. He was prepared to go to blows if needed, disregarding all rational thought. It was solely through the captain's words that his arms yielded their grip. "You gotta let him go," he told TJ. "You just gotta let him go."

PART SEVEN

Empty-handed I entered the world
Barefoot I leave it.
My coming, my going—
Two simple happenings
That got entangled.

—Zen teacher Kozan Ichikyo

❧ 66 ❧

All day long, cars honked and neighbors cheered. Celebration crammed the sun-drenched streets of Boyle Heights. They were the same, no doubt, as every city in America.

Creak, creak . . . creak, creak . . .

Maddie swayed in her rocking chair, still wearing her night-dress. She waited to feel even a prickling of the joy wafting through her bedroom window. "Victory over Japan Day." That's what the radio broadcaster had called it during the official announcement that morning. The last of the Axis powers had finally surrendered. The war was over.

When Jo phoned with the news, Maddie had infused a smile into her voice, another projection of appropriate behavior. Nearly three seasons of allotted grieving had passed, after all. Since that morning of Western Union's delivery, her feet had thawed and skin had warmed.

The numbness, however, remained. To this day, she scarcely re-membered the walk she had taken through the February snow, mindless, barefoot in her bathrobe—among the few garments she hadn't yet packed for their move. Ida had fetched her with a pickup truck, found her three miles down that Illinois road. Evidently Maddie had dropped the telegram onto Mr. Garrett's front porch. The clue had sent them searching.

She was relieved no one asked where she'd been headed. She hadn't known. Even now, there was no planned destination. She was merely putting one foot in front of the other. Any goals aside from rising out of bed each day had been shredded into scraps from a different life. No compositions to master. No conservatory to attend. The concertos that once played in her mind had fallen silent.

Maddie glanced over at her encased violin. It was a good thing, not hearing the notes anymore. Too many memories resided in those sharps and flats, the double-stops and trills. For six months she'd been back in this old house, which presented plenty of hazards. Every corner, every dust particle, carried a frozen moment if she let herself remember. She'd avoided visiting her father for this exact reason. Some things were best left in the past.

That was what she'd told herself when Lane's letter had arrived. His final letter. Dewey Owens had passed it along after her husband's death. She had yet to break the seal. What difference would a message from the grave possibly make, except to rip open a barely healed wound?

Maddie resumed her chair rocking. She averted her attention from the night table, where that letter remained stored. The same as the framed military portrait she'd retired from display. She didn't need a daily reminder of what she was missing. The numbness wasn't thick enough to shield her from more devastation than what greeted her each morning anew.

Naturally, she shared none of this with her brother, who would soon return from a long stay at an Army hospital in Hawaii. She actually went to great lengths to assure him of the opposite. In weekly posts, she made it clear that she and Suzie were fine, that TJ wasn't to blame for whatever had happened during the raid.

Someone was to blame, of course. Someone was always to blame. But it wasn't her brother.

"Shh-shh, Suzie-*chan*," Kumiko said, appearing in the room. She picked up the toddler from the crib in the corner.

Maddie tugged on a smile. "Oh, I didn't hear you arrive."

"Yoshi yoshi, daijōbu," Kumiko soothed, patting Suzie's back. Perspiration darkened the girl's little summer dress, matted her auburn hair. She sniffled back her tears.

Maddie had forgotten Suzie was in there napping. How long had she been crying?

"I guess my mind was wandering." Maddie offered her hands. "Here, I can take her."

Emma peeked in. "Everything okay?"

Before Maddie could say yes, Kumiko handed Suzie to Emma and said, "Baby hungry. Milk in kitchen."

Emma nodded, and Yuki pranced after them down the hall.

"I'll come help," Maddie called to them, rising, but Kumiko stopped her.

"No. We going to talk."

Since Lane's death, the woman had retreated into herself. But gradually, having Nobu and Emma to mourn with, she had again torn down her shell inch by inch—which was why her sudden coolness threw Maddie off. All this for not greeting them at the front door?

"Sorry I didn't hear you," Maddie appeased once more.

"You will sit."

Maddie recognized that voice, from their early days together. A voice that wouldn't budge. Although reluctant, she lowered back into the chair.

Kumiko perched herself on the corner of Maddie's bed and took a breath. "In camp, always we say, *'Kodomo no tame ni.'* For sake of child. You are mother now. For Suzume, you must wake up. Be good mother."

Maddie bristled. "Are you saying I'm a bad mother?"

"No. But you are walking in sleep."

Suddenly self-conscious—hair unbrushed, not dressed for the day—Maddie folded her arms over her nightgown, and tried to play it off. "Suzie was up and down last night," she lied. The restless one had been Maddie herself. "So we just got a late start."

"Bea tell me, this morning she come here. Bring you pie. She say you know she is coming, but you not answer."

Oh, no . . . the visit had slipped Maddie's mind. She must not have heard those knocks either.

Still, that had *nothing* to do with the devotion she held for her daughter. And who was Kumiko to criticize the skills of another mother? How dare she sit in judgment.

"I must have dozed off when she came by, that's all."

"For long time, I am asleep too. Asleep with eyes open. I feel alone because baby die. I forget rest of family."

"Yes. You did," the retort flew out. Maddie immediately thought to retract the snipe. But she didn't have the strength, or the inclination.

After a moment, Kumiko's tightened lips relaxed. "Soon, we go back Japan. I have to know you be okay. And Suzie-*chan* okay."

"We'll be *fine*."

If the woman were truly concerned, she would have refused Nobu's suggestion that their family repatriate. Only two days after the second atomic bomb dropped on Japan, sealing the Empire's demise, the couple began making plans to move themselves and Emma back to their decimated homeland.

Granted, resettling in California wasn't all peaches 'n' cream for many Japanese Americans. There were cases of burned-down houses and defaced gravestones. Groups like the American Legion and the Native Sons of the Golden West made no secret of their hopes to keep the returning families out.

Yet for every opponent, a staunch supporter surfaced—like Major Berlow, a Marine who had served with Lane in the South Pacific. The man had seen to it that the Moritomos received top priority for housing nearby in Aliso Village. The American Friends Services had even offered to help Nobu find a job.

Regardless, Lane's parents had made their decision. In a matter of weeks, any semblance of family that Maddie had come to cherish would vanish.

"If you'll excuse me," Maddie said, rising from the chair. "I need to go take care of my daughter." She stressed the sentence to make a point.

"We not finished."

"Oh yes we are. You and your husband are making sure of that." As she started to leave, Kumiko stood to block her.

"Look yourself in mirror," Kumiko demanded. "Takeshi no want you live like this."

A fizzing of emotion shot up from the base of Maddie's chest, an eruption from a dormant volcano. "Your son," she spat out, "is the reason my life is ruined!"

The slap to Maddie's face came in a blaze of fury. Bent over, she grabbed her cheek with both hands. With every throb, bottled sorrow poured into her muscles, her limbs. Anger and guilt pumped through her in beats that echoed in her ears.

Only then did Maddie realize she'd actually wanted to hate Lane, to blame him for everything, just so she wouldn't have to face how much she'd loved him. How much she *still* loved him.

Slowly she forced her head up. Kumiko's eyes awaited, but rather than a deserved rage filling them, there were tears of grief and, more than that, empathy.

Maddie shook her head as moisture glazed her vision. "I didn't mean . . . I just . . . ." Her voice and lips quivered. "Lane saved my brother, and I'm grateful for that. I'm so very grateful. But what I don't understand is . . . ." She pushed herself to finally craft the words. "Why weren't we enough? Why wasn't *I* enough to keep him here?"

A long unreadable pause followed. Then, for the first time ever, Kumiko reached out and enfolded Maddie in her arms. Together they sat and cried, over the tragedy that had passed and the unknown that lay ahead. And as the freeze of Maddie's heart melted away, she felt again the warmth of a mother's love.

✌67✌

This was the first place TJ had promised himself he'd go the minute he made it back. Now here he was, across the street from Jo Allister's house.

The sun was settling in behind the trees. Orange and pink and purple streaked the sky in watercolors. Summer flowers scented the air. All those nights while in that godforsaken prison, this was the moment he'd dreamed about. In large part, it's what had kept him alive. The thought of coming home, of marching up to that door all spit-shined and gallant in his uniform, of spinning that sweet gal around in his arms and keeping her there forever.

Of course, TJ's dreams had changed since then. His mind, in the sporadic hours he managed to sleep, had become a movie screen showing only two reels. A double feature of that last night on Magtulay. Occasionally, the guard's bullet would hit TJ instead. But more often, Lane was the one who got shot and the guy who pulled the trigger was TJ.

It was this second vision that woke him night after night in the hospital, his pajamas soaked from a cold sweat. The three extra months he'd voluntarily stayed in the ward hadn't done much to help his insomnia. Not to say that's why he'd waited to leave until an Army doctor booted him out. The real reason was that he couldn't stand the thought of facing Maddie. Or Suzie. Or Lane's family.

In letters, Maddie had done her best to alleviate his guilt, with no success. If there was any man good enough to marry his sister, it should have been Lane. TJ had just been too stubborn to see it. Too afraid that one more change in his life would have eliminated the few sureties left.

Now everything he'd ever known had changed.

The one constant seemed to be the view in front of him. Aside from some weathering of the roof and loosening of the screen-door netting, Jo's house looked no different than when he'd shipped out. Although he'd never asked, Maddie—who clearly knew about the short-lived romance—had been inserting tidbits about Jo in her letters. How the gal had been on dates here and there, but no fellow had truly caught her fancy. That she'd been running the hardware store on her own, even though the three brothers who'd served had made it back, and outside of her ball career ending early, her life was going oh-so-splendidly.

Maddie's intentions in those updates were transparent. They were a way of explaining that his own life could resume as smoothly. But suddenly, reflecting on all she had written, he found a glaring reason not to knock on the Allisters' door: Jo didn't need a payload of his unresolved issues to disrupt her oh-so-splendid life.

Just then, someone turned on a lamp in the front room. TJ slung his duffel bag over his shoulder. In his spit-shined uniform, he turned away, rounded the sidewalk, and boarded a bus headed for what should have been his first destination.

The hall grew longer and starker with every step. Two visitors at the rest home smiled in passing and continued toward the exit. Guest hours were nearly over, which wasn't a problem. TJ wouldn't be staying long. Truth was, he had no idea what he was going to say to his father.

At the entry to Room 33, where TJ had been only once before, he slowly opened the door. No light shone from inside. The man had to be asleep. Coming back tomorrow would be better. Why talk to a person who wasn't awake? Whatever he had to say could wait.

He turned to leave, but his eyes, adjusting to the dark, caught a clarified view. The bed was empty. In fact, the whole room was empty. What had happened to his father?

If his health had gone south, Maddie would have told TJ— unless she didn't want to say in a letter, saving him from more worries while in the hospital.

Oh, God . . . no . . .

No, no, no!

TJ took off for the lobby. "Nurse," he called down the hall. "Nurse!"

A staff woman came out from a room on the right. "Sir, residents are sleeping."

"Jacob Kern," he blurted. "Where is he?"

"Sir, please quiet down."

"He's my father. His room is vacant." Standing before her, he said, "Please, tell me he's not . . ."

Apparent understanding ironed the crevice splitting her brow. She shook her head and squeezed his uniform sleeve. A gesture of compassion? A condolence?

"Water was leaking from his ceiling," she explained, "so we moved him to Room Ten to allow for repairs. I'm afraid we just haven't gotten around to moving him back yet."

"So—he's alive?"

She smiled tenderly. "I'm sorry we caused you a fright."

A wave of gratitude washed over him, so strong his knees almost buckled.

"You're welcome to peek in," she said, "but I believe he's sleeping. Would you prefer to talk to him in the morning?"

TJ didn't think twice. "It has to be now. I've waited too long already."

Seated beside the bed, TJ struggled with where to begin.

He studied the profile of his father's features, the wrinkles smoothed by a mask of moonlight. This was the man TJ remembered from his childhood. This was the guide he'd relied upon to determine right from wrong, to direct him toward the road worth traveling.

Please tell me where I'm supposed to go.

There was no answer. His father's husky breaths continued to flow in and out, and his eyes, like his mind, remained shut to the world.

TJ rubbed his palms on his trousers. So as not to disturb his father, he spoke in a hush. "It's been a while, huh, Dad? Not sure if you remember, or if you heard me at all actually, but . . . I've been away because of the war."

As TJ hunted for the right words, it struck him how similar their journeys had become. Somehow they'd both survived tragedies in which others hadn't, left behind to agonize over the casualties. In addition to Lane, an Army Ranger and two POWs had also been killed during the raid. Four American lives lost.

"You know, I've been banging my head here, trying to figure out why some make it and some don't. Military officers, they'll tell you it's just the nature of war. Other people will say it's all part of God's plan."

The theories seemed to work for most folks. To TJ, they were loads of bull. Simple things people say when they don't have hard answers. There wasn't anything natural about war. And after two years of living in that blasted POW camp, he knew for a fact: God was nowhere near the place.

That didn't stop TJ from wanting to make sense of it all. Laws of physics could explain how any pitch would fly, or calculate its trajectory off a bat. But no formula could enlighten him on the logic of death.

Looney was a perfect example.

"Word has it that during the raid, Looney—that's what we called the camp commander—apparently he knew he was done for. So he hugged a grenade and yanked the pin. Turned out to be a dud. How you like that?"

Now the asshole was facing a trial for war crimes. Some called that justice. Maybe so. Maybe it was pure dumb luck. Then again, luck was supposed to be a good thing. Same went for survival.

So why did survival feel so unlucky?

With a heavy sigh, TJ leaned forward, elbows pressed into his knees. "All I know is that I'm tired. . . . I'm just so tired." The guilt fastened to his back made every movement a drain to his body, his spirit.

Gently he touched his father's hand. The skin was rough and aged but warm. From the simple contact, images that had haunted TJ for years rose in a mental mural, still locked behind a cage. His mother's wracked form, the endless rain, the twisted mess of metal. In his mind he saw the key turn and the door swing open, and in a plume of darkness they drifted free.

"It's time to forgive yourself, Dad. It's been long enough."

Perhaps it was wishful thinking, but the sound of his father's breaths seemed to stretch into a deeper, more peaceful rhythm. As TJ sat there listening, he couldn't help but wonder if he too would ever forgive himself for what he'd done.

❧ 68 ❧

"Watch out!" Maddie cried.

With a jerk to the handle, Emma swerved the wagon just in time to avoid colliding with the Ovaltine display. She brought the wheels to an abrupt halt in front of Maddie. Seated in the Radio Flyer, Suzie released giggles that filled the supermarket. Her eyes sparkled like firecrackers.

"I'm just keeping her entertained, like you asked," Emma reasoned.

Maddie tried to keep a straight face, yet how could she possibly? Between Emma's sly smirk and Suzie's lopsided piggytails, Maddie found herself giggling with them. The feeling was wondrous. She couldn't recall the last time she'd actually laughed so freely.

Within seconds, however, a prick of guilt deflated the moment. It didn't seem right, enjoying what Lane would never see.

Maddie grasped the handle of her shopping basket, maintained her smile as best she could. "Em, could you grab a box of gelatin? I think I'll make a spinach mold for supper."

"Yuck!" Suzie puckered her face.

Emma bent over to meet Suzie's eyes. "Ah, c'mon, shortcake. Don't you wanna be strong like Popeye?"

When Suzie adamantly shook her head, Emma warned her, "You know, if you don't eat your spinach, you won't be strong enough to do things like . . . *this!*" With that, Emma darted down the aisle with the wagon, causing Suzie to squeal.

A pair of elderly women pointed at the girls and whispered to one another. Maddie didn't have to hear them to know what they were saying. An interracial child spurred plenty of attention, even after the war. Maddie prayed nightly that societal acceptance would evolve long before her daughter could comprehend her differences.

Refocusing, Maddie turned to the crates of fruit. She sifted through the muskmelons and tested a few with a squeeze. Her mother had taught her not to judge on appearance alone. So Maddie followed her instincts and chose one for tomorrow's breakfast.

She was moving on to the apples when she spotted the rhubarb. TJ's favorite kind of pie. She added a bundle of stalks to her basket. She hardly expected a dessert to free him from the quiet anguish that kept him cocooned in their house, blatant since his return a week ago, but she was willing to try.

On occasions when she'd felt the strength for it, she had risked broaching the subject. Yet he would quickly divert. And she'd let him, as it wasn't an easy topic for her either. In its place, they would discuss the weather and Bea's latest gossip from the shop. Then TJ would grab their father's old toolbox and busy himself with repairs in the basement, where he could be alone.

If only she knew how to reach him.

"Madeline."

The sound of her proper name was jarring. Though even more startling was the sight of who'd said it, a person she hadn't seen in eons. "Mrs. Duchovny," she replied, and a genuine smile curved Maddie's lips.

Pecan curls brushed the collar of the woman's dress suit, clearly tailored for her robust shape and bordering on too fancy for a supermarket. With rouge highlighting her cheeks, her polished appearance differed vastly from their last run-in.

And then Maddie remembered. She'd been delivering Donnie's favorite shirt, in time for his funeral, when the woman tore Maddie's pride in two. Even on that day, she understood it was grief that had propelled the mother's outburst. Still, Mrs. Duchovny's cruel judgment—her blind hatred of Lane, her piercing references to Maddie's parents—rose now like a welt.

Maddie angled toward the produce, unwilling to meet her gaze. This person was no longer her benefactress; just a former customer of her father's. Someone she used to know.

"Madeline," she tried again, "what a delight to see you." Unease seeped into her voice, which then dropped into silence. Once known for her endless supply of chatter, Mrs. Duchovny seemed at a loss for words. "So," she said, "I hear you have a daughter."

Maddie stiffened, although she shouldn't have been surprised. The scandalous news, about "that half-breed" in the neighborhood, had no doubt garnered sneers among the local uppity circles. "I have shopping to do," she bit out. As she started to leave, Mrs. Duchovny tenderly grabbed her arm.

"Please."

Without looking at her, Maddie asked, "What is it you want?"

"I just wanted to say that . . . well, Bob and I . . . we were very sorry to hear about your husband."

Maddie snapped around. "Were you really?"

"Yes," she affirmed. "We were."

That was all. She added nothing more. But in that brief sentence, Maddie heard it. Like a quarter rest in a musical piece, the message was soundless though present. *We're no different now, you and I. Our loved ones fought, and sacrificed, for the same cause.*

Perhaps Maddie only imagined these words, these alms of understanding. All the same, their evident truths shed a layer of her resentment. How could she truly blame the woman for lashing out at the time? Effects of tragedy can vary. Maddie saw that now. From losing her mother, as well as her father, the sorrow had been tremendous. Yet with Lane it was worse. She had spent the better part of a year actually blaming the person who'd died. The whole world can become the enemy when you lose what you love.

Softening, Maddie nodded in response, acknowledging the sincere condolence.

Mrs. Duchovny smiled with her ruby-red lips.

When Maddie stepped away again, the gal ventured, "Is there any chance you could join us? For supper on Sunday? Your daughter too, of course. About six-thirty?"

Something in the invitation jostled a memory. A vision of Kumiko burning a letter, moving on from her past.

Maddie felt herself nearing her own flame as she considered her reply.

While tentative, she swiveled back and said, "That would be lovely."

As hard as Maddie tried, she couldn't concentrate on anything but the task waiting at home. Her exchange today with Mrs. Duchovny had made clear what she needed to do. All else became buzzing to her senses—at no benefit to Emma.

Throughout the stroll from the market, Emma voiced concerns about living in Japan, a country she had never even visited. Would her Japanese be good enough? Would the kids treat her poorly? She didn't complain, just sought assurance.

Maddie would typically oblige, despite her desire that they stay. This time, though, her offerings ran thin. Her mind had fixated on an unsealed envelope, and the pages inside, which, for better or worse, could change her life.

Finally, alone in her bedroom, Maddie dared to open the nightstand. With a cautious hand, she pulled out Lane's portrait. His eyes gleamed with such pride for the uniform he wore.

She had been jealous of that uniform, for the shiny, starched enticement that had taken him away. First, to another country, then from this earth. Somehow, she'd thought that shutting Lane out, along with that dratted uniform, would keep her pain at bay. She hadn't realized that by doing so, she had trapped herself in that drawer as well.

Perched on her bed, she set his envelope on her lap. She paused to prop his frame on her night table. She would need Lane beside her, now more than ever.

After a careful breath, Maddie broke the seal. At last, she began to read.

⤜69⤛

TJ pounded out his frustrations over the news. He snagged another nail from between his lips and hammered it into the wooden bracket on the wall. Adding shelves to the basement was the latest chore he'd thought up, to kill time, to give him purpose. But thanks to a phone call from Ranieri, the shelves would likely end up cockeyed.

Stupid Italian know-it-all, shoving his nose in everyone's business. What right did he have giving updates on people TJ would rather forget? Just about the last person he wanted to hear about was Eddie—or "Dopey," as Ranieri knew him. Apparently, as a result of Eddie fetching help during the raid, G-2 had discovered he was American and the circumstances of his draft. Cleared of any potential war crimes, he was given the chance to come home.

A swell thing, right?

Oh, but here's the kicker. He'd said *no*. With his mother and sister living in Nagoya, he had chosen to live there instead. In the country he should have hated. Surely he could have brought his family to California too, if he'd wanted.

Just didn't make a lick of sense. None of it.

And what bothered TJ most? That it bothered him at all. Why'd he care what the guy did anyway?

"TJ!"

He swung toward the yell, his heart in an instant gallop. Maddie stood at the base of the stairs. His sister. Not a prison guard with a bamboo stick. "What's the matter?"

She smiled. "Nothing. I just couldn't get your attention."

"Oh. Right." He sighed, relieved, embarrassed. How many times had she called his name before he'd heard her?

"Here," she said, handing him a glass of lemonade. "Emma made a fresh pitcher. I'd almost forgotten how good it tastes with the full portion of sugar."

TJ finished his drink in three swallows, barely tasting it, and returned the glass. "Thanks." He wiped his beaded forehead with a dirty rag. Dust from his handiwork floated in the afternoon light, a dim stream through the smudged window, causing him to cough.

"Dinner will be ready soon," she said. "You should come up and join us. Get some fresh air."

By "us" she meant Suzie and Emma, two people worth avoiding, the same as Lane's parents. Not just for the painful reminders stirred up by their presence, but for the family's warmth he didn't deserve.

"Actually," TJ said, "could you, uh, leave it out for me? I want to get this done before nightfall." He angled back to the boards that needed to be cut, and sketched pencil marks on the top piece.

"All right," she said halfheartedly. "If that's what you want."

After a pause, her footsteps climbed the stairs, only to stop midway and descend again. He could feel a confrontation looming, the topic obvious. He placed the saw on a board's edge and heaved the metal teeth into motion. Back and forth he pushed and pulled, generating noise too loud to talk over.

In the corner of his eye, he could see her knee-length skirt. Her legs went still as beams. She continued to wait . . . and watch. TJ's nerves jittered beneath the skin, scratched at the surface, until agitation won out. "Is there a problem?"

Maddie answered in an even tone. "I got a letter."

More news he didn't need. He lined up another board.

"It was from Captain McDonough. He was one of the Rangers who helped lead the prison raid and—"

"I know who he is."

Maddie pressed on, unfazed. "He said that if you and Lane hadn't run into the guards that night, they would've caught up to the other prisoners who were with you. And that a lot of those guys probably wouldn't have reached the rescue point."

"I *know* all this, Maddie." He tossed a finished board onto the cement, grabbed a new one. "Told us everything at the hospital."

"Oh," she said. "I didn't realize . . . I thought . . ." Her attempt crumbled away. TJ hoped she'd take her cue and leave him be.

That hope lasted mere seconds. A rustling of paper indicated she had other plans. She was pulling pages from her pocket. Did she really think showing him the captain's letter would make everything better?

Feeling bullied into a corner, he verged on shouting. "I told you I don't want to read his goddamn note. So stop pushing."

She looked at him, a calm determination in her eyes. No suggestion of a flinch. He'd never seen her this strong.

"These are from Lane," she said. "It was his farewell letter."

TJ's shell of mettle cracked and shattered as Maddie crossed the room.

"It wasn't until yesterday that I had the courage to open it. Now that I have, I think you ought to read it too." She held out the pages, displaying the familiar handwriting.

Desperate for escape, he twisted away from her. He placed a shelf on the brackets and stood there gripping the board.

"Please," she said, suddenly right behind him. "Read it."

"I can't," he whispered.

"TJ . . . I'm asking you to do this one thing for me."

He glanced at the stationery. Every word would strike like a whip. Yet after all he had stolen from her, how could he refuse?

A stretch of silence passed before TJ accepted the pages. Then he lowered himself onto a stool, mustering what was left of his strength, and honored his sister's wish.

My dearest Maddie,
*   I write this letter to you now in the event I don't*
make it back. Tomorrow I leave on a mission that offers

a great deal of danger. For this reason, I've given plenty of thought to changing my mind. Believe me, sweetheart, the easiest thing would be to bow out and head for the States, where you and Suzie and I could finally start life together as a family. If I did that, however, I fear a burden of regret would grind away the husband and father I'd otherwise be, and both of you deserve better.

In spite of these ominous and necessary words, my hopes are high that you'll never have to read this. I had actually written a final letter to you before, prior to my first deployment. I've asked Dewey to throw it away and keep this one in its place. What I thought was important back then has come to mean little. Proving myself a loyal American is nothing compared to proving myself a worthy man.

I had enlisted in the Army to do my bit, but also to show others that I wasn't the "enemy." In the end, I discovered that's indeed what I was—an enemy to myself, I mean—and long before the war began. For so long I've been rejecting my heritage out of shame and fear of being different. What I didn't realize was that I was only denying the person I really am, equally Japanese and American. I had such dreams of changing society's views through votes and speeches, yet the one who needed to change first was me. Beyond any lesson I've gained during this crazy war, our "baby bird" has taught me that.

You see, Suzie is not just a gift to us, darling, but to the world. She is living proof of the beauty that two sides, even in the midst of warring, can create through love and peace, understanding and compassion, and, most of all, forgiveness. Please instill in her the deep pride that took me far too long to find. And whether I'm there or not, I ask that you tell her the truth about me. I want her to know that her daddy was a real person, both flawed and blessed, and not some fantasy of perfection. That's the only way our dear Suzie will know that it's okay to stumble as she finds her own path through life.

Heaven knows, I've stumbled plenty over the years. I would venture to guess no one knows that better than TJ. I hope he'll be home safe and sound very soon, and eager to share some of those tales with her. Through good and bad, he never stopped being part of me, and despite my occasional doubts, I know in my heart it's been the same for him. TJ is my brother, in every way that matters, and I'm so sorry that for a time I had forgotten that.

Please send my love to my parents and assure them that any strength I now rely upon, and good character I might possess, is because of them. I am truly honored to call myself their son. Also, please tell Emma it's been a privilege watching her grow up into the beautiful young lady she has become. I have no doubt she will change the world for the better.

And finally, I ask that you forgive me for any hurt I have ever caused you. You are and will always be my greatest reason for living. Even if I am not at your side, know that I'm at peace and keeping watch over our family. Until we meet again, I wish you nothing but the happiness you have all given me.

My love for eternity,
Lane

The pages trembled in TJ's hands. From one look at his sister's moistened eyes, the tears he'd worked so hard to keep inside poured freely down his face. He tried to speak, but Lane had managed to say it all.

"We're going to be okay," Maddie told him, and assured him with an embrace. At that instant, TJ knew she was right, for he could feel with everything in him that Lane—forever his friend, his brother—was looking on with a smile.

"Bubba-skosh!" Suzie's butchered version of the word helped relieve Maddie's apprehension.

"It's *butterscotch*," Maddie corrected gently, yet the girl paid no mind. She just continued her hopping about on the nursing home's checkered lobby floor.

"As a matter of fact," Bea said, appearing before them, "we just so happen to have butterscotch *and* bubba-skosh pudding." She extended her hand toward the toddler. "Shall we?"

Suzie latched onto Bea, and the two of them turned for the kitchen.

Maddie found herself wishing for an excuse to delay this visit. Really, after not seeing her father for so long, what difference would one more day make?

"Are you sure you're not too busy to watch her?" she called out. "We could always come back tomorrow. . . ."

"Take all the time you need, sugar," Bea replied pointedly. "Suzie Q and I are gonna have ourselves a feast." She winked at the little girl. "Isn't that right?"

Suzie nodded, and off they trotted around the corner, leaving Maddie alone.

Well, not completely alone. She peered down at the violin case in her hand. "Guess it's just you and me again, huh?"

An elderly gal in a wheelchair cast Maddie a queer glance. No question, she wondered if Maddie was as senile as half of the residents here. Why else would a person be conversing with an instrument?

Maddie smiled tightly at the woman before gathering herself and forging down the hall. The place looked the same as she remembered, except smaller. There was a huge world outside these walls, this city, that she had now sampled. She wondered how much of it her father had ever experienced. . . .

A thought occurred to her: Maybe his enthusiasm for Juilliard had been less about her music and more about life; for not even Mischakoff could have taught her the lessons she had gained.

It was certainly a pleasant theory.

At the door to her father's new room, she announced her arrival with a knock. He sat by the window, staring out, just like before. He had a different colored chair now, upholstered in blue stripes rather than gray.

Maddie cleared her throat. "Hi, Dad."

She considered giving an update, like she used to, but too much had happened. No summary seemed adequate. Instead she would gift him with a performance, asking nothing in return. Her only hope was that somewhere deep inside he would hear her.

"I thought I'd play one of your old favorites." She offered a smile and walked to his bed. Setting down her case, she noted its grooves and scratches. Her fingers traced the marks, each one bearing a story.

From Lane's letter to TJ's talk, to supper with Mrs. Duchovny, the message had been clear. *Life goes on, despite our misfortunes.* The first challenge was to survive. The second, to keep from losing yourself. Conservatory-bound or not, Maddie would always be a violinist. Even Kumiko had tried to tell her so, through the painting of Benzaiten, the goddess of music—

Stop this, she told herself. *Focus.*

She hadn't practiced enough to play decently without keeping her mind sharp. Case hinged open, she rosined her bow then pulled out her violin. She tested the strings, adjusted the tuning pegs. Though she missed her instrument's original tones—the desert weather had affected them permanently—she was learning that "changed" wasn't the same as "ruined."

Maddie fanned out her music sheets. Bach's Third Partita in E major. She settled the violin beneath her jaw. Her internal metronome ticked with the briskness of three-four time. The opening measures danced through her head, accompanied by a faint ringing. The bell of doubt. She muted the sound, her eyes on the notes, and began.

The prelude had returned to her remarkably well while rehearsing at home. Her muscles had weakened from time away, but they did their job, so long as she didn't think. Such a task wasn't the easiest with the ache in her shoulder, fingers sore at the tips. Runs of sixteenth notes were turning her hands cumbersome and stiff.

Keep up with me, she urged, and pushed them through the challenging phrases. Errors were accumulating as she trudged from one page to the next. Acutely aware of her father's presence, she cringed at the lazy slur, the poor intonation.

She attempted to block these out and drift into the piece's mathematical precision. For years, notes of the like were keys to a passageway, to a dimension of reprieve from all that overwhelmed her. But she had been gone too long, and the door had rusted. The lock wouldn't turn.

Frustration mounted from her mistakes—a sharp not C-natural, forte not piano—until a failed roll produced a screech, and her bow, without planning, stopped. It hovered in mid-air, as though Bach, reaching from heaven, had grabbed the horsehairs to end the mutilation.

Out of habit, her gaze dropped to her case's interior, to the home of Bach's portrait, where she expected a look of disgust. But the composer wasn't there. Nor was the rest of her critique panel. She had gradually replaced scrutinizing eyes and high collars for images of greater inspiration: her wedding photo in the minister's house; a day at Manzanar spent with unexpected friends; her brother in his dress uniform; a family gathering at the farm before Thanksgiving dinner.

Although Ida and Mr. Garrett lived half a country away, and Emma and her parents would soon cross the Pacific, that family would remain in Maddie's heart. The same place her parents and husband would always dwell. Music, she now realized, would keep them close. Songs evoked memories with each person in those photos. The practice pieces for TJ, the Irish jigs at the farm. Japanese folk tunes with her newfound family, and with Lane, it was the final movement of Bach's Second Partita. The Chaconne.

Maddie lowered her violin, recalling Mr. Garrett's tale—about the Chaconne being Bach's expression of grief, a story of his wife's death and the seven children left in his care. It was a testament to loss and survival and hope. Maddie's ears had been deaf to the true beauty that had been there all along. She had toiled for hours upon hours, ignorantly plucking away at the technical masterpiece, attempting to mimic what she couldn't possibly.

She suddenly looked at her violin as more than an instrument. With a body and neck, a rib and a waist, the wooden form represented the person who guided it to sing. To keep her loved ones alive, Maddie would tell their stories—and her own—with the voice inside and the strings in her hand.

And so, once again, she found a home in the chin rest. She studied her pictures a final time before closing her eyes. She didn't need score sheets to guide her. No metronome dictated her pace. Faces rather than notes floated through her mind, and that's when she plunged into the Chaconne. Not Bach's version. Not that of Yehudi Menuhin, a virtuosic recording from Mr. Garrett.

This one belonged only to Maddie.

Fear and tragedy spilled from her fingers. Four years of injustice and disappointment, death and destruction, rode the bow's jabbing movements. The stanzas descended into a headlong dive without a net.

But then, at last, darkness lifted. Light broke through a clearing in the storm. An opportunity for reflection, on herself and her journey. It was a season of change and redemption and, in the end, triumph.

Maddie barely felt her fingers graze the strings. There were no aches in her shoulder or tenderness of her skin, just a release of heaviness while she held the final note.

Exhausted yet satisfied, she opened her eyes. Moisture streaked her cheeks. She had finally discovered her voice. Never again, she vowed, would she silence the song within.

After gathering her belongings, Maddie stood beside her father. "See you Saturday, Dad." Then she smiled and kissed him on the temple. She was heading for the door when Suzie burst into the room.

"Mama!" She hugged Maddie around the thighs, the best kind of hug.

"So how was your butterscotch?"

"*Oishi,*" she declared, a mumbled "yummy" in Japanese. Pudding tinted her cheeks. "Hoo dat?" She pointed to Maddie's father, asking who he was.

Maddie squatted down and said, "That's Grandpa Kern. Remember? He's the one I talk about at bedtime. We should let him rest now, but we'll come visit again in a few days. Okay?"

Bea arrived at the door, a bit out of breath. She held a crushed napkin in her hand. "Lord 'a' mercy, that girl gets faster by the day. She shot out of there before I had a chance to clean her up."

Maddie suppressed her laughter. As a mother, she had to be firm when needed, no matter how entertaining the circumstance. She faced her daughter. "Suzie, you have to listen to Aunt Bea, now."

The toddler dashed off again. This time, over to Maddie's father. "Bye-bye," she exclaimed, and she wrapped her arms around his waist.

Maddie's heart warmed and expanded, leaving no room for a lecture, although she soon remembered the girl's cheeks. A nurse would have to launder his robe if Suzie nuzzled her face in the fabric.

"Hey there, peanut," Maddie said, stepping closer—yet that's as far as she got. Her father's hand had moved onto Suzie's shoulder.

A random physical reaction, Maddie presumed, until he tenderly patted the girl's back, not once but twice.

An instant quiver shook Maddie's chin. "Daddy . . ."

In slow motion, he turned his head. Tears glistened in his eyes as if he'd heard Maddie's voice, and even her story. As if awakened by his granddaughter's touch.

Regaining her bearings, Maddie walked over and knelt at his side. She held his hand for the first time in years. "Dad, can you hear me?"

He didn't nod. He didn't speak.

But when his lips curved up, just the slightest amount, the fog seemed to fade. The cobwebs began to clear.

❧ 71 ❧

After TJ left the rest home, where he'd reveled in his father's progress as much as his sister's joy, the first face that came to mind was Jo's. He couldn't wait to tell her the news. He nearly raced straight over, but a thought stopped him.

His father's car.

TJ couldn't move on with that rusted chunk of metal chaining him, and his family, to the past. So he returned home and phoned the local mechanic shop. He didn't go into detail. Didn't need to. The town's memory was long and wide.

"Got an old car I need towed to the junkyard," was all it took. Within hours, the grizzled guy in a jumpsuit came to his aid, and TJ watched the sedan roll down the street and out of sight.

The sole evidence left was a heap of tarp beside the house. He worried the vacant spot would feel empty. Instead it felt open. Like a window raised in a stuffy room. Finally he could breathe.

Nobody answered at the Allisters'.

TJ knocked louder. The lights were on inside, and he had no intention of leaving without seeing her.

Soon one of Jo's older brothers swung open the door. "Yeah?"

"I'm looking for Jo."

"She ain't here."

"Know when she'll be back?"

"Dunno."

"Any clue where I can find her?"

The guy scratched his forehead. "Hard tellin'. She went on a walk."

TJ wanted to probe more, but Jo's granddad called out for some water, and it didn't seem right to hold up his request. Besides, TJ could take a wild guess as to where she'd gone.

"Thanks," TJ said, and the door closed.

Through the darkened streets, he strode toward the old sandlot, sorting out what he would say. Lately any plan he'd created ended up screwy. He was probably better off trusting his instincts. In baseball, at the peak of his career—through every no-hitter, every shutout—that's what he'd done. It was time he applied the same theory to his heart.

From the edge of the park, he could see the shadowed outline of a person lying on the mound. Wearing a baseball cap. Staring up at the summer sky.

"That's my Jo," he said to himself, and smiled. As he quietly approached, certainty over his assumption wavered, until he was close enough to make out her features. Ah, yeah. He knew that face. The narrow chin, smart bronze eyes. He'd reviewed them in his mind so often, he could spot her in a crowd fifty years from now.

He was about to toss out a greeting, eager to surprise her, when she beat him to it.

"Take a wrong turn?" she asked dryly. She kept her gaze on the sky, fingers knotted behind her neck.

"Your brother told me you went walking."

"And?"

"And . . . I thought you might be here."

"Yeah, well, you found me. I'll put your prize in the mail."

So much for not harboring a grudge.

"Listen, I can see you're still sore at me. But give me a chance to explain, all right?"

She shot him a hard look. "You explained enough already."

He'd prepared for irritated. He'd expected stubborn—it was one of the traits he loved about her. What he hadn't anticipated was the arctic glare in her eyes. A dagger of a message that said it was too late.

Maybe it was. Two whole years had passed. She too had done her share of living, according to Maddie, with plenty of hardships. Her granddad's health, a dream career squashed. She hardly needed this curveball thrown at her.

Let him go. You just gotta let him go. Captain McDonough's words repeated in his ears, and they related no less to Jo. Holding her close inside had kept TJ going. During moments when he'd otherwise have suffered alone, she had been there. She'd become the tune he'd lost, the hum that rose from deep down. She was the song that strengthened him.

How could he ask her for more?

She'd given him enough.

"I'm sorry I bothered you," he said at last. "It won't happen again."

Although it pained him, he turned and started back. The fact she didn't ask him to stay confirmed he was doing the right thing. She deserved someone who made her happy, a guy who had his stuff together. For the time being, that obviously wasn't him.

Almost at the sidewalk, TJ glanced down at his shoes, among the many things he'd taken for granted before the war. They'd seemed unfamiliar when first reuniting with his feet. But a normal fit had since returned, and once again they were running away.

Was he still too chicken to take a risk? Lane would call him a chump for it. He'd tell him to go after the girl—just like Lane had persisted in the rescue. The guy could have given up, for lots of good reasons, and he didn't.

Drawn by the thought, TJ gradually wheeled around. Every day he faced the harsh reality that Lane was gone. Nothing would change that. In the end, TJ had no choice but to let him go. When it came to Jo, though, he had a choice. Unless he wanted to rack up more regrets, he'd hang on to that girl. Or at least go out swinging.

His determination doubled as he charged toward the mound. Jo was now sitting upright. She gazed off into nothing, hugging her trouser-covered knees. TJ was a few yards from her when he said what he should have from the beginning.

"The three stars in a row, those are Orion's belt. And next to that is the sword he's using to fight Taurus. The hunter's guard dogs are at his side. And the top one? That's your father, the brightest one in the entire sky."

She stared at him with lines on her brow.

"Jo, nobody in that prison knew if we'd ever make it out. Worse yet, there was nothing to show that anyone remembered us. But then I'd look up at night, I'd see those stars, and I knew you were out there. It was you, Jo—you were what brought me home."

Crouching down, he reached for her hand.

She pulled away. "Please don't do this." Sadness filled her eyes, her voice. He'd hurt her with that last letter more than he had ever imagined. Ironically, it was the only message that hadn't been true.

"I was scared," he admitted, "plain and simple. If you want to know how I really feel—"

"You died," she burst out.

He stalled on her words, trying to comprehend.

"There was a mix-up. The cable for Maddie, it should have been forwarded to the farm, but it came to your house when I was there. They said you were KIA."

TJ hadn't thought of anyone except his sister being affected by the false announcement. Those blasted miserable telegrams.

"Maddie said it was a formality, because of how long you'd been missing, and that we shouldn't believe it. But to me, TJ—you died." She jerked her gaze away and her volume lowered. "I lost my father, I almost lost Gramps, and then . . . I just can't go through that again."

In the silence, he studied her. They were so much alike. Both concealing scars, having every reason to prevent another wound.

TJ sat beside her on the mound and explained, "I understand wanting to protect yourself. I've been doing that for years. But look where it's gotten me."

Her face remained to the side.

"Lord knows, there's fellas out there who'd be a lot easier to handle," he said. "This might come as a shock, but I do realize I'm not completely flawless."

Her chin crinkled from a smile creeping onto her lips. Boy, how he loved that smile.

With care, he took off her baseball cap, and was relieved she didn't resist. "Take a chance on me, Jo. I won't let you down again."

He stroked her cheek with the back of his fingers. More than from any ball game, more than his ship docking in the States even, he felt a sense of coming home.

At last, she turned to him, a growing gleam in her eyes. "Okay," she whispered.

TJ smiled, and nodded. Then he drew her face closer and tenderly kissed her lips; they were soft as cotton, her breath warm and sweet. A rush of desire tingled through him. Yet he harnessed his willpower, eased himself back. They had a long journey ahead and hurrying would mean missing the enjoyment of every step.

"Come 'ere," he said, guiding her head to rest on his shoulder. He savored the lemon scent of her hair as he curled his arms around her.

And they started to talk.

They traded stories about family and Hawaii and the hardware store. He made her giggle with tales about Ranieri and Tack, who both had a hankering for Hollywood starlets and were counting down the days to visit. She recounted highlights from the All-American Girls Baseball League, and of losing to the Racine Belles in the World Championship.

Finally, when he remembered to ask, he discovered that Jo wasn't short for a longer name, rather a tribute to her dad's favorite pitcher, the great "Smoky Joe" Wood.

TJ laughed at the revelation. He should have known all along.

"Something wrong with that?" Jo playfully challenged.

"Nope," he replied with sincerity, "it's a perfect fit." As was she.

When the time came, he held her hand and walked her home.

Every block produced memories, good times shared with Lane. In the midst of remembering, he caught a flicker in the air, a white wink from the North Star. It glowed high and bright, a compass in the sky.

That one's your father, he would tell Suzie someday. *Whenever you feel lost, he'll always be there to guide you.*

∾72∾

The impending ceremony made today the most appropriate for removing her ring.

Seated at her vanity, Maddie fastened the clasp and wistfully admired the golden loop. Her wedding band, like a cherished locket, hung from her necklace once more. Unlike before, though, she wouldn't hide it beneath her blouse; she'd wear the keepsake proudly and always close to her heart.

"Maddie!" TJ hollered from downstairs. His footfalls pounded up the steps. "You up here?"

He must have received an answer.

She crossed her room anxiously and met him at the door. "What did they say?" His expression gave no hint.

"Counselor tried his best to pull some strings. To get me into the classes I still needed." He suddenly beamed with a smile that took years off his face. "Still have some paperwork to do for the GI Bill, but otherwise, I'm set for fall term."

Aside from Kumiko's announcement that morning, this was the best news Maddie could have hoped for.

"That's not all," he added.

At the suspenseful pause, she showed her palms, pressing him to finish.

"Coach Barry's back from the Navy."

His old coach, his favorite of all time. "Gosh, TJ! That's marvelous. Will he be at USC again?"

"They've actually invited him to help with all three sports."

"Well?" she said. "Have you seen him yet?"

"No, but—"

"You should make an appointment. As soon as possible."

"Maddie, I don't need to see him."

She folded her arms, pinned him with a glare. "Thomas James Kern. If you think I'm going to sit back and watch you hem and haw about playing again, just so you can mope around this house come March—"

"I don't need to see him," he interjected, "because I already talked to him on the phone." His mouth settled into a smirk. The old TJ was definitely shining through, barring their apparent reversal of roles.

"So," she drew out. "Do I have to drag the story out of you? Or are you going to fill me in?"

"Coach Barry said he had to chew it over with Coach Dedeaux, but—if I worked at getting back in shape—I'd be welcome at spring training."

"Oh, TJ. Congratulations!" Maddie went to hug him until he stopped her with a warning.

"This doesn't guarantee I'm making the team. Just that he's giving me a second chance to try."

Second chances, she'd learned, were a luxury many would never have. Her brother understood that better than anyone.

"You'll be on that team," she told him with absolute certainty. "And we'll all be in the stands cheering for you."

TJ didn't argue, or downplay with sarcasm. He merely looked at her with gratitude.

"Mama!" Suzie's munchkin voice pulled Maddie's attention. *"Iko."* She stood in the hallway with a paper lantern in her arms, underscoring her plea to leave. She resembled Lane more and more each day.

"Is everyone ready?" Maddie asked.

The girl nodded her head in excitement. To Suzie, the event was purely a celebration. For others, it wasn't that simple.

"In that case . . ." Maddie borrowed support from her brother's eyes. "I suppose it's time."

They walked in twos down the slope toward the riverbank. All of them but Suzie carried an octagonal lantern atop a wooden square. Nobu held her little hand, leading the way. He stomped at occasional strands of overgrown grass invading the dirt path, their blades brown from the late summer heat. Behind the pair, Yuki padded alongside Emma, and TJ escorted Jo with a hand on her lower back. Shades of a sunset smoothed the sky.

September had arrived, weeks past the annual Obon festival. Yet Emma's suggestion of a belated rite, in honor of the deceased, seemed fitting in spite of tradition. Kumiko had agreed, to the surprise of everyone except Maddie, who felt it made sense. Not only had Lane's mother shown acceptance of past tragedies, but her penchant for strict rules, as well as superstitions, had clearly waned.

Perhaps it was the thousand stitches that had failed to save her son. Maybe she had just grown weary of allowing fear to dictate her actions. A good lesson, actually, for them all.

Halfway down the hill, Kumiko stumbled slightly. Maddie grabbed the woman's closest kimono sleeve. Wooden *geta* weren't ideal shoes for the rocky trail.

"Daijōbu?" Maddie asked.

Kumiko gave a small bow of her head, affirming she was fine. She looked more than fine. In the ornate floral garment with a wide orange belt, black hair bound into a soft bun, she was the picture of elegance and beauty. Was this how she used to dress before leaving her homeland? Would she regret not returning as she'd always desired?

Maddie had rejoiced as much as Emma when Kumiko declared their change of plans: They were staying in California for good.

But now, seeing the woman in such a complementary garb, the essence of another existence, Maddie questioned if they were making the right choice, and for the right reason.

"Mrs. Moritomo, I was wondering . . ."

"Okāsan," Kumiko corrected, a directive to call her *Mother.* She stared straight ahead as she walked. No sentimental outpouring. Just a statement of fact.

At the unexpected gesture, Maddie nearly forgot her question. "Didn't you say that . . . you've always dreamed of moving back to Kyoto?"

"Mmm."

The familiar address of *Okāsan* further tempted Maddie to let things alone, yet she had to be sure. She refused to be another barbed-wire fence entrapping the woman's life.

"The reason I ask is—well, I want you to know that Suzie and I would be all right. Don't misunderstand, we'd miss you all terribly. You're our family. I just don't want to keep you from going back home, if that's truly what you want."

"Mmm," Kumiko said again, and added, "You want to know why we change mind?" Her even tone indicated Maddie's presumptions might have been wrong.

Maddie shifted her grip on the lantern and answered, "Yes."

Pausing her steps, Kumiko angled to face her. "Is true, always I miss Japan. *Demo,* Takeshi fight for America, die for country. Finally I see, this is home. Family is here. And always, Kyoto inside, *ne?"* She patted the chest of her kimono. *"Wakatta?"* she asked.

Maddie smiled in reply. Indeed she fully understood.

The group gathered beside the river, and with lantern candles lit, they began Tojo Nagashi, a ceremony of setting spirits free.

Emma went first. In honor of Mrs. Garrett, she placed her lantern on the water. She asked for the woman's blessings on Mr. Garrett's behalf; he and his bride, Ida, were now expecting a baby. As the glowing structure floated down the stream, Maddie somehow had a sense his late wife would be pleased.

TJ went next, offering a lantern for his and Maddie's mother. Without question, she was smiling down on them, overjoyed her husband would soon be moving home. This time, at the mention of her, Maddie smiled too. The wringing in her chest, a usual cost of recalling her mom, was gone for good. She simply felt serenity, and a deeper connection from their bond of motherhood.

Jo followed with a tribute to her parents, and Nobu with an acknowledgment to the lives of all those lost in war—a war that, God willing, would never be repeated.

Approaching the water's edge, Kumiko touched the painting she'd added to a lantern wall. On the sheet of rice paper, a sparrow appeared alone, but its wings were spread wide, as if soaring through the heavens. Suzume, at last, was free.

Then came Maddie's turn.

With Suzie at her side, she retrieved from her pocket a medal belonging to Lane. The Distinguished Service Cross, awarded after his death. She ran her thumb over the golden eagle, across the ribbon of red, white, and blue. She'd first considered keeping it, but decided she didn't need an object to display her husband's valor. His devotion and bravery lived on in every memory, and in the freedom he'd helped secure for their child.

She set the decoration on the wooden square. With a joint nudge, she and Suzie released Lane's lantern toward the sea. As it drifted away, his soul aglow on the reflective current, Maddie's ears caught a sound. A melody in the breeze, forever there for those who listened.

THE BRIDGE BUILDER

by Will Allen Dromgoole

An old man, going a lone highway,
Came at the evening, cold and gray,
To a chasm, vast and deep and wide,
Through which was flowing a sullen tide.
The old man crossed in the twilight dim—
That sullen stream had no fear for him;
But he turned, when he reached the other side,
And built a bridge to span the tide.

"Old man," said a fellow pilgrim near,
"You are wasting strength with building here.
Your journey will end with the ending day;
You never again must pass this way.
You have crossed the chasm, deep and wide,
Why build you the bridge at the eventide?"

The builder lifted his old gray head:
"Good friend, in the path I have come," he said,
"There followeth after me today,
A youth whose feet must pass this way.
This chasm that has been naught to me,
To that fair-haired youth may a pitfall be.
He, too, must cross in the twilight dim;
Good friend, I am building this bridge for *him*."

AUTHOR'S NOTE

The premise of this novel began with a vision of two brothers, one fighting for Japan and the other for America. Years ago I had learned of siblings who, during World War II, found themselves in this extraordinary predicament.

I was fascinated by the discovery—in no small part, I admit, on account of my shameless infatuation with the *North and South* miniseries. (Patrick Swayze in a uniform was awfully tough to resist.) Yet, in the midst of research, I stumbled across another find that ultimately set the course of my story: a brief textbook mention of roughly two hundred non-Japanese people who had lived voluntarily in the internment camps, refusing to be separated from their spouses.

Being half Japanese myself, and with a father whose birthday falls on the anniversary of the attack on Pearl Harbor, how was it I had never heard of this before?

Intrigue propelled me to investigate these unique spouses further. Showing the internment experience through their eyes, I thought, could provide readers with a fresh yet accessible perspective. Unfortunately, I located very little information documenting the couples. Nevertheless, I forged ahead, and under every proverbial stone I unearthed more shocking elements of history.

Among these were cases of Japanese Americans who became stuck in Japan after America declared war; at age twenty they were conscripted into the Imperial Army or Navy, forced to fight against their own country, left distrusted by both sides. I went on to fiercely scribble notes regarding battles in the Aleutian Islands, including the infamous banzai charge on Attu. How ignorant I'd been of the war coming so close to the U.S. mainland.

My studies soon led me to accounts of Japanese American linguists who had served in the Military Intelligence Service (MIS), a secret U.S. Army branch perhaps best known for their employment of Native American "code talkers." Thanks to the Go For Broke National Education Center, I had the privilege of interviewing several of these Nisei WWII veterans. I listened in awe as one particular gentleman described watching his unit shoot down Japanese fighter planes, unaware until later that his brother was among the enemy airmen killed.

Reinforced by books like James McNaughton's *Nisei Linguists,* my admiration swelled over their courageous feats in the face of diversity and danger. Never will I forget their treacherous accounts of "cave flushing," nor the unspoken rule for those who fell into enemy hands: *Save a bullet for yourself.* No less memorable are such heroes as Master Sergeant Roy Matsumoto, a Nisei linguist with Merrill's Marauders, whose imitation of a Japanese officer's order to charge prevented his unit from being overrun. As the saying goes, reality is often stranger than fiction.

In my attempt to do justice to that reality, I ventured to Los Angeles and strolled down First Street in Little Tokyo. Engraved into the sidewalk before many stores' entries are historical captions of livelihoods lost: details of an FBI raid that resulted in the arrest of Japanese businessmen and community leaders, names of shops that had been closed due to the evacuation.

As if following in the former store-owners' footsteps, I made the lengthy trek through the barren deserts of eastern California to join an annual pilgrimage at Manzanar—a place to which I, too, might have been banished with my children only decades ago. On the perimeter stood a lone, empty guard tower, reminding visitors of a history too often glossed over. Relentless winds whipped dust into my eyes while I walked alongside former camp residents. Above all, I had hoped to gather insights of their time spent in the tarpaper barracks that once lined the rocky dirt roads.

I soon found, though, that much of the older generation, even all these years later, preferred to remain silent about what they had endured. Despite their internment ultimately being ruled unconstitutional—and the fact that not a single person of Japanese ancestry was ever convicted of espionage or sabotage against the United States—they showed no signs of resentment. Perhaps, instead, an undeserved shame lingered beneath the surface.

Fortunately, a voice that wouldn't be quieted spoke on their behalf. Through a biography titled *The Red Angel* (by Vivian McGuckin

Raineri), I at last learned about the late Elaine Black Yoneda. A political revolutionary, she had refused to stand by and watch her husband, Karl Yoneda, and their "half-breed" son torn from her life. Rather, she became one of the few Caucasian wives to insist upon living at Manzanar, where she worked at the camouflage-net factory, entrenching herself in the community. When her husband enlisted in the MIS and the camp riot erupted, the Yoneda family allegedly appeared on the Black Dragons' death list. Many of the details I relied upon in this regard, including the subsequent evacuation to Death Valley, appeared in Mrs. Yoneda's testimonies. For her strength and inspiration, a cameo in my story was the least I could offer.

Yet another area of research that made a lasting impact on me was the subject of Allied POWs in the Pacific. Their stories illustrated the horrors men are capable of inflicting upon one another and the utter lack of humanity that occurs during wartime. I will point out, however, that although Japanese-run prisons indeed bore brutality in each of my readings, I have learned enough about WWII to know that atrocities happened in every theatre and by every "side"—the same for acts of compassion.

As I hope my writing makes evident, I take great pride in historical accuracy. (Granted, riding in the nose of a B-17 and compiling airmen's tales of parachute thefts and practical jokes were more fun than work.) The few liberties I have taken include the following inventions: a small storage shed near the chicken ranch at Manzanar; the island of Magtulay (meaning "to bridge" in Filipino), fashioned after Cuyo Island in the Sulu Sea; and the climactic prison raid, which was inspired by the U.S. Army Rangers–led raid on the Cabanatuan Prison, successfully freeing five hundred POWs who had survived the Bataan Death March. I also took creative license with time line pertaining to the theory of a secret epitaph woven into Bach's Partita in D minor for solo violin; not until around 1994 did Professor Helga Thoene announce her conclusion.

In contrast, superstitions are in fact prevalent in Japan to this day, often illustrated by the omission of the unlucky numbers four and nine in everything from parking garage spots to hospital rooms and floors. My late paternal grandmother subscribed to many such beliefs. Given the symbolic importance placed on earlobes in her culture, as seen on most statues of Buddha, you can imagine her displeasure over my ears being pierced as a youngster. No doubt, for redemption's sake, she would be delighted my novel includes seven parts for good fortune, along with a spotlight on the Seven Lucky Gods. When I first began writing this book, I was somewhat familiar with these deities but had no knowledge of Benzaiten. A river goddess known to carry a stringed instrument and representing all that flows, from music to speech to fine arts, Benzaiten naturally completed the puzzle of Maddie's story.

Other essential pieces that enabled my characters' journeys stemmed from a long list of wonderful memoirs, biographies, and documentaries. A few that demand citation are: *Devil at My Heels* by Louis Zamperini, *Violin Dreams* by Arnold Steinhardt, *Only What We Could Carry* by Lawson Fusao Inada, *Last Roll Call* by Kenneth S. Tucker and Wanda Tucker Goodwin, *The Head Game: Baseball Seen from the Pitcher's Mound* by Roger Kahn, and *We Refused to Die* by Gene S. Jacobsen. I am a better person for having read these works.

Finally, I would be remiss not to mention a deep connection to sparrows that runs quietly through my story. In 1958, intent on bettering his nation, Chairman Mao Zedong led the charge to rid China of sparrows, labeled an agricultural enemy for their consumption of grain. Citizens were commanded to join an anti-sparrow army, utilizing weapons, sentries, and even propaganda. The war began with the sounding of bugles and cymbals, the banging of pots and pans, to scare the birds into flight. Once their wings tired, they either dropped dead from fatigue or were entrapped for easy elimination. Nests were discarded, eggs destroyed, nestlings killed. And not until the species had reached near extinction did experts discover their grave error: Sparrows ate vastly more insects than seeds; the targeted enemy was instead an ally.

Indeed, history has much to teach us, if only we are willing to learn.

ASIAN-FUSION RECIPES

The bridging of cultures can nurture not only the soul, but also the body. *Yoshoku,* a cooking style that combines Western and Japanese dishes, provides a perfect example of the harmony created by blending the best of both worlds. In America, socializing and dining go hand in hand, while elegant meals in Japan are meant to be savored by the eyes as well as the mouth. In this tradition, and to celebrate the remarkable mending of ties between these countries, please enjoy the following dishes and drinks with your friends, family, and book club members.

Lemon-Ginger Cake

1 cup unsalted butter, room temperature
2½ cups granulated sugar
5 large eggs
1 teaspoon vanilla extract
½ cup lemon juice
3¼ cups all-purpose flour
½ teaspoon baking soda

½ teaspoon baking powder
1 teaspoon salt
1 tablespoon finely grated lemon zest
¼ cup minced crystallized ginger
¾ cup sour cream
1 cup powdered sugar
2 tablespoons lemon juice

Using an electric mixer, beat butter and granulated sugar in a bowl until well blended. Add eggs one at a time, beating after each addition. Mix in vanilla and ½ cup lemon juice. In a separate bowl, sift together flour, baking soda, baking powder, salt, lemon zest, and ginger; add to butter mixture in three parts, alternating with sour cream (beginning and ending with dry ingredients). Spoon batter evenly into a greased and floured bundt pan. Bake at 350°F until a tester inserted into the cake comes out clean, about 1 hour. Let cool 10 minutes, then remove from pan and cool completely on a wire rack. Combine powdered sugar and 2 tablespoons lemon juice to create a smooth glaze; drizzle over cake.

Green Tea Cookies

1½ cups sugar
1 cup butter, softened
1½ teaspoons vanilla extract
1 egg
2¾ cups all-purpose flour

1 tablespoon green tea (*matcha*) powder
½ teaspoon baking soda
½ teaspoon baking powder
pinch of salt

Using an electric mixer, beat sugar and butter on low speed until smooth. Stir in vanilla and egg. In a separate bowl, blend the remaining ingredients; gradually stir into butter mixture. Roll into walnut-sized balls and place on an ungreased cookie sheet. Flatten by depressing a fork twice on each dough ball, creating a crisscross pattern. Bake at 375°F for 10 to 12 minutes.

Japanese-Style Potato Salad

1½ lbs. large potatoes
½ lb. large carrots
1 teaspoon granulated
   chicken stock powder
⅔ cup cucumber cubes,
   peeled and seeded

⅓ cup thinly sliced onion
1 cup Japanese mayonnaise
   or Miracle Whip
salt and coarsely ground pepper

Steam-cook washed, unpeeled potatoes and carrots until done; peel when slightly cooled. In a bowl, break up potatoes, mix in chicken stock powder, and set aside. Cut carrots in half lengthwise; slice into thin pieces. In a separate bowl, sprinkle some salt over cucumber cubes and leave for 2 to 3 minutes to soften, then squeeze to remove excess liquid. Soak thinly sliced onion in water to reduce bitterness; drain and pat dry. Combine all vegetables when potato is cool. Stir in mayonnaise or Miracle Whip. Salt and pepper to taste.

Cherry Blossom Cocktail

¾ cup chilled plum wine   1 cup peach juice
½ cup chilled drinking *sake*   1 cup sour cherry juice

Combine all ingredients. Divide among four tall glasses filled with ice cubes. (Note: If you can't find sour cherry juice, double the amount of peach juice.)

Crispy Prawns with Japanese Tartar

For Tartar:

½ cup mayonnaise
1½ tablespoons dill pickles, finely chopped
1 tablespoon rice vinegar
1 small handful parsley, finely chopped
1 scallion, white part only, finely chopped
1 garlic clove, crushed
salt and ground white pepper to taste

For Prawns:

all-purpose flour, for coating
salt and ground white pepper
1 lb. raw jumbo prawns with tails, peeled and deveined
1 egg, lightly beaten with dash of cold water
sesame seeds, panko, and/or flaked almonds
vegetable oil (for deep-frying)
¼ cup sesame oil

In a small bowl, combine all tartar ingredients; chill until ready to serve. Season flour with salt and white pepper; use to lightly coat prawns, avoiding the tails. Dip into egg mixture and press into sesame seeds, panko, and/or flaked almonds (for a lovely presentation, serve all three variations on one platter). Refrigerate prawns while preparing oil. Fill one-third of a medium saucepan with vegetable oil, add sesame oil, and heat to 350°F. Deep-fry prawns in batches until golden. Drain on paper towels and serve immediately with the tartar sauce.

Zesty Karaage Chicken

Great as appetizers, this is a tasty Asian twist
on all-American fried chicken!

4 large garlic cloves, peeled and thinly sliced	salt
	½ cup cornstarch
2 oz. fresh ginger, peeled and thinly sliced	⅓ cup all-purpose flour
	vegetable oil (for deep-frying)
1 cup light soy sauce	½ cup Miracle Whip
1¼ lbs. boneless chicken thighs with skin on	2 tablespoons lemon juice
	½ tsp chili powder

Combine garlic, ginger, and soy sauce. Set aside for half a day to deepen flavor. Cut chicken into bite-sized pieces. Marinate in 2 tablespoons of the soy sauce mixture, 5 to 10 minutes. Add salt as desired. Coat chicken in mix of cornstarch and flour. Deep-fry in hot oil (350°F). When chicken is fully cooked, carefully remove from oil and drain on a paper towel. Place chicken pieces on small wooden skewers. Serve with a mixture of Miracle Whip, lemon juice, and chili powder.

Curry Deviled Eggs

6 large hard-boiled eggs, shelled	1 teaspoon curry powder (or wasabi)
¼ cup Miracle Whip or mayonnaise	salt and pepper
	toasted sesame seeds
1 tablespoon minced onion	

Cut hard-boiled eggs in half lengthwise. Scoop yolks into a small bowl and mash with a fork. Add Miracle Whip, onion, and curry powder; mix thoroughly. Season with salt and pepper. Fill the egg-white "boats" with the yolk mixture and sprinkle with sesame seeds.

Sweet Sesame Glazed Squash

2 lbs. kabocha or butternut squash	1/4 cup superfine sugar
	1 tablespoon light soy sauce
1 1/2 cups water	1/4 cup toasted sesame seeds

Peel squash, remove seeds and pith, and cut into 1-inch-square pieces. In a saucepan, combine water, sugar, and soy sauce. Heat to a boil, then add squash pieces. Once the liquid has reduced, stir constantly to prevent sticking or burning. Remove from heat when all liquid has been absorbed and squash is soft and sticky. After squash has cooled, toss in sesame seeds.

Wasabi Mashed Potatoes

*A fabulous variation on a holiday classic,
the wasabi adds mild but memorable flavor.*

2 lbs. (about 5 to 6) russet potatoes, peeled and cut into 1-inch cubes	1/2 cup butter, softened
	2 tablespoons wasabi paste
	salt and pepper
1 cup sour cream	

In a large saucepan of cold salted water, heat potato cubes to a boil. Cook until fork tender, about 20 minutes. Drain well and return to pan. Add sour cream, butter, and wasabi paste. Blend with a hand mixer until fluffy and smooth. Season with salt and pepper.

* * *

Some of these recipes were adapted from the following cookbooks: Harumi's Japanese Home Cooking, Everyday Harumi, *and* Yoshoku Contemporary Japanese. *For more unique recipes, special reading group features, or to invite Kristina to visit your book club in person or via phone/Skype, check out www.KristinaMcMorris.com.*

BRIDGE OF SCARLET LEAVES

Kristina McMorris

ABOUT THIS GUIDE

The suggested questions are included to enhance
your group's reading of Kristina McMorris's
Bridge of Scarlet Leaves.

Discussion Questions

1. The title *Bridge of Scarlet Leaves* was inspired by an ancient haiku. Describe the symbolism of leaves in the story and possible reasons they would be scarlet. What thoughts and/or emotions did the opening poem (by Deanna Nikaido) evoke both before and after you read the book?

2. *Bridge* conveys a variety of meanings in McMorris's novel, many of which relate to connecting hearts, people, and cultures. How did each major character fulfill the role of a bridge? Who or what do you view as the most significant bridge in the story?

3. In the 1940s, interracial marriage was illegal in more than thirty American states. Given expectations placed on Caucasian females during this conservative era, how do you feel about Maddie's hesitation early in her relationship with Lane? Would you have made the same daring choices that she did over the course of the war?

4. Several of the characters' lives often parallel throughout the story. Discuss such instances found in TJ's military training and tour, Lane's and Maddie's Manzanar experiences, Mrs. Duchovny's tragedy, and Dopey's assignment to the POW camp.

5. While working at the camo-net factory, Lane ponders the irony: "Here they were, unjustly imprisoned by their own country, contributing to the fight for freedom and democracy." In Lane's situation, would you have enlisted in the U.S. military? If drafted, would you have refused to serve?

6. Japanese honor is a major element in the book, as exemplified by Lane's confrontation with the *sōchō*, Happy's cere-

monial sacrifice, and the Japanese Americans' general compliance to evacuate. One could say it's a privilege lost by standing out from the group. Discuss how the concept of honor—as a burden versus a reward—contrasts between the Japanese and American cultures.

7. The final scene of Maddie sitting at her vanity creates an echo of the book's opening scene, her reflection having vastly changed. In fact, every character experienced a tremendous amount of growth. Of them all, who do you believe transformed the most? Whose journey was your favorite?

8. A great number of historical facts and events, along with cultural tidbits, are woven through the pages. What was the most surprising or intriguing piece of information you learned?

9. Translations of the names Suzume and Orochi are included in the story. Other names that bear meaning are: Tomo ("friend"), Takeshi ("warrior"), Kumiko ("longtime beautiful child"), Nobu ("faith"), and Kensho ("self-realization, awakening"). To what extent do these names fit the characters?

10. Often the key to empathy lies in uncovering traumatic events that have shaped another person's life. Did your impression of Kumiko change once she revealed her past? Have you ever encountered a similar situation in which a discovery altered your perspective of a person?

11. At what point in the story do you believe Lane and Maddie's relationship truly became love? Do you believe Maddie regrets her choices? Reflecting on your own life, if you had foreseen the path ahead, would you have made the same decisions? Are you glad you didn't know beforehand?

12. In writing, Lane explains to Maddie that he had asked Dewey to throw away a previous letter. How do you think the discarded message differed from the one Lane ultimately sent?

13. Do you wish the story had ended differently for any of the characters? If so, how would that have affected the growth of the others? How do you feel about Dopey's decision after the war? Do you agree with Maddie's choice of placing a keepsake on the floating lantern?

14. Adhering to Kumiko's superstitions, the book is divided into seven parts to incite good fortune, just as the following bonus question effectively prevents this list from ending on #13: Which two minor characters from McMorris's debut novel, *Letters from Home,* make a cameo in *Bridge of Scarlet Leaves?*